Stephen Benatar was born in 1937, to Jewish parents, in Baker Street, London.

Although he started writing when he was only eight, 'The Man on the Bridge' wasn't published until he was forty-four - and even then, if it hadn't been for the kindness and concern of Pamela Hansford Johnson, the novelist wife of C.P. Snow, this might never have happened.

Since then, however, there have been eight novels - one published by a borough council, the first and only time a council has produced a work of fiction. There have also been two plays and two children's books. In 1983 he was awarded a £7000 bursary by the Arts Council; and Boston University in Massachusetts is now the repository for all his papers and manuscripts.

He was married for twenty-nine years to Eileen, with whom he had two sons and two daughters - has taught English at the University of Bordeaux, lived in Crete and Southern California, been a school teacher, an umbrella salesman, hotel porter, employee of the Forestry Commission - and at long last, in his retirement, has become a full-time writer, and now lives in west London with his partner, Aaron.

Also by the Author

THE MAN ON THE BRIDGE
'Great understanding and depth of feeling.' *New Statesman.*

WISH HER SAFE AT HOME
'A masterpiece … matchlessly clever … wholly original.' *Professor John Carey, chairman of the Booker McConnell panel in 1982.*

'With this marvellous book, character and poetry return to the English novel… Rachel is one of the great English female characters, like the Wife of Bath or Flora Finching: both an individual and a species.' *Times Literary Supplement.*

'This is a most original and surprising novel, and one difficult to forget: it stays in the mind.' *Doris Lessing.*

(Shortlisted for the Booker McConnell, 1982. Runner-up to the James Tait Black Memorial Prize, 1982. Recipient of a £7,000 bursary from the Arts Council.)

WHEN I WAS OTHERWISE
'This book is remarkably convincing... One's first reaction on finishing the novel is "Goodness, how sad!" One's second is "Goodness, how funny!"' *Spectator.*

SUCH MEN ARE DANGEROUS
'A heartfelt piece of writing, at times even surprisingly powerful as a rallying-call.' *Times Literary Supplement.*

FATHER OF THE MAN
'Benatar's writing captures the absolute dailiness of real life without being in the least mundane itself... He is particularly good at catching life's small uplifts and cringing embarrassments.' *Sunday Times.*

RECOVERY
'A beguiling masterclass in modern fiction. Tension inexorably builds toward a gripping conclusion… the sort of book you start reading especially slowly as the final pages arrive.' *LBC Radio.*

NEW WORLD IN THE MORNING
'A breathtakingly accomplished work from one of our finest postwar novelists' *Sunday Express.*

LETTERS FOR A SPY
'Impossible to put down. A terrific story, beautifully told, and I recommend it highly.' *Historical Novels Review.*

ON CHASING BRAD THROUGH PURGATORY
Already published in the United States; soon to be published in Britain.

BEFORE GETTING RID OF GIL AND JOSH

and

ABOUT A BOAT TRIP, A HOLD UP, A STRIP SHOW AND YOU

STEPHEN BENATAR

Matador
9 Priory Business Park,
Wistow Road, Kibworth Beauchamp,
Leicestershire. LE8 0RX
Tel: 0116 279 2299
Email: books@troubador.co.uk
Web: www.troubador.co.uk/matador
Twitter: @matadorbooks

ISBN 978 1789015 188

British Library Cataloguing in Publication Data.
A catalogue record for this book is available from the British Library.

Printed and bound in the UK by TJ International, Padstow, Cornwall
Typeset in 11pt Adobe Garamond Pro by Troubador Publishing Ltd, Leicester, UK

Matador is an imprint of Troubador Publishing Ltd

For Kimberley Lawson,
whose friendship, kindness and
encouragement over the past several years
have perhaps meant more to me than she realises.

Also – naturally – for Aaron.

Contents

BEFORE GETTING RID OF GIL AND JOSH

Part One

---

as related by Tom Ralston.

One

My brother Max was thirty-eight when he died.

And when he died I was virtually the same age. The older by a few minutes.

Essentially, we were identical.

There's supposed to be a very special bond between twins but I had never liked him. He had been a selfish child and had grown into a highly selfish adult. All right. Yet I had never envisaged a day when I should want to kill him.

Literally, I mean. *Kill* him.

"Good morning, Claude. We need to talk."

Only God knew why he found it amusing to call me Claude – my name being Thomas. He'd been doing this for months. Claude had superseded Young Pedro. He had told the two boys there was a song called Pedro the Politician.

These weren't the reasons I wanted to kill him.

My study wasn't a place for socializing but, typically, he hadn't knocked. Heedless to all the papers on my desk – although Sophie must have told him I was hoping to get through most of them by lunch – he actually pushed some aside so that he could perch facing me, with his left foot resting on the floor. "Salud, amigo!" He sipped from the tumbler he had brought.

"No," I said, "whatever we need to talk about, Max" – I had parodied his pretentious, irritating claim – "we can do it this afternoon. So now if you don't mind…"

"But that might mean in front of your wife and children."

"What of it? I have no secrets from Sophie and I can't imagine either Gilbert or Josh being in the least bit – "

"It's about Jack, you see."

"Jack?" My cool, dismissive manner disappeared. "Jack who? I must know roughly half a dozen."

"Roughly? But you don't mean *all* in the biblical sense, surely? What a man you are! In that case, won't the others feel slightly slighted" – he grinned – "if we concentrate on only one?"

"Max, you're burbling! Jack who?" In fact, I'd seldom called him anything but Jay.

"Linden."

He waited for me to react but I'd had plenty of time to prepare myself.

"Jack – or Jay – Linden," he said. "Twenty-nine. Blond, nice-looking. Tall, athletic. Aspiring actor; currently 'resting'. Lives at No 6 Beaumont Street, London West One. I know you do your best to see him every two or three days but this week it's been difficult. Today is Sunday and you haven't met up since Tuesday – no wonder you're edgy! Am I ringing any bells?"

I said nothing. There seemed no point. Every detail was correct.

"What do you do, amongst other things? Cap quotes from Oscar Wilde? Analyze *The Importance*?"

"When did you find out?"

"Ah, good, you're being sensible. About three weeks ago. I almost walked into the pair of you."

He sipped some more whisky – again with leisurely appreciation – put his glass down on another indifferently cleared patch, then took a diary from the inside pocket of his jacket.

"May the fourteenth to be exact. You were strolling through Leicester Square. On your way to the Warner, as it turned out."

"Then wouldn't the normal thing have been to stop and say hello?"

"Oh, no, is there any such thing as normal in such a…queer… context? You were both so lost in your own little world – even had a card hanging from its doorknob. *Do not disturb.*"

"So you followed us in and chose the seat immediately behind?"

"Would that have been possible? I assumed you'd be sitting in the back row. Don't tell me when you forked out your ten bob you were actually meaning to watch the film? Anyway, I had an appointment. But after a couple of hours I feigned sickness – left my lady friend disconsolate; especially as it was she, dear thing, who had offered to foot the bill – and was back outside the Warner reading *The Evening News* when the last performance ended. I think it was *The Evening News*; it could have been the *Standard.*"

My God, was he enjoying himself!

"Then I followed you back to Beaumont Street. Good healthy exercise! But the next day I decided to borrow enough cash to make a small investment. Went to a private dick and asked him to get me the lowdown on the blond, nice-looking, tall, athletic young gentleman who lived at No 6; to keep note of all his visitors, et cetera." He put the diary away. "Incidentally, I thought it expedient to strike a deal with this character – scary though he undoubtedly was; tattooed like a railway navvy, or some hulking great sailor under Captain Cook; even if in truth I daresay he hardly knows who the prime minister is, let alone which party he represents, let alone any of his…*currently*…more up-and-coming MPs."

It was very clear where all of this was leading. Maybe in time people would grow more tolerant. But this was 1954: only three years after all that Burgess and Maclean business. If you were married and you were in parliament – I mean *especially* if you were in parliament – it was bad enough to be caught out with a *woman.*

But with a man! The following example has to be extreme; I realize that. Yet by no means unique. Soon after my demob what did my parents tell me? They told me about someone who… was what, did what?…they couldn't even bring themselves to complete the sentence, although they somehow managed to hint at something quite unmentionable. But then this young man had been killed, at El Alamein. "Which was maybe the best thing that could have happened to him!"

Sweet Jesus! Yet instead of being openly disgusted I'd only murmured indistinctly and hurried from the room. However, when I discovered they'd never treated Max to this particular anecdote – and by then I couldn't remember at all what had given rise to it – I became worried. Why me, not him? In my teens I had played a lot of tennis and had surely become just as fit. My own war had been spent in the navy, *his* in the army, but I don't suppose I'd ever been thought of as effeminate, any more than he had. If anything, he kept his hair longer than me and once, even, had daringly experimented: gone fair for a week. Plus, he used cologne – which I never did. In the Thirties, too, he had tended to be a dandy, while I had trained myself to dress soberly, even at Oxford. So what had my parents seen in me that they hadn't seen in him? I'd always been so careful to conceal so much of what I felt.

But on May 14th, almost nine years after demob, I had clearly lapsed – no matter how briefly. The one certain giveaway: that sparkle which almost invariably steals into the eyes of somebody in love. The eyes of somebody, in this instance, seen walking unhurriedly through Leicester Square. We'd been a little early for the film.

"Okay, Max. So how much do you want?"

I had half-expected him to aim as high as five thousand. After all, you could buy a house for five thousand, rather a nice one too, in quite a reasonable area. But I felt certain he'd settle – finally – for something a lot less. Possibly a fifth.

"Claude, what I admire about you is the way you always go straight to the heart of things! Blackmail *is* blackmail; why should either of us try to dress it up? In which case, please, a one-off payment – and, yes, I swear you won't ever be troubled again – a one-off payment, please, of twenty thousand pounds."

I honestly thought he was joking.

"I intend to go to America, you see, perhaps become a partner in some thriving enterprise, marry a rich woman, a young rich woman." For some reason he emphasized the word 'young' and seemed to put it in the wrong order. "In short, the kind of life I was cut out for: challenge and adventure and escape. But I'm not naive, Claude. I know I ought to buy insurance (perhaps 'buy' isn't exactly the right word?). I mean – in case thriving enterprises, not to mention rich young women, don't rush to meet me off the boat. I might have to wait a day or two."

"I think I could probably manage fifteen pounds a week. For life."

"Fifteen pounds?"

"A week. For life. And if Sophie ever found out – although I honestly don't see why she should (not until I died, at least, or went senile) – she might simply put it down to brotherly affection. Brotherly affection, my God! But believe it or not, Max, Sophie actually likes you. Why else do you suppose that you're invited here on Sundays?"

"And would that sum be subject to inflation, Claude? Mm. A whole fifteen pounds a week! I wonder what that is in dollars?"

Then his manner changed.

"Stick to this, my son, and you'll be lucky to find your half-witted little self with fifteen *pennies* a week!"

"But I can't see what good that could possibly do *you*."

"Can't you?"

"Other than the satisfaction you'd receive from denouncing me."

Pensively, he finished his whisky. The change had been brief. That sardonic smile was back in place. "Should have brought the whole bottle! Don't suppose you'd feel like running down to fetch it?"

He reached across to pick up a framed photograph of Sophie. The strain began to tell.

"I wish you'd take your dirty hands off that!"

"Oh, come now, Claude, temper, temper!" But at least he replaced the picture. "You see, we *can* get along, isn't that so? And Sophie has money, of course – in marrying a rich woman I'd only be following in my brother's footsteps."

I felt almost as sullied by his insinuation as I had by his handling of the photograph. It was true that Sophie had money. But I hadn't realized this until after our engagement.

"For God's sake, you don't think I'm going to tell Sophie, do you?"

"Naturally you're going to tell her! I never thought for one moment that you could raise the money on your own."

"*Her* life, then, to be overturned as thoroughly as mine? The one person who truly likes you? Who doesn't yet see you for what you really are?"

"Oh, I can assure you, there are many who truly like me. Whether they yet see me for what I really am or not…? Well, who ever sees anyone for what they really are?" He gave a smiling shrug, as though the consideration of such issues provided his most stimulating pastime. "Anyway, isn't that what marriage is all about? For better for worse? For richer for poorer? A problem shared…? You could even think of Jay Linden as your problem. *He* could now become your Sunday visitor? Also, I've known Sophie long enough to fully appreciate how broadminded she is. Broadminded and beautiful and rich. Perhaps I'd better marry her myself!"

"Oh, shut up! You make me sick!"

"Yes, there's a thought. If Sophie did decide to ditch you, don't you think she might do worse than marry me? Quite as good to look at – well, that goes without saying – indeed fairly similar all round, except that I might be a little more stylish, a trifle more amusing and wouldn't always be running off to my constituency (which I know she does occasionally complain of) or running off somewhere else, a bit less noisily; and except, too, that I'm a red-blooded male, wholly heterosexual and willing to convince her of it possibly a little more often than you..." He paused. "Oh no, forgive me, I mustn't appear to be celebrating my own bold masculinity whilst commiserating on the failing health of yours! What atrociously bad form! You'd think I was appallingly *nouveau riche*, wouldn't you? – so unfair, since I'm not riche at all... although hoping very soon to be facing in the right direction."

Patently, I was yearning to hit him. But I suppose what largely stopped me was the notion that this might be the very thing he was desiring. Trying to needle me, at moments we were unobserved, had always been one of his favourite occupations.

And where would it have got us? My hands were clenched but I'd been careful not to let him see this.

"Obviously, you'll have to give me time to think."

"Yes, obviously! And please don't fret. I can easily hold off till pudding."

"Very well, then. We'll settle on exactly one calendar month from today. Let's say the sixth of July."

"Excellent! Or, even better, let's say next Sunday."

"You suppose I can see to all of this in seven days? You honestly suppose that?"

"Oh, yes, brother mine! Just follow my example. Try always to think positive!"

He stood up, glass in hand.

"Time for a replenishment – and who can think more positive than that? I'd offer to fetch you one, naturally, but I feel you should be aiming to keep a clear head – do you *really* have to read all of this? I'd cheat if I were you. Winston will never know."

Two

At lunchtime Sophie noticed I wasn't eating very much. "Darling, you don't feel ill?" I told her that my appetite had gone.

"Mine hasn't," said Joshua, smugly.

"We can all see that," replied his mother.

"What about your manners, though?" asked his uncle. At present Josh was mashing his peas and spreading them onto his well-done slice of beef – which he'd flatly refused to have cut up. "Are we all expected to look at that disgusting mess and appreciate its beauty?"

"Yes!"

Max was sitting next to him. He made a play, with his napkin, of mopping something from his eye. "That's not only gravy you're splashing about but bits of mustard and horse-radish sauce all mixed in – it stings!"

"You're fine, Josh," I said – for all the world as if his face were starting to pucker and he was about to throw a tantrum. (Instead, he merely looked proud of his creation: an artist whose work was on display in a public gallery and was beginning to draw attention.) "If you want to do that, you just go right ahead and do it. Nobody tells you how to behave in this house except for your mother and me. Or Ruby, if we're not around."

Everybody looked at me.

"Darling! Are you certain you're okay? You wouldn't like to lie down for an hour or two?"

"No, thank you. I wouldn't."

More than a little stroppy.

Sophie said to Max: "Tom drives himself too hard. He really needs his holiday."

"Mummy, do I need mine, as well?"

"Of course you do, Joshie. Who's learnt to tell the time, to tie up his shoelaces and not wee-wee on the floor of the lavatory? And all within the past two weeks? Of course you do, my love."

"*And* to tie up my tie and read Babar the Elephant and count up to a hundred thousand million!"

"Exactly. Exhausting!"

"And not to ask anyone what 'fuck' means, even if you do say it's intelligent to ask questions."

"I'll tell you what *really* takes it out of you," volunteered Gilbert. "Having to put up with a chatterbox younger brother all the time."

"Yes, sweetheart. You need your holiday, too."

But there was small doubt, despite the scrimmage that then broke out across their uncle's lap and which he rapidly put down – and also, of course, despite a two-year difference in their ages – that on holiday they'd be more or less content to spend most of their time together; or that when they grew up they'd be likely to remain friends.

I loved my children and was proud of them. I loved my wife even more, if such a thing were measurable. Today she was wearing a red dress, one of my favourites, which always made her look not simply beautiful but glamorous. She wasn't Scandinavian but was often mistaken for being so, slim, gently tanned, smiley, vivacious, and with so much more warmth in her eyes than was commonly associated with the colour blue. She was the ideal wife; the ideal mother. There was no way I was going to lose her.

I apologized for my tartness and assured her I was fine. Then set about trying to prove it, by making myself eat.

"Oh, well done, Claude! Yes, you have to keep your strength up!"

Josh paused in his art-gallery activities. "Why do you call Daddy Claude?"

"Oh – Cyril Scatterbrain! You must have asked me half a dozen times."

"I know but I keep on forgetting the answer."

Gilbert now supplied it. "Because there's some upper-class twit who acts in films whose name is Claude Hulbert – isn't that right, Uncle Max?"

"And whom Daddy doesn't in any way, shape or form resemble. I wish you wouldn't do it, Max. It was never very funny; now it's only irritating. Josh is going to ask in a minute what upper-class means."

"What does upper-class mean, Mummy?"

"It means you stop playing with your food and either eat some more of it or just put down your fork and spoon and quietly wait for pudding. That's what upper-class means."

"As ever, may you be forgiven! Yet if – "

"That's what it means today," said Gilbert. "But I wonder what it's going to mean *next* Sunday." He gave a patient nod, as if planning to compile a list of definitions.

"Gil, you've just interrupted your uncle! That was rude. Say you're sorry."

At Sophie's behest he did so at once – and very willingly.

"Not of the least importance, Gilberto. I was only going to say that of course I shan't do it any more…not if your mother thinks it's irritating."

"Oh yes, Max? As though you've never heard me mention it before!"

14

"But now you have my word on it. Children, no more addressing your father as Claude, please. If you do so, I shall personally pull your tongues out."

"They never did," I said, not wanting to leave Sophie unsupported even in this very silliest of subjects. "I asked them not to do so and at least you couldn't override me *there*!"

"I'm sorry, Claude. What was that?"

Both the boys giggled uncontrollably. Even Sophie laughed. But much as I begrudged him his success I couldn't hold his audience responsible.

Indeed, even at this quite singularly inauspicious moment, I distantly enjoyed their giggling and their laughter.

And to every problem I'd ever had, no matter how apparently insoluble, there had eventually come a solution. Don't forget that, Tom Ralston. Just have faith and remain strong.

Everything has its solution.

Naturally, despite the intensity of my current shock and pessimism, I hoped, vehemently hoped, that I *wasn't* going to lose Sophie – why had I let the phrase so much as enter my head?

Yet even if – no, not if, *when* – such a hope were fulfilled… Well, the pain which she'd have had to endure in the meantime, the lessening of her trust, the undermining of her certainties! What in heaven's name had she done to deserve any of that? I wouldn't let it happen.

No. Whatever misery was going to lie ahead, unquestionably I was the only one – apart from Max – who had caused it and deserved to suffer. I'd been weak, I'd been irresponsible.

Yet even now, God help me, I couldn't entirely regret the stupid thing I'd done; still couldn't quite believe, in fact, that it *had* been so very stupid or regrettable.

And in my fevered protection of the four who meant more to me, though in a different way, than even my own parents or those kind, kind relatives I'd known in childhood, I was now going to show myself so far from weak, so far from irresponsible, that no concept of guilt or even of loss or just deserts would be allowed to enter into my mind again.

Yes, Max, you're right. Think positive. Nothing whatsoever to be gained from feeling guilty.

So now it was almost with equanimity that I could watch the destroyer being charming to my wife and like a storybook uncle to my boys, agreeing to kick around a football in the garden after lunch and – a plan quite soon to be abandoned – then take them to the Heath and allow them both to treat him to ice creams; three, because that way he could have vanilla, strawberry and chocolate all at the same time, a lick from each in strict rotation, and not even once be asked to share by any greedy little boys who might be watching…his licks being so very loud and slobbering and juicy, spraying just as far as any watering can. ("But three!" repeated Josh, who nearly always had an answer. "Then they'd melt and drip all down your trousers and it would look as if you'd done a pee. And that's what we'd tell everybody you *had* done – wouldn't we, Gil?" Gil also had his reservation: "Only watering can? Not garden hose?") I could console myself with the thought that, come what may, this might be one of the last occasions he would ever have a seat at our dining-room table; indeed, ever set foot again inside our house.

Charming? He was even charming to me – and also to Ruby every time she came into the room: Ruby who still in 1954 insisted on wearing a maid's uniform. He asked which Bond Street salon had given her that perm (most of which, indeed, was hidden by her headdress) and were they now paying her to walk round Hampstead and to make them famous. He fulsomely praised her Suffolk Pond Pudding and begged her for the recipe.

We were still finishing that pudding when the telephone rang. It was my mother, inviting my father and herself to tea. And not only them – Sophie's parents as well, to whom they had been giving lunch. Apparently, they were drinking coffee right now but they could be with us in half an hour. Or would that be an imposition?

It was Sophie who'd gone to speak when Ruby told us who was ringing. Had it been me I'd have made some glib excuse, no matter how rude it might have sounded; I wasn't in the mood for further visitors (plus dog). Sophie, on the other hand, would have been characteristically welcoming.

"They're going to bring a cake," she said, on her return. "'Tell Gil and Josh that – never mind all this horrid rationing! – it's been made with lots of chocolate and should be really nice and gooey.'" The boys had often heard my mother's complaints about the rationing and for some reason took a sympathetic interest. ("How do you find the rationing today?" Josh would ask. "You little monkey!" would come the invariable reply.)

"Oh God, I shall lock myself in my study. You'll have to tell them that I've far too much work to be sociable."

"I already have. But undertook to have you appear for a twenty-minute cup of tea. No more than that; it was accepted without compromise. I'll even set the alarm!"

She was a woman impossible to argue with.

Three

When I came down at half-past-four – Gilbert, with grave and endearing face, had been dispatched to fetch me: "I know it must be a nuisance for you, Daddy!" – there followed all the usual greetings and commiserations. "Tom, you look worn out! When the Queen next opens parliament we're going to add a new clause to her speech." Clearly – like mother-in-law like daughter-in-law. Maybe like grandmother like grandson. I was just so unutterably blessed. How could anyone have thought (least of all, me) that I was ever going to imperil even one jot of it?

Earlier, I may have given a wrong impression about my parents. They were late Victorian, that's all. It was the same for Sophie's. All four were lovely people – generous, funny, opposed to such barbarisms as hanging and the cat-o'-nine-tails. What I mean is, I'm sure my mum and dad wouldn't actually have stood by what they'd said about that young man killed at El Alamein. And yet, for all this, they were still Victorian in their attitudes to sex. Even murder was a subject more suitable for conversation.

Therefore the topic presently under discussion – broken into by my arrival but shortly afterwards resumed – should have been surprising. In fact it wasn't. I knew, absolutely, its instigator. The one surprising thing, within this company, was the interest it generated.

Presumably, as soon as Gil had reappeared and the discussion seemed likely to develop, the children had been sent out in the garden, each with his cucumber sandwich and scone and slice of cake.

So had Rufus, with his maybe less interesting Boneo but – also presumably – one loyally protective eye on both of the boys' plates. They'd all have been very willing to go.

When I'd actually walked into the room, the grown-ups had been talking about the Home Secretary.

"First-class man, Sir David," Sophie's father was saying. "His exact words: 'a new drive against male vice that will rid England of this plague.' His exact words, mark you. 'Rid England of this plague!'" It wasn't a long sentence but in the brief moment before everyone turned to welcome me I wondered how many would have been able to quote it so fluently.

"Well, if it isn't Colonel Blimp!" I exclaimed.

My own father bridled on the instant. "You change-coat! You fickle, fair-weather friend! I thought *I* was Colonel Blimp."

"You so reliably bring out the worst in one another, you'd better share the distinction."

It was at this point that those greetings and commiserations briefly intervened, and that allusion to the Queen's speech. "Yes, somebody said the skies over…Chelsea, was it?…are now quite black with people having to burn their love letters." (To say the very least, it would have been an *unusual* opening to parliament.) But my mum, like my dad, had plainly become adept at quoting – had there been a Mrs Blimp? – that is, once she'd been given her second cup of tea; having made sure, from Sophie, that *I*, her older son (by several minutes), had received my first. She gave a not unkindly smile, over that image of the shredded love letters. "All those leftwing young men in the Grenadier Guards; I think those were the ones that the 'somebody' had in mind."

No, not the Queen, although she was undoubtedly close to the Grenadier Guards.

My mother had certainly made progress over the past nine years. Sentences could now be completed. Even on the trickiest of subjects.

"Why leftwing though?" It was Max who asked that, apparently with interest.

Our father chortled. "I notice he doesn't say why the Grenadier Guards!"

"What I don't understand…," murmured Sophie's mother. "What I don't understand is…what do they actually *do*?"

There was an embarrassed silence. Even Mrs Templeton must have realized she had gone too far. "Was that a shade indelicate?"

"Most decidedly, my dear."

"I *am* sorry."

I smiled at her. "Yet it must be the question half the world would like an answer to but doesn't have the courage to ask." I had no idea whether this was true or not. Why should half the world be interested?

"Can *you* enlighten us, Tom?" For once I heard my proper name issue from my brother's lips.

But it was Sophie who replied. "Oh, for heaven's sake, Max! And I think it's high time we changed the subject! Another piece of cake, anyone?"

"Sophia" – he pronounced the last two syllables to rhyme with fire – "how would you feel if one of the boys turned out to be a homosexual?"

She answered briskly and without thought. "I hope I'd never need to know."

"My dear sweet sister-in-law…surely that isn't like you? And besides. There'd naturally come a point when you must begin to wonder. No girlfriends; no plans to marry; a certain flamboyance to the style of dress."

"My dear sweet brother-in-law…aren't you now describing yourself?"

"Oh, I've no shortage of girlfriends, don't worry! But let's go back to what I asked. You wouldn't be able *not* to know. There'd be hundreds of telltale little signs."

"Well, I certainly wouldn't love him any the less, if that's what you're implying. But I do admit I might be disappointed."

"For his sake or for yours?"

"Well, both, I suppose. Tom and I will one day want grandchildren, won't we, darling?"

"There'd still be one of our sons who'd probably give us those."

"For his sake of course," supplied our father. "No way for any man to be! It's unnatural. It's abhorrent."

"Unnatural, Sophia? Would you agree?"

"I don't know; I'm ashamed to say I've never thought about it. But didn't the Greeks…or was it the Romans…? Perhaps I'll pop into the library at some point and see if they can find me anything to help."

"What do *you* think, Claude?"

I answered him only because I had to. But scarcely glanced in his direction.

"I take the view that for some people – I believe it's about one in ten – it does appear to be completely natural." I looked at my father. "And not in the least abhorrent." I, too, had made some progress over the past nine years.

Perhaps it was I who'd now gone a bit too far. But if so I really didn't care.

"About one in ten? My word, how well-informed you are! But actually, Sophia, I may have been mistaken." The rest of the room remained silent while Max continued to detain Sophie on the stand; there was obviously a distinct fascination even for Victorians – especially for Victorians? – in this pursuance of a

21

taboo subject: polite society venturing into hitherto unknown territories, teacup still in hand. "There might have been no signs whatever. I believe there've even been cases of respectably married men, loving husbands and fathers, upholders of the faith, pillars of the community and so forth, who've suddenly trotted over to their wives to reveal their big bad secrets and to hang their naughty heads in shame. So Sophia? How would you feel if it wasn't one of the boys but Claude himself who proved to be the villain?"

"Villain? Oh, stop it, Max – at the moment you're the villain! And I thought you told me you weren't going to call him Claude any more. So much for *your* assurances!" Which, regrettably, hadn't been said with any discernible annoyance. She turned to the rest of us for support. "But on to more interesting matters! Is it going to be Drobny or Rosewall; and how can someone born in Czechoslovakia be allowed to play for Egypt – that's what I'd like to be told!"

Yet for the minute Wimbledon didn't hold much appeal. I did my best to help.

"And do you realize, everyone, that today is already the tenth anniversary of the Normandy landings!"

Of course they did. One couldn't switch on the wireless or pick up a newspaper without soon being reminded. But they had probably been discussing it all over lunch, these two ex-officers and their loving wives, and their comments now were practically as burnt-out as those regarding the tennis.

Sophie and I smiled at each other. "Well, no one can say we didn't try!"

And then our smiles turned to laughter. That was exactly what eight years of marriage could do to you: we had come out with the remark in unison.

But none of our parents seemed to notice our laughter. Only Max may have done; and, if so, probably wouldn't have been too pleased by it.

"Isn't there something called aversion therapy?" Sophie's father, once again. "You show the fellows pictures – you know the sort of thing – having first given them some sort of tablet to make them want to vomit, so that forever afterwards they associate…"

But now, thank heaven, this was finally enough. "Lloyd, we do *not* wish to hear about anyone's wanting to vomit while some of us still have Martha's delicious cake sitting on our plates. Really, dear! Whatever next?"

Whatever next turned out to be the boys (and Rufus) tumbling in through the French windows hoping there might be further slices of that selfsame cake; and also turned out to be, scarcely ten seconds before this, Sophie's reminder that I was now free to go: my twenty minutes had been more than honourably observed.

I made my escape with two kisses and two handshakes. I ruffled the boys' hair and gave Sophie a quick hug. "Love you," I whispered. Didn't acknowledge my brother in any way at all.

Right then I didn't know it, but this was the last time I would ever see him.

Four

They were all gone. The children were in bed. There was a Sunday-night play which Sophie wanted to watch.

"Do you mind, then," I said, "if I simply leave you to it? I've a bit of a headache. Need to get some fresh air."

"Oh, my poor love. I'm not surprised. Stuck in that gloomy old study all day long."

"I don't think of it as gloomy."

"No, I know you don't. And it isn't, either. But it made me sound slightly more sympathetic, my expressing it like that. By the way, did it annoy you very much when Max came up to you this morning? I did my best to head him off."

"Well, I could certainly have done without him."

"Yes, he's been in a rather funny mood today, hasn't he? Not so much at lunchtime but look at all that business over tea. What do you think got into him?"

"Maybe my brother Max has homosexual leanings?" I enjoyed saying this, remembering the pride and one-upmanship that he'd revealed in asserting his 'masculinity' – which, in his eyes, meant bedding women, only women, and having to pick his way through all the dozens who could endlessly be seen drooling after him. "Maybe he was wanting to find out how the rest of us might feel about it? You, in particular."

"Why me in particular?"

"Because you're lovely. You're intelligent. You like him." I'd refrained from saying, "I mean, intelligent in every *other* way."

"His love affairs are no concern of mine."

She gave a shrug and picked up the *Radio Times*; then suddenly she laughed.

"My God, though, wouldn't your parents both have heart attacks! Can't you jusr imagine it?"

"And yours, too. Disgrace by association. They could all have their heart attacks together."

"But not in our house – oh no, dear Lord, please not in our house!"

"Yet, on the other hand, it probably does them good to talk about it. A sort of softening-up process? The more familiar they become with the whole idea of it…?"

I realized I might be sounding wistful.

"Darling, the only softening-up process around here is taking place inside your own brain. Just ask yourself how it would be if next time we're all having tea Max prances in unexpectedly with a nice effeminate young man and introduces him as somebody very special." She again began to laugh. "Oh, my sweetheart, it could almost be worth it! Maybe Max wouldn't agree – so as a precaution will you stand by ready to take over? Upholder of the faith, pillar of the community, respectably married man, loving father and so forth. Shall we make it next Sunday?" She leaned back in her chair, put one hand over her mouth and surrendered to her giggles – just as Gil and Josh had surrendered to theirs at lunchtime. "I feel that things may never be the same again."

For a moment it made me wonder… A heaven-sent opportunity? My own introduction of somebody very special?

"Though why effeminate?" I asked. "That's such a stereotype."

But, no, this wasn't the time for it. There was too much going on already.

And in one sense, of course – quite different to the one she was thinking of – things would most definitely never be the same again. If public opinion entailed my resignation, it was nonsense to think that everything else wouldn't be enormously affected. And not just by a fall in our standard of living. That really wasn't it.

In any case, I lost my nerve.

"Enjoy your programme, then."

She was still giggling as I bent to kiss her.

"And don't wait up for me. You know how sometimes I can practically forget to stop walking."

"It's just that I can see their faces!"

She found a handkerchief and wiped her eyes, then unexpectedly stood up and accompanied me to the front door.

"Have you taken any aspirin? Would you like me to run up and get you some?"

"No, I'd like you to stay exactly where you are…and let me put my arms about you just like this…"

Our leave-taking turned out to be a throwback to all the leave-takings of our earlier years – or perhaps more to our arrivals than departures.

"Maybe you ought to get headaches a little more often?"

Or shocks? Shocks that suddenly stopped you taking all the simple things purely for granted?

"I would say let's go upstairs but I *do* want to see that play…"

For that she received a light slap on the bottom. Then I left. Conveniently I was able to pick up a taxi on Rosslyn Hill, although otherwise I'd have been quite prepared to walk; I could probably have done it in forty minutes. As it was – quite late on a Sunday evening, the roads all fairly empty – we got there in around ten. Sophie's play would hardly have started yet. *Anastasia*. I hoped she would enjoy it.

I'd phoned Jay twice during the past twelve hours: the first time soon after nine, knowing he'd be awake, and my simply wanting to hear his voice; also wanting to know if he were likely to be at home that evening.

Then following Max's visit to the study I'd rung again, this time *needing* to hear his voice but not yet feeling equal to telling him why – well, certainly not over the telephone. He'd swiftly sensed that something was up, however. "Nothing which means we'll have to stop seeing one another?"

"No – good heavens, no!"

"Nothing *I've* done?"

"Stop it, my darling. It's nothing like that at all."

"Sophie's not found out?"

Despite being able so easily to allay his fears it now occurred to me how selfish I'd been to contact him that second time, without the existence of any real necessity – only the comfort of knowing he was there and knowing he was strong and steadfast and committed.

Though this was nothing compared to how selfish I'd been on the evening we had met.

It wasn't the first time I'd seen him. Towards the end of March, Sophie and I had been to a play at the St James's in which Jay had been cast as a medical student honeymooning in a residential hotel by the sea. It was only a small part but every time he appeared I thought how attractive he was. There was nothing unusual in this: on the rare occasions we went to the theatre it would have been less usual if there hadn't been some young actor I rather fancied. Yet this one impressed me more deeply than any other. It wasn't merely the look of him, although that naturally played its part – it was something about the personality which shone through his performance; shone through it so strongly that after Sophie and I had gone to bed that night – and, incidentally, made love – I found myself inventing crazy pipe dreams in which, naturally, he always starred. At first such dreams didn't appear in the least harmful but later I began to find them disturbing on account of their persistence. I mean, some four or five *days* later. And not only did they cause me to feel discontented, and more questioning of my sexuality than at any time since adolescence, they even made me wonder if I had done right to marry Sophie; made me speculate on the kind of life I might now be leading if I hadn't.

But *of course* I had done right to marry Sophie. Sophie herself, in everything she did and said and was, provided constant reaffirmation of that. Gilbert and Josh – except perhaps when they were squabbling or being unusually irritating in any of three or four other ways – lent irrefutable support to it.

And, basically, I was a happy man. Happy with my wife and family. Happy with my home (obvious tautology), happy with my career. With just about everything.

Which meant that after a week or so I was at last on the road to recovery, starting to laugh at myself a little, without being overly judgmental. It didn't even faze me too much when Sophie looked up from the *Standard* one evening to observe we'd been lucky to catch that play when we did, since it was due to close on Saturday. Admittedly, I then spent a few more minutes thinking about him, but only a few. The notes had said it was his first West End appearance; patently I hoped it wouldn't be his last. The paper didn't mention whether the play would now be off on tour, so I thought in all likelihood it wouldn't – and at once felt obscurely glad he wasn't about to set great distances between us. But that was it, more or less. I was ninety percent cured.

And then what happens? Oh, lead us not into temptation, Lord. But why should he want to do that? Any sort of real test and he already knows we're going to fail. Or, at any rate, he already knows *I'm* going to fail.

We were quarter-way through April, it was the year's first truly spring-like day. Having now bathed the children three evenings in a row I'd decided I was going to walk home. And even then I might well be back by the time they were ready for their story. In Weymouth Street I passed a pub which was painted bottle green, had bits of relieving gold here and there, window-boxes, hanging baskets, an attractive sign. *The Good Companions*. It looked clean and colourful. Inviting.

I'd almost reached the bar when something made me wonder if I'd just passed somebody I knew. Delayed reaction. I swung round – and supposed for an instant it was only because I'd had him so very much in mind. He was reading a paperback, sitting on his own at a small table.

"My God," I said.

Understandably surprised, he looked up.

"You're Jay Linden, aren't you?"

"Do we know each other?" Even while asking, he had risen to his feet. The sure sign of a gentleman.

"No, you don't know me but just the other night I saw you on the stage." It had been about three weeks before but I didn't feel I had to be exact.

"That's extraordinary," he said.

"Why? Thousands of others must also have seen you. Not necessarily the other night."

"No, what I meant was, you're the very first person who's ever recognized me. Other than my mother and perhaps a great-aunt or two."

"I have a thing about great-aunts." Straightaway he was as easy to talk to as that. "So, naturally, I'll need to have your autograph!" This last bit was a joke; even as a boy I hadn't been interested in autographs. "And you'll have to put exactly what you said just now: 'The very first person who's ever recognized me.' Then add: 'In a line that's going to stretch for miles.'"

"Oh, I couldn't! The sheer swank of it! But what I *can* do is buy you a drink. What will you have?"

"No, the play's off, isn't it – which means you may be out of work? What kind of beer is that? I'm not up on beers. I'm a whisky man myself."

I was served immediately; the pub wasn't busy. When I rejoined him – my heart now thumping in a way it never thumped when I was getting up to put a question or to table some amendment – I belatedly introduced myself. We reached across to shake hands. "Tom Ralston. But *does* it mean you're out of work?"

"Yes. Yet who knows what's just around the corner?"

"I like a man who displays optimism." It occurred to me that, close-to, he was even more attractive than from the fifth row of the stalls.

"Thank you for that, and for the line that's going to stretch for miles. And thank you for the beer." We touched glasses. "Cheers."

"Cheers."

"You know, you look familiar, too…? I'm sure I've heard your name, as well…?" He seemed to be searching for clues in the details of my dark suit, white shirt, blue tie – I'd left my hat, coat and umbrella at the office. "Have I seen your picture in the papers? I'm afraid I'm only guessing but I think you may be some big wheel in the City."

"Not quite. I'm in politics."

"What, civil servant?"

"No – MP."

"Great Scot! Then plainly *you're* the famous one at this table."

"Not a bit of it."

"Which side of the floor?"

"Government."

"Oh dear."

We laughed. "Okay," I said, "you've convinced me. I'll turn Socialist tomorrow."

And that was the last word either of us spoke that evening on the subject of politics; although not from any lack of opportunity. After we'd each had a second drink – which Jay had insisted on paying for (I'd switched, without his knowing, from Glen Fiddich to Bell's) – I phoned Sophie to say I'd been delayed at work. Sophie was always the easiest woman to warn of delays; what difference did it make if all my reasons had previously been true? Although she now said she could tell I'd fortified myself against the task – and I'd asked for what other reason would one ever keep a bottle in one's desk – I knew it wouldn't have crossed her mind I could be lying. "See you before midnight," I said. "Give the boys kisses. And don't worry about feeding me. Susan's been out for sandwiches." (She said she hoped Susan had been permitted to fortify herself as well. I said of course she had: a bribe to go and fetch the sandwiches. Lies have a habit of expanding.) It may sound paradoxical that even at such a moment I should feel so very loving towards my wife; so keenly aware of her trust and general niceness.

I hadn't told Jay whom I was phoning, hadn't even told him I was married. At that stage I'd believed this could only be a very brief encounter: a fling that at the outside wouldn't last longer than a month (I hadn't even asked, wanted to know, whether he himself were married); an affair – if it actually became one of those – that was going to harm nobody; would be in such a good cause that even archbishops and popes might fervently campaign on its behalf. Basically designed, they'd say, to get something out of a person's system. Something which needed to be got out – just once – and then quietly left behind.

Yes, certainly selfish, naive, rationalizing – call it what you will. But I simply didn't realize.

I know that doesn't make it any better.

And when I did realize, fully realize, it was by then far too late. I mean, in the sense of my being able to run out of that examination hall in the sure knowledge I had scored an A-plus. Or even a D-minus.

It didn't take long, that full realization. It happened over dinner. Dinner at the Duck Inn. And when I say too late, I don't mean merely for me, I think I'm speaking for Jay just as much as for myself. We clicked; gelled; continued on our voyage of discovery. Received unending confirmation of what we had straightaway suspected.

That, yes, we were undeniably kindred spirits.

Just like it had been with Sophie.

Obviously there'd been girlfriends before Sophie – when she and I had met I was twenty-seven – but Sophie had been the very special one, the wholly new and different one, the first to make me feel intoxicated in a manner quite unlinked to alcohol. And in essence it was totally the same with Jay; it could have been lemonade we'd ordered at the pub.

Does it need to be said I'd never dined alone with a man, discounting the occasional dinner to talk shop, or the equally occasional meal with my father or a school friend or suchlike? But it might have been a woman I was now sitting across the table from, if that makes any sense, a woman every bit as pretty and vivacious and easy to talk to, and flirt with, as Sophie herself. Yet, in his plain white T-shirt and well-cut jeans, Jay was unmistakably a man: just one who didn't continuously talk cars or girls or money, or cricket or racing or football – *or* politics! – which up to then had been fundamentally all that I'd expected from a man.

Often, when comparing certain occasions (for example two absolutely incredible first dinner dates!), one is forced to say, "No, not better; not worse; just different," and even before that initial evening with Jay was over I was already thinking, "With two such wonderful people in my life" – two such adults, I meant, I wasn't forgetting the boys – "how could I ever ask for even one more thing to make me happy?" (I knew, of course, I could – *and* would.) Before we left that restaurant in the High Street I felt as if I'd finally come home in time for Christmas.

And – yes, even on this peculiarly upsetting Sunday night, some eight weeks later – it was still Christmas and I was still returning home. (What a particularly confusing sentence that must be, when only a short time earlier I'd been seen off on my own front-door step with a very loving kiss and, almost, an invitation to go upstairs and make love!)

Anyway, Beaumont Street was as deserted as most of the other streets my taxi had skimmed through. The busiest had been

Marylebone Road but even that had been untypically quiet. The High Street seemed nearly village-like.

And, of course, all this Sunday-night tranquillity suited me just fine: Max's private detective – large and scary, I remembered, tattooed like a sailor – might not have been especially knowledgeable re politics but my photograph *had* occasionally been in the newspapers and several times, too, I'd been briefly interviewed on television. Whenever I'd called on Jay during the week, I had pulled down my hat and turned up my raincoat collar – all very theatrical – but tonight I wasn't even wearing a hat and certainly had on no coat of any kind, nor yet a jacket and tie. This seasonal evening in early June was almost balmy and I had thought I ran little risk of being recognized.

Jay kept me on the pavement barely fifteen seconds. And as soon as he'd closed the main door we stood together in a minute-long embrace. (If anyone had put a key in the lock behind us, or had been coming out of one of the flats, we'd have had plenty of warning.) Eventually we started up the narrow staircase, Jay's hand periodically placed on my bottom, as if to help somebody elderly.

"Would you do that to your grandmother?"

"The small of her back, maybe. Although she might well have enjoyed having my hand a little lower down. I'd have needed to inquire."

He added that actually his grandmother had never visited him here and now perhaps wasn't all that likely to do so (as far as he knew) since she was dead.

"By the way, I can now provide you with your own key. I've at last remembered to have one cut."

When we had reached his flat and were lying together on the sofa, each with a glass in his hand, he referred to that morning's second phone call.

"All right, then. Shoot!"

Jay, like me, was a lover of film, particularly American film. The second time we'd met – in fact, the first time we had spent a night together – I had finally let him know about Sophie and Gilbert and Josh. There'd been disappointment and tears on his side…and, on mine, a load of apology and self-recrimination (together, of course, with tears – you should have seen us – two great big sniffling Nancy-boys) but he had rallied remarkably fast.

"So long as you don't start to call me Irene!"

"Irene?"

"Are you trying to tell me you've never seen *Back Street*? Irene Dunne as the woman who has to make do with second best and spend the rest of her life in the role of devoted mistress? Because I'm already hooked, you know – just as she was."

He hadn't intended it but this was simply a further instance, to add to all the others there had been throughout that long day, of my being freshly appalled by this bitter-sweet thing I'd set in motion – and which I now knew, better than ever, I'd never find the strength, nor the altruism, to be able to pull out of.

"Jay, it isn't going to be like that. *Second* best? – don't you dare say it! *Equal* best or nothing! I've read a French novel published a couple of years ago – I'll have to get it for you. *Jules et Jim*. About two men and a woman living together. When I discussed the book with Sophie she claimed she didn't see why a *ménage à trois* couldn't be a great success. That in fact it had the potential to be thoroughly life-affirming. Whether two men and one woman or two women and one man – depending, of course, on their personalities. I promise you, there's no way I'm going to let you spend the rest of your life in a back street!"

Fighting words…and a problem I'd now been thinking about for quite a lengthy time – until temporarily eclipsed by another, which had turned up that very morning.

"Shoot?" I repeated, perhaps referring back too far for many but in full confidence that between ourselves… "If that's a piece of advice, it could hardly be more apropos. Just hand me a gun."

"Who do you want to shoot?"

"Whom. My brother Max."

"But you can't. Not him. You say he's the spitting image of yourself. There's not so much beauty in this dreary old world that you can afford so recklessly to squander it."

"Thank you – but my brother Max is not beautiful. Not on the inside, where it matters. He's utterly selfish and always has been. Utterly fixated on himself."

"Then there's clearly no resemblance. Have you enough bullets, in case at first you miss?" He reached over to my cheek, brushed it with the back of his fingers. "Tom, what's brought this on?"

"He's found out about you."

"Does that matter so much? After all, he *is* your brother."

"And now he wants to go to the media…"

"Oh, God." The motive was instantly apparent. Most of the consequences soon became so.

"…unless I put twenty thousand pounds into his sweaty little palms…and let him fly off to a new existence in the New World."

"Twenty thousand pounds! Oh, my sweetheart!" He whistled.

"Exactly."

"Can't you put it there in ha'pennies?"

He apologized.

"So what are we going to do?"

I liked the 'we'. "God knows. We've got precisely one week in which to make up our minds. He wants an answer by next Sunday."

"And then…if we aren't going to meet his terms…?"

I nodded.

"We've somehow got to stop him." He was stating the obvious but even so there was a quality of reassurance to it – as though the mere expression of such a statement was making it appear practically achievable.

"Yes. Go fetch that gun."

"A bit drastic, love. They'd hang us. And even if we went together – an early-morning walk, hand-in-hand, singing 'Even when the darkest clouds are in the sky…' – no, I'm just not sold on it. Couldn't we simply hit him on the head; not hard enough to kill him but hard enough to bring on amnesia?"

"There might be quite a science to knowing where the line was."

"That's true. But they may have a bulletin board in the library."

"And while you're there you might bump into Sophie." I briefly told him why. "And see what *she* could suggest. The more the merrier."

"But too many cooks spoil the broth. Not the brother."

Actually I was now discovering – contrary to what I'd have thought – that a light-hearted approach was possibly the best antidote. Maybe it was the whisky but something was making me start to relax, even to regain a sense of perspective.

"Besides," I said, "the amnesia mightn't last. In that case – back to square one!"

All right, perhaps for the moment this *was* the way to look at it.

But at the same time I knew I had to be driving into Buckinghamshire the next morning and holding a surgery for three hours, then attending in the evening what was likely to be an exceedingly boring town meeting. I knew that reality would surely have returned by the time I awoke (supposing, I mean, I'd actually managed to sleep) and that the whole day was likely to be one of battling against worry and despair and inattention. I'd never once suggested the following idea to Jay – such a suggestion would have seemed a gamble even at the best of times – but now, when it had suddenly come to feel riskier than ever, I said it anyway.

"Will you drive down with me tomorrow and supply masses of moral support?"

"Of course I will. And now let's go to bed for an hour. To hold each other very close."

Five

In the end, however, I decided not to take him. To become all devil-may-care at this stage would not be sensible. When I phoned him a little before seven Jay reluctantly agreed. But we arranged to meet about an hour later, at a workman's café in a side-road off Gloucester Place, and to continue racking our brains over a large fried breakfast – which was a form of recklessness that seemed not merely acceptable but called for. Almost an act of defiance.

We sat at a formica-topped table in a corner by the steamed-up window, drinking dark brown tea from thick white china cups; and waiting for eggs, bacon, fried bread, all the rest of it. The place was full and we'd been lucky to get the table we did. The atmosphere was noisy and cheerful and although there were men so near we could almost have reached across to help ourselves to *their* sausages, tomatoes and mushrooms, we still felt we were as private here as if we'd been walking through Regent's Park, which was very close by.

"I'm sorry I called you so early."

"You could have called me any time. I wouldn't have been asleep."

"Perhaps I should have tried to keep it from you?"

"If you had you'd have been in big trouble." He grinned. "Bigger trouble."

"Do you know – I'm fighting such an urge to take you in my arms? Are these the best surroundings?"

His own question was more serious. "Did *you* manage to sleep?"

"I don't think so."

"Then why is there nothing on TV – nothing but that boring old test card? Wouldn't you think they'd spare some thought for all of us poor victims of blackmail and extortion? Why does there even have to be a shutdown?"

"Another question for Queenie to ask in parliament. I can see your mind's been working overtime. Anything else occur to you?"

"No."

"I may have had *one* idea," I said. "Not a startlingly useful one but at least…"

Our breakfast came. The fried bread looked good. In fact, all of it looked good. I remembered I hadn't eaten much the day before.

"More tea, my loves?"

"Yes, please," said Jay. He added – as the woman moved away, carrying our emptied cups – "You see? I *can* show initiative."

"I'm glad. Especially since what I came up with hinged on your showing a lot of it."

"Good. Whatever happens in this you're never going to find yourself alone. The three of us against the world!" He invariably aimed to include Sophie. I never drew attention to it but that was one of the many things I loved about him. "And this time I won't say shoot. Merely, *spill the beans*. This time, you see, I'm speaking metaphorically. At least, I think I am." He picked up his plate and tilted it, then decisively shook his head.

"Well, I don't know what it's going to achieve, this idea of mine, but we have to do something. We can't just lie down and take it."

"Too right we can't. What d' you want me to do?"

"Tail him."

Our fresh tea arrived.

"Okay. Anything. But ignoring the fact I've had no training, he also knows what I look like." He paused. "Though for God's sake I'm an actor, aren't I? A dark wig, a Trilby, a moustache – *three-piece suit*, if I must... Good Lord, I could call on my dear old mum in Preston and she'd only say, 'No, not today, thank you. I already have more than I require. *Good* afternoon!'"

"I can almost hear her! What would you be selling? Encyclopaedias?"

"No. Contraceptives. It's good to hear you laugh."

"One of these days I hope to meet your mum. Also, of course, your dad."

"I want that, too. What's this plan of ours?"

"To start to wage a war of nerves. For which you'll need no suit, no Trilby, no moustache. No training."

"In other words...no talent? I'm your man!"

"Yes. You are. You're very much my man."

"Thank you. But stop it. You'll give me a hard-on."

"Then why should I stop it?"

"Because there's only the top of the counter. And we'd have to mind the tea urn."

"The thing is, my love, we'd *want* him to know you're following him. Right from the beginning. Especially when he's waiting to cross the road or standing on some busy underground platform. Yes, that's when we'd want him to be most strongly aware of your presence. Rush hour will be your time; but in fact any hour could be your time."

"For what? I hope you're not going to say what I think you might be going to say."

"No. Simply your time for looking big. And looking dangerous. Chock-full of menace. Be wearing one of your T-shirts – just as you are now, in fact – but first remove the sweater. Let him see your biceps."

"You mean, starting today? But how long do I have to keep it up?"

"All week? It would be good if his eyes met yours every time he looked around. As you know, of course, he's a salesman at Fortnum's. Well, you're invariably standing there and staring at him silently. Leaning against something? Arms folded? Chewing gum?"

"Until he brings me to his supervisor's attention?"

"I'll supply you with cash. You ask the supervisor which would be the best this or the best that – the one *he'd* particularly recommend – and then of course you buy it. A gentle answer, especially when coupled with a banknote, turneth away suspicion. It's as good as the other cheek."

"*Anything* he recommends? I hope Max doesn't work in the white goods department?"

"I don't think there is one. No, he works in Provisions. On the ground floor."

"And suppose he himself comes up to me? 'I know who you are. What the hell do you think you're doing?'"

"You deny every word he utters. You look all innocent and bewildered. 'Jay Linden? Who's Jay Linden? *I* don't know any Jay Linden!'"

"Oh, darling, have a heart! Ask me anything but that! If it ever got back to my agent…!"

"You can improvise a little."

"'You mean – Jay Linden, that brilliant young actor currently tipped to give the best Hamlet of his generation? Jay Linden, whom Richard Burton would consider it a privilege to understudy? *That* Jay Linden? Oh, I wish I were!'"

"Are you through?"

"Almost. 'My mother thinks he's wonderful!' I must get that bit in. What happens then?"

"You give it a rest for a while, maybe wait until the store closes. But in the meantime… Max lives in a flat in Maida Vale. Sophie looks after his spare key – which, as it happens, I've now borrowed from her…although I think I may have forgotten to let her know."

I handed it across.

"And what am I supposed to do with this? Trash the place?"

"No. All you'll do is to move a few things around. Ornaments. To begin with he may not even notice but when he does… All part of a gradual wearing-down process."

"But do we have the time for gradual?"

"I hope that next Sunday I'll be able to stall him."

"When he *does* notice will I be his favourite suspect?"

"Not instantly; not if you've been subtle. *Tomorrow* evening he'll find his toothbrush on the floor, although in a spot where it could easily have fallen. Cap off the toothpaste, or *on* the toothpaste, depending on whichever way you've found it. One of the windows left ajar."

"Yes. That might start to unnerve him. I think it would me."

"Something taken from the fridge and left out on the table. In his rush that morning he just *might* have forgotten to put it back."

"But all of this and the knowledge he's being watched and threatened – you think it's going to affect him…how?"

"Make him jumpy and short-tempered and not his usual sophisticated self."

"As a prelude to what?"

"I don't know. As I said, all this might achieve nothing. But I'm only hoping it will start to rattle him. And when we're rattled we sometimes make mistakes. Don't ask me what kind of mistakes. I'll tell you when I find out."

I'm only hoping! Good grief! But actually, in the end, I had rather a nice day. An hour spent with Jay and his continuing resolve to smile at our predicament without ever losing sight of its importance…this again relaxed me. For no proper reason, other than of course because I loved him, I felt practically sanguine as I drove towards the Hendon Way, his sweater folded neatly on the passenger seat, almost a talisman, the next best thing to his presence. The sun was shining and I simply couldn't believe evil was about to triumph. For Max *was* evil: the happiness of five people – certainly of three – clearly meant nothing to him; which suggested the happiness of five million wouldn't have meant a great deal more. During my hour-long drive I found myself talking to God about the whole sad situation, about my infidelity and what my infidelity had given rise to, whilst not letting him think for an instant that even in hindsight I'd have played that scene in the pub any differently. And God seemed to be listening. Seemed to be listening, just as I, a bit later (no comparison intended), was also in a position of listening to the problems some of my constituents had waited patiently to set before me. Although all of these problems were relatively petty – last week, I thought, they mightn't have appeared so – I was assiduous about my note-taking and honest about my assurances of help. After the surgery I had a pleasant meal with several friendly and interesting colleagues – following which there was even an unplanned visit to a bookshop – then took a short but refreshing stroll in a small woodland area with two stern-faced yet sympathetic secretaries…and found that even the scheduled meeting of the evening was a lot more stimulating than anticipated. In fact I was astonished by how little my previous night's lack of sleep seemed to have affected me.

And this may sound smug but I actually came up with a couple of remarks that gave rise to prolonged laughter, which wasn't (I believe) merely sycophantic. The adrenalin was running.

It's true that on my way home I stopped in a lay-by and closed my eyes for half an hour – and briefly held Jay's sweater to my nose before closing them – but I could most likely have managed without; I was only following Sophie's impassioned advice, given nearly fifteen hours earlier, to please darling be sensible. And sensible I was.

Arrived back in London, or rather on the outskirts, the first thing I did was to call Jay. But he wasn't home. I tried again, twice, before reaching Hampstead, and held on both times to a slow count of twenty – just in case – yet there wasn't any answer. Clearly, I'd have to wait until the morning for the update I felt so anxious to receive.

And in the morning, although I'd slept much better, I was again showered, shaved and dressed well before seven. But I delayed phoning Jay until eight; he, too, might have slept better. Therefore, while Sophie was seeing to the boys' breakfasts – Ruby didn't sleep in, unless we wanted her to babysit – I rang him from the study.

He still wasn't there.

Six

Thankfully, however, *he* rang *me* at half-past-eight. By good fortune, I was just then collecting papers – again in the study.

"Oh, thank God! Are you all right?"

"Yes, fine. But I've been having adventures. If I grab a taxi, I could get to Hampstead in fifteen minutes. Might we meet for coffee in that little place we went to before? The one opposite the Everyman."

He'd underestimated the amount of traffic at that time in the morning; his journey took him half an hour. I'd ordered for us both but since Mitzi, the owner, had stood for some time making friendly conversation – mainly about Sophie – our coffee and Danish arrived only a short while before he did.

I said: "I was so relieved you telephoned."

"It went off like a dream. Well, anyway to begin with." He was wearing the same white T-shirt; it had lost that freshly laundered look.

"Did he challenge you at all?"

"Yes, he did. But – like you said – it was his word against mine and the customer's always right. What could he do but back away in defeat?"

"He hadn't tried to have it out before that?"

"I could see that he'd wanted to. In the tube. With both of us strap-hanging and at least a dozen others in between. But at that stage I was being careful to keep my distance, although whenever he looked my way – which was often – he found my gimlet eye resting upon him. You could tell he wasn't enjoying himself."

"Yet when you both got out? Couldn't he then…?"

"No, because I'd decided to go on to the next stop. After he'd left the train he looked back a bit too late – he'd been caught up by the crowd! I gave him a nice big wink, though. And the next time he set eyes on me I was looking at various kinds of tea."

"He must have loved that."

"He went very pale. He left the department and I thought he was going to be sick."

"How long was he away?"

"I'm not sure. I went out for a bit and when I came back he too had returned. In fact I popped out several times; thought it might be more unsettling if he kept thinking he'd got rid of me." He sighed. "But I suppose this was what finally allowed him to give me the slip. I asked for him by name; was told he'd probably gone to lunch. So I decided that was my cue to head back to Maida Vale. I let myself in; had a mosey round; knew I wouldn't have to hurry."

"But something went wrong? It all went like a dream, you said. *Anyway – at first.*"

"I'll say that something went wrong! I told you how pale he was looking. Halfway through lunch he must have thrown up or something. At least, that's what I thought: that he must have been instructed to come home. And, as it turned out, he got there not a great deal later than I did. I could have waited for him on the doorstep."

"Oh, bloody hell!"

"Yes, instant paralysis! I froze. I heard that key turn in the lock and didn't stop to think *Hey, what's the panic? You're as big as he is*! I felt just like a boy again, as though it was my old headmaster about to walk in and find me altering exam results. My only thought was where to hide. I was standing in the kitchen. Thank God, there was a second way out – no, not an exit, I don't mean that, but a box room with a load of junk in it…and a handle that came off in my hand as soon as I'd jerked the door shut. Never mind; for the moment I was safe. When Max came into the kitchen he had no idea that we were so lovingly close or that I could hear his every movement. Even watch it to some degree, by squatting at the keyhole."

"I take it he didn't stay in the kitchen for very long?"

"On this occasion, my love, you are so terribly mistaken! He stayed there for the remainder of the afternoon – and for much of the evening, as well."

"But why? Doing what?"

"Preparing a meal for his lady friend. Clearly, he wasn't sent home because he'd been sick; he must have *feigned* sickness, possibly as the result of an unexpected phone call, a promise he may playfully have been reminded of, a need to show he was always – but always – a man who honoured his commitments. I could see a couple of carrier bags on the kitchen table. They were filled with meat and potatoes and cream and stuff and it occurred to me that if he hadn't stopped just now at some of the local shops I'd have let myself in and probably found him waiting for me with a carving knife. And, because by then he was hating me so much, he might very well have used it."

"And it was I who involved you in all of this!"

"Yes, it was. Bear that in mind if I ever start to seriously piss you off! But at first, you know, it was quite interesting. I could hear his mutterings. Did you realize he muttered to himself?"

"He used to, as a child. I assumed he'd grown out of it. Perhaps because he's getting stressed…?"

"Yes, he's getting stressed all right. Every so often he'd begin to pace. 'Fuck him!' he'd say. 'Fuck him! Fuck them both! My God, I'll make them pay!' Actually, it wasn't that interesting; you'd think he could have varied it a little – for his own sake if not for mine. And then, till the next time, he'd just go back to the cup of tea he'd made, or later to his glass of wine, and continue with the rather fancy meal he was preparing. He had two recipe books to help him."

"Well, he'd certainly started on it early enough. Was it yet three?"

"But that was evidently the fault of his visitor, who not only arrived at a very strange hour for dinner – half-past-five or so – but would be needing to catch a train from Victoria shortly after nine. She lives in Eastbourne and for the moment couldn't stay overnight because…oh, I don't know, something about her maid being away till Saturday and there being a very important delivery expected in the morning. Important, she said, because it happened to be a small present for himself. Well, no – actually not so small, she told him, not in terms of size."

"Then you learnt all this from *her*?"

"Yes."

"Something tells me that she isn't young?"

"About twenty years his senior, at a guess. Surprisingly, she seems quite nice and not at all as stupid as you'd think… considering she's a rich widow falling for the charms of a pretty unmistakable fortune-hunter."

"But she wouldn't need to be that stupid. Only lonely and trusting. I wonder how they met?"

"In the shop. I inferred she comes up from Sussex two or three times a month. It's my belief it started out with little chats which soon turned into light lunches at the Kardomah and after that progressed to dinner at the Ritz. I know there've been three weekends in Eastbourne. I know, too, that he has the day off on Friday and will be going down there again: both to find out the nature of his 'small' surprise and also because…'Well, because there've been certain silly irritations I'd like to get away from.'"

"He actually said that?"

Jay nodded. I now remembered he was an actor – and one, I saw, who could convincingly and quite without parody, without even needing to raise his voice at all, differentiate between assured and sophisticated man and subtly less confident older woman. "'What kind of irritations?'"

"'Oh, all tied up with something I can't discuss at present.'"

"'But if you want to get away from things like that which bother you, silly or otherwise, why won't you come back with me tonight? We'll say you've fallen ill.'"

"'Oh, I wouldn't give them that satisfaction!'"

"'Them?'"

"'And in any case I have a means of dealing with it – or of having somebody else deal with it – that ought to quickly put an end to further repetition.'"

"'But just in case it doesn't…Eastbourne on Friday?'"

"'Yes, I expressed myself badly: apart from anything else, I'd still be wanting that. And very well you know it, my dear seeker of reassurance – my dear fisher of compliments.'"

Jay had come to the end of this particular exchange.

"Sweetheart, you mustn't go back to your flat today. Obviously."

"Don't worry: his 'means of dealing with it' won't include any attempt at elimination – think how that would jeopardize his bargaining position! Oh, and by the way, he also made it clear he needs to return to London first thing on Sunday. There's a pressing family engagement he must attend!"

"And all this happened in the kitchen?"

"Yes. Gourmet meal, tablecloth, candlelight, champagne – 'and even, afterwards, your disgusting amaretto!' – but all in the kitchen because it was less formal than the dining room and he didn't want to treat her as a guest. 'Besides, to be honest, my sweet, I didn't have the time to clear it and transfer things to my box room before a final sorting out.' Thank God! He actually said he'd considered it and that the very next time she came…"

"It makes me cold just to think about it."

"Oh – and one last detail! 'I want to thank you for that crazy, wonderful thing you said you might be going to do for me before the summer's out.'"

"Hell's bells, when it comes to quoting, you can beat even my father-in-law. We'll have to organize a contest"

"I may have paraphrased a little."

"'Before the summer's out'? What's going to happen, I wonder, before the summer's out?"

"Maybe she'll agree to let him whisk her off to somewhere in the New World?"

"No, I don't think so. On Sunday he was hoping for a rich *young* woman to rush down longingly to the quayside."

"Also, this gift that's being delivered – it struck me as something not readily transportable. I hope he doesn't mean to disappoint her."

"He's *bound* to disappoint her."

"I suppose he is. Well, at any rate she enjoyed her meal last night. And I have to say that it smelt good. An exquisite form of torture; Max would have been delighted." He inhaled, with closed eyes, like the Bisto Kid. "May I have another Danish?"

"When did you last eat?"

"It doesn't matter. Another Danish will be fine."

"Yesterday's breakfast? God, I'm such a brute! How can you ever think me worth the saving?"

"I don't know. Maybe I'll come up with something after I've had that Danish."

At least I ordered him some scrambled egg and bacon – a double portion – and a plate of wholemeal toast, with more coffee and a glass of orange juice.

"They had wine," he said, with downcast eye and glum expression. The wistfulness extended. "Not to mention amaretto."

"'Disgusting' amaretto."

"You don't have to concur with absolutely *every* word your brother may be heard to utter!"

"Besides, it wasn't nine o'clock in the morning when they were imbibing all that alcohol, or even" – I glanced at my watch – "oh, for heaven's sake, very nearly ten! But what else did you find out with your sweet little ear glued to that box-room door? Did you happen to hear her name?"

"'My dearest Olivia,' he said at one point. 'Or may I call you Mrs Prescott-Ames?'"

"Olivia Prescott-Ames? Well done. But tell me something, Jay. He must have taken her to the station? Why didn't you make your escape?"

"Well may you ask."

"I *am* asking!"

"I was asleep."

"You were…what?"

"After dinner they went off (I'd imagine) to the bedroom. By then I'd been cooped up for over four hours – and without even a chair. But when there wasn't anybody nearby I could at least clear a bit of a space on the floor…and sit down…or even lie down… You forget, I hadn't slept the night before and what with all the excitement of the morning…"

"No, I don't forget."

"When I awoke he was doing the washing up; and it was after ten."

"My brother Max doing the washing up? Though I suppose that even Adolf Hitler, on occasion, may have done the washing up? But after that didn't he have the decency to go to bed?"

"Possibly."

"So…?"

"Well, for a politician, Tom, you may have quite a good memory – and there may sometimes be one or two things you *don't* forget but… That handle which came off in my hand?"

"Oh, God! That handle which came off in your hand."

"Which meant the door could only be opened from the outside."

"Sweetheart…!"

"And I had no idea how long it would take to break it down. Long enough to phone the police and have me arrested? And what story could I ever have told the police? Or long enough to be waiting there with that afore-mentioned carving knife? Oh, yes, most certainly."

"So…what, then? You just went back to sleep?"

"Did I hell? But luckily there was at least an old vase I could take a pee into. Oh, it's just occurred to me: I didn't empty it after my breakout!"

"Which, in the end, took how long?"

"Fifteen minutes? I know he left the flat at ten-past-eight. What time did I phone you?" Ruefully, he rubbed his shoulder. "Every square inch will be forever bruised. I hadn't any tools and I couldn't even use my feet – not in these shoes!"

"You'll have to get something at the chemist's. Is it painful?"

He assured me that it was. "I'm no hero. Don't ask me to be brave. I'll soak it in a bath as soon as I get home."

"You're not going home. You'd better move into a hotel for the next week."

"You mean, because you think he'd shop me to the coppers? With all those thousands of fingerprints flying around? But he won't do that. Suppose they discovered my motive?"

"No, I mean, because of what he said about dealing with annoyances – or having somebody else deal with them. Anyway, even if you hadn't overheard that, I still wouldn't have wanted you to go back. "

"What, not simply for a hot bath and to throw a few things into a suitcase?"

"When I suggested this whole crazy scheme I clearly wasn't thinking straight. Isn't that a perfect illustration of what stress and lack of sleep can do? Please forgive me."

51

"Perhaps I'd better go to Eastbourne? Sun and sea and Beachy Head."

"Perhaps you better had." Neither of us meant it at the time. "No, darling, who knows what contacts he may have? Contacts capable of being activated by just a speedy phone call? You can buy whatever you're going to need. You can stand under a hot shower at the hotel."

"Shall we say the Ritz? It's already been mentioned once this morning. Could be a sign."

"If that's where you'd like to be that's indeed where you *shall* be."

"It was a joke."

"You know, Jay, there's something I can't help wondering. Why, if he's got a rich widow all ready for plucking – why do you think he's also chasing us?"

"My dearest Tom! Sorry to labour it, but hearing you put a question like that really won't inspire me to change my vote at the next election!"

I laughed…and that was the very moment when Sophie walked in.

Seven

S he was accompanied by Miriam, our nextdoor neighbour. The two women were thinking – not very seriously – of writing a book about coffee places in the north of London, and every ten days or so sallied forth on their research, combining it with bits of non-household shopping and with having a very leisurely lunch out. It simply hadn't occurred to me that they might drop in on Mitzi, who'd been at school with both of them. Perhaps I was still too tired to allow for every contingency. It was stupid of me. Jay and I could have met at the workman's caff where we had breakfasted the day before.

"Tom! What on earth are *you* doing here? Why aren't you at work?"

Sophie turned to her short, slim, ginger-haired companion. "Didn't I always say I was married to a skiver?"

It struck me there was something just a little unnatural about her; just a tiny bit off-key.

"No," said Miriam. "But that doesn't mean you aren't. Or that most of us aren't, come to think of it. I suppose that's why they call us the weaker sex. We have to work twice as hard to make up for it."

"Well, *I'm* not to blame!" I protested.

I had by now stood up – which wasn't as easy as it sounds; there wasn't much room between the table and the vinyl-covered bench placed against the wall. Jay had risen, too.

"It's this man here who's the real culprit."

"Tom may not be a skiver," murmured Miriam, admiringly, "but you can see how he's ended up in parliament!"

There weren't normally this many jokes in the course of just an hour or so concerning my chosen profession. But whoever had made them – whether Jay or Miriam – I felt they symbolised a lightness of touch, or of atmosphere, which, less than forty-eight hours ago, neither Max nor I would ever have considered possible…not right now, not in *this* branch of the Ralston family. In fact I tremored on the brink of feeling cheerful. *So what do you say to that, you non-prophetic scumbag?*

"Darling, don't you recognize him?" I said to Sophie.

Sophie was gazing at Jay. "Yes, I think I do recognize you. I'm sure I do. Oh, this is going to sound rather rude – but I'm afraid I'll need to be given a clue."

"In the meantime do you mind if we join you? Then you and I" – Miriam was addressing Jay – "can talk about the weather, while these two have their little parlour game."

"Back in March," I prompted.

"I can't think of a thing we did back in March, other than attending Lucy's wedding and – oh, yes, just the evening before that, when normally we don't leave the house more than once in any century – going to the theatre."

"You're now so warm you must be burning."

"My God, you were in that play, weren't you? You were the student with the young bride!"

Jay held out his hand. "Correction! I was the young student with the old bride – Jessica's nearly five years older than I am! Jay Linden," he said.

"And this is my wife, Sophie Ralston. And our friend and neighbour, Miriam Roberts."

"*Now* may we all sit down?" asked Miriam, when she too had shaken Jay's hand. "And you and I, Jay, are still going to talk about the weather, or any subject that you choose, other than anybody's age – because, frankly, you're the handsomest man I've met all year! Tell me what the play is and this evening I'll be sitting in the front row blowing kisses."

"Oh God," I said to Jay. "What have I got you into?"

"I'm afraid the play's finished. Otherwise that would have been wonderful and I'd have been blowing them straight back."

"I truly never thought," I said, "when we started talking in that sweet shop…"

"Sweet shop?" exclaimed Sophie.

"I was looking for a packet of cough lozenges."

"Why, my poor love, do you have a sore throat?"

But although her tone appeared concerned, somehow it also sounded mildly ironic…almost as if she already saw through… But how could she? It had to be my guilty conscience.

"I thought I did, but now it's all completely gone. We ought to patent a medicine called Distraction. I even forgot about the lozenges."

"Well, what an unexpected pleasure this is," declared Miriam, as though she were a hostess attempting to cover a slightly awkward pause.

"Tom's been telling me he's a politician," said Jay at nearly the same moment.

"Though when I told him I was Tory…"

"…this meeting very nearly didn't take place!"

"Me, I'm a confirmed Socialist," lied Miriam, gazing at my lover with limpid eyes. (I felt so proud of him – what did it matter if today of all days he had to look scruffy and unshaven?) "Or do I mean Liberal? Communist? Independent? Actually I'm thinking of starting my own party. Only waiting to find someone to come in with me."

"Your husband?"

"You mean, *that* skiver? Oh, just in time I had it pointed out to me. I owe it all to Sophie. How can we ever repay her?"

"Well, talking of skiving…" I again stood up, a little awkwardly. I'd been about to ask Jay if I could offer him a lift but had abruptly changed my mind. I took a five-pound note from my wallet and handed it to Sophie, along with a rather bulky though attractively wrapped package which I took out of my briefcase. "Open this later, after you get home." (Always unfailingly obedient, she opened it in the lavatory at Mitzi's.) "Jay, is it safe to leave you in such company?"

"Darling, I'll do my very best to protect him," promised Sophie.

I shook his hand. "Me, I'm awfully glad this meeting did take place. You must come to dinner one evening. Mustn't he, sweetheart?"

"Of course he must. What about tonight?"

How unbelievable it sounds: I felt so happy as I waved through the window (and was buttonholed by Mitzi returning from the Express Dairy across the road, a bottle of gold-topped milk in either hand). For a minute I didn't care about my career; I didn't care about anything other than the four people in my life – and, just for that moment, about Miriam too, who in her good-natured overwhelming fashion had eased the way into an encounter which could have been disastrous. I got back in the car and had negotiated even Swiss Cottage, not to mention Fitzjohn's Avenue leading down to it, and Finchley Road leading away from it, before I realized I hadn't a second's recollection of my having done so. This frightened me and I remained alert from then on but my awareness of a desire to run, jump, touch the sky, not easily accomplished in traffic, remained undiminished.

Later on, of course, I heard what had happened after my departure. Jay had said he'd be delighted to come to dinner; whereupon Miriam, not to be outdone in this matter of delivering invitations, had suggested that the three of them should walk to

Kenwood – this made a pleasant walk across the Heath – where she would be happy to buy them all lunch.

And then Mitzi unwittingly took care of their agenda for the afternoon as well, by saying she had seen such a good double programme at the Everyman the night before: *Spring in Park Lane* and *Gentleman's Agreement*.

Sophie had also asked Miriam and Alastair to dinner.

"But oh dear – this is so tragic! – we're due to attend my mother's birthday party. And can't you see from Jay's face how bitterly and eternally disappointed he is, poor lamb? Will he *ever* forgive me?"

"I don't know. The poor lamb is just waking up to the essential duplicity of women. You said you'd have been blowing me kisses from the front row."

"Oh, it's true. In *spirit* I would have. Noel Coward drew on me for the role of Elvira in *Blithe* – "

Mitzi happened to be passing. "Are you sure, dear, it wasn't for the role of Madam Arcati?" Miriam put out her tongue.

Jay turned to Sophie. "No, I'm afraid it's only men in my life from now on. With the single exception of yourself, naturally."

Sophie accepted this. "Well, in that case may I still go to phone Ruby to tell her to lay an extra place for supper?"

"And I suppose we do have to make allowances," sighed Miriam. "No women in his life? After all, he *is* an actor."

At first Jay didn't realise this could have been taken two ways. "Oh, Miriam!" he responded. "I'm glad my friends Sir Laurence and Sir Ralph can't hear you!" (That evening he admitted to me he might have been somewhat stretching a point but at least he had once met them both, he said – or at any rate viewed them from a fairly short distance – at last year's theatrical garden party.)

But it was only over lunch that he suddenly thought of something.

"Oh my God, Sophie, I've just remembered – I'm afraid I'll have to cancel this evening! You see, there are renovations being made to my flat and I'm supposed to be looking for somewhere to…" He shrugged, felt tempted to say *hide out*, before Miriam took advantage of his brief hesitation. "To lay your hapless head?" she sympathised.

"But that's ridiculous," asserted my wife without hesitation. (That's symbolic of one of the many things I love about *her*.) "*We* have enough room to put you up, Jay, both for tonight and however long you need."

"And so do we!" inserted Miriam.

"Sophie, are you sure? You've only just met me. How do you know I'm not a monster?"

"If we do discover that, we'll swiftly offload you onto our nearest neighbour."

"Most people would know at once that he's a monster."

"Tom wouldn't mind?"

"Tom wouldn't mind."

"Neither would Alastair, I can assure you!"

"That's so lovely of you. So lovely of you both." He couldn't omit Miriam. "After the film I'll stop to do a spot of shopping."

"Why? Tom will be able to lend you anything you need. You're roughly the same size."

"Alastair, too! Or, at least, we could stretch him a few inches. I'd be perfectly happy to stretch him a few inches, if the two of you would lend me a gentle hand." She turned to Jay. "Without my knowledge, he took our two sweet and innocent young children to the Chamber of Horrors at Madam Tussaud's. We could give him an abiding insight into how it really felt to be stretched upon the rack."

"Oh, Miriam, stop it!" exclaimed Sophie and Jay in unison.

"Under those circumstances," murmured Jay, "I don't think I'd want to borrow his pyjamas."

"And anyway," said Sophie, "by the time we'd finished, the shops would probably be closed. I think you'll do much better helping your mother cut the cake at her seventieth birthday party."

"And passing round the trifle. Oh dear. It must be karma. One can't ignore the Fates."

And so arrived another wholly memorable evening; Max Ralston notwithstanding. When I got home, a little before eight, it was to find Jay sitting with both the boys on his lap and in the midst of reading them a William story. They were enthralled and of course I could totally understand why. Not only Mr Brown and Robert and Hubert and every other male character leapt vividly off the page but so did Mrs Brown and Ethel and Violet Elizabeth – they all became real people with real personalities. When I was doing the reading, or even Sophie, they all, both male and female, remained caricatures. Again, I'd almost forgotten that Jay had been to drama school.

But not only that. Sophie told me how he had bathed them and got them ready for bed, overseeing the teeth-cleaning and the prayers, and how he had taught them to sing *There's a hole in my bucket, dear Liza*. And throughout the entire process there hadn't been even one squawk of protest, nor of squabble. She said: "I have a proposal to make. Shall we hire him while he's out of work – and then send his agent off to Australia?"

Both Gilbert and Josh wanted to know if he'd be the one to take them to school in the morning, and collect them in the afternoon, and bath them and read to them in the evening, and neither Sophie nor I had ever known them go to bed with less fuss, not even on Christmas Eve.

"Yet obviously it won't last," predicted Jay and we knew he was completely right; but it was still something to be wondered at and made the most of while we had it.

He'd even tidied up their clutter – with Sophie lazing in an armchair, glass in hand, legs resting comfortably on footstool. And languidly pointing a tired finger.

"No, I'm sorry, Mr Linden, this will never do! Don't you realize you've missed one – that soldier with the broken arm? Oh and good heavens! Please don't tell me that's a Dinky toy I can see poking out from underneath the curtain! *Who* was it who wrote your reference?"

"Tomorrow," I heard him say – as I came back into the room in more casual attire. "Tomorrow we get them to do all this by themselves."

"Now you're getting *really* carried away!" she informed him. "Despite what Josh said to you earlier."

Naturally I asked what that had been.

"And how did you get such very big muscles?" our younger son had wanted to know.

"By eating up my spinach and Brussels sprouts and carrots and peas and cauliflower…"

"And your broccoli, most definitely," said Sophie.

"And my broccoli, most definitely," agreed Jay.

"Mummy, may we have spinach and Brussels sprouts and carrots and peas and cauliflower for our supper tomorrow night?"

"And broccoli most definitely? We'll have to see. But how about taking some salad to school in your packed lunches?"

"Salad?" checked Josh, gazing at Jay, while Gilbert looked on in gently smiling tolerance.

"Oh, certainly. I couldn't live without it!"

And soon after I'd got home but hadn't yet been up to change, "I'm afraid I've got to send you *both* in to say goodnight. Jay, are you certain you'll be able to stand a full week of this?"

"With two boys as beautiful as those?"

"Humff," said Sophie. But you could see that she was pleased. "I'm still not sure, though, that you'll ever get them to clear up everything themselves."

"There are ways. No new song if they don't. No new William story. And perhaps I shall give them a very small hand."

"This man is *ruthless*," Sophie said to me. "I feel we'd better not tell Miriam."

"Ruthless? May simply be that he's never had any children of his own. Hasn't yet been more or less worn down by them."

However that might be, after we'd closed the boys' door behind us – they no longer insisted on having it ajar; a nursery light was now sufficient – we stopped at a place round the corner from it, secluded enough for a second quick hug. (The first had been downstairs while Sophie was tucking up the children, despite Jay and I having agreed that a cuddle in *my* sitting room – well, Sophie's and mine and the two boys' – somehow seemed a little more underhand than a cuddle in *his*. Was this irrational? Anyhow, we'd promised ourselves we'd soon get over it.)

Now, on the landing, we felt less compunction. "Darling, you've been fantastic," I said.

"Not difficult in these surroundings."

"But how on earth have you kept going? Did you sleep in the cinema?"

"I thought I might but in the end it wasn't necessary."

"I see. Every now and then you touched your stubble and just the rasp of it was enough to keep you awake? Ah, what it is to be young!"

"Yes, those nine years make all the difference! I could even hear the dialogue I'd drowned out for everybody else."

"Oh – and by the way – how did you get such very big muscles?"

While we were going back down I warned him, though still in a reasonably low voice, that there was one question he ought to be prepared for: when was he going to have children of his own?

Despite our eight years of marriage, though, Sophie clearly wasn't that predictable. There wasn't a single question concerning either children or girlfriends.

I'd brought home a magnum of champagne and we had some Château Margaux in the cellar. I'd determined, though – and so, I could see, had Jay – we ought to be careful about how much we drank. But being careful was no hardship. Our laughter didn't become silly and it didn't by any means follow each remark any of us made – as you sometimes hear in restaurants and which, for outsiders, can rapidly grow tedious – but there was still a lot of it. And we completely ignored the telephone ("They're out!" said Ruby every time), knowing it could never be so interesting as the conversation it aimed to interrupt. Ours was a three-way first dinner date: a metaphor I've already hinted at. Different – but on this occasion, anyway – exhilarating.

Exhilarating!

It was only when we'd left the table and taken our coffee into the sitting room that – not so very carefully, after all – I tried to put it into words.

"One of the three most enjoyable evenings of my life!"

Sophie showed no sign of wishing to dispute any such rather sweeping claim. She merely asked: "And which were the other two?"

I reached across to take her hand – we were both on the sofa.

"Oh, that was simply a number I plucked out of the air! But one of them just has to be the evening of our first date. Remember how we didn't get to bed till nearly four?" I smiled at Jay. "Though I don't mean together – unfortunately!"

"Which now leaves one." She still kept hold of my hand although holding hands wasn't something we normally did a lot of. "Don't try to tell me it was purely random. Three is *not* a number you just pluck out of the air."

I smiled at Jay again – a smile, perhaps, to indicate husbandly tolerance of such tenacity. "Well, I think it must have been something very similar to that? Our wedding night, maybe?"

"Okay. That'll do."

"Yes, all for one and one for all!" And this time, when I could really see no logical connection between wedding nights and musketeers and might have been seriously stumped if she'd asked me to provide one (I'd have had to say it was clearly the influence of the figure three) she didn't think to question it.

Or possibly she did. Possibly it was only a somewhat startling interruption that stopped her. Not the telephone this time, nor yet Ruby having come to tell us she was off and would see us in the morning, but the sudden hurling open of the door by two smilingly daredevil rascals who – side-by-side – now threw themselves into the room.

"And what is the meaning of *this*?" demanded Sophie. "Do you know what time it is? Why aren't the pair of you fast asleep and dreaming of rabbits and things?" These were all exclamations rather than questions.

"That's dogs, Mummy, not children." Gilbert was being as indulgent with his mother as he'd earlier been with Josh. It seemed to be an evening for quiet toleration all round.

In the meantime Josh himself had padded over to Jay and put a small hand on his shoulder; a shoulder which – thank heaven – now appeared to have stopped aching.

"He wants to ask you something," explained Gilbert, from his place by Sophie's chair.

"And what is it you want to ask me, Josh?"

"Why don't you live here? I really wish you would."

Jay made no answer but put one arm about him and scooped him onto his lap. Three seconds later, as had been the case when I came home, his other knee was occupied as well.

Eight

I'd said I would take him down to Westminster and give him a guided tour of my workplace – or as much of it as was allowed – so I waited until he'd returned from walking the children to school…and no doubt being shown off in the playground: now all clean-shaven and wearing *my* white T-shirt, *my* blue jeans, *my* brown loafers (purchased only the previous Saturday). Sophie waved us off from the front door and blew us extravagant kisses.

"I can't lose all this," I said, as we turned the corner at the bottom of our road.

"Tommy, you won't have to."

"Promise?"

"Well, what I *can* promise is that yours truly doesn't intend to get lost and I now feel as confident as can be, having learned at firsthand how the four of you interact, that Sophie won't intend it either; which means, of course, those two pesky and rambunctious brats are still going to be around for at least the next ten years, to plague the living daylights out of both you, Sophie, and whoever else happens to live within a five-mile radius. Oh, yes, there are bound to be shock waves – anguish – exhaustive discussion. But

Sophie's not the girl to give up on what anyone can see is the love of her life. The love of both our lives."

"You don't happen to be fishing, by any chance?"

"And whether I do or not, you sound like Max talking to Mrs Prescott-Ames." He laid his hand lightly on my wrist. "All for one and one for all – remember?"

"You know something? I'd kill him if I had to."

"Me, too."

We had crossed a line. I think we both knew we had crossed a line. We were meaning what we said. "Tom? Shall I go to Eastbourne?"

"What would you do in Eastbourne?"

"Try to find out what she's worth? And if it's more than twenty grand…try to find out whether our blackmailer can be blackmailed?"

He paused.

"Or, failing that, just push him off Beachy Head."

"And who do you suppose is going to tell you what she's worth? Certainly not her bank – even if you knew which one it was."

"Granted, old doubting Thomas, but just the look of her house might give us an inkling."

"What – with the amount of outstanding mortgage helpfully pinned to her front door?"

But all the same I was warming to his proposal. It had occurred to me we shouldn't even need to ascertain if our blackmailer could be blackmailed. It was indisputable he could.

Nor, indeed, should we need to ascertain what the lady was worth.

"I think we can assume she's rich – and possibly to the tune of a bit more than twenty thousand. A lot more than twenty thousand."

We were waiting at those continually busy traffic lights which yesterday I must have driven through without a particle of conscious thought.

"And perhaps…if only it were possible to make her see the kind of person he is…? Jay, you've hit on it! Blackmail the blackmailer! Why didn't we think of that before?"

"Because we've been too nicely brought up. Blackmail wasn't on the school curriculum."

"But this means you needn't go to Eastbourne. I'll speak to Max tonight. Or, better still, we'll visit the bastard. Apprise him of the scheme we have in mind."

"If only that handle hadn't been defective…"

"What?"

"How profoundly satisfying it would have been! He wouldn't have had the slightest clue we even knew of her existence, let alone could have provided him with her name and her address." In fact, we hadn't yet checked on the address but were confident we'd find it in the East Sussex telephone book, which of course they'd have in any main post office or library. "I mean, wouldn't it have been good if he could have found out only tonight, while we were standing right in front of him to witness his expression!"

"Yes – true. But it's only the element of surprise that's missing. He'll still know we have him."

I was getting quite excited.

"Do you realize, Jay, we're off the hook? We've actually escaped him? And all thanks to you, my love. Entirely thanks to you. Oh, God, you're such a marvel!"

"It does almost seem like it? No, I don't mean that last bit."

"Well, you should, you should! Dear Lord – it's incredible – we're free of him! He hasn't any comeback. We shan't ever need to set eyes on him again, not ever!"

"Apart from tonight, that is."

"Yes, apart from tonight. Oh, I wish I could express what I feel! My gratitude. Relief. I think even *you* are never going to know how much you mean to me, when really I'd like to express it to the nation. To the world! I'd like to copy the Queen at Christmas – Home Service, Light Programme, the lot! Except that *I* might take it a degree further. *I'd* do it on TV, as well. "

"Mightn't that just *slightly* defeat the object of the exercise? But, still, I appreciate the thought. Of course – if you really want to express it – you should know that right now, in default of the BBC, I'd probably settle for a nice hotel room."

"Oh you slut! You tease! Sweet heaven, how I wish we could! But you're well aware it's not possible."

By now we were nearly at Orchard Street.

I saw an empty phone box.

"You know what? I'm going to ring him! Make sure he'll be at home this evening. Tell him to expect us."

"But surely he won't be home now?"

"I'll leave a message at work."

"Then better not say to expect *us*. He'll think we mean to beat him up."

I parked in Portman Square, alongside the railings that bounded the square and under the overhanging branches of a couple of plane trees. Perversely, neither of us had any coppers but a shop called Daniel Neal, at which Sophie and I had bought the boys' school uniforms, gave me change of half a crown.

In the still vacant booth, I consulted the second of the four directories; and the woman on the Fortnum's switchboard, instead of writing down my message, put me straight through to Provisions. I hadn't realized I would need to speak to him.

One of his colleagues answered. But apparently Max wasn't serving anyone at present – I heard him cheerily greeting somebody as he approached the phone. It seemed he wasn't in any very great hurry.

"Well, well, if it isn't my own dear Claude! To what do I owe this most unexpected pleasure?"

I told him.

"A visit? How nice! But I must be perfectly honest – I can't lure you over under false pretences. It's all been taken care of."

"Been taken care of? What has?"

"Why, all that business you were wanting to speak to me about. Naturally. What else?"

"You've no idea what I was wanting to speak to you about."

"Oh, but I think I have. And you see, because of that, I've already had a good long conversation with Olivia."

My confidence had ebbed. All sense of triumph. All sense of well-being.

"But, again, how I admire you! No prevarication. No 'What do you mean?' No 'Who's Olivia?' Claude, you're a lesson to us all! And how are my two gorgeous nephews…not to mention my even more gorgeous Sophia? Of course, I shall be able to see for myself on Sunday – as well as to engage in sunny conversation with their happy lord and master; their *present* happy lord and master? That arrangement still stands, naturally." It wasn't a question.

"And what exactly did you tell her?"

"My even more gorgeous sister-in-law? Oh, nothing – promise, promise! – I haven't yet asked her whether she's sex-starved; haven't yet asked her to marry me."

"You know who I mean."

"Shouldn't that be *whom* you mean? But who am I to quibble? You're the one who went to Oxford and got that glossy black-gowned seal of approval."

I felt so tempted just to slam down the receiver.

"Oh, are you still there, Claude? Such a waste, if not – I feel sure you haven't had your four pennies' worth!" Not hard to understand why he'd assume I was calling from a public box.

"I asked what you had told her."

"Ah…the lovely Olivia? Mrs Prescott-Ames? In short – my intended? Well, let me see now. What *did* I tell her? Not the easiest thing to summarize but basically I just gave her the facts, sir – I just gave her the facts!"

"What facts?"

"Embroidered slightly, I admit. Depression, jealousy, a fondness for the bottle. Sexual deviancy. Fundamentally, I believe,

I delivered a novel by Dickens: a newly discovered manuscript that ought to be worth thousands. She was appalled...and gripped...by every single page. Oh, what a cliff-hanger; I think I could probably have made him fairly popular – Mr Dickens."

"In other words, you told her a pack of lies." But that was merely talk just for the sake of it. What else had I expected?

"And his hero on this occasion? A bit more complex than either Copperfield or Pip, and I can't say she's actually looking *forward* to meeting him, but if it can't be avoided at least she's going to be prepared. And to be forewarned is... Why do they say *fore*warned? You'd never do that, would you, Claude?"

Now I did put down the receiver. The man who emerged from that phone box was quite a different person to the one who'd entered it. I got back in the car, but even before I'd done so, Jay knew of my depression; merely that six-second walk across the pavement had informed him. "Oh, you poor old love!" He now laid that comforting hand upon my knee. "Tell me what's happened." My résumé sounded very lame.

Jay's response didn't. "Oh, that's such a load of nonsense! She'll never believe a word of it – not when she actually meets you, not after the first ten minutes or so. She isn't stupid."

"Well, maybe she isn't. But she's in love with him. He's no doubt told her how plausible I am and how I'll stop at nothing to scupper any chance he has of real happiness – having always, of course, been such a stranger to real happiness myself."

"No, he can't risk it! Tommy, you have integrity. How can he possibly think that, given time, this won't appear to Olivia? Or that at the very least there won't creep in some tiny niggle of doubt? He must already be scared but point it out to him again...I mean, in the note you ought to write, the one I ought to put through his letterbox this morning. (No need to mention integrity, I'm sure he doesn't know the word.) I'm sorry that I'm sounding bossy but I think it's imperative. Say you'll now give *him* a week for reflection: a week starting Sunday – you're more generous than he is! With time, he's bound to see the game isn't worth the candle. Apart from anything else, if by then he's grassed on us…I mean, grassed on us to the press…well, that's scarcely likely to advance his love suit, is it? Tom, you're holding all the cards; you only have to understand you are. Please don't get depressed. I know it's useless to say it but getting depressed isn't going to help anyone."

He was right: about twice a year I did suffer from depression – only mildly, though – a day or two each time. I wondered if Sophie had told him.

"No," he said, lightly, "Sophie didn't tell me. I'm just insightful. Intuitive. And in love with you…which it's not impossible may have a bit of bearing on the case."

I managed to summon up a smile. In a moment – solely on account of my looking at him and digesting what he'd just said – my smile grew broader.

"That's better," he exclaimed. "That's much better! What's more, right now I'm having another hunch. It's again telling me I ought to go to Eastbourne."

My smile faded. "Why?"

"I'm not sure. Might it help if I could somehow get friendly with Olivia?"

"Well, who knows? At any rate, I don't see how it can do us any harm." I was aware of my voice still sounding lifeless, even grudging. "Do you *want* to go to Eastbourne?"

"I want to do anything that might help."

"When would you go, then? This morning?"

"No, it's important I deliver that letter. Besides, I told the boys I'd pick them up from school. But tomorrow? I'd still get there a whole day ahead of Max. And otherwise what? What would I be doing here?"

I shrugged. "At least I know what *I'll* be doing here. Seeing if I can borrow twenty thousand pounds from the bank."

"But that won't be necessary."

"Jay, don't you see, we have to explore every possible avenue?"

"Okay then. Giving the house as collateral?"

"Well, certainly not my cufflinks…if that's what you happen to be thinking."

He was very forgiving; showed no sign of being offended. I silently pleaded, while there was yet time, that whatever happened I mustn't grow depressed. (Had the happy thought of adding: *Besides, Lord, what a victory that would be for brother Max!*)

"I'm sorry," I said. "Just being snotty. Pay me no attention."

"No – I asked a silly question; received a funny answer."

I didn't believe him but acted as though I did; and suddenly – hallelujah! – I knew that I was out of danger. It was almost as if a heavy curtain had been raised.

"Yes, my love, offering the house as collateral! Sophie and I have joint ownership." My voice had regained its vigour, despite a strongly self-evident rider. "Which unquestionably means that if they say, 'Well, of course, old boy, delighted!' I'll be having to forge her signature many times over!"

"Yes, you will, won't you? Do you think you're up to that?"

"Perhaps easier than pushing him off Beachy Head."

"But not so much fun."

"That's what you *say*; but if it actually came to it… Though it beats me how, with his knowing Mr Jay Linden's in the vicinity, you would ever get him within two hundred feet of the edge! Or let's change that to yards – far more realistic!"

"Yes, that beats me a little, too." Between our seats and well below the level of the windows or the windscreen he squeezed my hand. "So it's becoming increasingly clear. What we need now is a hit-man."

"Do you know any hit-men? Are they listed in the Yellow Pages?"

"Maybe not. But my Aunt Madge has a very wide circle of acquaintance."

"Jay, if you don't watch out, we can forget Max, you'll be the one with the knife sticking out of your back."

"Or the pair of scissors. It's ironic, isn't it, that the night he saw us going to the pictures, the film in question should have been the one it was?"

"*Dial M for Murder?*"

"Even the telephone exchange was right. Maida Vale. But rather more to the point…"

"Yes?"

"The potential killer was someone entirely unconnected with the victim. What conceivable motive could he have had for bumping off a complete stranger?"

"I suppose your Aunt Madge herself wouldn't contemplate a spot of temporary employment?"

"To be entirely accurate," he amended, "I should have said my *Great*-Aunt Madge."

"Oh, that's better still! How could you ever have known it? I have a thing about great-aunts." We grinned. I had incontestably recovered.

"Even Great-Aunt Madge wouldn't necessarily qualify. 'Your motive, madam? Well, now! Wasn't Mr Linden your very favourite nephew? Isn't it widely reported you were rather apt to spoil him?' And – come to think of it, Tom – Hitchcock's previous film was making the same point. Two men who meet on a train and talk about exchanging murders. Apart from that initial encounter – and who really notices what's ordinary? – nothing to suggest a connection."

"Then perhaps there'll be someone when you travel down to Eastbourne? Just so long as he isn't too handsome… That's all that I insist on."

It was certainly a strange week: our propensity to treat things either like Victorian melodrama or Whitehall farce; the shifts between despondency and hope. Perhaps – as Jay seemed to have understood from the beginning – it was sometimes only humour, even gallows-type humour, that could sufficiently thicken the skin, and by reducing the seriousness of reality make it feel a lot less frightening.

He caught a train to Eastbourne on the following day. I drove him to Victoria. He thought that at the other end he'd maybe hire a car.

It might have seemed frustrating to be able to do nothing more than stop beside the barrier and shake hands. Lucky Ingrid Bergman and Gregory Peck in yet another Hitchcock movie who had gone into a pretty firm embrace – twice! – so very close to a surprised yet indulgent ticket collector. But actually it wasn't frustrating. As much warmth could pass between hands and eyes as between arms and lips; and probably no one noticed how long the contact held.

"I'll telephone tonight," he said, "no later than eleven."

"It doesn't matter how late. Half-past-four and you would still be wonderfully welcome. But, for heaven's sake, don't do anything foolish!" I meant risky and he knew it.

"Give hugs to Sophie and the boys."

"See you just the day after tomorrow. Or Sunday morning at the latest."

"Yes."

"I love you, my precious."

When he did phone – and it was well before midnight – I was working in my study.

"So? On the train? Did you meet up with either Robert Walker or Farley Granger?"

"No. But possibly the next best thing. After I got here."

"Tell me."

There were phone calls from him on Friday, too, and on Saturday. Especially on Saturday.

And, bit by bit, the full story would emerge.

It wouldn't make for easy listening.

Part Two

---

as related by Jay Linden.

Nine

As predicted, Tom, she wasn't difficult to find; there were only two Prescott-Ames in the directory: herself, Mrs R (her husband had been an insurance broker named Richard) and her son, Philip. For some reason I hadn't thought of her as having a son. In every play or film featuring some merry widow earmarked for destruction – as well, of course, as in the operetta – the ladies hadn't been provided with family: possibly convenient to themselves, unquestionably more so to any ill-intentioned suitor. (There was one exception, however. In 'Cast a Dark Shadow' there'd been a deeply and correctly suspicious younger sister. Perhaps Olivia had a sister? It could certainly prove a help.)

Anyway, I first went to look at her home. Oddly enough, I discovered right outside that both my shoelaces had worked themselves loose. I had to squat down to retie them.

Whilst carefully attending to their knots, I saw that the house was rambling, gabled and pleasantly ivy-covered; that it had a brick path meandering up to its front door, daisies and buttercups in the grass, beds of various-coloured roses along one of the garden walls.

I also saw that the relatively modern garage, with its separate short drive and own exit onto the roadway, was nicely unobtrusive. I might have supposed the property far too large for merely one occupant – although I suddenly recollected that madam had a maid – but if I'd been rich and currently in the business of house-hunting I think I'd have fallen in love with it even from where I stood (or squatted) by the gate.

I'm confident Max would have been equally impressed; and that it might likewise have crossed *his* mind the place looked entirely too rambling, entirely too spacious, for just one owner. Most likely he'd already used that well-known phrase, 'rattle about', in some of his conversations with her.

As a matter of fact, this query regarding the house – named End House, for obvious reasons – was even touched on by her son, Olivia's son, after I'd phoned him and he'd given me in oft repeated and practically insulting detail, yet clearly well-intentioned, the number of the bus that would take me across Eastbourne to the part where he himself lived: where to catch the bus, roughly how often it ran, how long it would take, and where to ask to be put down. Although I wasn't yet ready to talk to Olivia I hadn't felt at all nervous about ringing Philip. I don't know why. And he, too, was obviously more than willing to hold a meeting.

He lives in a bungalow in a dull and narrow side street; virtually as different, Tom, to his mother's house as – well, I don't know – a prefab to a palace.

Now, what can I say about Philip? Perhaps he's one of the least image-conscious people I've ever met; and yet there assuredly *is* a trace of vanity, as I very soon found out. So do I mean one of the least anxious to impress? Ingenuous? Artless?

Almost childlike? Almost…well, little boy lost?

Yet, anyhow, I liked him – and think that you would too. Liked him; felt sorry for him. He's thirty-three, short and a bit on the weedy side…even though he does claim to be a very good long-distance swimmer.

Also, he's both diabetic and manic-depressive – which means he's had problems holding down a job: mainly in the handmade furniture industry. When he was young he chose to train as a carpenter and in his home he has a kitchen table and a set of chairs he was plainly eager to show off. Luckily my admiration was real and I could gush over them a bit. I don't think I normally gush – do I? – but he really lit up and you could tell it was fulfilling a need.

However, I wouldn't have been able to gush over his wife; and she'd have been a great deal harder to show off. They don't have any children and I can't believe they ever have any sex – but, honestly, who *knows*? And this is one of his periods of unemployment, which may be responsible for a lot of the tension flying about – no wonder the poor man gets depressed!

Though no wonder *she* gets resentful!

Her name is Edna. On my arrival she was out. She'd gone to Sainsbury's; actually, when I telephoned, she'd only just left. Which was fortunate: *she* wouldn't have been nearly so forthcoming, *he* would have been immeasurably more reserved.

The story I'd told on the telephone was true. I said I'd seen his mother in London and been worried about her association with someone called Max Ralston. Edna might have asked me what business it was of mine – or at the very least *where* I had seen his mother. I was all ready to say at the house of a friend but was glad I didn't have to.

Shall I tell you though what *Philip's* immediate response was? "Oh, that bloody man! I'm sorry but I hate him!"

"Well, that certainly gives us something in common," I said.

And he'd at once supplied me with all those directions on how to get there. Even had a pot of tea waiting and a plate of biscuits. We sat in the living room – well, he called it the lounge – and he closed the lid on his gramophone and put away the Deadwood Stage. "Oh, I shouldn't have said what I did! You might have been a friend of his."

"Well, I suppose the man must have friends, because *everybody* has friends, but I can tell you *I* would never choose to be among them."

"Oh, you can say that again! I've met him just the once – at my mum's – and he was rude to me. Which isn't the only thing I've got against him, not by a long chalk."

This might have made me smile. I could picture Max having quite a shock when he met Philip. Put Philip and Olivia at different ends of the same room; listen to the way they spoke, look at the way they dressed…you'd never think, "Ah, *yes*, mother and son!" Philip's accent is provincial. Left to himself he would never – you could almost guarantee it – become stylish. And Max is undoubtedly a snob.

"In what way, Philip, was he rude to you? Anything specific?"

"Yes."

He'd stopped nibbling around the outer bobbles of his Lincoln.

"You see, I'd said that along with my woodwork and listening to records, swimming was one of my favourite pastimes and because of this I was always glad I'd been born by the sea. Well, he just looked me up and down and said he wouldn't have thought I had the build to be a swimmer. That was all. I just thanked my lucky stars I hadn't mentioned – as I very nearly had – that it was my dream one day to swim the Channel."

"But what did your mother say?"

"Oh, she'd been pouring out the tea. I don't suppose she even heard what he said. She only knew what the subject was and she asked him when she handed me his cup (I'd like to have thrown it at him!) whether he himself enjoyed swimming."

"To which I assume he answered yes? Johnny Weissmuller! A very manly type of sport! Something to impress the ladies."

"And although he was sitting down at the time, cramming his mouth with buttered scone and cream and strawberry jam, you should just have seen the way he puffed out his chest; should just have heard the way he gave that silly little laugh of his. 'Actually, I *have* been told – more than once, in fact – that I should've trained for the Olympics; won us a gold medal back in '48.'

"'Why not '52?'

"I think my mother was teasing him, meant it as a joke, but he replied as if she was all serious and had only forgotten the main point.

"'In 1948 the Games were being held right here on British soil,' he said. '*That* would have suited me – hearing the loving roars of the home crowd!'

"'Mm.'

"'Mind you, I could then have won again in Finland, couldn't I? Yes, why not? Oh damn! Missed opportunities!'"

Philip pulled a face.

"Oh, what a liar he is," I exclaimed, with a look and in a tone I knew were bound to be appreciated. "What a braggart! The extraordinary thing is, I know his twin – know him pretty well – and he's not like that at all. In fact, if you tried for a hundred years, you couldn't come up with anyone more different in disposition."

"Perhaps all the good's gone into the one, then," he suggested, "and all the bad's gone into the other?"

Out of the mouths of babes and manufacturers of kitchen furniture! "No *perhaps* about it," I said.

(I'm only reporting this because you don't know how much pleasure I derived out of just being able to talk of you. Even to a stranger.)

"I knew he had a brother but wasn't aware this brother was a twin. I'm sure my mother doesn't know it either. What a funny thing to hide from people…as though you don't want them to think you feel any special closeness, not like twins are supposed to feel."

"Like a form of divorce?" I said. "An act of dissociation from the norm? But, Philip, you said the man's rudeness wasn't the only thing you had against him?"

"No, of course not. He's after my mother's money."

"Yes, naturally he is. But doesn't she realize that?"

"Well, how couldn't she? But shall I tell you what *I* think, Mr Linden?"

"Jay."

"I think she doesn't mind. After all, he's handsome, isn't he? And he's tall and has broad shoulders. All that sort of thing. And he knows how to make compliments. Mum likes that. She likes going out and having a good time. Not since my dad died has she ever gone dancing again, or horse-racing, or cruising round the Med. Dad and her, they were always off somewhere together. And the fact he says he likes older women – finds women his own age boring… Yes, I mean it. I don't think she minds."

"She has the money and might as well spend it?"

"I've often heard her say that thing – you can't take it with you."

"So, Philip, if you understand all this so very well, and your mother obviously likes him, even loves him, then what's your main reservation? What makes you hate him?"

"Nothing to do with his age; nothing to do with his being poor and looking for some well-paid job. But *I* wouldn't hire him. *I* wouldn't trust him not to be slacking the very second he was off probation – not to be lolling back half the time and swirling the brandy round his glass and reading all the wanted ads."

I nodded. "Yes, I think you've got the measure of the man."

"Nobody deserves such disloyalty. Not even when they're so completely without… "

He broke off and left me unsure if he were going to say 'without loyalty themselves' – or, possibly, 'without any discrimination'. He struck me as a strange mix. At one moment – objective, articulate, insightful. At another – vulnerable, looking for guidance, looking for reassurance.

But, come to think of it, what was so strange about that? Weren't all of us to some degree – ?

"Philip, do you *like* your mother?"

He took his time about answering.

"I used to. But then…I don't know…things changed."

"After your father died?"

"Dad's been dead for ten years. It was a long time after that."

"Were you close to him?"

"Yes. I was close to both of them. Ten years ago I was still living at home."

I hadn't told him I knew where that home was and that I'd even been to take a gander. If he'd asked me why, what could I have said?

All blackmailers – reciprocal or not – had to use a bit of subterfuge.

"But I suppose that with your father gone the house became too big? Your mother decided to look for something smaller?"

"No, my dad was born there, spent his life there, she'd have thought that selling it was like betraying him. And she'd never betray my dad. Or at least that's what…"

I wanted to say: Philip, please try to finish your sentences. "That's what…?"

But he only shook his head. I felt scared he might clam up altogether and I could scarcely have blamed him. I was asking some extremely personal questions. I must have sounded like a policeman.

In fact I wasn't even sure why I was asking them. Was it because if one were inexperienced one never quite knew what could prove to be illuminating? Or was it because if one were inexperienced one never quite knew what actually *needed* illuminating.

"Anyhow, that's really good, Philip! It means your father's house will one day become yours?"

"Does it?" Clearly, my fears had been justified.

Or possibly they hadn't.

"Become mine and my brother's?" he added, in a tone that sounded unmistakably sarcastic.

"Your brother's?" But there hadn't been any third Prescott-Ames in the directory. "Does your brother live in Eastbourne?"

"No, he lives in Battle."

"Just along the coast? On the other side of Hastings?" A new line of questioning. (Leading to what?) "I suppose in that case you get to see him fairly often. And your mum does, too?"

"I see him from time to time – not all that often. My mum doesn't. Doesn't see him at all. He's a pervert. John's a pervert."

"Oh," I said.

"He lives with a man."

I nodded again – as if enlightened by the explanation.

"And he could go to prison if anyone found out."

I was uncertain how to follow this. "Do *you* mind that he's…a homosexual?"

"*I* don't. And Edna doesn't. My mum says it's disgusting. The same as my dad did. She hasn't spoken to John for nearly thirteen years. He didn't even come to the funeral." There were a few seconds of silence, apart from a little reflective munching; by this time he had worked his way through most of the biscuits. "So she won't leave John the house."

"It might be a long time before she dies. Couldn't she have changed her mind by then?"

"Though, naturally, if she left it to me I'd see that he got half. We'd have to sell it and I'd see that he got half."

"That's very nice of you. And would your wife agree?"

"Oh, yes. But the trouble is Mum may not leave it to me either. My wife doesn't like her. She doesn't like my wife. They've never hit it off, not from the beginning. We went to the house together just once, Edna and me, and Mum says Edna stole one of her brooches. Since then they've refused to have anything to do with one another – and that was over six years ago."

And did she, I wanted to say…*did* your wife steal one of her brooches? Yet, in the face of all expectation, there are some questions which even I find it impossible to ask.

"But do you think that's enough to make her cut you out of her will? Because you still go to see her, don't you? Then surely she wouldn't…?"

"That might have been how it was *before*. But *now*? Now that she's met this man?" He saw my look of disbelief. "Yes. She's as good as told me so."

All right, it *had* been a look of disbelief; yet at the same moment I found myself thinking – perhaps a shade paradoxically – about something else altogether.

I was remembering that the other night Olivia hadn't struck me as a woman who'd be difficult. My judgment might have been at fault but otherwise it now seemed sad, contrary to the law of averages, that out of her two children – beloved offspring, I supposed, of a beloved husband – she should have one son whom she'd come to consider a pervert (and could I ever feel grateful enough that my own parents, unlike Tom's and unlike Olivia herself, were so very understanding?) and another whom she'd come to think was married to a thief.

I was obliged to reconsider. Yes, she might have money and a lovely house and all of that, but would it be so astonishing if having been offered one last chance at happiness she'd prove dead set against the likes of you or me, Tom, trying to wrest it from her? Especially in view of her attitude to homosexuals, an attitude that no amount of integrity (yours) could ever hope to override? Indeed, she might even believe a prison sentence for the pair of us could be fully justified. She might regard Max's potential revelations as something that a dutiful and law-abiding citizen actually owed to British society, even if she hadn't quite been able – and would never allow him either – to denounce her own son.

But for the present I couldn't bear to feel so defeated. So defeatist.

"Do you think your mother's conduct to…Edna?… and through Edna, of course, to you…could ever be thought reasonable?"

In other words: do you reckon your wife *did* steal that brooch?

It was an unplanned, unfair and fairly unforgivable question.

My only, very tame excuse was the fact I couldn't countenance that final crushing of our hopes. For I suddenly knew – knew beyond a doubt – there was no way Olivia Prescott-Ames would ever be swayed by anything that you, Tom, might ever find to say to her. I thought she wouldn't even agree to meet you. And as for my supposing *I* could exert some sort of influence…well, what arrogance, what presumption! I felt ashamed of even thinking it were possible. I felt ashamed of even being in Eastbourne.

But luckily I'd scarcely completed that question before Edna herself returned.

She started calling Philip from the hallway before she realized that he had a visitor. She was asking him to come to help her with the shopping bags. I wondered why she hadn't simply rung the bell but then remembered he'd left the door open in order to let through a would-be, highly welcome, current of air.

Perhaps *asking* wasn't the best way of putting it.

"What do you think I am, some kind of bleeding social worker? Some kind of bleeding home help? Cart-horse? While you sit there with your feet up, knocking back the bleeding beer and listening to your bleeding girlfriend, Miss Doris bleeding Day – "

"Edna! We have a visitor!"

He was saying it even as he hurried out; but didn't just leave it at that – he gave a loud, rueful laugh. Wholly unexpected.

"Edna, it's the vicar!"

Since the next voice I heard was also Philip's I could envisage her gaping at him.

"The one from that church in Uckfield Road," he said. "You know, the one on the corner by the Spar shop."

His voice projection would have been sufficiently strong for the theatre in St James's. Not hers. Her comeback was so quiet I barely caught it.

"Well, why didn't you say so, you daft apricot?" And for a moment I almost liked her.

But, when she came in, her looks partly put an end to sympathy. She was older than him, maybe by ten years; and although with a softer expression – and a more flattering hairdo – she might have been considered pretty, the smile which she'd put on her lips didn't reach her eyes, not even in the presence of a clergyman, nor did it express anything more than a general sense of regret.

"Sorry about the language. It's hot outside and the bus was full."

"And the bags were heavy. That's quite all right, Mrs Prescott-Ames" – how strikingly the name didn't suit either one of them! "I've heard much worse in my time – and some of it from my own wife, after *her* struggles home with the week's shopping!"

While I was aware of Philip grinning in the background I thought hard about the ordained father of a school friend and somehow managed to preserve my gravity and to extend my hand.

"My name is Johnson. I'm sorry I'm not dressed a bit more formally – but, yes, at the moment we're certainly experiencing some very warm weather, aren't we?"

She waved my apology aside, just as I had waved hers, and glanced without reproach at my somewhat less than appropriate clothing – my sympathy advanced again – perhaps she wasn't actually so awful.

"Well, Ed, I'll just nip into the kitchen and fetch you a cuppa? And then I'll put the shopping away." He turned back to myself. "More tea, vicar?"

I thought he was going to spoil it – I thought we both were; I was reminded of many wet and ill-attended matinees in places like Hull and Wolverhampton, where there'd often been a colleague trying to get the rest of us to corpse. Highly unprofessional – and fiercely resented by somebody as priggish as Jack Linden – but actually of value in the end. A good training.

"Thank you, Philip, but I'm afraid I have to be off. Thank you, though, for saying you'll join me in a swim tomorrow morning. Shall I call for you about eleven?"

To my great relief there was no noticeable hesitation. "Half-past would be better. That'll be all right, won't it, Ed?"

"Don't ask me, you daft apricot! Aren't you the master in your own house?"

I doubted it but, even so, I thought she might be much nicer to him than at first I had imagined. I recalled his laughter at the front door and I liked the repetition of her silly little endearment. Nor, apparently, was she antagonistic towards her homosexual brother-in-law. I revised my earlier assessment. Perhaps they did occasionally have sex.

But, as I walked away, I still couldn't help wondering again about that brooch – and thinking what a most unfortunate blunder it had been, if it had actually occurred.

Ten

Naturally we had no intention of going swimming – although for Edna's benefit he had brought along his trunks rolled in a brightly coloured towel. Today he was wearing short sleeves and looked considerably less weedy; his arms were muscular – not in a bulky way but in a hard and well defined one. This pleased me. I was able to feel a lot more trusting about the claim he'd made.

The pub we went to was on a promontory and had a large and fairly sloping garden. Soon after twelve we were sitting on a bench which overlooked a sea so sparkly I'd have felt tempted – I mean if there'd been any menswear shop sufficiently close by – simply to run down the hillside, throw off my clothes and leap joyfully and forgetful through all those tiny shimmering waves. I'd have wanted to slice along beneath them…well, either through them or beneath them…for at least the next couple of hours.

But that, Tom, would have struck me as monstrously unfair.

So we just sat and proceeded with our conversation.

This had started up in earnest – following a few forced jokes about the vicar and the likelihood of Edna's ever finding out – soon after our leaving the bungalow.

"Philip, you know he's down here again – Max? May even have arrived already. Goes back on Sunday morning."

"No, I didn't know that. How did you?"

"Just something I overheard."

Which reminded me of something else I'd overheard.

"He thanked her for that 'crazy, wonderful thing' she might be going to do for him this summer. Have you any idea what?"

"Changing her will? At the moment everything goes to a charity for the homeless and to cancer research. "

"Yes, that's what we thought, Tom and I – that it was something to do with changing the will."

I explained who you were; I mean, the twin – not my lover. And how we thought Max was solely preoccupied with building up a fortune. I didn't go into detail but that couldn't stop me *thinking* about the detail: the twenty thousand pounds he was hoping to procure from you; the larger sum he'd now be counting on from Philip's mum; and any other potential sources of income he might at present be single-mindedly investigating.

He was evidently determined to lead an exceedingly secure old age – without neglecting the chance, while he waited, of a middle age that would also prove to be comfortable.

"Is there no stopping this man?"

I hadn't known I was going to say it, let alone exclaim it with so much passion.

It was a bitterness, of course, in which Philip shared.

"Do you know something, Jay? Mum deciding she didn't want to leave John or me her money…well, that's okay, she had her reasons, why shouldn't she decide like that? And honestly I wouldn't have minded if every last farthing had gone to charity – I promise you I wouldn't!"

He kicked a small stone out of his path – kicked it with more vehemence than I knew would otherwise have been likely.

"I think she'd have wanted to help out with cancer – that's what my dad died of. And she always felt sorry for the homeless, anyone without a roof to protect them from the wind and the rain and the biting cold."

He was repeating himself – he was the kind of fellow who frequently repeated himself, obviously anxious to eliminate all possibility of a mistake – but this time I guessed he was quoting directly.

And this accorded far better with the impression I'd formed of his mother in Maida Vale; far better than revelations about stolen brooches or homosexual sons.

"But I'm telling you, Jay, the thought of her money going to the likes of *him* – my dad's money; that really makes me want to…I don't know…do something which is…violent."

I wasn't loath to underline things. Emphasize the obvious. "So it's not only you and your brother he'd be stealing from. He's stealing from cancer sufferers and the dispossessed and maybe many others who would have stood to gain from…?"

"Even a home for dogs and cats," he assured me. "*Anything* would have been better!"

This time I said it more levelly. And with far more deliberation. "Philip? Is there no way of stopping this man?"

But by now we had reached the pub. It was good timing: the landlord was currently opening up. I bought two pints and two packets of crisps. We carried them outside.

"Cheers!"

"Cheers!"

These salutations seemed a little out of place.

After we'd been silent for a while he turned to me abruptly and took up my own uncompleted refrain.

"*Is* there no way?"

"Yes, there is." I felt I was saying it to you, Tom, just as much as to him. "There has to be!"

Where there's a problem, you'd said to me on Sunday, where there's a problem there is *always* a solution.

This wasn't profound. But often the truth doesn't need profundity.

"This time… well, no more playing at it! I'll swear to that!"

"This time?" asked Philip. "Playing at what?"

I didn't answer. It seemed unimportant that he must have thought I was talking to him. The thing which appeared to matter at this juncture was – above all – a clear and convincing statement of all the main issues. I had to know where I was going.

To be honest, Tom, when you first mooted this idea last Monday – my God, was that only four days ago? – I simply hadn't believed in it. Yes, I played along because we couldn't think of anything better. And, as you said, because we'd needed to be doing something – *anything*; we couldn't just sit there and twiddle our thumbs.

But now I suddenly saw the potential.

This time we'll really put Max in fear of his life! On a daily basis and in such a way he'll never know where the danger may be coming from – real, real danger, not playacting, no longer the wink and the ironic smile – and to such an extent that he'll no longer have the courage even to leave home!

In fact, I hardly knew *whom* I was talking to; or, indeed, if I was talking at all. I was already thinking of the speeding car, the ruthless mugger, the falling flower pot: all staples of the action movie, the dime novel, the television episode.

But for the time being, I thought, we'd just have to make do with those tired old clichés. I had nothing against a good cliché whether it was overworked or not. A lot of them had proved their worth.

Anyway, Tom, within days – scarcely weeks – he's going to wake up to this one hard and incontestable fact: that if he ever again wants to lead a free and normal life he has, ultimately, only a single option. To abandon at least one of his schemes to become Paul Getty. "Philip," I said, "here is what's going to happen. Here is what *must* happen."

I saw his confusion disappear. We were back on solid ground. I was the general on the battlefield, laying down my orders for the following day, giving firm and concise directions before climbing back in my jeep and driving off across the desert. He was the private waiting to be led. We both felt very sure of our positions.

"Tomorrow morning you'll go to your mum's house" (perhaps I didn't sound absolutely and unmistakably like Monty), "pretending to be unaware of Ralston being down here again. Presumably your mother will be feeling happy – she'll be pleased to see you. Probably she's wanting you to get to know him better and have a further opportunity of witnessing just how lovely he is. She wants you to appreciate him. She wants the two of you to gell."

"That's true enough. She does."

"So you join your mother and Max for the cup of coffee you'll almost certainly be offered. Maybe in the garden if the weather holds? Let's hope the weather holds."

"Why's that important?"

"Because you're going to get all chummy with him, that's why. No matter how he treats you – although I don't think he'll patronize you to the same degree if he knows your mother's paying attention. It's not in his interests to make waves."

I lingered a little over that expression; rather wished I hadn't used it.

"All right," said Philip. "Him and me, we're suddenly best mates? What happens then?"

"You say to him something like this. All confidentially – despite the nearness of your mother. You say: 'You know what upset me last time? The way you laughed when I mentioned being a good swimmer. Well, that's all in the past now, we can start again, but I'd really like you to see I wasn't boasting! I want to challenge you to a race.'"

"Go on."

"Well, from what I know of her, I think your mum will enjoy that. Her son and her boyfriend bonding! And Max will enjoy it, too: the thought of putting *you* in your place and at the same time impressing *her*! Added to which, the weather's warm and I'm sure he does enjoy swimming. Probably more interesting than just sunning himself in the garden."

"You mean, tomorrow morning? Tomorrow afternoon?" His tone sounded panicky.

"Yes, definitely tomorrow! Tomorrow afternoon. We haven't time to mess around. And *he's* here, *I'm* here, the weather's good! What's wrong with tomorrow afternoon?"

"Oh, I didn't understand that; you'll be here as well?" I hadn't realized I might need to emphasise that fact. The panic in his eyes receded.

"To be exact," I told him – and, as I did so, I pointed, "I'll be behind that very large rock that we can see over there. Is it about a mile from shore?"

He nodded.

"Are you capable of swimming a mile?"

"I think I'm beginning to see what your plan is going to be."

"If you have to, are you capable of swimming a mile?"

"You sound like Max!" Then unexpectedly he laughed. "Of course I am! I'd have liked it to be twice as far!"

"Good. Well, here's what you have to do. You'll challenge Max to a race. You say you'll be ready to bet a fiver on it – even a tenner – the bigger the bet the more excitement you'll create! And then you tell him about that rock out there and about this pub – this pub, where you'll treat him to a glass of something, either beforehand to wish him luck or afterwards to commiserate; *that* should provoke him to some kind of interesting response! And you tell him about the stretch of beach that we can see below us…which looks practically perfect, doesn't it? Even if tomorrow – being Saturday – it's likely to be much busier."

"No, it's a fair distance out of town. Not many holidaymakers seem to know about it."

"Which suits *us* fine…but on second thoughts don't talk about its quietness. To Max that might translate only as a scarcity of onlookers – of admiration! Obviously your mother knows the way?"

"Oh, yes. And it shouldn't take her more than fifteen minutes." I thought of the *fifty* it had taken me.

"And do you happen to know about the tides?"

"Of course I do. There are plenty of signs and if you swim a lot you make a note of them. High tide tomorrow at about one. You can see it's nearly high tide now."

I couldn't, not really: both unable – because of the overhang – to see the full extent of the beach and not knowing how much of it the sea was due to cover.

"Great, that's great. So, Philip, I'll give you the number of the place where I'm staying and you'll let me know more or less at what time you'll be entering the water. Whatever time it is, I'll have swum out to the rock some twenty minutes earlier. Make sure you either beat him in the race or are pretty close behind. Yes, let him beat you but be *very* close behind. It's going to need the two of us."

"What, to duck him, hold him down?"

"Yes, to hold him down within an inch of his life. I've heard it takes three minutes for a man to drown, so we'll have to give him at least one. It's going to seem like a hell of a time and it won't be easy but we'll have to be thinking the whole while of how he's brought all this on himself and what a swine he is and how he really needs to learn his lesson."

"Will you be keeping that watch on?"

"Oh, don't worry, we'll know exactly when he's had enough. He'll have stopped struggling; he'll have gone quite limp. Philip, we're going to know all right!"

"It sounds as though you've had a lot of practice?"

"No, he's going to be my first this week."

But that didn't come, Tom, half as naturally as it would have done with you. Perhaps we were too close to being called on to take action. Perhaps we hadn't known each other long enough.

We fell silent again; went back to staring at the sea.

"Clearly, it's going to happen well out of sight of anyone on shore. We'll just have to hope there are no speedboats or fishermen or people in pedalos all vying to obtain the best view. When you get to the rock you'll swim a short way behind it, to find out whether you get the all-clear or just an urgent shake of the head."

"Okay."

"If it *is* a no-no, then whatever you do, don't let *him* swim behind it. That's why you need, if you can, to be very close. Or if he does swim behind it – if you can't prevent him – I'll just have to do my absolute best to circle. You see, he knows me. It's far better he shouldn't be aware that *you* do. Not if it's unnecessary."

"But if it's the all-clear…"

"Yes? What?"

"Jay, will you be strong enough to help him swim back? I mean, when one's been almost drowned…to within an inch of one's life…?"

"I don't know. Obviously he'll need time to get over it. But after that… Anyway, I'm sure I would be strong enough." No matter, I thought, how very little I'd like the idea of having to support him throughout the course of a long swim.

And suddenly I felt sick. Could I really go through with it? Even one full minute, as we'd just said, was going to feel practically endless. I grabbed our empty tankards and hurried back inside the pub.

By the time I'd been served, however, I felt sufficiently recovered to return. And to appear confident.

"Yes, all we must think about is the people he's robbing and – if we don't do what we can – the people he will go *on* robbing. Your mother, first and foremost, and even members of his own family. And then the homeless. And then all those whose lives could have been saved, or could *still* be saved, by generous bequests to medical research."

I hesitated.

"And talking about lives being saved…"

"I know what you're going to say."

"What, that I'm not even sure how safe your mother's life would be, once she'd actually got round to changing her will?"

"I've wondered about that too."

"A fall downstairs…a slip on icy steps? Some fault with the electrics…a bit of interference with the car?"

I'd been speaking largely to persuade myself. A pep talk. Happily, it had also persuaded my companion.

"Even a proper drowning would be too good for him!" he now declared – and I hoped the look on his face would be something Max would see following the pretend one. "But how come you believe just *this* will be enough to make him finish with my mother?"

"It won't immediately but the plan is – "

"He'll tell her I tried to murder him."

"Will he? But why should she believe him? After all, you already know you won't inherit. And simple jealousy…is that enough of a reason to take anybody's life? (Well, yes, perhaps it is. But I don't mean to be offensive – would your mother ever reconcile something so very *fiery* and *passionate* with either of the two boys whom she accompanied every day to kindergarten and made up little lunch boxes for and frequently waved to as they rode upon their father's shoulders?) And what else could there be: that's what she's going to ask."

I paused; again slipped into different roles.

"'Concern for the safety of *my* life? How ridiculous! Why would Philip think that?'"

"'Because there may be people like my brother who've told him how unscrupulous I am.'"

"'You know *I'd* never believe that!'"

"'But you're not Philip.'"

"'Then, Maxie, there's only one solution, isn't there? I can still enjoy the pleasure of your company for years before I need to change my will; and I don't suppose that in the meantime there are too many charities likely to come and push me down the stairs!'"

I finished my second pint.

"No, Philip – all things considered – I'm not sure that he'll actually rush to tell her."

After this, there was nothing further we needed to discuss. Our scheme was pretty straightforward. I gave him the number of my B&B so that, at probably around twelve the following day, he could let me know the time decided on. He could even leave a message. 'Half-past-two' – 'three o'clock' – 'four'. There would be nothing too incriminating about that.

"Should we run through it all again?" I'd put it as a question but I knew it was essential that we should.

I accompanied him most of the way back. We shook hands by a pillar box. He seemed nervous once again. "So this is the very last time we're going to talk, Jay… before…?"

"Well, I can't think of anything else we need to say – apart, that is, from your phone call. But if anything goes wrong – "

"Like the two of them having other plans for tomorrow afternoon?"

"Yes. Or if there's some particular point you might want to discuss…? And, Philip, you can ring at any time. If I'm not there I'll phone back as soon as I get your message. And naturally I'll remember to be guarded…bearing in mind that Edna could possibly overhear."

"You still have the number?"

I assured him I had.

"Oh, something I've been meaning to ask… When you phoned yesterday you said you'd met my mother and were worried by finding out she knew Max Ralston; and last night, thinking about it in bed, I suddenly wondered where you'd met her."

"Philip, I'm afraid I told a lie. I've never met her. But I couldn't think of anything else to say since I didn't know how you felt about Max Ralston. Or whether you even knew of his existence."

"Oh."

"And although I discovered very quickly how you felt about him…well, it's a long story and not actually all that relevant. But, if you like, we could begin to walk some more and I could tell you about it. You see, he's actually blackmailing his own brother – "

"The twin? The good twin?"

I'd forgotten, of course, that you might have had another brother. Or even brothers. "Yes."

"Is it some sort of crime that he's being blackmailed for? Is he in prison and that's why it's you instead of him who's come to sort things out?"

"No, nothing like that. Tom's a bit like your own brother. He has a very lovely wife but in fact he likes men as well as women and, like your brother, he *could* be sent to prison. That's what Max is threatening him with, if he doesn't pay up."

"His own twin?"

"Yes. His own twin."

"Okay. That's all I need to know. We're going to be doing the world such a big favour, aren't we?"

"Let's hope the world will be suitably grateful."

"But, do you know, by the time we do talk again – I mean, if there's no reason for us to do so before properly…before…"

"Yes? Go on."

"I was just thinking. We're going to be two very different people by then. For the rest of our lives, I mean. We're going to be two very different people."

"Are we?" Despite the heat, I gave a little shiver. Luckily, he didn't seem to notice. "Yes, I reckon that you could be right."

As I say, he's quite an interesting mix, is Mr Philip.

A bit of an unknown quantity.

(Though – and I repeat myself here – aren't we all?)

Eleven

The next morning appeared interminable. I'd had hardly any rest but at about half-past-five decided there was no point to my staying in bed. I felt sluggish – filled, moreover, with a sense of dread, even one of doom – and wondered if I'd ever sleep peacefully again.

So I showered, shaved, softly closed the front door. From the railing of the promenade the sea looked a long way out but I still thought about heading across those acres of hard sand and finally wading in. Yet there'd be no means of getting dry and if I now went back for a towel I'd have to ring the bell. Not a way to make myself immensely popular.

What to do, then, but wander around the town until I found some workmen's café open, like the one in Gloucester Place?

Again, this one supplied cups of a dark and powerful brew in thick white china that was slightly chipped – were the chips mandatory? I sat a long time over two such very good-sized cups and a persistent thought I had whilst doing so prevented me from worrying (too much) about the lining of my stomach and the colour it might gradually be turning – burnt umber, raw sienna?

My thought was more to do with this: the question of how men could ever positively choose to become torturers, whether in times of war or of purported peace.

Or, if not actually making a conscious choice about it, even allow themselves to be coerced into the role – apart from anything else, to begin their training in an observational capacity and be shown what were currently considered the most effective techniques? Was it nothing but sadism and/or a hankering after power?

In any case, I didn't want to be amongst their numbers.

Yet now I'd have to be. At my own instigation, Tom, rather than at yours. So should I simply pull out? Let Philip down in the same way that I'd be letting *you* down? Was there no alternative?

Because this man somehow had to be stopped.

Tom, he simply has to be stopped!

Or might there, in fact, be some acceptable alternative? What I mean is: how long do you think it would take to raise the money on your house?

And, come to that, even if it proved impossible to raise enough…well, would Max really start to circulate those rumours? Could he know for certain how it might affect Olivia?

Since yes, okay, she had undeniably broken with her older son, John, but she hadn't gone so far as to shop him. And, after all, in some people's eyes family was family, no matter what. If Max were to inform on his own brother – on his very own brother, no less! – and to become a driving force in having him committed to jail… Well, that was something you just didn't do to family. You might hate the sin and even feel incapable of ever forgiving the sinner – never wish to set eyes on him again – but someone who could actually bring down disgrace and imprisonment upon another child of his own parents… Perhaps Olivia would never trust him again. Could Max be wholly sure how such an action might affect her?

I almost smiled. What an exquisite form of revenge! In trying to snaffle a very much smaller fish, Max could lose his grip on the one that might truly have safeguarded his future.

Oh, wouldn't that be wonderful?

Yes, but it wasn't the essential thing. What's really at stake here, Tom, is the matter of your whole career. That, and what will happen to Sophie and the boys once innuendo starts to be unleashed.

Not to mention my own rather uncertain future. But that's all right. I don't give a damn about my own rather uncertain future so long as you and the others will come out of it all right. I mean, come out of it unharmed – well, basically unharmed. A prison sentence for myself honestly isn't going to amount to – what is it now? – isn't going to amount to even a hill of beans. (Thank you, *Casablanca*.)

But how can the four of you come out of it unharmed? How on earth would I define that? Oh, just talk about the woolliness of some glib little phrase.

I sat over those cups of tea and felt bewildered. Helplessly bewildered. The trouble was – a small part of the trouble was – I just felt so unbelievably *tired*.

But back to the boarding house and to a breakfast which I also lingered over. Fried bread for the second time in six days. (Not so good as Monday's!)

Then up to my room…which I didn't need to vacate until midday.

I brushed my teeth, lay down on the bed, and miracle of miracles…I slept!

Only for forty-five or fifty minutes, though: awoken by a Hoover. But even forty-five or fifty minutes was a shining gift. After I'd recovered from my initial state of grogginess – and renewed sense of impending doom – I felt much better than I had felt when I'd first got up. I walked back into town and bought a pair of swimming trunks and a towel; tried not to think about the first time I might be using them. Spent a further half-hour wandering around Eastbourne and yet another half-hour dawdling over coffee.

But, almost incredibly, when I returned to the B&B it was still only a quarter-to-twelve.

"Any messages?" I asked.

"No, sir."

"I'm expecting a really urgent call. Will it be okay if I settle up now, and then wait in the lounge until it comes through?"

"Of course it will. We'll know exactly where to find you."

Twelve o'clock. A quarter-past-twelve. Twenty-minutes-to-one. One o'clock. A quarter-past-one. Twenty-minutes-to-two.

I gave up trying to read the paper, went out to buy some apples and a sandwich.

Because I had to keep up my blood sugar, didn't I? Had to try to maintain my physical strength – as well as my moral. (I wasn't too sure I was maintaining *that*.)

Or would my physical strength no longer be a requirement?

He rang at twenty minutes past two.

"Four o'clock, Jay!"

This information acted as both a relief and a depressant – I couldn't have said which was the stronger. Shamefully, *not* having to torture a man might have seemed like something of an anticlimax.

He apologized for being so late.

"My mother invited me to stay for lunch. I'd already said that Edna had gone into Hastings so I couldn't pretend to be phoning *her* – and, anyway, there's a new extension; wouldn't have been safe. So now I'm phoning from a callbox. Made out I needed some cigarettes, when it's nearly a whole year since I gave them up. Not that I couldn't do with one right now, if you want to know the truth!"

"Philip, think about this. Do you believe Max would ever let your mum know he was threatening his brother with imprisonment? Would she carry on liking him and trusting him if he did? I'm sure she'd never have wanted John – did you say your brother's name was John? – to go to gaol."

He did think about it. For over a quarter of a minute he thought about it. I didn't hurry him. There wasn't any rush.

"I don't know, Jay. John is her *son*; she and my dad used to love him, she knows he has fine qualities. So it might depend on how Max has spoken of his brother. If she thinks he sounds bad enough all-round and that he really does deserve... Remember how my mum considers Max so special, and truthful, and deeply loving."

"Even although she knows he's probably after her money?"

"Yes, even although she knows that. The two things can sometimes go together."

I remembered *Gentlemen Prefer Blondes*. That had been very much Marilyn Monroe's point of view. Her about-to-be father-in-law had respected her for it.

"Besides, Max could be her last chance," continued Philip. "It might take a lot to make her change her mind."

He added – it was almost a non-sequitur – "She even believes all that stuff about the Olympics!" I could hear the residue of bitterness.

"And you think, then, she wouldn't try to dissuade him from going public?"

"Perhaps he hasn't said that's what he intends to do. You might suppose that he'd discussed it with her but can either of us honestly be sure?"

"That's certainly the impression which he gave his brother: that they had discussed it."

"And Max would never think of telling a lie, would he, if he felt it might assist him in some way?" It was the first time I'd heard him being sarcastic.

"If it does happen do you imagine she'll forgive him?"

"She's in love with him," he told me simply. "Or, at any rate, seems to be. And like I said just now – this man could be her last chance."

"Okay, Philip. All questions answered. Thank you." I took a deep breath. "What do you mean to do about your swimming gear?"

"We'll have to drive past the bungalow. That's all right – with my mother thinking there's no danger of her meeting Edna. And

Max actually brought his with him; went for a dip as soon as he arrived. Swam halfway to France, he made out."

"Oh, and by the way. I've decided I *shall* wear my watch and that we'll only hold him under for forty-five seconds. That ought to be enough."

He nodded. "Hope it's good and waterproof," he said.

"So… See you, then, around four."

"Yes. See you, Jay. Good luck."

"Good luck."

The thoughtless and virtually automatic things we say! One could really wish we didn't. *Have a nice day!* – at least we kept away from that.

I went into the lavatory by the front door. It provided barely sufficient room to change. Maybe my new trunks ought to have been black but they were rainbow-striped and it seemed more fitting when my jeans were back in place.

Underpants, neither black nor rainbow-striped but plain white, went into my overnight bag…which I then left with the landlady's auburn-haired daughter. All I took out was the new towel. To have been walking along the shore carrying an overnight bag…toothbrush, shaving things, all the rest of it… well, who in his right mind (and particularly when anxious to maintain a low profile) would ever have wanted that sort of city-boy encumbrance? Who *in his right mind*, I thought.

It took me about an hour to reach my destination. I undressed, made a bundle of my clothes and trainers. Lay down on the towel; had about thirty minutes to wait. Fidgeted; just couldn't keep still. When ten of those minutes had elapsed – or maybe twelve or thirteen – I left my bundle, threw the towel carelessly across it, and walked down to the water's edge.

There weren't too many about: a father paddling with his three kids, an elderly couple snoozing in deckchairs, a group of youngsters – maybe students from the local university – laughing and talking amidst the debris of their picnic. Admittedly some in that small group of friends might have noticed me in a casual sort of way, but I don't think anybody else did – and would it have mattered if they had? Low profiles notwithstanding?

It occurred to me I was behaving as though an actual crime had been committed – not some sort of safeguard being set in place to *discourage* an actual crime but already something which the police would soon be needing to investigate. I shook my head. Fundamentally, I still felt tired.

The water soon came up to my waist. I was aware that it felt cold but I welcomed such coldness…thinking partly perhaps of its capacity to revive but also no doubt of its capacity to numb. So, after I'd lunged forward, I didn't aim for speed. I aimed for clarity of style: long, clean, reaching movements, as if I were again being used as a model at the Seymour Place swimming baths. I hadn't thought in years of the P.E. teacher who'd been getting me to illustrate the various points of technique, but although Mr Finbow was universally unpopular, like the loud-mouthed drill instructor in the first reel of a film about the army, I was actually glad to be thinking of him now. Especially so when I discovered that time had repented of its behaviour in the morning…and that I'd all but reached the rock.

There was a young couple sunbathing up there.

Naturally I wasn't aware of this until I was practically upon them: the summit must have been a good four feet out of the water and I'd been doing the crawl – my face had been well down.

Can you imagine my shock? I'd actually got my hands on the side of the rock and was ready to hoist myself up.

"Oh, dear God," I exclaimed.

Clearly, the two occupants wouldn't have been in the least shocked; they would certainly have heard the splash of my approach. But all the same they must have been quite seriously put out.

So what should I do? Merely turn around and start on my journey back, making a detour so as not to meet Philip and Max?

"Really sorry. Didn't mean to disturb you."

I smiled and shrugged – anyway, it felt as if I shrugged, although I'm not sure I actually could have done – and was just about to lower myself.

The young man jumped up. "As a matter of fact, we were already talking of leaving."

"Are you sure?"

Are you sure? My God, we might have been back in the Kardomah! *Would you both mind awfully if I came and shared your table?*

He pulled his girlfriend to her feet. They bade me a hasty farewell and dived in. Can you believe it: I felt *guilty* at having hastened their departure; at having marred their afternoon.

After they'd gone, though, I too lay down; what else could one do? A lot of the surface was smooth and one's back soon adapted to what little bumps and hollows there inevitably were. Even at such a time as this, it was pleasant to stretch out and feel the sun. I suppose the ultimate irony would have been if I'd fallen asleep.

But even had I been wanting sleep the mewing of gulls would have kept me wakeful. And at least every three minutes I needed to sit up to see if anyone was coming.

I heard a sound that steadily grew louder.

It was made by a helicopter.

Max and Philip were due at any moment and here was this suddenly materialising machine now flying in my direction.

But appearing to take forever to reach me.

It flew not exactly overhead but assuredly near enough and low enough for the pilot to give me a smiling wave.

"Wish I could be down there with you!"

He may not actually have said this but such was clearly the thought he had in mind.

However, he did gradually move off…even if it seemed to take another half-hour for him to become at last no bigger than just a neutral and unthreatening speck.

I need hardly say that throughout all this my gratitude and my frustration continued to wage war. Again, I'm not sure which was paramount at the moment I finally saw the line of spray I'd been expecting – and realized that my long wait was over.

No need to be specific about the next few minutes...apart from, obviously, having to highlight one unspeakably awful detail. (Though maybe this suggests that *every* detail wasn't awful, from the first instant I saw Max without his clothes: a confused montage of head, throat and shoulders, and raised arms: which was ten or twenty seconds before he saw me, so there wasn't any surprise or fear in his expression, just pure enjoyment of the exercise or pleasure in his winning of the race. But what I mean to say, Tom – it could have been you! It could so easily have been you! I hadn't prepared myself for any such unnerving similarity.)

But don't be so stupid, I told myself. In essentials this man is as different to Tom as any person possibly could be!

And luckily (*luckily?*) he then did something to emphasize the fact – again, before he noticed me – by looking back at Philip with the makings of an undisguised sneer...visible even before his head was fully turned.

"So there you have it, baby shrimp! Though why was proof *ever* asked for? You only had to take your shirt off!"

Yet this isn't the detail I've referred to: the one that was completely unforeseen and – beyond all others – excruciating.

You see, I could probably have handled Max on my own. I mean, when you've taken into account the factor of surprise, his consequent lack of readiness.

But we'd arranged that Philip should go straight for his ankles...or at least for one of them, if both legs were instantly flailing. In theory – me at the head, him at the feet – it should have been simple, it should have been fast.

Yet it wasn't simple and it wasn't fast; and in his uncertainty and panic Philip got muddled and did quite the craziest thing that, imaginably, he ever could have done.

Somehow – and God knows how – somehow in all the confusion – and plainly these things can't be choreographed or rehearsed – somehow at some point…

Philip, not I, was up by Max's head.

And he was close to the rock.

And he banged the head against the rock.

I think I heard the skull crack.

There followed a moment of utter stillness and suspension.

I suddenly felt a long way off. Enclosed in a soundproofed bubble. My view out of it, this bubble, receded and advanced, receded and advanced, and I thought I was going to faint. I thought I was going to throw up.

Yet neither of these things happened. The world recovered some of its stability. I heard again the slosh of the sea and the mewing of the gulls. Max sank into the water.

He didn't sink far. Beneath the surface, yes – a very short way beneath it – but some part of him must then have caught on something.

Philip and I were gazing at one another.

We were treading water and gazing at one another.

"I didn't mean to do that," he said. Said? Whimpered.

A further long moment went by.

Long? Well, who knows? But then at last (ten seconds after that audible impact of bone upon boulder? thirty? more?) I gathered my wits – or some of them – and started feeling for Max's pulse and heartbeat.

Nothing.

I tried to pull his head clear of the water but met only with resistance. The fact I had one hand beneath his chin, the other behind his neck, instead of holding him firmly under both arms, showed that I plainly wasn't with it.

Anyhow, it wasn't going to make a difference.

I had a vision of his head coming away in my hands – and grinning at me, maliciously.

I didn't give even one second's thought to resuscitation.

Philip said: "I've killed him, haven't I?"

I couldn't answer.

"I didn't mean to. He shouldn't have made that jibe. He shouldn't have called me puny."

Had he called him puny?

In any case, right now, Max wasn't calling anybody anything. He was staying absolutely quiet, as if intent on surveying some interesting form of marine life just below the waves.

I again hoisted myself onto the rock. I had to sit and think. Philip followed me; also sat. The helicopter returned. The pilot waved again. I waved back to him.

Philip did the same. What else could either of us do?

The pilot may have wondered where this second man had come from. With luck, though, he wouldn't have noticed any third one, on whose presence he might more worryingly have speculated.

I spoke at last. "I planned to frighten somebody. But look what happened. I took a human life."

"It wasn't you. And that life wasn't human. It was worthless."

Philip's voice, too, seemed to advance and retreat in waves. In echoes. *That life wasn't human. It was worthless.*

But was it? Did we know for certain how Max might have felt about Philip's mum? Did we know for certain that there couldn't have been – if not a powerful love – at least a fragile affection, incipient tenderness, which could conceivably have flourished?

That was a thought I already knew was going to perturb me. I didn't want it to be true…and perhaps this, too, was something which ought to have perturbed me. Probably would.

"And Jay, you know, he was asking for it! He was really asking for it!"

Yes, he was. Philip was right. I had to pull myself together. I had to get rid of this nausea – disorientation. This woosiness.

I said: "Except that no one asks to be murdered."

But I can't have been *that* much disoriented. Through it all I realized exactly what had happened and realized that I was the one responsible. Without my presence in Eastbourne there was no way Philip would now be sitting on this rock.

"It wasn't murder!" he said. "It was an accident."

"*Accident?*"

"Yes." His voice became wistful, almost dreamy. "A body drowned at sea. Mightn't get washed up for weeks, if ever… And when it does…*if* it does…"

"But, Philip, don't you get it? Haven't – you – begun – to – *get* – it?"

I could have cried. Cried out of guilt and remorse and also – suddenly – out of sheer exasperation. Out of an almost uncontrollable anger. Levelled only at him. At Philip.

But that anger may have done me good. What had he done, other than what the moment had driven him to – what the whole situation, coupled with his instinct or automatic reflex or snap judgment, had driven him to? Unconsciously, he had only done what he thought was going to help me – and help you, my love – at least as much as it was going to help himself and his mother. There was no point in my trying to apportion blame.

"Philip, we have to think. We have *got* to think."

"But it could have been worse, Jay. It could have been worse… couldn't it?"

Now, belatedly, he was beginning to sound anxious. Little boy lost again. In obvious need of reassurance.

And undoubtedly this helped me.

"Yes, Philip, *much* worse! But even so… We're still left with one enormous problem. We'll have to unhook his body" – it was his nylon trunks which had become caught up – "because if we leave him here he's going to be very soon discovered. Less than an hour ago there was a nice young couple on this rock. Sunbathing."

Thankfully, mercifully, everything was now beginning to come clear again. As far as I could tell.

"But if we do unhook him," I continued, "and then he *is* washed up on shore – as the chances are he just has to be before long – they're going to know at once that this wasn't a simple case of drowning. The post-mortem won't point to tiredness or cramp, or to a stroke or heart attack. The post-mortem will point to a broken skull. The post-mortem will point to murder."

We didn't talk again for a while.

"I'm sorry," he said.

"I know you are."

"Couldn't he maybe have bashed his head while diving? There must be other dangerous rocks round here. Smaller ones, below the surface?"

This suggestion struck me as inventive. Surprisingly – perhaps unsuitably – it triggered a memory.

Edna, it's the vicar!

"Or couldn't his head," he persisted, "have knocked up against something after he was dead?"

"I think they can tell about that sort of thing. I'm not sure but I think they can." I paused. "But it's an interesting idea. Just *might* be feasible."

"If only we could do something."

"Yes, if only we could."

Those two words now reverberated in my mind, although linked to a different subject. Or – of course – a different aspect of the same subject. "I suppose you ought to be getting back to your mother. She must be starting to wonder what's become of you. Of *both* of you!"

"My mother isn't here."

"What!" His mother's presence on the beach – or, rather, my strong desire for her absence from it – had comprised the sole content of that latest (and *if only*) heartfelt plea.

"She'd eaten something which disagreed with her. She thought she might be going to get diarrhoea. Max told her it was all in the mind. He got quite shirty about it but she still decided not to come."

"Then thank heaven for whatever disagreed with her!"

And now – cause and effect? – my brain showed definite signs of being about to function again. I might previously have 'gathered my wits' but the harvesting had plainly been premature: my wits hadn't appeared robust enough or in any way obligated.

I asked Philip to remain quiet for a while. He stayed completely silent.

And eventually:

"You know what? I suggest we swim back to shore, get dressed, and then walk up to the pub."

"Yes…if you like." He seemed baffled.

I'd have felt disappointed if he hadn't.

"From there you can ring your mother and tell her it's on behalf of Max – your new chum. (You can tell her he won the race and sound all smiley about it; that ought to please her.) But you've got to say he met a friend on the beach – someone from Fortnum's, why not? – who asked him back to his hotel for dinner. Naturally Max was going to ask for your mum to be invited too; but then remembered her wonky tummy. Anyhow, he'll be home a little late but will be thinking of her every moment he's away. He sends great smacky kisses."

"She won't be happy though. How late?"

"You can tell her that, expressly to make up for it, he won't go back to London till tomorrow night."

"Well, that would certainly help – yes – but…"

"I'll fill you in while we're walking to the pub. Philip, I really think that this is going to work! I hope your brother's home at the moment? Hasn't gone on holiday."

"No, he won't be on holiday. His boyfriend has a son who lives with them – and who'll next year be sitting for his GCE. Which means that *this* year they wouldn't think of letting him miss school. Patrick's very strict."

"Fine. Good for Patrick! Beat you back to the beach, then."

But I didn't. He couldn't be allowed to lose twice in the same afternoon; although in fact (but I didn't mention this yet) he might still find himself with a further chance of victory – later on, and once more during the outward trip.

Yet that wouldn't be until after the sun had gone down; or at any rate until after the beach had cleared. At nine or twenty-past, let's say. Though, naturally, it was far too much to hope that the pub garden would also have cleared by then.

However, despite its vantage point over the sea, even as far as the rock the pair of us had just quitted, no one in that garden could really expect a perfectly clear view – either of three late-in-the-evening swimmers or of two dripping men needing to support, even half-carry (certainly across that part of the beach which wasn't obscured by the overhang) their obviously exhausted comrade.

Furthermore, it would be impossible for anyone not equipped with strong binoculars to identify, later on, those two staunch helpmates, presumably conveying their friend to a waiting car.

Another small risk we'd have to take was that no one would come rushing down the hill to act as Good Samaritan.

But small risks were inseparable from the whole business of living. The whole business of living or – as in this case – dying.

We got dressed. We bought our half-pints of shandy. Philip made his phone call.

And I made mine.

Both proved satisfactory.

*

Then, with not much reason other than to pass the time, we made for a restaurant which he knew of – situated practically an hour's walk away – where we ate lightly but nutritiously. Sustainingly. And on our way back we stopped off at a pub larger than the one above the beach, in which they had a jukebox and TV and a pinball machine – and in which none of the three barmaids seemed to think it strange we ordered only drinks that weren't alcoholic. ("Driving, you know." "My goodness, sir. You are being careful!... Mitch, are you listening to this gentleman?") The pub was full and there was a nice Saturday-night feel to it. We must have heard 'Unchained Melody' about a dozen times.

Yet only once did we allude to that afternoon's events, and that wasn't in the pub but during our journey to the restaurant. Philip asked if I thought it probable anyone would have swum out to the rock after we ourselves had left it.

No, I didn't think it probable. This was partly because of the distance and partly because – the day having lost a great deal of its heat – even the most determined of sunbathers would no longer feel drawn to it.

In any case we'd taken Max round to the back and had again discovered a convenient protuberance on which to hook him; a convenient and, of course, *submerged* protuberance. We'd indeed be unlucky if anyone spotted him this evening. And for the moment, definitely, the current wouldn't be strong enough either to unhook him or to carry him away.

I think I must have made a good job of allaying Philip's doubts. After that, as if by some binding though unspoken agreement, neither of us referred even indirectly to what had gone before.

That is, neither of us referred to it until the time was well after nine and we were heading back towards the beach on a grisly mission of hopeful – yet far from thoroughly assured – investigation-proof achievement.

Part Three

as related by Tom Ralston.

Twelve

I should have felt relief at learning that Max was out of the way – and I did, to some degree, naturally – but this was suddenly offset by memories of certain escapades the two of us had shared as boys. Why should life be so contrary, choosing to remind you of such things only after somebody has died?

And then my relief was offset, even more so, by my anxiety regarding Jay's predicament.

Philip's predicament didn't worry me so much. Damn it, if it hadn't been for him… Also, I hadn't met him yet.

When I did meet him I could see why Jay liked him. He struck me as both well-intentioned and unassuming and I could believe he felt absolutely no resentment at the way his mother had treated him. How many could you say that of, when the only thing they'd done wrong was to marry unsuitably in their mother's opinion but just this had been sufficient to deprive them of their inheritance?

And of course I needed to be just as worried by *his* predicament as I did by Jay's. The two were tightly intertwined.

On the phone we'd agreed to meet that same evening, Saturday, at eleven – outside the main entrance to the station. Or as close to eleven as we could all manage. Jay had rung me at about six and, in view of what was going to be necessary, timings had been difficult to determine on.

In fact I could have met them earlier – twenty minutes or so – but as it turned out they couldn't have met *me* any earlier. They didn't get there until nearly a quarter-past. They arrived in Olivia's white Jaguar.

This was the same car in which they'd earlier carried Max's body to a nearby beech wood – and, whilst there, made pretty shoddy work of burying it.

However, it had never been intended as anything other than shoddy. So long as Max wasn't going to be discovered until latish tomorrow evening it really didn't matter when he was going to be dug up.

All that mattered was that his death should be established as having occurred after 7pm on Sunday; Max would have been waved goodbye to, by Olivia, shortly *before* 7pm on Sunday. Post-mortems couldn't always be accurate. The loss of a day wasn't by any means unheard of, especially after a body had spent a fair time in the sea.

Despite this, I ensured that practically the first thing Jay and Philip did on arrival at the station was to book their train tickets and strike up a friendly conversation with the clerk. They were to ask him for the time and make a big performance out of being surprised.

Then Jay would be catching the last train back to London and doing all he could to talk to people on the way, as well as to the taxi-driver who drove him from Victoria. Safety in numbers.

At Hampstead he'd be welcomed home by Sophie. 'Welcomed', I wasn't so sure about, not at nearly three on a Sunday morning – although Sophie being Sophie, I could almost afford to be sure of it. Welcomed home with the news of myself having been called away at ten-past-six on a Saturday evening. (And here is what I'm told she actually said, more or less.) "Jay, would you believe it? – called away on some trumped-up piece of utterly meaningless constituency rigmarole! I think I shall probably join you and Miriam in your new independent party. Please bring me a membership form."

Of course, there'd been a bit of laughter and some lessening of her indignation.

"Well, at least he stayed to bath the kids and get them into bed, then stop to have his supper with *me*: a little treat for both of us which I'd taken most of the afternoon preparing. (You should have told us you'd be home tonight; I'd obviously have saved you some.) 'Yes, damn them!' he cried. 'Let them wait!' He held out his glass and made this little gesture of defiance (not like him, Jay, not like him at all) – 'Let the country topple!' – which nearly turned that miserable phone call into something *marginally* worthwhile! The only thing missing from all of this was *you*!" Pause. "Though please don't tell me that I muddled the time of your return – and that it was meant to be today, not tomorrow! I had something special planned for tomorrow night as well! *Had*? No, *have*! And Tom thinks he should be back by ten."

Well, then, so much for Jay and me.

What about Philip?

Philip would have caught a slightly earlier train in the opposite direction; and from Hastings he, too, would have taken a taxi and made sure he chatted to the taxi-driver. (Everyone knew that an alibi provided by a spouse was largely worthless. Therefore he was going to make it known to his brother – and to his brother's partner and to his brother's partner's son – that he had quarrelled with Edna and had decided on a short break.) The name of the town where John and Patrick and Terrence lived seemed unexpectedly appropriate.

Battle!

Obviously we hoped that all this endeavour at alibi-making would in the end prove needless. But that would depend, absolutely, upon the next phase of our plan. And the next phase of our plan was…well, to say the very least…open to catastrophe.

"No, Tom," Jay said. "You're going to romp home."

"Am I? Tell me that again."

"Sweetheart, you're going to be wonderful."

He quickly changed it.

"Oh, what am I saying? You *are* wonderful; and whatever happens, nothing in this world so far as I'm concerned – and so far as Sophie is concerned – is ever going to change that."

No, my darling, you don't gush (to answer again that earlier question of yours) but you do have this way of saying things, potentially schmaltzy things, sometimes way-over-the-top things, and turning them very much into the simplest, most convincing and most encouraging statement you could possibly have made.

I put you onto the London train, secure at least in the knowledge that, come what may, I'd be seeing you again in less than twenty-four hours. Just hold onto that thought, I told myself.

And then I tried to enter still further into that state of mind where failure was a concept I couldn't allow myself to entertain. Not for so much as a second.

I had, of course, changed into Max's clothes and shoes, even into his underwear and socks; exchanged his wristwatch for my own; put everything of mine into a large carrier bag for Jay to carry home. I'd also exchanged our wallets, Max's and mine, and everything that they contained – apart from a pound note and a couple of ten-shilling notes which Max had had on him; myself, I'd hardly brought enough to cover Philip's fare, which wasn't very bright of me; and, lastly, I'd swapped over our key-rings and carefully pocketed the ignition key Philip had handed me.

I drove along the route he had proficiently outlined, found End House and parked inside the garage, which I was pleased to find unlocked. (There were so many things I hadn't thought to ask and probably so many things Philip hadn't thought to tell.) Then I went round to the back of the house and let myself into the kitchen, also unlocked. Went through the kitchen and into the capacious hall. "Livy, I'm home!" I knew that Elizabeth, the maid, whose mother lived in Portsmouth and had recently been ill, wouldn't now be back until Monday. I was alone in the house with my benefactress – who now called back to me.

"What sort of time do you call this?" But then her tone softened appreciably. "Hello, my little Maxie!"

"Your *little* Maxie, be damned! Your great *big* Maxie, if you please!"

I thought myself perfectly safe in making this correction. But also I wanted just to be talking – talking any kind of nonsense – before I went into her bedroom. I felt that by then I needed to have established a definite flow between us.

It was a large house, with several doors opening off the landing, but even if I hadn't been schooled I'm sure I'd have known which door to choose. Not only was it the only one not fully closed but her voice, while I was still on the stairs (she'd wanted to know if I'd had a nice evening), would have been a sure-fire indicator.

She was sitting up in bed, wearing a pink frilly nightgown that was probably expensive, certainly quite pretty and – I was undeniably relieved – not all that revealing. She herself was actually quite pretty, younger-looking than I'd imagined, with softly waved fair hair and strikingly blue eyes. The hair was maybe dyed and the blue might have been enhanced by contact lenses but the overall effect wasn't in any way unpleasant. She'd been reading a novel, a hardback that appeared new, and after I'd kissed her, first on the cheek, then on the lips rapidly turned towards my own, I almost asked her if the book were any good…until I recalled it was one of Max's boasts that he neither read novels himself nor, by his appearing in the least bit interested, ever encouraged anybody else to do so.

Not that it would have mattered. People act out of character when aiming to impress.

"Livy, about this evening – sincerest apologies! This fellow George, he's quite an entertaining idiot and I thought you might rather enjoy meeting him – his wife's a hoot – until I suddenly remembered… How're you feeling by the way?"

"Oh, much better, thank you. You were absolutely right. I should have listened."

"Of course you should have listened! Well, never mind, even the Prescott-Ames-es can maybe live and learn. (What sort of awkward name is that? Can't you do any better?) But I shouldn't have said 'by the way', should I? Not 'by the way' at all."

"Max, you're very sweet."

"And to say 'I suddenly remembered' wasn't right, either. But you know how it is – Phil and I, we'd just had our little race – "

"*Phil?*" she repeated, laughingly.

"Well, why not? Livy, I think I may have totally misjudged him. It was all very exciting and in fact I only *just* beat him. So much wished that you'd been there!"

"He enjoyed it, too. Sounded all bubbly on the telephone. Darling, do come and sit beside me."

I'd been about to choose a small chintz-covered armchair but she patted the bit of the bed right next to her so I sat and held her hand. Gave it a loving squeeze. Returned to the story of my evening.

"Indeed, I felt *so* guilty, not saying I'd rush straight back and caressingly soothe your fevered brow! But you know how it is: after they've poured one GNT down your throat, you feel you can't just dash off without trying to return the compliment – "

"And, Max, *you* know how it is: one returned compliment follows so hot on the heels of another…?"

"Why, Mrs Prescott-Ames! Are you suggesting…surely you're not suggesting …?"

I released her hand and stood up; walked across the room in an exaggeratedly straight line…if straight lines can actually be exaggerated. It had suddenly occurred to me she might want to smell my breath.

"Madam, I hope you feasted your pretty little eyes on that? Are you now feeling you've wronged me in heart and mind and spirit?"

"I did. I am. Can't wait to meet these lovely friends of yours. "

"You will. They stay quite often at the Grand."

"Perhaps next time they'd like to stay here? But for the moment never mind about walking in straight lines. Why don't you just come to bed?"

So far so good. But Philip hadn't known, obviously, whether Max would retire to the dressing room or bathroom – or simply get undressed in front of her. Myself, I didn't feel that Max would have turned his back on any opportunity to flaunt.

But, again, never mind. *Variety is the spice of life; variety is the type of berry scattered on your cheesecake.* That would have to be my line.

"First, Livy dear, may I go to take a little nightcap – since I've been so very, very good – and maybe fetch a teeny one for you as well?" I could scarcely go wrong in assuming there would be a drinks cabinet in the drawing room.

"All right, my pet. That does sound nice! You can bring me up my usual."

I should have seen that coming.

A moment's hesitation…before I took the chance.

"I suppose you wouldn't join me in my own wee dram? Have a proper manly drink for once in your short life?"

"No thank you."

"You insist on that same boring girly little beverage?"

"Maximilian, don't think you can shame me. I've already heard you call it far worse than that. I've heard you call it disgusting."

"What? Me? No! Never! *Would* I?"

And yet 'disgusting' triggered something. Suddenly I was back in Mitzi's, with Jay, last Tuesday. Before Sophie and Miriam had walked in. And he was describing to me –

"All right, my pet. It shall be done!"

"Don't forget the ice."

"I swear to you, my love: the ice shan't be forgotten!"

"Oh – and Maxie – "

I was already on my way down.

"Yes, Livy?"

"While you're downstairs, will you give me a little treat, show me you still appreciate that nice new shiny toy of yours?"

Oh, Jesus.

I went down the rest of the stairs a lot more slowly. Philip certainly hadn't said anything about a nice new shiny toy. Perhaps he hadn't been told of it? Which meant, more than likely, it would be small and easily overlooked – but in that case why would it be kept downstairs?

I went into the kitchen, took the ice cubes from the freezer, knocked their tray on the draining board.

Looked frantically about me.

Perhaps some sort of kitchen appliance? Max had given her a gourmet meal? – yes, right – but what type of small treat could you whip up whilst you were in the midst of pouring a couple of drinks?

I carried the ice through to the drawing room. Head turning to left and right with every step. A set of golf clubs? Had Max been thinking of taking up golf? A new umbrella? Some rare, exotic pot plant? But could a vase or a cigarette box or a Royal Doulton figurine; even a pot plant or an umbrella – unless this last had a sword tucked away inside it! – be designated 'toy'? And again, in any case, where was the lady's small treat to be looked for?

The television was impressively wide-screened but would surely be too cumbersome to carry – besides, wouldn't you expect it to be still in its wrappings? (Or wouldn't he be meant to take it back to London?) The record-player also looked stylish, state of the art, but the same absence of packing materials had to be considered – sadly, because a record played on it, a record of her favourite tune maybe…'Our very own song, my sweet one!'…?

On Monday she had spoken of needing to be at home next morning when something was to be delivered. Deliveries were generally large. A small present, hadn't she said…but not in terms of size?

I continued to look about me.

And it was certainly shiny. Looked new. Could easily have been spoken of as nice. (Yet how had Philip overlooked it?)

Not overlooked it, possibly – in the midst of everything else, just hadn't thought to mention it.

I sat down.

Said a little prayer; then raised the lid and flexed my fingers.

'Don't throw bouquets at me; don't laugh at my jokes too much.' It might not be *the* one – how could it be? – but it might at least be one of them.

Despite my nervousness I played it well. Sophie was always saying I should somehow find time to teach Gil and Josh. They might be more amenable to the idea of their dad teaching them than 'some silly old woman we don't even know and can't get all cross at'.

"That was really lovely," said Livy when, still feeling more than a little apprehensive, I returned. "Thank you so very much."

"Thank *you* so very much! What an incredible present! My goodness, how you spoil me!"

"I think you're worth the spoiling."

"I think you haven't yet noticed how your ice has melted!"

"I'd much rather have had 'People will say we're in love' than all the unmelted ice in the whole of Eastbourne!"

She'd noticed, however, that my 'own wee dram' wasn't quite so wee as she might have expected. Neither was her amaretto.

"Oh, Maxie, it's just occurred to me. If you were drinking gin earlier, should you now have switched to Scotch?"

Something had occurred to *me* too: that the apparent mixing of my drinks might provide a reasonable excuse if, before too long, a reasonable excuse were going to be required.

I had the distinct feeling that it was.

"I'll be all right. But thank you for worrying about me."

"I'm glad that you and Philip are becoming such good friends. I hope we'll now be seeing a little more of him…?" Her tone grew suddenly arch. "I mean, Max, after you've packed up your job and your apartment in that wicked and stuffy old city and might then be – ?"

I interrupted. I was sure it was exactly what my brother would have done.

"Now, Livy…!"

Perhaps it was only the whisky but I was getting to feel a lot more confident: just following my instincts and now believing that, basically, I was going to get through all of this.

Which meant that Jay and Philip were also going to get through all of this. If anything went wrong, I told myself, it would be salvageable. Following the piano and the amaretto I felt more or less impregnable.

"Now, Livy, we don't want to rush things."

"*You* may not." She gave a little giggle.

"Bad girl. Be good."

"You may rely on it, I fully intend to be." It was a passable imitation of Mae West. "And please don't forget, big boy, that little thing you mentioned to me only yesterday."

"What little thing did I mention to you only yesterday?" I considered this permissible. "What particular gem out of all those many thousands?"

"Don't tell me you mean to renege! It was a promise; I've been looking forward to it all day! Your Saturday night strip, my little darling one!"

Oh, help!

Oh, all you saints in heaven – *help*!

And yet at the same time I couldn't deny a distinct quiver of excitement. I had sometimes performed a striptease for Sophie. I'd kept in reasonably good nick and felt proud of it. Also – well, let's face it – I was something of an exhibitionist.

Plus, it would certainly get rid of that quandary which had faced me earlier: whether Max had taken off his clothes in the bathroom or the bedroom – and, if in the former, whether he'd then have wrapped a towel about him.

"Very well. If you insist. But you mustn't keep using the word 'little'. And in any case I'm going to need a refill."

She didn't object; and even the small matter of my mixing drinks appeared forgotten.

But, even so, my striptease – when it began, some ten minutes later – barely got off the ground; and I don't say this merely on account of the fact that Max's suede shoes and yellow socks were the very first things to get discarded.

We should have had some music. I had to supply my own… which was a disadvantage, certainly, but might not have been insuperable. My sweater then came off and was swung – by the cuff of one sleeve – in absolutely the best Hollywood tradition (or perhaps the best non-Hollywood tradition, I had never actually seen a live stripper, whether male or female) and after that the zip on my trousers was lowered very, *very* slowly, only to be raised a lot more quickly, in the parody of a highly knowing, smirking, cocksure tease… But then – the thing that really put an end to it: a jarringly premature end to what was shaping up to be quite a reasonable performance – for about three seconds I didn't even realise what this thing was. I had slowly unbuttoned my shirt, equally slowly shrugged my way out of it, with my turns and my dance-steps pretty much in rhythm to the music issuing from my lips…which should all of it have been okay…perfectly okay… when…

Well, even before I'd begun to twirl the shirt – preparatory of course to slinging it off in the general direction of the sweater – Olivia gave a gasp.

At first I thought (oh, the presumption of the man – and I'm talking here of Tom, not Max!) that she was gasping at just the sight of my pectorals; and I suppose I felt a bit smug.

But then I found out that what she was gasping at wasn't their development. She was gasping at their covering of hair.

It wasn't a particularly *thick* covering, I'd have thought, but that was beside the point. It was dark and it was noticeable. And for some reason my brother Max must either have shaved himself – perhaps he knew a lady who preferred smooth skin – or had simply never grown any chest hair in the first place. My twin brother Max.

But these weren't considerations I could admit to. I remembered my own advice to Jay on the morning he had gone to Fortnum's. If challenged in any way – deny it! *Deny it!* Never back down.

Your word against anyone else's! Absolutely anyone's!

And now I felt very mean. But what else could I do?

"Livy, you're imagining it! You have to be! Only a werewolf can grow hair that fast."

I chided her.

"So are you saying I'm a werewolf? *Are* you? Well, I ought to tell you something: werewolves are *extremely* good at tickling!"

She wasn't happy and she didn't look convinced but obviously she saw that she was in the wrong; just had to be; what other explanation? I didn't like what I had done (didn't like what I was doing) and my hand reached out to her: my hand attempting to communicate sympathy – no longer my claw-like, werewolf fingers, poised to scratch and tickle.

Poor Livia. (Suddenly I wanted to provide her with a nickname of my own. Suddenly wanted, in every way, to dissociate myself from anything of Max.)

"I could have sworn," she said.

"Livia, this sort of thing…it's often happened to myself."

But fortunately she didn't seek examples. I couldn't have given her any. She was clearly being short-changed all along the line.

"What's wrong with me?" she asked.

"Perhaps it's merely that you don't like body hair and up to now have somehow blocked it out?"

"How could I not have liked it? My husband had body hair."

"There you are, then! A psychiatrist might say that – this way – your subconscious would feel a lot easier about letting any other man…"

I know! I know! I know! I felt so guilty, so blameworthy, so thoroughly ashamed – not only for what had passed but for all the confusion and self-doubt which was clearly going to hang around – that after I'd been to pee and used my index finger to smear toothpaste round my teeth, after I'd joined her in bed and put my arms about her, after I'd become aware of the wetness on her cheeks, I ended up by comforting her in the only way I could think of; and actually it seemed completely natural, there in the dark, and I thought, oh hell, Sophie need never know and nor in fact need Jay. Even before the lamps had been turned off, no other presence of hair seemed to have presented any problem and if Livia hadn't by this time guessed the answer to her conundrum (which I felt sure she hadn't; although – like all these things – it appeared so glaringly obvious to anyone already in the know) then I doubted she was ever likely to.

In any case, Jay would hardly have thought that I'd done wrong. And if Sophie had known what was involved – the saving of the lives of two essentially innocent young men, one of whom not only she but her children liked very much indeed, she would scarcely have blamed me for it either. She might have said, "I hope you closed your eyes and thought about the Conservative party – your constituency – the House of Commons!" and I might have told her the room had been in darkness anyway, but I probably wouldn't have mentioned that Livia had been very soft and giving and responsive. And, also, that she'd smelt extremely nice.

Afterwards, after all the pillow talk and our decision to spend tomorrow driving through the Downs and maybe having lunch at some charming riverside inn, with later on a cream tea in some equally pretty village (for Livia was a true romantic), I found myself drifting off to sleep more peaceably than I had done in the whole of the past week.

But was then jerked fully awake, feeling even more of a heel than I'd felt earlier.

And here was the reason. Because of everything else, I hadn't really been thinking about what Jay must be going through at the moment, the *hell* he must be going through at the moment… although I knew full well that the horror he'd endured had all been faced on *my* account, not on his own.

He'd been present at the killing of a man.

But here was I talking about riverside lunches and cream teas; and my motive for doing so presented not one crumb of mitigation.

Yet, now my guilt had started up again, that was simply the beginning of it.

And the ending?

After I'd heard two o'clock strike – three o'clock – four o'clock – my thoughts finally returned to, settled on, this sleeping woman by my side.

Well, my thoughts had actually been shooting off all over the place, with lots of repetition but hardly any orderliness or logical progression, so to speak of 'returning to' or 'settling on' – to speak of beginnings or ends – was utterly ridiculous.

Yet anyway…

Before she'd gone to sleep Livia had told me how different I seemed.

"All the time, my love, you're growing nicer and nicer. I wouldn't have believed it possible!"

Never mind her complete misapprehension. The crucial point, it seemed to me, was that she'd been saying this to my bastard brother, whom she'd be driving to catch his train some fifteen hours from now but after that would never see again.

She would hear there'd been some botched attempt at robbery – Max had certainly *looked* as if he might have money – and forever afterwards would mourn him as this wonderful man she might have married and been extremely happy with.

That was a desperately sad reflection. Sad and sick. She would measure all others against this tragically wronged hero and inevitably find them wanting.

I told myself I couldn't let that happen.

But how to prevent it? What could I do? I remembered a technique I had sometimes used in my teens and twenties, to prepare myself for difficult situations: school debates, university interviews, boardroom conferences. In my head I wrote a film script.

I wrote one now: *Disillusioning Olivia.*

6pm - return from pleasant day in country.
Man steps out of car: "I'll go pack my bag, then I'll be off."
Woman: "Wouldn't you like a drink before I drive you to the station?"
"No need. I want to walk."
(Disappointed) "It's a long walk. Take you half an hour."
"I'd still prefer it." (Man leaves her in car; runs up to fetch bag. She remains in driving seat; gets out when he returns. Voice sounding rather flat) "Don't forget your raincoat. And I've bought you something to take back to London."
"Don't want it."
"What's happened, Max? What have I done? Why won't you let me drive you to the station?"
"I can't marry you, Olivia."
(Pathetic attempt at humour) "That's really not a condition for my driving you to the station."
"Not now; not ever. It's better I should say it. I shan't be coming here again."
(Woman now starting to cry. Rummages through handbag. Sits down on little wrought-iron bench)

"What have I done?"

"I don't love you. Nothing more to it."

"I know you don't love me. I'm not a fool. But I thought we got on and I thought the fact we always seemed to have a good time…" (Still hasn't found her handkerchief)

"Oh, take this, for heaven's sake! Keep it as a souvenir!"

"On Friday you seemed so very pleased with the piano."

"Then find someone else who'll also seem so very pleased with the piano!"

"And I thought that my simply having money… I told you, Max, I've even changed my will."

"Oh, damn your money! Leave it to your children. That's the natural thing to do." (Starts to walk off.) "Besides. There's someone else. And always has been."

"But I don't understand. The way you made love to me last night… And after we've had such a very pleasant day, as well…?"

"Oh, grow up, Mrs Prescott-Ames! You've got children. Be a natural mother. Then at least you may have *somebody* to love you in your old age. Correction. Older age!"

(Leaves her. Doesn't look back.)

Yet I wouldn't be able to do it.

Who could? Who could?

And Olivia wasn't my problem.

Jay was my problem. Even Philip was my problem. But his mother most definitely wasn't. I might like her; I might feel desperately sorry for her. But she really wasn't – was not – my problem. I had more than enough already.

And at the moment I couldn't take on any extra.

Small wonder that in the end that night – and after what had appeared such a very promising beginning – I hardly slept.

But again, as had occurred after an equally wakeful night last weekend, the day that followed was an unexpectedly pleasant one – despite the fact I still felt that I ought to be saying *something*. At least ought to be *trying* to say something.

"Livia, I'm surprised at you."

We were returning home and she was at the wheel. All day we'd shared the driving.

"Why? What have I done?"

"Phil told me that you've cut him out of your will."

Actually, Philip had told Jay and Jay had told me.

"And that you've also turned your back on your other son. Can that be true?"

"Maxie, you haven't met Philip's wife! I hope you'll never need to. And my older son – I'm ashamed to have to tell you this – he lives in sin. But not with a woman. With a man."

"And why is that so shameful?"

I didn't know if it would occur to her how *truly* out of character this was; forget the novel-reading and suchlike.

"Some men," I said, "like women. Some men like men. That's just the way it is. One isn't any more shameful than the other – or any less wonderful."

Oh Max, Max! Can you only hear yourself?

"And as for Edna… Philip was clearly looking for a mother. That's quite a compliment to you. What's more, I'd have said that it was fully deserved…until you took it into your head to behave in this remarkably foolish fashion."

"She stole my brooch."

"All right, not proven, but let's just suppose she did? Aren't there worse things than being desperate for a bit of money? I once stole twenty pounds out of my father's sock drawer."

"Oh, Max! You didn't?"

It was an utter lie, both on my own account and, so far as I knew, on Max's.

"All of us do silly things at times. Perhaps that's what makes us human."

"Did your father find out?"

"And talking of silly things – do you know what Edna sometimes calls your younger son? 'You daft apricot!' I feel a woman who calls him a daft apricot can't be *altogether* bad."

A silence lasting about three minutes.

"I suppose you do realize, Maxie, that you're arguing against your own interests?"

"No, I haven't forgotten you said you might be going to leave me something…"

"Darling, why do you say 'might'? You *know* I've already done it. Or are you just giving me a chance to tell you again? Because I was cross with myself for not being able to hold back on the telephone?"

"No – because I hope your will won't come into force for another forty years! Because I myself could well be dead by the time it does!"

"And not just something. *Everything.*"

"I don't know what to say, Livia."

"You've already said it. Many, many times."

"It's just that I feel so sorry for your sons. I really do. And, Livia, please remember this – that if anything should ever happen to me, anything at all, it would be my very dearest wish… Sweetheart, I've come to like your son. I *like* Philip. I feel I could almost be his second dad."

"Do you know, Max, I'm seeing such a different side to you this weekend?"

"Just remember that, Livia. Will you promise me?"

"Yes – you daft apricot! But nothing *is* going to happen to you, my dearest. I wouldn't let it!"

I felt satisfied. I wouldn't now have to turn into a complete bastard before she left me at the station – and, obviously, by doing so, hurt her very deeply indeed. I kept remembering how happy she must have been when she awoke on Friday morning.

So, all right, let her always remember my brother as a saint. Perhaps there were worse ways of living your life. For instance, as a cynical and embittered old woman who would never trust any man – anyone – ever again?

Perhaps it *was* better to believe in fairy tales…even if they had to include on occasion a cunningly sharp-toothed wolf lying in your grandmother's bed, wearing her nightdress and bonnet.

Rest in peace, Max.

Thirteen

The police arrived late on Friday evening, very late: Detective Inspector Wilby – probably in his mid-forties, tall, moustached, pleasant-looking; you could imagine him at home, sitting contentedly over breakfast with his pleasant wife and pleasant teenage daughters, a family man who looked quite forward to retirement – and Sergeant Trip, who was possibly fifteen years younger, also amiable but with a far more alert expression, a constantly roving gaze, which suggested promotion might be far more what *he* had mind; and that it wouldn't be too long, either, before he achieved it.

Jay had answered the doorbell. In theory he had moved back into his own flat on Sunday but it seemed to me he need scarcely have bothered – Sophie had invited him to dinner on both Monday and Wednesday; he had slept over on both Monday and Wednesday; it was more than likely he would sleep over again tonight. It was as though a pattern were being established. The children were at last in bed and the three of us had been having a drink before our somewhat belated dinner. Jay performed the introductions.

"Would you like me to leave?"

He asked it in an innocent way which implied a visit from the police must have something to do with matters at Westminster and certainly couldn't be meant to include outsiders. Socialists, at that!

"No, sir. Neither you nor Mrs Ralston. I'm afraid there's nothing confidential about this." The inspector looked apologetic…as though he really regretted his errand could *not* be viewed as confidential.

On the other hand, Jay looked curious and even mildly pleased. All those years in repertory were obviously a help.

The inspector chose an armchair, while the sergeant – a bit gingerly – sat on the edge of a sofa.

"What may I offer you?"

Sophie was no doubt aware of what the stock answer had to be; she indicated the alcohol only vaguely. "Or could I make you both a cup of tea or coffee?" Which was noble of her: I could tell she had no wish to leave the room.

But in any case her offer was declined.

"I'm afraid it's about your brother, Mr Ralston." Clearly, those first two words made a combination the inspector used a lot.

"Oh, yes? What has he done now?"

I'd been anticipating this moment and felt that I, like Jay, had sounded fairly natural.

Sophie, of course, had no reason not to sound natural.

Inspector Wilby smoothed one side of his moustache. "Why, sir, what has he done before?"

"Oh, nothing. That was only a very feeble joke."

"Ah yes, of course." Now, with the same index finger, he smoothed the other side.

He was nice but I wanted him more businesslike, less leisurely. Later I repeated to Jay what several times I'd probably heard or read about: that lengthy pauses on the stage were far more testing for an actor than his having lots of dialogue.

"I'm afraid, Mr Ralston, I have to inform you that your brother has disappeared."

"Disappeared?"

The importance of the word – the drama of that moment – was either completely lost on Sophie or, perhaps a little more likely, unwittingly held at bay by an anxious interpolation.

"Darling, I told you he hadn't shown up for lunch."

She turned to the Inspector.

"Sunday lunch. You see, I'd thought it a firm invitation but that evening my husband told me that possibly it wasn't."

"That evening, sir? Why did you wait until that evening?" Wilby, it seemed, was fully prepared to adjust to a digression; even, perhaps, to welcome one.

Again it was Sophie. "Tom had been gone all day, Inspector. Constituency business. A politician's life must be a bit like a policeman's? Always being called away at the last moment."

"Ah yes, madam. I see."

On the sofa, now sitting less gingerly, Sergeant Trip vigorously nodded his agreement.

I shrugged. "It was foolish of me not to have told my wife that Max had been planning – or, at any rate, half planning – to spend the weekend away. I thought she knew but I'd forgotten she hadn't been with us when Max had spoken of it."

"When was that, sir?"

"When was what, Inspector?"

"That he had spoken of it."

"Oh. The previous Sunday."

"And did he say where he was going?"

"Yes. To Eastbourne."

"Ah." This syllable seemed also to recur with some frequency. The inspector's moustache again received a moment of attention. "And did he mention whether he would be spending the weekend there on his own or whether he might be going with friends? Or meeting friends? Or possibly *staying* with friends?"

I felt tempted to say, "Well, *that* just about covers every base!" But at the same time I didn't want to appear frivolous, nor did I wish to detract from the importance of my answer.

"I believe he was staying with a Mrs Prescott-Ames. I think that was the name he mentioned."

"A Mrs Prescott-Ames? Ah, thank you, sir! Now indeed we may be getting somewhere."

"Olivia Prescott-Ames. He called her Livy. I sensed he knew her rather well."

"Darling, why didn't you tell *me*?"

"Sweetheart, I assumed Max would have done so – or, if he hadn't, it was something that he didn't want too widely known."

"*Too widely known?*" Sophie addressed both Inspector Wilby and Sergeant Trip. "And my husband's a politician! Some foolish people might think politicians were the same as diplomats!"

The inspector himself responded diplomatically; and perhaps a little smugly. "My wife would take it just the same way, I feel sure."

The sergeant also smiled. "Mine, too!" He had now brought out a notebook and had written down the name. "Livy, sir, with one v or two?"

"Heaven knows. The Roman historian had only one but I don't suppose Mrs Prescott-Ames falls quite into that category."

He grinned. "Well, I reckon it isn't too important. Can you give me the address?"

"I don't know it but it's bound to be in the local phone directory." I added to Sophie, "I must say I was a little surprised you didn't mention it after everyone had left."

"And you – for once – the very soul of discretion! Where was I when he told you?"

"Downstairs, I imagine. He came up to the study before lunch. I wondered why you hadn't stopped him."

"Ah, yes, I remember. I tried to, but… Well, you know Max."

Knew Max.

A small conjugal vignette. Maybe providing a touch of authenticity? It was useful to have one member of the team left in happy ignorance. Happy?… obviously a moot point.

"Anyway, Inspector. It really doesn't appear as though my brother can be missing after all. If you'd like to use the phone here and check with Directory Inquiries…?"

"That's very kind, sir, but it's something I can see to at the Yard." He didn't say *prefer* to see to at the Yard but such was definitely inferred.

"In any case, who reported him missing?" Jay was tending to address the younger of the two policemen but it was the older one who replied.

"His supervisor. Naturally, at the beginning, Mr Sutcliffe supposed the absence due to illness, even if it's a policy of the store that anybody sick phones in to say so… Of course, it still isn't the case that everyone has access to a telephone but apparently Mr Ralston was one of the luckier ones in that respect."

"Was?"

"Apparently Mr Ralston is one of the luckier ones in that respect." This time it was the turn of the left eyebrow to receive the tidying-up treatment. "And it seems that – more than once each day – Fortnum's Personnel did its level best to make contact with *him*. Finally Mr Sutcliffe grew worried enough to drive out to Maida Vale himself. This occurred on Wednesday evening."

The inspector thought about it.

"Well, now. In addition to ringing Mr Ralston's bell he rang the bell of his nearest neighbours. It seems that all of them were at home but that they couldn't supply him with any information. Then yesterday he got in touch with us. You know, Mrs Ralston, I think I've changed my mind. I wouldn't say no to a drop of that Scotch if you could still manage it?"

"Of course."

But it was Jay who jumped up to take care of this – and obviously, as well, to give some to the sergeant.

After he'd provided us with a few more details, none of which appeared particularly germane, Wilby sipped appreciatively, then reached his conclusion.

"So we went along to Elgin Avenue – I don't mean *we* did, not we two personally – and finally forced the door."

I thought: not the first door to have been forced in recent weeks in Elgin Avenue! "And found nothing but an empty flat?"

"That's right, Mr Ralston. Found nothing but an empty flat."

"But surely, Inspector, it's plain that he's decided to take a short holiday. We've been having a heatwave. It must be pleasant by the sea. I know that Max likes nothing better than a good swim."

"Yet that sounds just a smidgen irresponsible, sir – wouldn't you agree?"

"Well, I'd guess my brother left a message which never got passed on. We hardly need to know the reason…only the result."

"You mean, someone had forgotten?"

"Exactly. People do forget. And I still don't understand why it should ever have become a police matter. We're always hearing that dozens go missing every day but that you people seldom see it as much of a priority."

I wondered if I should be showing a little more concern over the fact my brother *could* be missing – and a little less, maybe, over police attitudes in general.

"Ah, yes, but that would depend on the situation. And we really can't subscribe to your theory, sir, of his having left a message which someone may have forgotten to pass on. Even if that had happened in the first place…well, don't you see that as soon as questions were beginning to be asked…?"

"Possibly the culprit felt ashamed? He or she didn't like to admit to…?"

No, I told myself, you really must stop. To be making such a point of it might be starting to sound suspicious.

The inspector took another appreciative sip of his whisky.

"You know, sir, madam, this is really very good!" He must have seen my quick look of exasperation. "But, as it happens, sir, we can set aside the question of the message. A friend of your brother's had indeed mentioned that he thought Mr Ralston might have gone to the seaside. And not just the seaside, either. To *Eastbourne!*"

He gave a smile that might have been one of general congratulation, even of minor triumph.

But no, as his next words made very clear, it couldn't have had a thing to do with triumph.

"And therefore – purely as a matter of routine, you understand – we put a call through to our colleagues in East Sussex. And from them, I'm afraid… I'm sorry now to have to give you news that will undoubtedly distress you. But, as I say, this only happened yesterday…"

"Please go on."

"Well, just the day before – Wednesday – they'd found a body in a local wood."

"Oh, no!" gasped Sophie.

"Yes – I'm so very sorry, madam. A body that had most likely been there since last weekend and the build of which seemed very much to tally with…"

He put down his glass, took out his wallet and drew from it a photo. Stood up. Came over to my chair.

It wasn't a good photo; or could the face of a dead person actually change so much…and in so very brief a period?

"Yes, Inspector. That's Max."

"Oh, no!"

Wilby also repeated himself.

"I'm so sorry, madam. But we thought it had to be. We showed the photograph at Fortnum's and, yes, they too seemed fairly certain. Although without clothes…and with his hair all disarranged like that… But then the moment I saw you, Mr Ralston… You and he were twins, isn't that right, sir?"

"No, don't show it to my wife, please!"

I was almost shouldering him aside as I hastened to sit down beside her, to put my arms about her. She too – like Sergeant Trip – was sitting on a sofa.

And, understandably, she was shaking.

"My wife was very fond of Max" – as though her reaction required some form of explanation.

The sergeant rose to his feet. "Shall I go fetch a glass of water?"

"I'll do it," said Jay.

But Sophie quickly put her hand up. "No, I'm all right." She lifted her tumbler, which still had some of her whisky left in it. "Though thank you both, anyway."

She said to the inspector: "I know you prepared us for it but even so…"

"Even so it comes as a bit of a shock when you actually hear it? Yes, madam, it always does. I'm afraid there's just no getting away from that."

"My husband didn't mean to be rude but he's right: I wouldn't want to see that picture."

"No, of course you wouldn't."

I stayed where I was on the sofa…now holding fast to Sophie's hand.

"Yet even in view of the likeness to yourself, sir, I'm afraid we shall still be requiring some formal identification. Would you be prepared to come down with us tomorrow?"

"I can go," said Jay.

Sophie looked at him in surprise. "But, Jay, they want somebody who knew him!"

It had clearly been a mistake but Jay absolved himself quite neatly.

"Yes, of course. Though on the other hand, Sophie, if Max was an identical twin, that's really all I need to know. I just thought – not being one of the family – it might be less horrible for myself than for Tom."

She smiled a wan apology.

"No, Mr Linden, I'm afraid Mrs Ralston is correct. It has to be someone who actually knew *him* – not merely knew his twin."

"Anyhow, thank you, Jay," I said. "But it may not be too horrible. Everyone knows that Max and I were never on the best of terms. Though perhaps you could come with me, as moral support?"

Being a dutiful and law-abiding citizen I glanced at the inspector for confirmation and he naturally acquiesced – why shouldn't he?

"So in that case I'll take my own car. Mr Linden and I will drive down together."

"Right you are, sir. But why is that?" For a moment the inspector's question quite threw me. "I mean, that you and your brother were never on the best of terms."

I hesitated and Sophie answered for me. "Oh, darling, you're only imagining it! He sometimes poked fun – like all brothers do – and of course you had your foolish little tiffs, yet basically…"

But Jay immediately shook his head. "No, Sophie, it was a lot more than that. Max was jealous of Tom; always had been. Resented Tom's success; hated the fact that he himself seemed such a failure…"

Do mistakes occur in threes? If so, he had another still to go. His words petered out with a look I recognized as one of sheer contrition at his own stupidity; I could only hope that neither the inspector nor the sergeant would have noticed it. (Yet how could they have failed to?) At least Sophie – thank God – on this occasion didn't question things. Well, anyway, she didn't question them aloud.

Because this was the point. Supposedly Jay and I had met only ten days previously. And yet he'd spoken with all the confidence of someone who'd been *au fait* with Max's character and with my own for very much longer than that. Less like a comparative newcomer, indeed, than like…well, like someone who felt he had the right and the authority to offer such a bold assertion.

More like an intimate than a newcomer. More like a lover.

He flashed me a smile of self-reproach which again – yes, they do come in threes – was quite the wrong thing to do; but I couldn't feel in any way resentful or annoyed. He had rushed to my defence with a haste which had given rise to misjudgement. But I loved the man – as much for that misjudgement as I did for everything else.

I saw Sophie looking at us. But it wasn't she who took the matter any further.

"Is that what it was, sir? Jealousy and ill feeling on your brother's part?"

"Well, let's just say we never got along…and in fact hadn't done so since we were children."

"And yet your wife doesn't entirely seem to take your view of it? Isn't that right, Mrs Ralston?"

I wondered what he had in mind. Possibly nothing other than a policeman's wish to understand every last detail, no matter how irrelevant it might appear to be.

"Max was unfailingly charming to me and a kind uncle to our sons. But quite honestly, Inspector, I suppose all of this was only surface stuff. What does a sister-in-law really know about those rivalries which may have been around for years and years?"

She shrugged and even smiled – albeit sadly.

"Besides which, he used to flirt with me; and what woman doesn't enjoy being flirted with by an attractive man? Even if he does remind you the whole time of your own husband?"

He nodded, also smiled, and turned back to myself.

"Then why do you think your brother chose to confide in you and not your wife?"

"I don't quite follow you, Inspector. Confide in me about what?"

"This lady. This Mrs…Mrs Prescott-Ames, was it?" He looked to the sergeant for corroboration. "Because it appears he insisted on disturbing you in your study – and when you were very busy – in order to do so? I think your wife had told him you were very busy."

Inspector Wilby might seem a little vague, even a little on the woolly side, but it was abundantly clear I shouldn't start to underestimate him. I took several seconds to consider my response.

"I think he may have wanted to impress me. To crow a little if you like. About this alteration in his prospects. Mrs Prescott-Ames is undoubtedly a wealthy woman and it seems she may have grown to be fond of him."

"He intended to marry her?"

"Perhaps."

Sophie again sounded peeved. "Then why couldn't he have told *me*?"

"Maybe, my dearest, because he liked you a fraction too much."

"What!"

"He once told me – and he wasn't joking – that if ever you were to divorce me he'd do his utmost to marry you himself." 'Once' wasn't precisely dishonest, even if it didn't quite convey how recently this claim, this boast, whatever it was, how very recently this idea had first been formulated. "And possibly it isn't tactful to speak of one prospective marriage…I mean, speak of it to a person who one day…"

"But why should he have thought I'd want to divorce you?"

"I don't know. Only, maybe that's why he meant to bide his time before telling *you*. And yet he clearly couldn't resist telling someone. That's the reason he had to rush up to my study even though you'd asked him not to."

"Then it almost sounds as though he thought I'd be wanting to divorce you very soon!"

"Yes, it does, doesn't it?"

"I wonder why," mused the inspector.

I suppose it was extraordinary how forthcoming the pair of us could become in the presence of two policemen. But presumably members of the CID were trained – like priests – to be patient, sympathetic, and adept at drawing people out.

"You haven't told us how he died." That wasn't me; it was Jay. "Did he have a heart attack or something?"

"No, sir, he was drowned."

"Drowned! And yet you said he was found in a wood? Didn't you say that he was found in a wood?"

"Yes, that's correct, sir. I'm afraid" – but now the inspector was again talking to us all – "it may not have been a wholly straightforward incidence of drowning. Mr Ralston had also sustained a blow to the side of his head."

"Then," whispered Sophie, "it was…? Are you really telling us that it was…?" She even had to pause again before she could bring herself to say it. "…*murder?*"

"It certainly does look like it. The post-mortem isn't quite completed yet but even if that blow happened *after* death… which seems unlikely…" The inspector spread his palms, without finishing his sentence.

Jay finished it for him.

"People who've been drowned don't usually walk off to bury themselves in some nearby wood?"

But he hadn't said it in a jokey way. Wholly matter-of-factly. Indeed, it now seemed difficult to believe that – even just between ourselves – we'd ever made light of any of it.

"But *why?*" asked Sophie. "Why should Max have been *murdered?*"

"Who knows, madam? Far too early to say. A robbery that went wrong, perhaps?"

"Max hadn't any money."

"But it may have looked as though he had. At this stage we have to suppose there could have been any number of reasons." He switched his attention back to Jay. "How did you know he was buried, sir?"

"I naturally assumed it. Isn't that what usually happens in a case of murder?"

"Yes, I suppose it is, of course."

"And he didn't assume it at first," I said. "He asked you if Max had had a heart attack."

"That's perfectly true. Yes, he did, sir."

His *right* eyebrow was now the one in line for the smoothing process: this time, with the middle finger of his right hand. Even in small ways he was plainly methodical.

"And you mustn't be offended, sir – this is something we obviously have to ask anyone who's in any way connected with the deceased…"

"You'll want me to account for my movements? But have you decided yet – more or less – when he died?"

"It won't take too long before we have."

"Excellent. Well, when you've narrowed it down just as far as you can…"

"Yes, sir, but in the meantime…"

"No, Inspector, you'll have to agree that my wife and I – and Mr Linden – have all been most co-operative. Now we'd rather wait until you lot can be a bit more specific. Then we'll endeavour to give you as full an account of our movements as we can. Nowhere near Eastbourne, I'm afraid." (I enjoyed using that little phrase.) "I haven't been in Eastbourne for years." I turned to Jay. "I wonder if it'll have changed much when we see it tomorrow?"

"Well, don't ask me. I've never once been there." (We'd told Sophie that at the end of last week he'd been at his parents' place in Preston. She must have been surprised at his arriving back at such an ungodly hour on Sunday – more surprised than she'd let on.)

The inspector stood up. "In that case, sir, we'll very soon be coming back if you don't mind…"

"And if I do mind?"

"Oh, please don't say that." We were both trying valiantly for humour.

"I think we'll still be coming back," acknowledged the sergeant, with a smile. He put down the glass he'd been cradling – careful to make sure it went on to a coaster, not straight onto the polished wood. "Mr Linden, if I could just take a note of your address…?"

Sophie seemed to watch the progress of his pencil.

"Inspector, what possible motive could any of us have?"

"Madam, I can't emphasize it enough. These questions are purely a matter of routine. They're going to be asked, quite literally, of dozens. Possibly of scores."

"All Max's neighbours and colleagues?"

"Along with most of the names we've found in his address book."

"Why only most?"

"I mean, we may not bother with the ones from overseas."

"Why not? Couldn't they have come and gone away again quite easily? I'd have thought that these days more and more of us appear to be travelling by air."

"A fair point. One we shall clearly have to bear in mind."

"Was he carrying his address book?"

"No, madam, we found that at his home. Along with his diary."

I had forgotten his diary.

"His diary?" I said.

"Nothing very helpful, sir. Not for the moment, anyway. May turn out to be more useful when we can start putting names to all the sets of initials. By the way, have any of you any idea who 'Claude' might be?"

Sophie looked back at him as blankly as I did. Both of us shook our heads. Jay, also.

"No, I rather thought not."

"Inspector, have you told my parents yet?"

"No, sir." He hesitated. "I was wondering if you'd consent to come along with us, if we go to see them now?"

"Yes, of course."

"Oh, poor Martha and Benjamin!" exclaimed Sophie. "May I come, too?" And then, perhaps remembering who had come out of this worse off than anybody – "And poor, poor, unfortunate Max! Always so very full of life! Yet now…! I still can't quite believe it."

"No, I'm not surprised." (Back to the moustache; I'm sure that if I spent much time with him I'd inevitably end up with chronic indigestion.) "When you saw him last, madam – the Sunday before last – did it strike you there was anything at all unusual about his behaviour?"

"No, I don't think so."

"You, sir?"

"No."

"Except…"

"Yes, Mrs Ralston?"

"Well, it's nothing really, but he did seem to be going on a little about homosexuals. Neither Tom nor I could begin to understand why."

"So he didn't normally do that sort of thing?"

"No – not at all."

"Ah, that's interesting. Very interesting you should have mentioned that." The other side of the moustache.

"Why so interesting?" I asked.

"What? Oh, no reason, sir. No particular reason. And was there anyone else present when he spoke on this subject?"

"Yes. Both his parents. (Who obviously are mine as well.) Both Sophie's, too."

"We almost wondered – Tom and I, after everybody had gone – whether Max might have been trying, in some small way, to pave the way for something."

"Even with this very rich lady waiting in the wings, so to speak, who he may have been desirous of marrying? You really wondered that, madam?"

"Yes," I said, while Sophie merely gave another shrug; "the whole thing is patently preposterous."

But all the same I was quite pleased when Jay pointed out that it wasn't unknown for men who were on the brink of…well, let's just call it, he said, a marriage of convenience...for them to start asking themselves what they might have been missing in certain other areas and then perhaps to embark on a bit of belated experimentation.

Wilby's attention returned to me. "Yet, as far as you know, sir, your brother didn't have any leanings that were...homosexual?"

"No, I'm sure he didn't. He often spoke about his girlfriends."

"Still..."

"Right, then. If that's all, Inspector...? Shall we go? Get it over with?"

Sophie made towards the door. "I think I'd better turn the oven off. Jay, will you have a biscuit or something to keep you going?"

"Yes, Sophe. Don't worry about me."

"Oh, one more question while I think of it. You see, we didn't find any of your brother's clothes. Mr Ralston was wearing only swimming trunks. You mightn't, I suppose, have any recent photograph of him in sportswear? The sort of get-up he might have had on when he went down to Eastbourne?"

We slowly shook our heads.

"Or – Mrs Ralston – could you describe to us what your brother-in-law was wearing the weekend before last?" He gave me a consolatory smile. "Women are generally much better at all this kind of thing."

Sophie justified such confidence. She was able to describe several of Max's off-duty outfits – colours and materials.

"One does rather wonder what happened to his clothes."

I could have told him. When I returned to London on Sunday I'd driven straight to Beaumont Street. Jay had actually been back there, very briefly, the night before, immediately after leaving Victoria. He'd deposited just inside his front door the carrier bag containing my own clothes, before leaving the latchkey under a piece of stair carpeting outside...further shades of *Dial M for Murder*! I had needed only to have someone let me into the building itself, which hadn't been difficult.

Max's clothes, therefore, had gone into that same carrier bag. (Max hadn't bothered with a raincoat.) Jay had taken both the carrier bag and the overnight bag – containing a change of shirt and socks and underwear, all washed by Olivia (shirt even ironed) – to a charity shop in Marylebone High Street. The keys and emptied wallet he had put into a dustbin. The shaver and some of the toiletries – plainly not Max's toothbrush nor his facecloth – he had put into his own bathroom cabinet. I think he was a little less squeamish than me. The Rolex wristwatch he had placed upon his own wrist.

"Not to mention his wallet and keys and wristwatch etc." The inspector added this in the same contemplative fashion. "Although I imagine all of those…if it was indeed a robbery… would doubtlessly have been taken anyway. Along with most of his clothes, maybe? But *socks*? *Underpants*? And the strange thing is, when my colleagues broke into Mr Ralston's flat, there was no suggestion that any thieves had been there ahead of them; they saw many valuable bits and pieces that most thieves would have found extremely tempting."

"Possibly he hadn't his address on him?"

"No business cards, Mr Linden? Well, possibly not…although these days…? Naturally, though, for the time being, as a matter of course, we're keeping his flat under surveillance."

"Yes, Max had cards." I stated it authoritatively. Anything to muddy the waters…to stir up clouds of silt. "I feel very sure, for instance, he'd have given one to Mrs Prescott-Ames. Tomorrow, of course, you'll be able to check with her in person."

Although I knew it was unnecessary I just wanted to keep them very mindful of Olivia. Once the police were aware that Max had been alive shortly before 7pm on Sunday, when she'd dropped me off at the train station and when, as soon as she'd driven away, I had hurried round the corner to the place where I had parked my own car – once they were aware of that, I wouldn't need to account for my movements either on Saturday evening or during most of

Sunday. It was fair enough that no one should have noticed me after 7pm while I was driving back to London.

While I was driving back to London, from my constituency in Bucks.

"Odd that her name and number shouldn't be in Mr Ralston's address book."

"Why should he need to have them there? I daresay *her* card was in his wallet." I added for good measure: "I hope that doesn't put her into any danger?"

"Oh, I don't see why it should, sir. Not really. Do you?"

Ah – and if only you knew, Mr Wilby! In all recorded history there was never anyone *less* endangered by the contents of a stolen wallet than Mrs Olivia Prescott-Ames, long-time resident of Eastbourne, in the county of Sussex.

"Poor woman, though," commiserated the inspector. "Let's hope she's feeling reasonably happy tonight – because little does she suspect how very *unhappy* she'll be feeling at this time tomorrow!"

"Yes," agreed Sergeant Trip. "It's one of the worst parts of being a policeman. Having to break bad news to loved ones."

He was saying this at the front door more to Jay than to anyone. "Good night, sir."

"See you again, Mr Linden." The inspector shook Jay's hand.

Jay said to Sophie and me: "Good luck, you two. I'll obviously be thinking about you. Perhaps especially about your parents, Tom. Oh, hell, what a rotten, lousy business! And I wonder how the boys are going to take it. I don't suppose they've ever known anyone who's died."

This last was the sort of banal observation which – more than anything else at the moment – revealed to me the true extent of Jay's anxiety for us all.

Fourteen

That night I said to Jay, after Sophie had gone to bed, "I think you should call on Olivia."

"Why?"

"To soften the blow. How do you think she's going to feel when the police arrive on her doorstep? That's enough of a shock in itself; forget all the rest of it!"

"We survived it."

"Yes, but we weren't alone. 'All for one and one for all', remember? And two of us were expecting it, anyhow, and felt downright relieved to be getting it over with. Also, I think, not all policemen will be quite as sympathetic as Messrs Wilby and Trip. Particularly not where certain stereotypes are concerned. Wealthy, middle-aged widow – with much younger boyfriend! Almost a figure of fun."

"But by the time we get to Eastbourne the police will have called on her? Surely?"

"We don't know that. And even if they have...well, won't she still be needing all the support she can get?"

"But, Tom, I don't *know* her! I'm a stranger. The last thing people want is the presence of a stranger…not when they've just received bad news. *Appalling* news. And why would it make it any better to have that news broken to them – no matter how sympathetically – by someone who has no reason to be there? I think you're wrong."

It only took me a few seconds to digest this. Then I gave a sigh.

"You're right, of course. I simply wasn't thinking. How stupid can a person get?"

"I'd rather have stupid than unfeeling. Any day."

"The thing is…well, I'll tell you what happened. I just had this *feeling*. Hunch, instinct, blind conviction – I don't know what to call it. This *feeling* that you ought to be there. And somehow it seemed to grip me with such power." I shrugged. "I may have *thought* that I was listening to logic but very clearly I wasn't."

"You were listening to love."

I'd never known him say anything so tacky. The effect on both of us was unexpected. We looked at one another and started to laugh. But not as either of us laughed in the normal way. It was uncontrollable; we found we couldn't stop. After half a minute we could neither sit nor stand properly. Tears were streaming down our cheeks; our hands were clamped across our mouths. At any moment we expected Sophie to come running down the stairs – Sophie or one or both of the boys – Miriam would be knocking at the front door. Were we hysterical? It didn't seem respectful to Olivia.

Gradually we calmed down.

"Jay, please warn me next time you're going to say anything like that. All right, I had a *gut* feeling. Will that do?"

"What about *my* gut feeling? Oh, so selfish! I think I was mistaken. You couldn't have been listening to love."

That nearly set us off again. But not quite – we ended up in a hug instead, and wiped each other's eyes, and kissed each other's cheeks. Then our mood became more serious and the subject soon got changed.

157

"To tell you the truth," said Jay, "I'd rather be anywhere tomorrow but in Eastbourne – I suppose that's at the bottom of it."

"At the bottom of what?"

"If I've been seeming uncooperative."

"Oh, piffle! You've been seeming as uncooperative as Harpo Marx when faced with a pretty girl."

"Exactly one week on," he said. "I'd rather be at Lord's or somewhere – in a crowd – in Oxford Street or Piccadilly Circus; anywhere I needn't think about your blasted brother and what happened to him."

I was immediately contrite.

"Darling, forgive me. Of course you don't have to come! *Isn't* there a match at Lord's?"

"You're wrong: I do have to come. I mean, I *want* to come – who suggested it in the first place? I'm just happy to have made my point, that's all. Sorry to be cranky."

"Oh, sweetheart!"

"I thought we agreed we weren't going to use endearments up in Hampstead? In case one slipped out in front of Sophie." He smiled. "You see, I'm still being cranky."

"That's okay. You have a right to be. You have a right to be anything you want to be. Or need to be."

"Then…in returning to the subject of our lonesome, lovelorn merry widow…"

"Or not so merry widow. You have a right to be anything you want to be except satirical. I know you didn't mean it, though. Not in all seriousness."

He assented to this. "But how would I introduce myself for heaven's sake? As a real close buddy of her late and much lamented boyfriend?"

"Why not? You can tell her you were going to write to her but decided you'd like to offer your condolences in person."

"Having just broken the news that her cutie-pie isn't with us any longer? Oh, my God!"

"Well, as you say – if it hasn't been done already. But I still can't help feeling that one of us ought to check up on her…and patently it can't be me!"

It occurred to me I had now moved away from contrition and was determinedly playing on what I knew to be Jay's weakest spot – his very loving heart. I even felt justified in doing so because of the sheer strength of my conviction, however irrational it might be.

"You see, I believe we can't simply leave her just to sink or…"

I grew flustered; hastily apologized.

"And, darling, there's no one in this world any sweeter or gentler than you are." I grinned. "When you want to be!"

"Hmm."

"She just couldn't find herself in better hands."

"Hmm," he said again. "Anyway, how would I have known?"

"That isn't difficult. You're an employee of Fortnum's."

"All right," he capitulated, eventually. Grudgingly. "I haven't yet received my pay cheque but I admittedly spent a lot of time there at the beginning of last week."

"They're probably a little slow up in Accountancy. I'll have to speak to them."

We arrived in Eastbourne shortly after twelve.

I said: "I'll do the mortuary bit this afternoon. While you're off visiting our friend. Let's find somewhere nice for lunch."

"On the other hand, if we get the mortuary bit out of the way to begin with, afterwards you'll be able to relax. You can spend your whole afternoon on the beach." He had insisted I bring my trunks; had brought his own as well. "I really do need to get back into the sea," he'd said, "and take a good long swim. Absolutely the best therapy there'll be. We mustn't let that word become taboo. And I feel you probably need it just as much as me."

"What? To strike out into cool, clear, cleansing water? But tell me something. Do you *ever* stop being considerate?"

"Max might have thought I did."

He added: "And not so long ago you called me cranky."

"No, you were the one who called you cranky. You'll have to check with Hansard."

However, he'd obviously decided that apparently careless, spontaneous, unselfconscious reference to the past, whether occurring frequently or not, might represent one way of coming to terms with it.

"Besides, it needn't be so awful, need it – the mortuary bit? You don't even have to look, not properly. We know damned well it's going to be Max who's lying on that slab."

We had been told to report to the police station, either to pick up directions or, if possible, an escort. Police station and morgue were close to one another.

PC Shaw was a smiley fellow who looked about sixteen – and I would have thought that, allied to these teenage looks, he didn't seem nearly tall enough to be a policeman. In fact he was twenty-one and I realised it was only because he was standing next to Jay that he might have appeared relatively short.

"Will you be coming in as well, Mr Linden?" We were standing outside the mortuary; the brightness of the sunshine seemed inapposite.

Jay looked at me.

"No need," I said. "It's going to take less than five minutes. You two stay out here and enjoy the fresh air; enjoy the smell of the sea. Besides, Jay never met him."

And even if he was prepared to talk about the incident, it now occurred to me, it might be a different matter actually to see again what seven days ago he must certainly have seen more than enough of – both in the sea and out of it. Would having to view it again prove quite so therapeutic?

But he was still looking at me to make sure I didn't mind going in on my own when a sudden female voice put an end to that rather lengthy pause.

"Good morning, Mr Linden. Fine weather still! Is that what's brought you here again?"

It was the owner's daughter from the B&B.

"And by the way we've still got those things of yours which you didn't collect! We were wondering what to do with them."

Jay had given his real name all right, but when asked to sign the register had put down neither his proper address nor proper phone number.

Fortunately she appeared to be in a hurry. She only slowed down, didn't totally stop. What else could he have done but nod and smile? "It was all so unexpected," he told me over lunch. "I just didn't have the presence of mind to…"

"To do what?"

He thought about it. "No, I couldn't have claimed she was mistaken, could I? She had actually used my name."

Near the entrance to the mortuary PC Shaw had smiled conversationally. "Oh, have you been spending a lot of time down here?"

Jay's reply had been nonchalant. "How often do we get a heatwave that lasts as long as this?"

There was no reason, I said now, why the constable should ever mention this to Detective Inspector Wilby. Probably didn't even know him. No reason why he should mention it to anyone.

"Yet if he does…? Don't you remember? I said last night I'd never been to Eastbourne."

"Yes, but not in response to any of their questions. And you only said it casually. They mayn't even have heard it."

"Sez who? And then they'll want to know why on earth I should have given a false address and phone number? Isn't that instantly suspicious?"

In my heart I felt that he was right but I still didn't believe it mattered. Why should either of those two young people think to mention such an extremely brief exchange? And even if they did – even if at the very worst it reached the ears of others who would see in it a contradiction – what was there to connect Jay's departure from a guest house on the Saturday afternoon to Max's own apparent departure on a London-bound train the following evening?

I wondered if before we started on our drive back home we ought to pick up the few things he'd left in the B&B? But I didn't speak of it.

We went to the stretch of beach where he had recommended I should swim – nowhere near the stretch of beach from which last week *he* had swum – and for a time we lay side by side on the sliding pebbles, with the sun tanning our arms and faces. He said he didn't know how on earth I was going to get changed, since the towel I'd snatched up as we left home had turned out to be a hand towel, and the shirt I had on didn't have any length to it. But the great thing was: he was laughing as we said goodbye and laughing even as he looked down a minute later from the prom; and I wouldn't have swapped that laughter for all the privacy a person could ever have asked for.

Besides which – as I'd told Livia – perhaps I *was* a bit of an exhibitionist!

"Just want to make things clear," he'd told me before he left the beach. "I'm still resistant to this."

"Just want to make things clear," I'd responded. "I love you very much. Love the way you always do what you can to please me, notwithstanding your resistance."

"Humour you, more like," he'd countered. "I just want to make things clear," he'd pointed out.

I had fully intended to drive him to End House but he wouldn't let me. After his farewell wave from the prom – and repeated snatch of laughter caused by my predicament – he walked there, as he had walked before, and even took the journey at an easy pace.

Nevertheless, he was still engaged in rehearsing his opening remarks and in thinking about the gentlest way of breaking painful news, when he found himself approaching the newsagent's where, a week ago, Philip had gone to buy unwanted cigarettes and to use the callbox on the pavement.

As he drew closer to the shop, almost parallel with it indeed, somebody came out. This was a large man who, above his scruffy jeans, was wearing a singlet which was at least a size too small for him and who, despite Jay's preoccupation, made him think of Ray Bradbury's *Illustrated Man*. Neither Jay nor I much cared for tattoos – we believed they marred rather than enhanced the appearance of a good physique.

Jay went into the shop.

He hadn't known he was going to do so – but, as he told me later, "We can all have our little moments of gut instinct. I don't believe they're the special exclusive property of Mr Thomas Ralston, MP."

"Don't you, now? Did you know that, even as late as Queen Victoria's time, people could still be hanged, drawn and quartered if found guilty of treachery?"

"Furthermore, not all questionable ideas to which a sensible person shows resistance have – necessarily – to emanate from that selfsame Mr Thomas Ralston. MP."

"At least I find that moderately encouraging."

But what did it all mean in this case? It meant that Jay simply didn't like the thought of turning up at anybody's house – in a context, naturally, that wasn't one of business – without some small offering like a bunch of flowers, a box of chocolates or a bottle of wine. It was practically second nature to him (he didn't say this) and to his unfailingly generous inclinations. So he wondered if there might be something here that he could buy for Olivia which…well, his brain told him this could easily strike a completely wrong note but his heart told him just to go ahead and do it.

The range of confectionery proved expectedly limited but – who knew? – for a change, this patron of Fortnum's might enjoy a few Cadbury's Milk Tray; and as he surmised that, except in the strange case of her children, she was the one who nearly always gave and very seldom received, he bought a big, flat, rather showy purple box. 'The lady loves Milk Tray!' an advertisement informed him.

Olivia's house was a little further up the hill, on the opposite side of the road. He stood outside it for a moment and admired it for the second time. The gate was open; he latched it tidily behind him. Before he reached the front door he'd decided not to ring or knock but just to walk straight round to the back. He had this picture of Olivia reclining in her deckchair – either, if the police hadn't been, sipping at a tall cool glass of amaretto and orange, or, if they had, simply staring straight ahead of her and sobbing. But either way he didn't want to bother with an intermediary – her maid, Elizabeth.

His assumption was partly right. Olivia *was* in her garden, and she *was* in her deckchair. She had her back towards him. But in her hand there wasn't any glass of amaretto.

And around her neck there'd been placed a length of cord, which was presently being pulled at either end by a large man in a tight red singlet – whose arms, upper chest and shoulders, possibly the whole of his body, were covered in tattoos.

Fifteen

"Well, of course, I flew at him.

"Circled his waist, yanked him back, threw him on the grass.

"Knew that the deckchair had also been yanked back – that it had collapsed with Olivia still inside it – but for the first moments I was aware of little else, other than of our rolling over and over on the dry ground, me and that thug, and of my feeling so… well, just so terribly *cross*. So utterly and overwhelmingly *cross*. Which was absolutely his undoing. Vicious, alarmed, desperate, whatever – he was no match for my feelings of sheer and almost incredulous indignation. And outrage. How *dare* he? And then I realized I was shouting, shouting for help – although I had no idea if there was any help available. But, yes, there was. Two women came running out of the house. I half-saw one of them ministering to Olivia, helping her up, while the other went racing back inside.

"Listen to this, Tom, the two of them, Elizabeth and her friend, they'd been sitting over cups of tea and *knitting* while that fellow was out there strangling our one and only alibi.

"But for now we were still rolling over and over, me and him, me and that oafish hired assassin, until at last I was sitting astride him, not simply pinning him down but actually digging my knees in, bouncing on top of him, doing everything I could to hurt.

"I was almost sorry when the police turned up."

*

"You must be the strongest man in the world," said Josh, when he and his mother and Gil had been privileged to hear a retelling. This was a version which – although edited – hadn't been stripped entirely of its more satisfying highlights.

"Yes, I think I probably am. Especially when I'm cross."

"So you'd better watch out," warned Sophie. "Particularly if Jay is coming to live with us."

"Is he *honestly* coming to live with us?" asked Josh.

"Well, it would seem sensible, wouldn't it? It'll save him lots of money – and we have several rooms we don't really make the most of. But what do you two think about it? Or would you rather tell me in private?"

"Why should we want to do that?" Gil looked perplexed.

"In case you'd be frightened of hurting Jay's feelings."

"And making him *cross*," said Jay. He casually extended both arms. "And then making him have to…oh, I don't know…yes, *pounce!*"

Which naturally elicited squeals of terror and excitement. "Will you always be as nice as you are now?"

"Oh dear. I can see this is going to be the toughest audition bar none! But possibly good training if they ever decide to make a film of Mary Poppins."

"Would you play Mary Poppins?"

"Mary Poppins is a *woman*, silly!"

"Oh, so she is, Gil. I knew there'd be a hitch. How silly we are, Josh!"

Jay added: "And I suppose there's another hitch! I actually think your father may be the strongest man in the world. I'll settle for being second."

Neither Gilbert nor Josh would settle for it, though, so Jay only shrugged and let them have their way.

"Sorry, Tom. I did try. But you can't argue with your fans. 'Ya gotta give the people…the ticket-buying people…'"

He was quite a talented song-and-dance man, too.

*

This was on Sunday afternoon, after tea. On Saturday evening – during our drive back to London – he'd told me what had taken place following the arrival of the police.

"After they'd pulled me off and I'd seen him handcuffed and marched away I suddenly went all weak at the knees and thought about what might have happened if I'd been just one minute later. Supposing I'd rung the bell; supposing I'd taken longer over my choice of chocolates? Actually, I needn't have wasted my money – wasted *your* money. Because stopping your hostess being strangled is possibly one of the best calling cards a person can produce. I didn't even have to worry about how I broke the news. Olivia didn't know already; there'd been no earlier visit from the police; but the shock of hearing about Max's death was somewhat mitigated, not only by the ordeal she'd just been through herself, but by the thug's confession that it was Max who'd hired him."

Though where, I wondered, did this leave that last-minute promise she'd made in regard to her sons? Well perhaps it would cause her to think – think both constructively and soberly. And this was probably the best that one could hope for.

"Tom, if Max could find a hit-man so easily – maybe not one of the highest calibre but even so – why couldn't you? Doesn't it make you feel just a soupçon inadequate? Perhaps I *should* introduce you to my Great-Aunt Madge."

"Yes, I'd like that. If you truly do possess one…a Great-Aunt Madge. In fact, I'd like to start meeting your entire family."

"You would?"

"Yes, I would."

"As an illustrious MP whom by lucky chance I just happened to run into? Or as something a little more than an illustrious MP whom by lucky chance…?"

"As something a whole lot more than that. I reckon that if you can take it, so can I."

Jay stared at me as though he were looking at some stranger in the driving seat.

"Please, love," I said, "don't start imagining things. I haven't suddenly grown brave. It's just that I reckon all those you'd feel inclined to tell – whether five of them or fifty – must be the sort who are reasonably sympathetic. Not the type who'd rush straight out to blab or would unexpectedly start to fancy a new life in the New World."

"That's true," he conceded. "But never on a Saturday."

"Never what on a Saturday?"

"I've just decided that it will be safer if I never leave my bed on a Saturday. Safer for me and for everybody else."

"I suppose I don't have to ask you why. Only one question I do need to put. May I join you there?"

"You have no choice. Not only are Saturdays going to be my *Back Street* day, back in my 'newly renovated' apartment, but it's a day when, clearly, I must always have an alibi. 'Officer, how could that have been me? I was in bed.' 'Can anyone substantiate your story?' 'Most certainly they can. Thomas Ralston MP. Alibi-provider."

At this point I myself took over. "'Oh, sir, not you again?' 'Sorry, Officer, let me hand you one of my cards; perhaps you can pin it on your notice board? *Alibis Our Speciality.*'"

Jay gave a nod, unmistakably ironic. "It must run in the family. I can tell you of someone else who certainly had the right idea regarding alibis. Even though it was his rich girlfriend who was about to be done in; even though it was he himself who was to be her single beneficiary."

"Can we be speaking of my one and only twin brother? Surely *that* can't be the case?"

"You're an amateur. *He* was a professional."

"Explain."

"Certainly. He had the best alibi ever. Watertight, irrefutable."

"How come?"

"He was dead."

*

Jay said: "Let's hope Olivia won't be asked to identify him. No hair on his chest."

I had obviously told him about that unterminated strip of mine – although not, of course, about what had followed on from it. ("Oh, you tease!" he'd remarked. "How *completely* you must have been in your element!")

I said now: "I shouldn't think she would be asked. He's already been identified. Besides, don't they only show you the face?"

*

In Eastbourne the police had told Jay – although not in Olivia's hearing – that they thought Max's murder might have been sexually motivated. His lack of clothing had been a pointer which they couldn't ignore. And they'd asked whether Max was queer. Jay had replied he'd never met Max and had never heard him spoken of in that way. But when he'd related this to me – although I knew I would never do anything, ever, to propagate such a story, any more than on the previous evening I had allowed myself to do so in front of Inspector Wilby and Sergeant Trip – his information made me smile. To myself; not to anybody else; not even to

Jay. I remembered Max's proud boast that he was a red-blooded heterosexual and the way in which this boast had incorporated a sneer. Shakespeare says the owl was a baker's daughter. Meaning we never know where we're going to end up or what kind of reputation we may acquire along the way.

"Oh, fuck!" I said – although not in relation to any of this. "We never retrieved your bag from that young woman at the B&B."

And even before I'd finished speaking I'd begun to turn the car around; but when a little later I phoned Sophie to inform her of our delay I simply said – since for the moment it was easier – that we'd spent longer in the water than we'd intended.

"I hope that doesn't mean the pub," she'd answered. "Darling, please be careful – I mean, whichever one of you is going to drive. You two are very precious, you know."

*

Back to Sunday.

Jay and I were walking on the Heath – would probably end up by having a whisky before returning home for lunch. Sophie, guessing that we might want to do this and guessing that we'd have a lot to talk about, had bribed the boys to help her make a cake and biscuits, and possibly some toffee. Ruby was visiting her parents.

"Jaybird – Sophie knows about us."

"Did you tell her?"

"Only when she asked. Perhaps 'asked' isn't the right word. She hardly needed to ask."

I nodded at some people I knew slightly and who looked as though they'd have been interested to be introduced to my companion.

"Last night," I said, "after I'd gone upstairs."

Jay smiled. "It's all right, my love – you don't have to be worried about saying, 'Last night in bed.' I assume that occasionally you need to go to bed."

"Just like to be a little tactful."

"How, then, could Sophie have claimed you weren't a diplomat?"

"Search me. One of life's small mysteries. But don't procrastinate; there's nothing to be scared of!"

"What made her speak of it?"

"You remember the morning you and she first met? Well, you should – it was less than two weeks ago. You'd phoned to suggest we have coffee, you and I, opposite the Everyman. When your call finally came through I picked it up in the study, thinking how providential it was that I should actually have been up there at the right moment. Little did I realise, though, that at precisely the same instant Sophie had picked up in the kitchen. That's why she and Miriam happened to drop in at Mitzi's – although Miriam had no idea it was for any reason other than to drink coffee and to see Mitzi."

"What had we said? Can you remember?"

"Nothing very much. But enough for Sophie to form an instant suspicion. More from our voices than from anything we actually came out with."

"Was it a shock?"

"Yes, naturally it was. But Sophie's a girl who can adjust. She said that if she'd discovered I was in love with a woman she couldn't have borne it – that she just couldn't have coped."

"What's the difference?"

"She didn't feel as if she'd be in competition with a man."

"Fuck! She's a marvel!"

"She said that at first she'd been flabbergasted to find out I liked men in that way – and frightened I might be going to leave her – but that she'd very soon realized I had no intention whatever of leaving her. And after that she was able to relax somewhat, take in all the positive bits, understand there wasn't anything negative she needed to be afraid of… Of course, if she hadn't liked you, it would have been a whole new ballgame…but how could anybody *not* like you? She almost fell in love with you herself that first day the three of you spent together, that first evening the three of *us* spent together. And naturally it helped a lot that Gil and Josh took to you so immediately – and so wholeheartedly – rotten judges of character that they are. But what can you expect at their age?"

I paused.

"Somehow, even by the time you and she and Miriam left Mitzi's, she already felt all right about it. Providentially I'd been allowed to choose the absolutely perfect moment in which to give her a present: a copy of *From Here to Eternity* with an inscription on the flyleaf: 'It's *all* in the title! From Tom, your oh-so grateful and *eternally* loving husband.' I'd bought it just the day before; still had it in my briefcase. Providential, in spite of all my worries about Max and you."

There came another pause. We passed a woman walking half a dozen dogs.

"And last night…? Tom, are you actually saying that she's willing to *share* you?"

We waited until a young couple had passed, with a toddler who was gazing at us – and at everything else – with wide-eyed curiosity.

"Well, we didn't use that actual word but yes…in practice… 'As long as you're not expecting us to fight over you, tear each other's hair out: *He's mine tonight – oh, no, he's mine – YOU had him last night!*'"

"That's incredible. That's really incredible! Hell's bells! *She's* incredible. Never been another woman like her!"

"Also, I told her about Max."

"Oh, God. She must have found that, as well, a tad difficult to come to terms with."

"Yes. A lot *more* difficult, as it happens. But in a way, once it all started, I felt that it was better…in spite of the fact *you* weren't there (I mean, weren't there to ask for your permission, for your go-ahead – and how I wished you had been!); felt it was better to get all of it out in one mad rush."

"I'm so very glad I wasn't there. If you were intent on doing that – no more nasty surprises, one shock supposedly neutralising another! – I imagine you told her how he died?"

"Yes."

"And what does she think of me now?"

"Just what she thought of you before. She thinks we were blessed to have gone to see that play. She thinks we were blessed that three weeks later I should have walked into *The Good Companions*."

"Even though if you hadn't…?"

"Even though if I hadn't…" Still a further pause, while two teenagers went by, dribbling a ball to one another. "Jay, remember it was Max's own choice to behave in the way he did. You and I weren't in the least responsible for that."

"Agreed, but perhaps we could have managed it a little differently."

I made no further comment; couldn't immediately think of one that might be appropriate – helpful, honest, satisfactory. But five minutes later: "Remember something else, my love. If I *hadn't* walked into that pub Olivia Prescott-Ames would now be lying in her coffin."

Yes, it seemed to me, Jay could most certainly draw comfort from that. I expatiated on it.

"And, apart from his legacy, what would there be to tie Max in with her murder? He'd no doubt arranged for himself the kind of alibi which Ray Milland had arranged for *himself*, while that so-called private investigator Max had gone to…"

Jay was incorrigible. "If it hadn't been for me he wouldn't have gone to him."

"Oh, my darling!"

"But it's true, isn't it?"

"Then undoubtedly he'd have found somebody else."

"How? You make it sound so very easy. I don't suppose there's another private dick in all of London who…"

"Well, maybe not. Who knows? Isn't it interesting, though, that you don't need any kind of qualification – you don't need any sort of licence – to set up in that line of business? Anyone can do it. People sometimes call them 'Guns for Hire'. Did you know that?"

"Interesting, you say? *Scary* is the word *I'd* feel more inclined to use."

"Yes. But no doubt things will change."

"You think so? Well, as my mother likes to say…"

Unexpectedly he grinned. Bless his mother. It was as though he suddenly realized that this morning was a happy morning – a happy, happy morning – a real turning point in all our lives: his, Sophie's and my own. It wasn't a time for wondering if one could have managed things better. Obviously one could have but so long as the hope had been there – at least the hope, the steadfast aim – of always doing one's best…

I smiled. "What is it your mother likes to say?"

"'When plums come to us without stones.' You see, a year or two back, she lost a tooth on some jam she'd just made. Before that, it used to be, 'When Tiggers can descend trees.' Or, occasionally, 'When women are allowed to marry one another…have someone else see to the laundry, washing up, cooking and cleaning…look after you, in short, like a mother.'"

"Is that what your mother likes to say? And does she add (I hope) that what's sauce for the gander…?"

"Oh, yes, she's always been very fair-minded. If women can marry each other – then quite obviously men can as well."

My smile extended. "Although in that case the subtext might need a spot of working on. But my goodness! No wonder you don't feel too nervous about introducing me to your family."

He acknowledged the joke, yet his manner was again quite serious.

"Honestly, Tom, do you feel that people of the same sex will *ever* be allowed to marry?"

"Not in our lifetimes, my sweet."

"A bit depressing – no?"

"But not for us. Because I'll tell you what *is* going to happen in our lifetimes. Starting almost instantly, indeed. Two men and one woman living together *very* contentedly. Throw into the mix – for twelve years or so, let's say – two lively, warm-hearted, funny, affectionate boys. Boys who'll turn into youths, youths who'll turn into young men – hopefully, adventurous young men. Five happy people altogether, all together. Happy and loving. That sounds good to me."

"Me, too."

"But, great Scot, did I say only twelve? No, they'll *never* want to leave. Who would willingly walk away from anything so wonderful? In fact I can foresee this as – eventually – turning into our next major problem."

"What, exactly?"

"Getting rid of Gil and Josh."

ABOUT A BOAT TRIP, A HOLD UP, A STRIP SHOW AND YOU

One

"Okay, Stella. Serious stuff! Please listen."

Now that I've reached middle age I'm not scared what people say about those who talk to themselves.

Nor do I ever shy away from cliché. "This is the very first day, indeed the very first morning, of the remainder of your life."

September 3rd 1986. 10.45 or thereabouts.

I don't shy away from brackets either or dashes or italics (when I'm writing stuff down, obviously) nor from using a conjunction to begin a sentence or a preposition to end it – although at school I was repeatedly told off for all of this. So, you see, we may live but we don't always learn. (The living bit is what concerns me now – but, yes, the learning too, of course; aren't the two inseparable? But learning not just anything; only things that matter.) The whole of Joseph Heller's second novel, *Something Happened*, was written in brackets; not one sentence which wasn't contained in a bracket. Did anybody tell him off? And as for clichés, I actively welcome a great many – recognise their essential truth and their readiness to share enlightenment; I know that even in something as simple as *my heart sank* I couldn't hope to make improvements. One doesn't break rules merely for the sake of it.

But how does a cliché get started? Catchphrases on radio or TV – yes, no problem. But otherwise? "Oh, good afternoon, madam. May I draw your attention to our exciting new line in flavoured yoghurts? 'Goodbye to our conservative past!' they declare. 'This is the first day of the rest of our lives!'" I feel there has to be a pretty sound marketing strategy in place.

Never mind. September 3rd 1986. Exactly forty-seven years since the outbreak of World War Two. One thinks of all those families sitting around their wireless sets and listening to Mr Chamberlain. Almost to the very minute – wasn't his broadcast at eleven?

I don't suppose many of his listeners were daring to think in terms of new beginnings then; how many would even be alive in six years' time? Not that in 1939 they'd have realised the war was ever going to last that long.

Whereas I, in 1986, can feel confident of at least another twenty years; maybe thirty, maybe longer; one grandmother and several of her sisters all lived into their middle nineties.

Indeed, forty-seven years *back*; why not forty-seven years *ahead*?

In 2033 I could be ninety-six. By no means impossible. Perhaps not exactly gallivanting but still, like Gran, hopping onto a bus from time to time and doing my shopping at Selfridges. Having tea in their Food Hall.

All right, not *hopping*. But still using a bus from time to time. Or the tube. And with a ready, cheerful smile. That's what counts.

Yes. Forty-seven years ago. On that day of the start of so much suffering and loss (how can any of us comparatively comfortable ones, on looking back, ever have the gall to complain about the silly little upsets of our own daily lives? But then it doesn't have to be war one looks back on – what about burnings at the stake, hangings drawings quarterings, crucifixions?) Anyhow, on *that* day was the morning as blue-skied and sunny as it is today? And if so, how many who lived in this area were saying, "Let's walk into Regent's Park and try to find tranquillity by the lake. Regain our sense of perspective through being close to animals and birds and things of natural beauty. Let's go into Queen Mary's Garden and smell the roses."

But it was a Sunday, wasn't it, and after the wireless had finally been switched off wouldn't people's thoughts more likely have turned to their already half-prepared roast dinner and to further numbed, half whispered – or suddenly defiant, loudly defiant – talk around the table?

Today is Wednesday and to my knowledge there's been no recent announcement of any big new global catastrophe; so the reason I'm now heading to Queen Mary's Gardens – if additional reason be needed, on a day when the weather's warm and the sun is shining – is purely personal and petty and unconcerned with world events. Actually it's because yesterday was harrowing and I thought that today I'd better treat myself to a good dollop of serenity. Serenity and contemplation. I find it's always easier to contemplate when I'm out of doors and strolling in a peacefully harmonious setting.

Or else sitting in one.

Of course, our garden at the back of the house is also pretty peaceful – I mean on the days when George our gardener isn't there; a really good-natured old chap but he loves to stop for a natter and I honestly can't bring myself to discourage him. At home, too, there's generally the idea of things nearby which you feel you ought to be getting on with.

Serenity and contemplation – and today, at any rate, positive appreciation. It was on Radio 4 this morning, while I was lying in my bath, that somebody uttered that old cliché which no one on the panel even bothered to respond to.

Naturally it wasn't something new to me. But it's like when you read all those self-help books. (*Feel The Fear And Do It Anyway* is one I've read three times.) There's very little that hasn't previously occurred to you but when you see everything persuasively collected in a book it somehow becomes more than a reminder, it turns into an imperative. "Why do I continually forget such very simple things?"

Anyhow – I repeat – yesterday wasn't a good day. Metaphorically I walked a long way down two avenues which maybe I wasn't in the proper mood even to set foot in.

No 'maybe' about it; I should have called a halt at the beginning. But I think I have a stubborn streak which tends to prevent me from admitting defeat – and in the end I barged into at least half a dozen offices of Hampstead estate agents. (Currently I live in West Hampstead. I have friends there and I know the area. I'm really not planning to move very far.) But all the furnished property at present on their books – I mean in the way of flats, not houses; smallish flats at that – seemed either inconvenient or unappealing; and if it wasn't actually furnished (but still for rent and not for sale) its photograph and somewhat perfunctory page of details proved scarcely more exciting. I tried to believe it would be fun to go to Maples or Habitat and buy lots of new things, especially with a friend like Maddie at my side. But I knew I'd have to do it on a budget, even if it were a budget of my own devising and not one laid down by Duncan – my husband has his faults but meanness isn't one of them. And Maddie works at two charity shops; she won't invariably be free.

Yet after leaving these estate agents I still hadn't the sense, whilst having eggs benedict and an espresso and crème caramel at a smart little bistro on West End Lane, the sense to let the contrariness of my mood deter me from opening my evening paper to look at whatever jobs might be available.

Situations Vacant stretched over several columns and several pages and my first reaction was one of relief. It shouldn't have been. I didn't drive a fork-lift truck; I wasn't a plumber, a maintenance man, a plasterer or a bricklayer. I wasn't a swimming-pool attendant. Indeed, I wasn't anything at all which it might have benefitted me to be. I left the bistro with a nod of good riddance to that aggressively demanding *Standard*, which I abandoned on my table.

I intended to work off my frustration by going for a long walk. But before I'd proceeded scarcely fifty paces I passed an employment agency where – having almost angrily retraced my steps – I was interviewed by an elderly and rather charming woman who would have liked so much to be of help (she told me this four times) but who resorted in the end to discussing the merits of *Hannah and Her Sisters*, which she'd seen only the night before. With the daughter of her former lodger. At the Odeon in Camberwell.

Following this, in the same desultory fashion, I went to look along the racks in a nearby Job Centre, which again I had walked past but had then conscientiously returned to.

Yet afterwards I felt guilty. When you realise you're competing against real desperation – no, let me change that, real material need; my own desperation seems genuine enough – then you feel spoilt and mean and grabby. Like someone sitting in Claridges and going on and on about life's enervating little hardships.

Besides, while standing in the Job Centre, I'd become distressingly aware of how well-cut my clothes were and that on the previous afternoon I'd had my regular Monday appointments at both the hairdresser's and the beauty salon. I beat a blushingly shamefaced retreat.

Not that anyone need have felt threatened. As must be plain by now, I possess neither qualifications nor experience. For the relatively short time between leaving Cambridge and getting married I worked in a West End shop that sold handmade chocolates. At college I'd read English, perhaps not the most relevant of subjects in our twentieth-century cut-throat business world. Admittedly I can discuss with confidence the weirdly erratic quality of Woody Allen – every bit as erratic as Alfred Hitchcock – but, in spite of this, employers aren't precisely going to fall over themselves in a mad rush to get me onto their team. Nor if all else fails are they going to wage a ruthlessly savage campaign to headhunt. I am not the girl most likely.

(*The Girl Most Likely* starred Jane Powell. I've been told I look a little like Jane Powell, although I'm not as diminutive as she is and, besides that, I have dark hair. I know I must have something though; at forty-nine I still get my fair share of appreciative glances – and not *just* from geriatrics! – and whistles from a building site. Often I used to wonder if the glances weren't due to a smudge somewhere but Maddie once assured me wolf whistles from on high weren't too noticing of makeup smears, or dust and smudges for which they themselves might be responsible. "I think that generally they're quite a broadminded lot.")

Anyhow, going back to my being unthreatening, I can't even type. I'd thought about enrolling on a course to make me computer-literate but I hadn't taken it any further than that – merely thinking about it. Therefore how committed can I truthfully claim to be? Stella, the games-player? Stella, the drama queen? Stella, the bridge-burner? All three of whom may only be sending out a cry for help…and a largely inaudible one at that.

(Stella, the cushion-plumper that I once accused my husband of trying to turn me into – despite our having Mrs Conway, who comes in daily and always keeps the house immaculate.)

Should I clarify games-player and drama queen? Both listed, even given pride of place, because I know this whole escape-route thing is going to be such an enormous gamble. And I'm really not that much of a gambler: only the odd flutter on the horses or the boat race, nothing more than that. I imagine that gamblers don't greatly mind the thought of losing; but I am not and never shall be a good loser. Not at heart. No matter what sort of face I may try to put on it. And I'm talking here even of a game of Scrabble or Canasta when there's nothing other than my poor wounded pride that's riding on the outcome.

So why am I even considering doing any of this?

Indeed, *am* I even considering doing any of this? Maybe, as I've already intimated, the whole thing is nothing but pure fantasy. Maybe it's symbolic that hardly ten minutes after leaving the Job Centre I find myself gazing at the pictures in the window of a travel agent. Stella, the woman who still yearns for that airline ticket to romantic places…? But if there haven't been many airline tickets up to now, when the actual wherewithal has never been anything of a problem, what on earth makes me think…? Oh, how I'd love to have a good rich suitor, one just as rich as my husband, who'd instinctively recognise all my needs and say, "There, there, my darling, your wish is my command. Forever and ever. Amen."

Or if only my mum were still alive. My father is – older son of the Selfridge-trotting grandma – alive and kicking rather querulously in North Yorkshire; but *he* has never been the kind to go "There, there!", and despite his essential integrity the two of us have rarely seemed to get along that well. My mother was the only person he'd allow to laugh at his pessimism and general tendency to be negative – perhaps he now lets his new wife do it, yet I neither know nor am much interested, not caring for her in the slightest. But ironically my mother has been dead for many years now and I still can't quite take it in. I mean, I'm always thinking of little things I want to ask her, small happenings in my day which I intend to share with her ("Oh, Mum is going to get a giggle out of this!"), before I suddenly and of course with a sharply renewed pang recall it's now too late. (I believe somebody once said *If only I'd done such-and-such* is the saddest short sentence in the language but I sometimes think *Too late* may equal it; or in fact are they roughly the same thing?) She was almost forty by the time I was born and both my parents had practically given up on the idea of their producing a child; but – cliché, cliché! – and this one's propagation is far more understandable – she was the best mother in the whole world, the wisest and most forgiving, the least judgmental. She would certainly have gone "There, there!" and her take on the situation – any situation – would undeniably have been the right one. Tender and constructive.

Anyhow, all of this (with little shortage of embellishment, you note – "Stella often finds it difficult to stick to the point," although Miss Shaw had never revealed exactly what the point should be) is why I'm now walking past the tennis courts and heading up to the Inner Circle.

So, then … Queen Mary's Garden. Here comes your mixed-up and adoring subject, Stella, in her perennial search for solitude, solace and balm. (Prennial? Well, these days it almost appears so – perennial, or should I only say ongoing?) But it seems like a definite touch of synchronicity that on this day the sun is warmly shining, whereas yesterday the sky was unrelievedly overcast, dark from beginning to end.

Or it *would* seem like a definite touch of synchronicity if I wasn't suddenly worried I might be using the wrong word. Perhaps I mean only symbolism. Boring old symbolism.

Shame. Synchronicity sounded so completely right. When I get home I shall have to look it up.

But first … Queen Mary's Garden … a brief bird's-eye-view of this park within a park.

To begin with, it's wholly self-contained, roughly circular, with things on its perimeter which don't at the moment seem quite relevant. The posh cafeteria, partly indoor, partly out. The Open Air Theatre, mainly concerned with Shakespeare – at the present, *King Lear*. The great fountain with its muscular bronze merman flanked by a couple of modestly breast-covered mermaids. And even a bit irrelevant right now, the thousands of rose bushes (more than four thousand varieties) which give the Gardens their name – in full, you see, it's Queen Mary's *Rose* Garden.

No, my own special part is a little to the right of centre (if you're standing with your back to those magnificent wrought-iron gates, black and gold – with a little golden crown placed on top – erected in the middle Thirties). There's a long broad pond near the foot of a green and leafy hillock – though when does a pond become a lake? – supporting an island of rocks and trees and shrubs that can be reached by a little wooden footbridge. In the water at the island's further end is a second bronze statue, this time of an eagle or a vulture – anyhow a bird with a very big wingspan, which is apparently perched on a tree stump and leaning down to scrutinise the darting shapes of fish.

And only a few yards from this statue, facing it and at the edge of a fairly narrow path which borders the pond, stands an isolated bench which is not only idyllically situated from a scenic point of view but always appears to be catching the sun whenever there's any sunshine to be caught. It is my favourite bench in all of London.

Or, rather, my favourite bench out of the many I've come across. Perhaps I ought to compile a guide. There've already been guides to all the pubs in London, and all the bookshops, and even all the public conveniences – would it be too mammoth an undertaking? A guide to all the most beautifully positioned benches, both those that bear inscriptions and those that rather sadly don't? I love the inscriptions set on benches, in commemoration of their having been so important a feature in the lives of those now gone. One can sit and share an experience with somebody one would have liked. Which, after all, is basically what museums are all about, isn't it? Connecting with the dead. Not all of whom, however – I'd stake my life on it – one would have liked.

But forget guides; I'm too little motivated, far too lazy. Let's concentrate on what I know. When I'm lucky, when all the gods are smiling down on me – which, in this respect, seems to occur surprisingly often – it's as if this particular bench, my favourite bench in all of London, remains half hidden by the very lushness of its surroundings.

It's as if – hallelujah! – there's no one as yet who's actually tumbled to the mere fact of its existence.

Today, though, somebody has. The bench is occupied. Delete that hallelujah.

(No, I'm sorry, Lord. Forgive me. One should *never*, of course, delete a hallelujah. There are far too few of them as it is. In fact, we must always do everything we can to add to their number.)

The trespasser looks about twenty-five. He's feeding the pigeons; the path has grown impassable. But I could very easily have made a detour round the back of the bench, aiming to disturb neither the nourishment of the pigeons nor the absorption of their benefactor. (Irrelevant: their darkly blond, nice-looking benefactor.) On his lap he has the remnants of a presumably stale white loaf and is removing one slice at a time from inside the wrapper – Mother's Pride? – tearing up each slice and throwing the pieces into every part of that jostling throng. There's something fascinating about this, the attempted precision, the care with which it's all being carried out. I stand and watch.

Yes, the young man's attractive, has a pleasant face and – so far as I can judge – a fine body; I form the impression he must be tall. But I swear that none of this is why I've paused.

Or perhaps I shouldn't swear to it. Can the kindness of someone's expression be separated from that person's face, whether handsome or otherwise?

In any case I suddenly realise something. Watching him I feel relaxed… preoccupied…almost happy. Helped by him of course – helped by him and his hungry pigeons – Queen Mary's Gardens are already working their usual beneficence.

Benefactor…beneficence…there appears to be a link.

Two

"I'm sorry! So sorry! I didn't realise!"

"I know you didn't. I'm enjoying it. That one seems to be missing out."

"Which?"

"There. The scrawny one with the brown markings." Fortunately it's easy to point to, being on the edge closest to myself.

For greater accuracy of aim he now stands – is even taller than I'd imagined, six foot four, maybe five? – and with demonstrable expertise throws the last of his bread.

Another bird grabs it.

"Oh, too slow, poor old thing, not with it!" He speaks with what sounds like a northern accent, although I'm not good on accents. "Just too dozy by half."

"Or too frightened of his peers, more like." It's stupid: I fully share his disappointment.

"Think he'll be all right?"

In truth I haven't the faintest idea. "Oh, at this time of year… And I'm sure by winter he'll have found his wings. May have got pushy himself by then. Or *herself*." How absurd: I must suddenly think it matters to establish this more-than-likely possibility.

"You're meaning…if the bird world is anything like ours?"

"Yes." I smile. "Exactly."

But now – no more food – the pigeons are starting to disperse.

"Would you mind if I joined you for a minute or two?"

"Oh. Please." He waits until I've sat down, then resumes his own seat – we're at opposite ends.

"Isn't this a perfect spot to have a bench?" I'd been about to tell him it was the bench I always made for but had then wondered whether it mightn't imply he was usurping.

"Yes."

He seems to be searching for something less monosyllabic.

"Yes. Looking at the water – and that statue of an eagle – and that bit of island we can see… And it also gets the sun."

"Thank you, Queen Mary," I murmur respectfully. "Thank you for placing it here."

"Yes, thank you, Queen Mary," he repeats. Then, to me, "You make it sound as though she did it herself."

"Well, perhaps she was good at delegation?"

"Getting others to do the work for you?" I have the feeling he didn't know the word but has made an intelligent guess.

"Delegation sounds a little more gracious, I'd say."

He nods. But while he'd been elaborating on this being the perfect spot (and now I rather like the idea of Her Majesty in long skirt, fur-collared overcoat and decorated toque being here to heft it herself and position it just right), while he'd been elaborating on this he'd been absentmindedly screwing up the wrapper from the bread; and now he's trying to stuff it into a pocket of his jeans. "Here, let me take that, it can go in my shoulder bag."

He hesitates.

"It would make me feel more a part of the enterprise." Me, who hadn't done a thing except stand and watch. (Next time I ought to do it myself, St Francis. I can't think why I haven't. After all, I *twice* took the boys to see *Mary Poppins*.)

"Then…thank you. Thank you very much."

It *was* Mother's Pride. I'd like to tell him he can do far better than that – from the point of view of health, I mean – but don't believe it's quite my place to do so.

Besides, he looks healthy enough. I notice he has nice clear eyes – blue but softer, less attention-getting than blue eyes sometimes are – and from the beginning, of course, I've been aware of how golden brown he is.

"Well, talking of catching the sun, one can see *you've* just come back from holiday!"

"Oh, what, the tan, you mean? No. I need to have that for my job."

"Your job?"

"Yes. I'm on the stage."

Although I know he's done his best to announce this quite matter-of-factly and without betraying even the slightest hint of pride he simply isn't up to it. He's probably younger than either of my own sons and he isn't fooling anyone.

"On the stage? Oh, how wonderful!"

I suppose that's a somewhat stupid and patronising sort of comment (would one exclaim to an accountant or a policeman or a street-sweeper in similar style?) but surely there are times when it's okay – at least, if it's not intentional – to be more or less stupid and patronising.

"Are you…are you…appearing in anything at the moment?"

Now *that* could have been far more the wrong thing to say; and I'm starting to worry, even before he's pointing to a nearby tree.

"Oh, look – a squirrel! They're pretty tame round here. I forgot: only a week ago, I saw a lady with a bag of nuts."

Remorsefully, I take my cue. "Then you come here often?"

"Not very. But it's peaceful. It's a place where you can think."

"When there isn't somebody stopping you!"

"No, I didn't mean that. It's nice to have company."

I decide to compound my mistake – only a mistake, I tell myself, because he's still so very young and insecure. After all, in the theatre isn't it a well-known occupational hazard: to be out of work a lot of the time – waiting on tables – 'resting'? Usually no one has much idea of how long a play is going to run.

"On the stage I would have thought you had plenty of company."

"Yes, you're right."

Well, that's fine then. My faux pas has clearly been forgiven. "You know, I myself always wanted to act."

"Did you?"

"And if I could only live my life again that's one of the first things I might change. I mean, at least I'd give it a shot. But what I was thinking just now…it was the comradeship that really appealed; the sense of everyone finding themselves in the same boat, all pulling together. Like in the war."

Yes, I am *wholly* in favour of a good cliché.

"Why didn't you then? Give it a shot?"

"No guts. My parents were both opposed – even my mother. And I didn't know then about drama schools or the possibility of ever winning a scholarship. I must have been pretty inexperienced. Sheltered. I must have been pretty docile."

But I don't want to be talking about myself. And he was the one who first mentioned the theatre – and did so with unconcealable pride. I decide to try again.

"What was the last thing you appeared in?"

"There wasn't any last thing."

Oh dear. I'm not doing too well at this.

"But there's a present thing," he says, "and I reckon that's what matters."

"Then you *are* in something at the moment? I'm sorry – I thought…! When I asked you before and you didn't answer I thought that I'd been tactless."

"No, it was just that…it was just that…I was scared…"

"*Scared*? What of?" I imagine it must be some form of superstition.

"That it might come across like I was showing off. Bragging or something."

"Good heavens, you've got every right to brag!" (Accountant, policeman, road-sweeper – please block your ears.)

(No – *how wonderful* to you lot too. Why on earth not?)

"That's very nice of you to say so. But it's not like being a doctor, is it? Or a dentist? Or a volunteer in Africa?"

I wouldn't have believed I could be co-opted so easily onto the side of the defence, trying to excuse, even justify, that earlier remark.

"Rightly or wrongly," I contend, "there's a glamour about the theatre." Oddly enough, I'm suddenly remembering plays I saw when I was young: *Where the Rainbow Ends*, *Peter Pan*, *Through the Looking Glass*, all of them suggesting that the world was colourful – exciting – enchanting. And, above all, *manageable*. "You tell stories and we all like to hear stories. *Need* to hear them. They're part of life's magic. I think the very existence of theatre – and indeed of any art, so long as it's affirming and inspirational – may even be what makes it possible."

"Makes what possible?"

"For people to become doctors and dentists and volunteers in Africa."

I don't know if I believe what I'm saying. I've certainly never said it before – nor even thought it, so far as I recall. And it's poorly expressed, I know. But there's something there which I *want* to believe in and later on must certainly return to. It's even something I could come to feel strongly about. This, I think, communicates itself.

"I hope it was implicit but perhaps I ought to emphasise it anyway. For most of the time – you give joy!"

"Thank you."

That's all he says but it's as if I've granted him some really big favour. I feel touched.

Then a few seconds later: "Implicit?" Most of us, I think, would either pretend, ignore…or make intelligent guesses. While I'm explaining, we hear the approach of a transistor (what else could it be?), not only loud but blaring. What's being played is a Beatles song; if the volume were turned down it wouldn't be displeasing.

And after a moment we see a young couple heading towards us, on the path beside the water.

"Shall I ask them to turn it off?"

"No, don't worry," I say. "I'll give them a withering glance!"

But – had I forgotten? – this is the first day of the rest of my life. Withering glances surely shouldn't have any place in a first day. The previous morning I could undeniably have done it well.

Besides, the young woman briefly turns her head and smiles at us. The young man follows suit. You can't answer a smile with a withering glance. Mainly, you can't answer a smile with anything other than a smile.

"Hey, you've got your music on a bit loud," drawls my companion – his voice sounds lazy, as though he's just been dozing. "You don't think you could turn it down a bit, do you? Or even off? This place is supposed to be peaceful." He rises, quite slowly, to his feet.

"Sure," says the lad. "No problem. Sorry."

John Lennon – or whoever – immediately gets banished after informing the world there's nowhere you can be that isn't where you're meant to be.

"It's easy!" I say – which is part of the lyric, no comment on our situation.

The young couple disappears around the next corner. "Well…! All you need is love! I can see I shan't have to teach *you* how to glare!"

He sits down again. "Oh, they'll probably turn it back on when they think we can't hear."

"No, I somehow don't believe they will."

"Nor me. They seemed all right didn't they? Just a bit young and thoughtless."

This amuses me. "Methuselah! Probably all of five or six years younger than you are! So tell me! What's the play you're in?" Now my eagerness is wholly genuine.

"What did you call me?"

"Methuselah. He was Noah's grandfather. Lived to be nearly a thousand."

"Oh! Right, then. Methuselah... Well, if those two were only five or six years younger than me, they aren't looking too bad on it. And what's nice: they were still holding hands. Nine-hundred-and-something and still holding hands!"

"And still enjoying the Beatles! Will you stop talking nonsense, please, and simply answer my question."

"Yes, of course I will. It's a kind of musical."

"Great. What's it called?"

"But it's *not* too late, you know; not if you really want it that much. 'If I could only live my life again' – that's what you said."

It isn't just an issue about bragging. He's obviously someone who likes to take his time over telling you things. Or perhaps he simply doesn't enjoy being the centre of attention. Perhaps he wants to emphasise that anyone else's affairs are every bit as important as his own – can he *already* have learned the truth of that? Whatever the reason I'm happy to accept it.

"Oh," I say, carelessly. "I feel that I didn't want it *enough*. Not at the time. And I feel, too, that it may have been for all the wrong reasons. More because I wished to be famous, like Audrey Hepburn or Grace Kelly, than because ..." Yet I can't think how to put it without my sounding wretchedly pretentious.

"But you want it now. That's what matters. And no longer for the wrong reasons."

"Far too late, though. I'm no longer seventeen."

"Well, who cares? Lots of people have started when they're much older than you."

"Name one."

"Well, I know they have. They must have. That's the time when they're getting…"

"What? Decrepit?"

"No. When they're getting more interesting. By then they've got character. By then they've had experience."

"I think I'd rather have hope."

I can tell he's not too sure how to answer that one. Poor love. Maybe I wouldn't be too sure either, but at least when you're older you can waffle. "Hope makes a good breakfast." I don't know whom I'm quoting. "But it's not much cop as a supper." (At this point I'm paraphrasing; the quote is probably eighteenth- or nineteenth-century.)

For a moment he considers this. "No, but why do people say then that life begins at forty? Proverbs don't catch on unless there's something in them."

"Perhaps people just like to be chirpy. Besides…unhappily I'm nearer fifty."

"Really?" His surprise doesn't sound put on but at the same time his demeanour suggests it isn't a question of much importance. "All right. So life begins at fifty. We can change it."

"*Nearly* fifty. Yet even so…too late to think of playing Juliet." I hang my head.

"Did you want to play Juliet?"

"Not in the slightest!"

He laughs and I look up again.

"But you haven't told me yet what musical it is. I haven't seen a musical in years."

"Don't you like them?"

"Oh, yes. But Duncan doesn't. My husband. Still, Duncan's away at the moment – so what has that to do with anything?"

"Perhaps it's not exactly a musical. Not a musical-musical, if you see what I mean. Not like *Oklahoma!* or *Singin' in the Rain*." He suddenly seems uneasy – is looking towards the tree which the squirrel had recently emerged from. "I've seen those films on TV."

I don't say anything. Merely look expectant.

"It's called *The Glory Boys*. Well...that isn't its full title. It's called *The Glory Boys Up West*."

Dear God. *The Glory Boys Up West*.

He briefly checks on my reaction.

"Oh. Oh, yes. Yes, I've heard of it." Not much of a reaction. "I mean, I've heard of you – *The Glory Boys*. No wonder you require that tan!"

"Sun-beds. At the gym."

That sounds anticlimactic. Or, at the very least, humble. I've just told him the theatre is magical; can a gym be in the same league? Again I remember the air of pride he'd done his utmost to suppress. And I struggle to find the right thing to come up with.

It isn't easy, despite that greater facility for waffle I was just now boasting of.

"Then you're a bit like the Chippendales?" I say.

"We're Britain's answer to the Chippendales!"

It sounds as if he might be chanting a slogan; a slogan either handed down by the producers or else employed in the publicity.

"And I thought you'd be American..." (I don't think I'd ever thought about it in any way at all.)

"We're Britain's answer to the Americans!" This time he gives a grin.

And then I discover that coming up with the right thing isn't truly so difficult ... where on earth could all my common sense have wandered?

It's not only easy but obvious.

"That's wonderful! You must be very proud."

He answers with a simplicity that's in some way a little shaming.

"Yes, I am. It's a tremendous bit of luck. A privilege. Most guys would give...well, nearly anything to be offered such a start. You see, in the end I want to be a proper actor. Like the one you just mentioned: *Romeo and Juliet*. Or *Hamlet*. If only I can manage to learn the lines."

He's thoroughly at ease again. And because *he* is...well, I am too.

"I certainly wish you plenty of success."

But oh dear my love – I think it's going to take a little more than only your ability to learn the lines.

"Thank you."

There follows a silence. It's lengthy but not uncomfortable. I'm the one who ends it, however – though without thought and in a manner I honestly hadn't intended. Not yet, I mean, with ease restored to us so pleasantly. And the sun still shining on us so very agreeably.

"Well, I suppose I'd better be on my way. It's been a really great pleasure meeting you."

"Oh…"

I'm sure I've heard a note of disappointment.

"May I ask your name?" I'm gathering up my bag, putting it back onto my shoulder.

"Vince."

"Vince what?"

"Peters. Why?"

"Oh, for when you become famous. I'll want to swank. I shall say, 'I once sat next to Vince Peters when he was feeding pigeons in the park. And I thought that he was lovely!'"

"Did you? I mean, is that honestly what you thought? What you think?"

Oh, *very* young; very vulnerable; *very* insecure. (But how on earth can he be insecure, doing the job he does and having such a fine appearance? Of course, they say that in private many actors lack self-confidence but that on stage, and watched by hundreds, they can then become so confident because they're hiding behind someone else's personality. Yet surely in revue it's not the same? You can't hide behind Romeo or Hamlet when you've taken off your clothes and are left with nothing but a loincloth…if even with so much as that. So I have to be mistaken – yes? Maybe he's no more insecure than the rest of us.)

Yet… *Is that honestly what you think?*

Oh dear.

"Yes, definitely." How else can one reply? I can't even remind him that 'lovely' has become hopelessly debased, along with countless other formerly meaningful words. "Yes, of course it is."

"Though a bit thick at the same time? 'I thought that he was very nice but also a bit thick.'"

Obviously I notice he's dispensed with lovely but that isn't now my primary preoccupation. Earlier, when he'd intimated I didn't look fifty – well, *nearly* fifty – his surprise had sounded genuine. Now I hope my own surprise sounds just as much so.

"Vince! Why do you say that?"

"Why not? It's what everybody else does. Look…only yesterday… I asked Mr Bielenberg if I was releasing a balloon in the right way (there's a scene where I have to let go of five yellow balloons, one after the other). 'Is it really okay, sir? Is it really as good as I can get it?' That's all I said. And he said, 'Yes, it's fine, it's perfectly fine.' But I saw from the smile that went between him and another director that they thought I wasn't very bright. I don't mind. I only want to get things right."

"And I'm sure he appreciates that." I hate Mr Bielenberg; I hate that other director. "Their smiles only meant, 'Here's someone who's truly keen to learn.'"

"My foster mother taught me another proverb. This one was out of the Bible. 'Be good, sweet lad, and let who will be clever.' You haven't told me *your* name," he tacks on.

"Well, I'm less likely to be famous. Stella. Stella McCabe."

There's a two- or three-second pause. "That's astonishing!"

"Why?"

"Because you're already famous. In a way. One of the songs in the show is called 'Stella by Starlight'. What's astonishing – it was only last night I learned its name."

"Well, there you are, then. Must be meant."

The words are scarcely out before I'm wishing that they weren't. In an attempt to cover up I talk fast, and without much punctuation.

"Yes I know that song, it comes from a film called *The Uninvited* made in the forties starring Ray Milland. The song's pretty but the film's about a haunting and even when I saw it just a few months back it was still quite scary."

Yet then I realise something. My statement had only struck me as dopy, or *mainly* struck me as dopy, because I myself half-believe in Dr Jung's theory. That one about meaningful coincidence. Not everything can be entirely random he suggests.

But if not everything – well, can anything? My woolly brain can't cope with it.

And perhaps Vince hasn't even taken it in, whether or not what I'd said was dopy. "McCabe? McCabe? That sounds Scotch. Your husband must be Scotch?"

"Not really. His *grandfather* was Scottish."

Then, after another five or six seconds, I stand. We both do. There seems no other option.

"My goodness but you're tall!"

"Yes. All part of my good luck. If I wasn't I couldn't be one of the Glory Boys, could I?"

"Or Romeo. Or Hamlet."

Oh, sweet heaven! Do I really say these things?

"Well then, Vince, like I've told you, it's been a great pleasure…" Then I hold out my hand.

But he doesn't take it. "Will it be all right if I walk with you a bit?"

"I'm on my way to Baker Street."

"Yes. Me too."

I wonder if I'd said St John's Wood, which lies entirely in the opposite direction… But I can't help feeling flattered and pleased and suddenly very grateful.

Grateful for the fact the sun is shining. Grateful for the bloody day I'd had yesterday, which had brought me into Queen Mary's Garden this morning. Grateful that I hadn't arrived earlier than I did and found my favourite bench unoccupied. (For I know that, if I'd already been sitting there, Vince wouldn't have intruded on me. He'd undoubtedly have gone away to find another spot from which, without risking anyone's desire for tranquillity, he could have scattered his benison before the multitudes…his benison whose wrapper I'm now carrying in my shoulder bag.)

And in fact I feel somewhat taken aback by the sheer intensity of my gratitude. "You, too? Very well. Then it's off to Baker Street we go."

As I announce this I almost feel we ought to link arms and skip off along a path which – but I suppose you can't have everything – isn't remotely yellow or anywhere made of brick.

And I'd be pretty surprised if we fell in step with a scarecrow who thought he lacked a brain.

Or a tin man who thought he lacked a heart.

Or a lion who thought he lacked the noive. (Not 'thought' in this case, 'knew'. He *did* lack the noive.)

Me, I sometimes think I lack all three.

I suppose the one which worries me most has to be the second. I watch such atrocities on the news and while I'm watching feel the usual sadness and the usual sense of solidarity – but how long do such reactions last? Less than an hour later I may be looking at something fairly light-hearted; I may be laughing. But how much I admire the person who is really inspired to make sacrifices – the person, for instance, who may indeed go out to be a volunteer in Africa.

Gut feeling tells me that Vince could be this kind of person. He may not know what implicit means – or delegation – he may never have heard of Methuselah. But gut feeling tells me that if the circumstances were right…

Though gut feeling at this minute isn't something I welcome. Suddenly I wouldn't even want him to go to Africa. Any more than I'd want Ben to.

Even less than I'd want Ben to.

Dear God! What can have got into me? What in heaven's name can possibly have got into me?

Three

The lake in Regent's Park – or *the* Regent's Park if we wish to be pedantic – isn't just a jumped-up pond, not like the one in Queen Mary's Garden. (Now I feel disloyal – I *like* the one in Queen Mary's Garden.) But the lake in Regent's Park, the parental park as it were, is undoubtedly the Real McCoy.

Vince and I are now walking beside the Real McCoy. Walking, not skipping. Strolling is perhaps the better word; strolling towards Baker Street. To the left of us are beds of gaily coloured flowers; to the right, a bandstand and deckchairs – with grass sloping down to the water and willows on the nearside bank. Several glimpses, in between those trees, of the elegant Nash terrace that forms a distant backdrop.

An aging painter with an easel is obviously hoping to encompass some of this beauty – and presumably to do it justice. But in all truth he doesn't stand a chance. Or does he? We decide we mustn't go too close in order to inspect (and thereby possibly inhibit) but we agree we want to be unfailingly positive – surely there must be others around today, conceivably many others, who won't have had the breaks, won't have had the recognition, but are basically just as good as Constable?

(Maybe the one person you can't put 'basically just as good as' right before his name has to be the bard…although I don't know anything about the worlds of music or of science. But otherwise a lot of it may be due simply to lack of opportunity. Which is sad. Very sad.)

There's also a young man lying on the grass, sunbathing, his head resting against the saddle of his overturned blue bike. And just behind that bike –

"Oh, look!"cries Vince. "See it? A hedgehog?"

"Where?"

He points excitedly, "There! There!", yet at first I still don't see it; I'm aware I'm beginning to need glasses for long distance as well as for reading. But then, thank God, I do see it…just before it disappears beneath a tall hedge and into the grounds of a magnificent white mansion, completely screened from view, which I believe used to be the residence of U.S. ambassadors – or could it perhaps have been the home of Barbara Hutton?

But I don't let on I've missed out on the detail and Vince seems as pleased about the sighting as he'd seemed about the coincidence of my own name. "You know, I haven't set eyes on another all the time I've been in London!" It instantly crosses my mind I should like to take him to the nearby zoo, although I've no idea whether the zoo actually has hedgehogs.

He comes from Manchester, has now been in the south for nearly eighteen months. Earlier he'd made mention of a foster mother but at the moment I don't like to ask him about this. It might seem too intrusive.

At the moment? That's a curious thing to think.

"How old are you, Vince?"

"Twenty-five."

I'm not always the most brilliant judge of age but for once I'd been spot on. "Oh, then, the same as my son – my younger son."

"How many have you?"

"Only the two. Paul and Ben. I'd have liked more. A couple of girls, ideally. But now we have a baby grandson."

"Nice. I bet you're very happy." A gently wistful response which for some reason I don't choose to answer.

For some reason? No, I know precisely what that reason is. I suddenly feel the need to be entirely upfront with this transparently unsophisticated young man, because I sense he'd be entirely upfront with me. And therefore he doesn't deserve to be palmed off with just the easy version – the polite, conventional version – even if he *is* a stranger. (I don't regard him as a stranger.)

But his expression changes and he looks troubled. Am I imagining it or has my lack of a reply not gone unnoticed? In any case I decide it's already too late to think up one that's going to sound convincing.

Anyhow, by this time we're back on the path, although for a while we'd been loitering on the grass, and I suddenly become distracted – yet again. (A lot of suddenlys, all of a sudden!) I realise I'm feeling rather proud to be seen in his company. People will of course assume that he's my son…well, okay then, who cares…who *cares?* I have the strong impression he's going to take my arm – or else offer me his own. Neither Paul nor Ben has ever, quite, filled me with the same awareness of my enjoyment of support. Or of my essential femininity. (Should a son, even a grown-up son, fill his mother with an awareness of her essential femininity? Well, no, let's merely stick with the fact that I feel proud.) Vince's appearance is far neater than that which either of my boys usually achieves – unless they're in dark suits, or tails, or dinner jackets. He's wearing only faded blue jeans and a yellow T-shirt, white socks and trainers, but the jeans look as if they've just come back from the cleaner's – although, thank heaven, they don't have any crease in them; how my sons would scoff at jeans furnished with a sharp crease! – and the white trainers, despite being obviously expensive and well looked after, and even quite conspicuous on account of their size, mercifully aren't *too* white, not glaringly so, which somehow I might have expected. Admittedly the T-shirt looks skin-tight and of course reveals a lot of bicep, but – well, after all – he *is* a Glory Boy, so why not? (I am momentarily amazed that such should be my attitude.) At least one can be thankful it hasn't any wording on it, advertising either the show or the company; and when eventually I hear myself comment on this – perhaps not so very tactfully – "Oh, yes," he says, "we're meant to wear our special T-shirts!" He gives me his infectious grin; I read the mischief in his eyes. "But I never do, not when I'm away from…" Without my having seen those T-shirts I feel it has to be a definite point in Vince's favour; *another* definite point in Vince's favour. His haircut, too, looks expensive – Mr Bielenberg may well send his boys to the likes of Vidal Sassoon; I'm liking Mr B a little better now – and Vince's fingernails, one of the first things I always notice about people, are certainly well-cared for. So, all in all, neat, well-groomed, clean-cut: somebody you might think was a model but without any of the knowingness perhaps unfairly associated with that profession; without any of the self-consciousness of your average very tall and well-proportioned model (unless you absolutely *must* count a figure-hugging T-shirt and its slightly turned-up sleeves). I mean without any of that knowingness appearing on his face. Maybe even with a touch of diffidence appearing there instead, which I vaguely hope he's never going to lose.

No, can it be surprising I should feel this sense of pride? In spirit I apologise to both my husband and my sons, and in fact to every other man I've ever known, that I should be reduced to such a state of girlishness over somebody I met no more than ninety minutes ago, and after the next thirty or forty shall probably never meet again. (The notion of the zoo was scarcely very serious.) Somebody who's twenty-four years younger than me and who in his own words – oh dear, poor Vince! – is perhaps a little thick and was brought up to think good a better choice than clever.

But on the other hand he has the sweetest and most winning sort of smile. (And, what's more, do I really mean 'on the other hand'? At my age I'm also beginning to value good a little more than clever. Or perhaps I always did, but simply didn't think about it.) He suddenly takes my arm.

"No," I say, "let me hold yours."

He immediately agrees.

Right about one thing, then, but maybe not so right about another. Is he quite so lacking in confidence as I'd imagined? *Did you? I mean, is that really what you think?* Doesn't it require a pretty solid base of security (or sophistication!) to take the arm of a very new acquaintance – purely on your own initiative, that is – and then instantly allow her to do a swap and to take yours? (Comparatively speaking, an *elderly* new acquaintance.)

"Tell me something, Vince. How long have you been with the Glory Boys?"

"Almost a year."

"And before that?"

"Oh, all kinds of different stuff. Labouring. Gardening. Stacking shelves in a supermarket. Or else plain unemployed. But I was always on the lookout for something more. Much more. And then I saw this ad – it was in the library, in a paper called *The Stage* – and I went for an audition. And that changed everything."

"But didn't you feel pretty nervous?"

"Gosh, yes. But everyone was very nice – well, nearly everyone. And before I saw the ad I'd even been thinking of trying for the navy or the police or the prison service. The timing was just right."

"'I trust in thee, O Lord. My times are in thy hand.'" I give a small laugh. "From one of the psalms. I've usually had a bit of trouble, though, in making myself believe it."

"Oh, *I* believe it. 'My times are in thy hand'… I must try to remember that. Those rowing boats look fun."

"What?"

"I know – that was a bit of a change of subject as my mum would often tell me!"

There are currently two rowing boats – also a skiff and a canoe – in the bit of lake that's visible between the trees.

"Yes, they do. I'm sorry – for a moment my mind was somewhere else. I believe they call it a kind of synchronicity when the timing's just so good. I mean careers not rowing boats." And belatedly I now feel convinced this is the right and proper word. Mum or foster-mum, I wonder.

"Hey, Stella. You wouldn't come out in one, would you?"

It's the first time he's called me that; and – would you believe it? – my stomach or my heart or something (could it be my soul?) at once gives a tiny flip…where is the cliché which can help me here? There's bound to be one.

Though possibly my rather daft confusion – *rather* daft? – is also due to the question which had instantly followed my name.

But why? I scarcely know. Obviously, for him, I should be somebody much younger; but I'm here and available and the youngest whom he knows in Regent's Park – and, anyhow, it's hardly like a date, is it? And I always tell myself that I *feel* like twenty-five. Have I been practising nothing but deception all these many years…and somehow escaped being challenged and detected? (I mean if you refuse to acknowledge such blatantly unfair intrusions as childbirth? My first experience of which was long and hard.)

(Though in neither experience of childbirth does the question properly arise. Even during my second time around I was less than twenty-five.)

Anyway, anyway. For boating I'm dressed a shade less appropriately than during those last few days of awaiting Paul and Ben.

Now I should've been wearing jumper and jeans without accessories – not the short-sleeved red dress which, admittedly, is simple enough but has black court shoes and black shoulder bag to go with it. All a bit fussy.

Yet Vince already knows how I'm dressed and he hasn't asked me to run home please and change. So why do I hesitate? It can't be a matter of propriety. Or convention. Or upbringing. It can't be from any ridiculous – *utterly* ridiculous – mounting awareness of unexpected danger. (I mean to me, not to him, and I'm not referring here to a mere wobble whilst I get into the boat, or a stumble of high heels on wet boards, or a humiliating loss of balance, possibly followed by an equally comic fall over the side.) No, I'm not referring to anything like that. Besides, I'm very confident that Vince would save me. Danger isn't at all the right word.

So I decide it must be more a matter of plain undiluted surprise that has to lie beneath it.

But oh Stella. The sun is shining, the lake is sparkling, and the last thing you'd ever want (twenty-five-year-old, irrepressible *you*!) is to be feebly and confusedly standing in any person's way – especially not in such an eager, vulnerable and treat-proposing young person's as this.

"Yes, I'd love to. I mean, if you're really quite sure…"

"Would I have asked you if I wasn't?"

"Then I gratefully accept. I think it would be fun."

So after we've crossed the bridge near the Baker Street exit (or entrance) we turn to the right and head smartly for the boathouse.

"Vince, you're going to laugh at this. But every morning when I first awake I unfailingly remind myself to gather ye rosebuds. Isn't this a brilliant day to be doing what we're doing? I'm so glad that you've suggested it."

"It's my first time," he says. "Is it yours?"

I would like to tell him yes. But I have to be honest; and memories have started to intrude.

Four

Before we married, Duncan and I had once come boating here.

We had a long engagement: he (and his mother!) wanted to make sure I was entirely suitable. Oh, apparently his mother allowed that I was pretty enough and that I knew how to wear clothes and maybe how to lay a table, but was I really going to be a helpmeet and was my temperament going to prove reliable?

She wanted to know: would I make a good housekeeper? Good hostess? Inventive cook? Would I make a good mother? – apparently housekeeper, hostess and cook took precedence. Was I well-read and intelligent or merely someone who knew how to bluff? (My own view is that it's exceedingly underrated, the ability to bluff.) At that time – he was twenty-eight – Duncan was interested in politics. Did I have all the makings of a P.M.'s wife?

I think the fact that Duncan himself shared some of these doubts – indeed, was possibly the one who'd instigated them – made me all the keener. For, in reality, he wasn't altogether my type.

Why not? Well, in the first place, he was a little staid. He rarely acted on impulse and would usually plan for the week ahead (or three weeks ahead), seldom for today or tonight or even tomorrow. He phoned me on Sundays and Tuesdays and Fridays – unless he took me out on one of those evenings – and didn't encourage me to phone *him*, on the grounds of possible inconvenience. He often said he liked to take things slowly, "especially in matters of the heart." That was honestly the phrase he used, not once but repeatedly.

Also on the debit side, he was possessive; he didn't like it if other men appeared to find me attractive. (I have to say, I didn't object to this at all – I mean, their maybe finding me attractive.) Plus, he had a collection of Royal Doulton figurines which he kept tucked away in a cabinet and only permitted to be viewed when – or if – close friends requested it. This I simply didn't understand; he hadn't acquired them for the sake of investment and when I suggested that because his beloved mum had fallen deeply in love with Harlequinade this would make a truly unforgettable Christmas gift, he sulked for three days: he would never, he assured me, think of parting with a single one of them – not to anybody. But, still. He very seldom looked at them.

Lastly – he used to sulk in fact rather often. He and our firstborn, Paul, are predominantly serious and far-thinking. Ben and I are seldom moody, and more or less serene. We're inclined to be spontaneous and on occasion – I know this isn't something to brag about – undeniably a bit reckless. Devil-may-care.

(Ben is shamelessly my favourite, just as Paul is shamelessly Duncan's. Obviously, we both do our utmost not to show it. One of the things that frequently makes me sad is that Ben now lives in Australia. He met and married Lucinda – and she's nice, they lead a pleasant and successful life. But oh sweet heaven…if it really had to be one of them, why couldn't it have been Paul? For one thing, Paul doesn't mind flying. Ben does. It's none too well arranged, Lord, that's all that I can say. Well, it isn't *all* that I can say; we both know you've had me bending your ear on the subject more often than perhaps you'd like…although we also know I wouldn't want to change a single thing in the matter if it's truly for the best. I mean, naturally, the best for Ben or for the children he one day hopes to have.)

Yet enough now. Enough of all the negatives. At twenty-eight Duncan was physically attractive. (Still is, I suppose, at nearly fifty-six.) He was roughly five-foot-eleven, which – until today – I've always considered tall. Also, he had a good lean figure, in part because he played badminton and a fast game of tennis and swam a great deal (although he did all this purely for the exercise and not – again somewhat perplexingly – because of any pleasure he derived from it); and in part because he was self-disciplined over what he ate and did his best, although with only moderate success, to persuade me to be likewise. In spite of my sweet tooth. He looked a little like Montgomery Clift but didn't like it if I called him Monty; very understandably, he thought that people might believe I was referring to a different Monty. This was unfortunate since he was vain and otherwise wouldn't have minded being compared to a matinee idol. He enjoyed flattery (well, don't we all?) and this was something I early on learned to take advantage of. He especially liked to receive it from girls in their twenties, so perhaps *early on* is the key phrase in that sentence. Even today, once a woman has turned thirty, Duncan will noticeably lose interest, even if he still perks up to flattery. Whatever source it may proceed from.

So, then, definitely nice-looking…and with just the right amount of body hair (you see, I'm holding nothing back); a good lover, if not a particularly passionate one or a frequent one, especially after the first ten years. But about all of this – well, it almost goes without saying – I knew nothing at the start.

There are two more things which influenced me to marry him.

One, the lesser but still of great importance, was his reliability. While he remained in love with me he was by far the most trustworthy man I'd ever known. If he made any sort of promise I soon learned I could rely on it. Perhaps promise is too strong a word but all other boyfriends without exception had said things like, "I'll ring you tomorrow," "We'll go there next week," "Shall I get tickets for such-and-such a show?" And all other boyfriends without exception had quite often forgotten or else for some other reason had let me down.

But even if it chanced that he were in one of his unhappier moods Duncan would never let me down, not ever, unless there were some indisputably valid reason. The only trouble was...the shows he said he'd book for – and in those days I never made a protest – were invariably highbrow, Wagner, Marlowe, Ionesco, Beckett; nothing undemanding nor, in *his* view, trivial. Even *Romeo and Juliet* could never be Tchaikovsky; it had to be either Shakespeare or Prokofiev.

But this was a very small complaint: it was only Wagner whom I found difficult and would most willingly have exchanged for Lerner and Lowe.

And we always, where possible, had the very best seats (and dressed accordingly). Just as we always went to the very best restaurants. And later, when on holiday, to the very best hotels.

(Except that we hardly ever went abroad. Duncan spent too much of his working life in aeroplanes and overseas. A holiday, to him, basically meant Britain. It was just a bit of a shame that 'abroad' was still a more exciting concept to myself and Ben despite Ben's growing fear of flying – oh, how very ungrateful that makes me sound! I ought to feel ashamed of myself. More ashamed, that is, than I frequently do feel.)

Anyhow, of course, we now come to reason number one.

Duncan was, and is, both generous and rich. A lot of the money comes down through his family but he's also done very well in his own right – probably far better than if he *had* decided to make a career in politics. I don't really understand what his work is; at the beginning he tried to explain and I did everything I could to make the right comments and to ask the right questions; but his degree was in Economics and mine was in Literature and both of us very soon gave up – although without even once making this explicit. (Symbolic, evidently. These days it seems we no longer communicate at all deeply about anything.) Suffice it to say, it's to do with financial dealings in almost every developed part of the world and if Margaret Thatcher ever needs a new Chancellor to talk gobbledegook at election time she could scarcely do better than ring for McCabe. He's obviously extremely good at his job.

Now this isn't something that I state with pride but at the age of twenty-one financial security appeared excessively important. My father hadn't done too well professionally and we were living in one of the cheapest parts of the country: Scunthorpe, in Lincolnshire. My mother would say there were a great many advantages to living in Scunthorpe – and she was undoubtedly right – but, still, it *was* one of the cheapest parts of the country, with everything which that entails, while at Cambridge (and this is the part where I feel most guilty) I was mixing with a number of exceptionally affluent types, the father of one of whom had offered me a job in his publishing company. (This later fell through and the post went to his wife's goddaughter… hence, for me, the handmade chocolates.) But the thought of returning to a relatively impoverished lifestyle at home – although I very much loved my mother – wasn't at all a happy one and may have depressed me more than I realised. There was also – and especially in my third year – the unremitting stress of work. I was a scholarship girl and always felt I had to show myself worthy of such privilege.

Or in saying this am I letting myself off too lightly? But temporarily at any rate I could have been slightly off-balance. And then, at a dinner party in London, given by the son of the publisher, I met Duncan. (He had Edwin's telephone number, of course, so he was able to deliberate a bit before asking me out.)

Incidentally, when my parents came down for the wedding, Duncan wanted to pay for them to spend a week at the Savoy. But in the end they stayed with my eighty-year-old grandmother in Golders Green. (By this time my three other grandparents were dead.) Thwarted, he then paid and made all the reservations for my mum and dad and Gran – along with seven of my great-aunts – to have *lunch* at the Savoy and then take in a matinee at the National. (While he and I were honeymooning in the Lake District – and so determinedly walking about that we both developed blisters!)

However, all of this is probably skipping around in time like a demented Dr Who. For here am I talking about Ben backpacking in Australia and meeting his future wife when I haven't even married his father yet and it will be at least a couple of years before Ben's conceived – although startlingly soon after the birth of Paul – and what's even more to the point at present, some eighteen months before the remembered boating trip took place when his father and I had been engaged for only a few weeks.

That afternoon, Duncan was by no means at his best. We'd arranged this excursion three days earlier; otherwise it most likely wouldn't have happened. It was even spotting with rain. We had the lake pretty much to ourselves and he rowed the full length of it, there and back, six times. It was obviously good exercise and helped him both to recover cheerfulness and remain warm.

Yet although I was dressed quite suitably for it, in cable-knit sweater, slacks and soft shoes, I could actually have done with a further layer of clothing and had acquired a rather runny nose by evening. He wasn't pleased. Nor was he pleased at my having developed a full-blown cold by the time we attended a very smart dinner party the following weekend – sniffles don't harmonize with evening dress and potentially important introductions.

But one thing: at least our boating trip, with the marked absence of other craft, hadn't given me much trouble with the steering and so had undoubtedly forestalled his usual irritation at feminine incompetence.

Oh – and another thing: the next time we met he had brought to the restaurant a very pretty pearl-and-garnet brooch as compensation for his grumpiness about my cold – we both knew this full well, although it was never actually acknowledged.

Anyway, irritation of the boat-related variety was effectively delayed until we again went rowing in Regent's Park, some seven years later and this time in the company of our two boys; presumably not thought old enough by their father to take on the task of navigation – the lake was admittedly quite busy.

But it was an outing which nearly ended in a stand-up fight (on the jetty) between the younger of them and Duncan, "because Daddy kept on being so rude to Mummy!"

Yet the memory that sparked off all this was only a disproportionately fleeting one. The point is that I'd been on this lake only twice, exactly twice, in over twenty-seven years; and in truth hadn't very much enjoyed either of those occasions. I had a feeling, though, that this time it was going to be a great deal different.

That's all I said to Vince; I knew he was glad to hear that it was *almost* like my first time. Then I asked him if in Manchester he'd rowed a lot and for the next ten minutes we spoke mainly about Manchester. We arrived at the boathouse.

Five

The chief reason I'm still not in line for any cox-of-the-year award is simply that I look about me too much – don't want to miss out on anything – and keep forgetting about rudders and suchlike. I also keep pulling on left when it ought to be right, and vice versa. Not that it matters, even when we go round in a complete circle – as we do, not merely once or twice but three times, *three* whole times – and notice oarsmen and passengers in other boats looking on in amused indulgence. We simply giggle. Vince does so unconcernedly, I do so with a tinge of embarrassment but not exactly beating my breast in self-recrimination. I think we're basically owning up to two rather amazing facts: (a) that we're practically resigned to our going around in circles and (b) that we must be bringing such a lot of entertainment into other people's drab existences…having mutually decided on the drabness, even though we see many smiles, hear many outbursts of laughter…not all of them, I hope, occasioned by myself. No, I'm clearly still no better at steering than I was at insisting, well trying to insist, that I should be the one to pay for our rowing boat.

Like Duncan, Vince is a very good rower. But unlike Duncan (who wouldn't ever consider performing any such eye-catching act in public) he has taken off his T-shirt – after asking me whether I minded – and now it's a pleasure to watch the easy grace of his movements and see the smooth play of muscle in his arms and chest and shoulders. I only wish I had a stomach which was half as flat as his…and I make a mental note to work on it more zealously in between my weekly visits with Maddie to our enjoyably invigorating yoga-and-exercise class. It would be enormously helpful of course if there were a *Glory Grandmothers Up West* attraction I could think about auditioning for in the near future.

But what about his love handles? I can't remember. At twenty-five haven't you as yet begun to acquire love handles?

At one point he briefly rubs his chest. Noticing I've noticed he clearly thinks he should explain.

"You see, I have to shave it all the time – and sometimes because of that it itches."

"Why do you have to shave it all the time? Are you a werewolf?"

His reply surprises me.

"No. I'm not American either. But at least I'm in London."

I laugh delightedly – although I feel a little naughty at having been surprised. (Oh dear, I'd even half-expected he might ask me what a werewolf was.) "Did you see it, Vince?"

"No. Did you?"

"No. Not really my sort of thing."

"Nor mine. I don't like horror not even when it's mixed with comedy."

Rarely can *not* having seen a well-spoken-of film result in such harmony. *The Exorcist* and *The Omen* are similarly disposed of, not to mention *Nightmare on Elm Street* and *The Texas Chainsaw Massacre*…even if we both saw (and enjoyed) *The Terminator*.

"Can't match *The Sound of Music*, though," I almost say.

"Who wants to see people having their arms sawn off? Arms, legs, all sorts of different bits?"

"I truly can't imagine. But, even so, those films do well."

"No – for real entertainment – give me *The Sound of Music* anytime."

"I was just about to say…" Now, of course, I feel annoyed because I hadn't done so.

"As a matter of fact we have a few songs out of that in our own show. And out of other musicals by the same composers. Richard Rodgers and Oscar Hammerstein…Oscar Hammerstein *the Second*! The same two guys who wrote *Oklahoma!*"

"Thank you," I answer meekly. "So…are you telling me you sing?"

"Not very well." But for a minute or two he rests on his oars and treats me to a sample. "'Shall we dance…dum, dum, dum…?'"

Therefore I have to ask myself again: lacking in self-confidence? And, by the bye, I used to reckon I was a reasonably good judge of character.

Fundamentally, though, in all the ways that matter, I'm sure I've read him right.

"'On a bright cloud of music shall we fly…?'"

He points at me.

And for once in my life I'm actually fairly quick.

"Dum – dum – dum."

At least the notes are *half*-sung (can one really call them notes?) and his smile is one of pure pleasure.

"'Shall we dance?'"

"Dum, dum, dum."

"'Shall we then say goodnight and mean goodbye?'"

"Dum, dum, dum." I'm really getting the hang of this and, in addition, once more feel quite proud – in that I don't even glance to left or right to see if anybody's listening.

"'Nor perchance…'"

But I feel I have to correct him.

"'*Or* perchance.'"

For a moment he looks puzzled but I quickly do my bit and so he carries on: "'…when the last little star has left the sky…'"

I'm not sure if he wants further backing at this point but when I look for guidance he gives another smiling nod – and then a couple of seconds later continues.

"'…shall we still be together, with our arms around each other, and shall you be my new romance?'"

Again I oblige.

"'On the clear understanding that this kind of thing can happen…'" But I'm not needed any more – not in my professional capacity. "'Shall we dance, shall we dance, shall we dance?'"

It's over. I mime applause.

He's a tenor, a perfectly pleasant and tuneful tenor, although the song isn't a testing one and it may be a wholly different matter when – doubtless with unimpaired clarity – it has to climb all the way to the upper circle.

I realise it ought to have been cringe-making – it ought to have been excruciating – to have someone serenade you in public (or even in private); moreover in a voice that, whether or not it's going to ascend to the gods, will perhaps – out *here* – have been wafted a not unappreciable distance.

A serenader who's strikingly bare-chested at that.

But – again – what's happening to me? What *is* happening to me? Am I still that same Stella McCabe who left home this morning in quest of a few quiet moments in the park, followed by a brief shopping trip to Selfridges, inclusive of a cup of tea? A woman who was looking about her, yes, but not desiring anybody to spend much time in looking back – more frequently than not (and perhaps a little paradoxically, in view of appreciated whistles from building sites and weekly visits to hairdresser and beauty salon) Stella is sometimes apt to feel self-conscious. Therefore, what in the name of all that's wonderful…? Because this woman supposedly now steering is so far from feeling self-conscious that she actually requests an encore – draws much satisfaction from her companion's evident gratification – and after a short while, spurred on by only his enjoyment, even raises her hands as though she were conducting him and almost as though she were exhorting others to join in.

And, yes, by the time we get to that final, threefold invitation to dance, there is certainly participation from at least five or six of our fellow lake-farers, distinctly uneven though most of it may be. I have the feeling, however, that it might rapidly have grown in strength had Vince not started to row again, with several nods of acknowledgment and farewell, and shortly drawn away from our very kindly chorus.

"In any case, I don't sing it on my own, nor any of the other songs – from *Showboat* and *South Pacific* and *Guys and Dolls* and *The Wizard of Oz*." He pauses and takes breath.

"*The Wizard of Oz*? 'If I Only Had a Brain'?"

"No. 'Somewhere Over the Rainbow'. Anyhow, what I was going to say was" – I hadn't realised I had interrupted – "all of it's ensemble."

I suspect that his vaguely inquiring look is to make sure I understand the meaning of that word. Oddly I don't find this at all offensive; on the contrary I find it endearing – I think by now I'm somehow programmed to find things endearing which previously, if they'd come from anybody else, I wouldn't have found in the least bit so.

And therefore, inside me, I can only repeat that same bewildering question.

Which naturally there's no one to respond to (but an understandably impatient self).

'Oh, for heaven's sake! As though you don't know! As though you actually need to be told!'

I then make matters worse by asserting – smugly? stubbornly? defiantly? – 'And into the bargain I think it's now too late to stop. Because apart from anything else… Well, just *look* at him!' It isn't only this, though – or even mainly this. 'And just *listen* to him, too! Just watch how he behaves!'

That's fairly comprehensive.

So perhaps 'too late' isn't necessarily one of the saddest phrases in the language. Sometimes it may merely provide an excuse; a dignified way of bowing out of blame and responsibility.

'And therefore isn't it lucky the pair of us will presently be saying goodbye? And that it's all so very one-sided?'

My answer doesn't end there; a further bracing word of philosophy. 'So in the meantime, Ms McCabe – since you needn't have any fear of repercussions – you're free simply to get the absolute most out of being with him. Why not? Rosebuds, rowing boats, rainbows – plus, the very beginning of the rest of your existence, the thought of making each day in some way special and different and memorable! All these things combining in a magnificent conspiracy: the what-might-have-beens of ships that pass in the night...of eyes that meet across the crowded room... or less conveniently across the crowded pair of escalators...of dreams that bring regret but can still enrich the diversity of your experience.'

(What balderdash! Do I even have a proper idea of what I mean? Bafflement and waffle don't often coalesce to give us the most rational and clear-cut thought processes of which we may be capable. Mine most assuredly don't.)

And yet...on the other hand...yes, I *do* have a proper idea of what I mean! I know exactly what each of those sentimental phrases signifies.

So forget inscriptions on London benches. Perhaps I ought to write a guide to what-might-have-beens, the what-might-have-beens across crowded rooms and busy escalators.

Vince nods. "Yes, all of it's ensemble. But are you sure it's '*or* perchance' and not '*nor* perchance'?"

"Absolutely. *Nor* perchance suggests inevitability; something *meant* rather than accidental. The meeting of Anna Leonowens and the King of Siam appears to have been a completely random one. By no means an encounter designed in heaven."

"How can you tell?"

I immediately capitulate. He's won his argument.

"No, you're right, Vince – I can't. No one can. I'm talking straight off the top of my head. I do that a lot; it's one of my greatest failings. My husband's always telling me to think before I speak."

"I don't believe I'd much like your husband."

"I don't believe I do. Certainly not at times like that."

He skulls for a moment in silence.

"'An encounter designed in heaven?' I like the sound of that."

"Yes, me, too." I say it with some feeling, remembering my thoughts – now abandoned (which, in the circumstances of course they had to be) – on Dr Jung and meaningful coincidence.

Synchronicity clearly isn't the first thing on Vince's mind, either. "Nobody's ever corrected me before, about using the wrong word."

"They probably don't hear it, not if you're all singing together. It would hardly be obvious."

"'Or perchance, when the last little star has left the sky...'" He seems reassured. "I hate to get things wrong. I think I may use 'nor' too much – I mean in ordinary conversation. Will you correct me if I do?"

"I haven't been aware of your using it too much. I haven't heard any mistakes."

"Thank you, Stella."

Again, that little lurch. I change the subject; or at least partly change the subject.

"This may amaze you, Vince – because in those days I wasn't such a whizz kid in the rhythm section – but Maddie used to sing that song with me when I was practising for natural childbirth."

"Maddie? Not your husband?"

I mutely shake my head. Indeed, it was she, not Duncan, who'd been with me throughout the births of both Paul and Ben.

Again his expression looks troubled: similar to when I didn't answer his remark on my supposed happiness.

"Stella?"

Yet again! Though nothing like so bad as before. And presumably it won't continue to happen for the rest of our time on the water. Or for the rest of our time while we're on our way to Baker Street.

But he's changed his mind about what he wants to ask; I feel convinced of it. Now he pauses as he formulates another question – possibly not less important but undoubtedly a lot different. "Something you said earlier…? About gathering one's rosebuds. Is that the same as counting one's blessings?"

"Almost. Not quite. It refers more to the possibility of any small treat or adventure arising during the course of that day. I remind myself each morning that I must always be on the lookout."

"But…why rosebuds? Nothing to do with our having been in Queen Mary's Garden?"

"No, not exactly. Although, yes in one way, *everything* to do with it. Watching you feed the pigeons…getting to talk to you… getting to like you so much…

> "'Gather ye rosebuds while ye may,
> Old Time is still a-flying:
> And this same flower that smiles today,
> Tomorrow will be dying.'"

I could have been tempted to spread my hands and become actressy; but almost at once I'm glad I didn't. It's a very simple message. It doesn't require embellishment.

"That's beautiful," he says. "That really is beautiful." For the moment he is resting on his oars again. He himself really is beautiful – though, I repeat, not merely in a physical sense. "Is there any more?"

"I only know the first verse and the last."

"Yes, please. I want to hear the last."

"'Then be not coy, but use your time;
And while ye may, go marry:
For having lost but once your prime,
You may for ever tarry.'"

At first he doesn't say anything. Slowly, he starts to row again.

"Why 'ye' all the way through, then 'you' right at the end?"

"I don't know. A good point. To be honest, Vince, it's never occurred to me."

He smiles broadly, a smile I'm sure he can't contain. It must be at the thought that he's noticed something which I haven't. My own smile – I can't contain that either.

"'Your' time, not 'thy' time." In my view, he's welcome to milk it. "Stella, what does 'coy' mean?"

"These days it means sort of shy but back then I think it must have meant hesitant or nervous. Too careful. 'So don't just mull it over but use all the time you have. Remember that every second counts.'"

"Which it does, it really does!" How I warm to his enthusiasm!

"Well, certainly it ought to. Isn't it awful when people say they're bored and don't know what to do with themselves?" I listen to the swish of the water and take a mental photograph of all the loveliness around us…as if trying to establish it forever: *I could never have been one of those people.*

"I've done that," he admits, apologetically.

"Me, too. I think we ought to be shot, both of us. Unless we now promise faithfully that we won't ever do it again."

"Yes, I do. I do promise faithfully."

"Mm. A little easier said than done, perhaps."

"We could help one another."

Dear Lord! Shall *I* have to be the one to say goodbye at Baker Street?

However, he doesn't pursue his idea of our furnishing mutual assistance. "'Then be not shy, but use your time…' I like that. I like it a lot. It must be Shakespeare." And *I* like the way Vince has used the word 'shy' in preference to all the others.

"No. Herrick. Robert Herrick. A poet born some thirty years after Shakespeare. But one who lived to be much older." I can almost *see* him taking a note of the name. "Though there's a couplet of Shakespeare's which always makes me think of that poem.

> "'Golden lads and girls all must,
> As chimney-sweepers, come to dust.'"

Again, a moment of silence. "That's nice as well. A couplet is something that rhymes?"

"Yes. And most often comes at the end of a poem. I think." It's dreadful how much I've forgotten. "Oh, Vince, I'm not quite sure; we'll have to look it up." I bite my lip; I don't think I've done that in many, many years – not since I first began to wear lipstick. "*You'll* have to look it up," I correct myself.

> "'Golden lads and girls all must,
> As chimney-sweepers, come to dust.'"

"You won't have any trouble learning your lines."

> "'Gather ye rosebuds while ye may,
> For time is still a-flying:
> And this sweet flower that blooms today,
> Will very soon be dying.'"

"Well, now you're just showing off – and getting some of it wrong into the bargain!"

"Yes, I know. I'm sorry, Miss Pincher. Will you write it down for me?"

"Who's Miss Pincher?"

He explains that she was his secondary school teacher in

English. "A bit severe she was, especially if any of us called her just 'Miss', and sometimes she would shout and lose her temper. But, underneath all that, she was really very kind." He assumes an expression which is knowingly sly. "*She'd* have written it down for me."

"Oh, you crafty old thing! Well, all right. I only hope I've brought my pen and notepad. But it might be better, young man, if we took the trouble to look in a bookshop and see what we could find *there*. Am I now sounding every bit as severe as Miss Pincher?"

"Oh, yes – and I think she could have been quite pretty too. If… Though not nearly as pretty as you."

"Thank you, Vince." I don't get many compliments at home, not these days, other than on occasion from Mrs Conway. "If what? Quite pretty if what?"

"If she'd wanted to be. Which I think is wrong – not to make the most of yourself. It isn't being vain."

"Something else we agree on."

"She may have been disappointed in love. And then she grew severe because of it. Because she was unhappy."

"Now then, young Peters, I won't have you discussing my personal life in this very impertinent and most improper manner! I'm severe because I think you boys require it."

"And girls." He laughs. "And you've actually remembered my name; you weren't just being polite! So even if you are severe I shan't be nervous; I shall use my time. Right now, you couldn't think of any more poems, could you? Or couplets? I mean, ones which you yourself really enjoy. This is, this morning is…"

I don't point out to him – it hardly even occurs to me – that we're now a long way into the afternoon.

"Well, I don't mind telling you, Stella. For me, this morning is fantastic."

I also hesitate but only for a moment. "So again we're in full agreement."

Unthinkingly, he's once more been rubbing his chest. Perhaps only because I feel very slightly but very pleasurably uncertain of what subject it's safe to bring up next:

"You'll be so relieved when you no longer have to shave that."

"But just a small bit worried as well. That by then the hair's going to have grown so thick… I'm scared that by the time I'm allowed to finish with the shaving it could have spread all over!"

Then, suddenly, I think he realises that what he's just said could be construed as being suggestive. I'd forgotten that he's only twenty-five and still quite capable of blushing.

"Into every nook and cranny," I want to add. Yet that would be not simply cruel but totally unnecessary – an instant later the boat is positively rocking with our laughter!

"One easy lesson," I finally get out, "it doesn't take six – on how to puncture the well-nigh perfect moment." Minimal pause. "Or possibly one easy lesson on how to actually enhance it."

You see? I really don't have any objection to breaking all the rules – whenever, that is, rules appear to require breaking.

Then immediately after this there's a different form of poetry which unhappily suggests itself. Lorenz Hart? It might be the very thing to sing at my audition for *The Goofy Grannies Up West*. Slip of the tongue, albeit the silent tongue (thank you, Ben). I mean – of course – *The Glory Grannies*.

> 'Falling in love with love
> Is falling for make-believe,
> Falling in love with love
> Is playing the fool…
> Caring too much
> Is such a juvenile fancy,
> Learning to trust is just
> For children in school.'

Ben used to have a model of Goofy on his chest of drawers; one Christmas I'd bought it as a stocking-filler. And quite often we used to call each other by this name. "Hello, Goofy Mum"…"How's my little Goofy Ben today?" I'm sure he'd never have thought of attaching it to Duncan.

(I only a few times addressed Paul in the same fashion. It simply didn't work: no in-kind response – just a slightly mystified and vaguely tolerant smile. 'Has my poor old mum now taken leave of her senses?' That's what it seemed to express.)

> 'I fell in love with love
> One night when the moon was full;
> I was unwise,
> With eyes unable to see –
> I fell in love with a love ordained
> And long-lasting…
> But love fell out with me!'

Not precisely Shakespearian perhaps but Mr Hart – although this song was written for the musical version of a Shakespearian play – would scarcely have been hoping to compete.

Just as well, when Yours Truly was needing further to paraphrase a little.

> *'I fell in love one day, one day when the*
> *   sun was high*
> *(But it isn't my aim or my mission to*
> *   cause you to wince.)*
> *I did not fall in love WITH LOVE on a*
> *   day when the sun was high,*
> *Oh no, Mr Hart – oh no, sir, you're*
> *   wrong! I fell in love with VINCE.'*

Six

I'm sure we must have overrun our hour. Will they be shouting
for us through megaphones – will they have sent out a squad
of river police to apprehend us? "It's all my own fault, officers.
Shall I compare thee to a summer's day? We've had Wordsworth
and Tennyson and Keats to lure us out of time, away from reality.
Reality, no; from the commonplace, yes! We've had Kipling and
Donne and Larkin, too. Betjeman and Dylan Thomas. Even the
ducks will quack to you in verse."

This is a bit of an exaggeration: they aren't even quacking in
prose although they've now joined Vince and me, and seem happy
enough to have done so, on that part of the lake, practically a
tributary, where there's a lengthy iron bridge which connects –
or almost connects – the sports fields to the rose garden…but
frustratingly has a sort of metal net beneath it, telling us we can't
go any further. (Is that why they're not quacking?) This is where,
some forty years ago, Trevor Howard walked into several feet of
water when *his* rowing boat – with Celia Johnson in it – became
entangled with the loops of heavy chain then employed for the
same purpose. She, I think, can't have been much more attentive

than I've been, to have got them into such a fix in the first place, but I too would probably have got the giggles – wot, me? – after watching him standing there in the prow in his business suit, leaning well forward to push back from the obstruction…and obviously unaware of the widening gap between the boat and that bit of the bridge against which he's pushing.

He had a nice sense of humour, though. He laughed as well, just as Vince would have done.

And although he and Miss Johnson (or Dame Celia, as of course she is now) were supposed to have been enjoying their boat trip somewhere in the north of England, the powers-that-be had evidently decreed it cheaper to film the sequence in Regent's Park, and also to film there the one immediately following, inside the bona fide boathouse – regrettably pulled down since then and replaced with something a lot less picturesque.

Anyway, this portion of the lake is where Vince and I (and ducks) now find ourselves – along with Masefield, Byron, Shelley and similar. I've spent a good fifteen minutes running through my repertoire – and ending up with other couplets, unashamedly improving, that owe little to any of them.

> "'What is this life if, full of care,
> We have no time to stand and stare,
> No time to stand beneath the boughs
> And stare as long as sheep or cows?
> No time to see, when woods we pass,
> Where squirrels hide their nuts in grass?'

"Yes, unashamedly improving – but I think none the worse for that."

"I want to be improved, in every way possible."

"Oh, don't we all, my dear? Don't we all?"

I then repeat to him a thought that had occurred to me earlier.

"I can't remember when I last recited to an audience. Not since Ben was about twelve, I'd say."

And that would have been when you, my love, were also about twelve.

But, in terms of encouragement, Vince has been an audience like no other. Perhaps I've taken a good half-hour rather than only a quarter, with one poem or scrap of poem inevitably putting me in mind of something else. How wickedly self-indulgent, I own, but how quickly the time passes when you're so happily engrossed and receiving such quantities of unwearying appreciation.

"Is Ben the one that's about my age? And does he know how lucky he is to have a mother like you?"

I make a suitably modest retort. Then Vince inquires about my own parents. I feel grateful for his interest but keep my answers pretty brief: he's the one I want to talk about – or, rather, to hear about.

"You've spoken of a foster mother. Does that mean…?" Yet I'm aware this could be painful to him. "Is it all right my asking you these things? We haven't known each other very long."

"I feel as though we have."

Although he's clearly giving me permission I don't instantly avail myself of it.

"Yes, it's silly to think it's been no more than three hours. I think we must have known each other in a former existence."

"Truly?"

He's taking me more literally than I'd intended but this doesn't faze me even if it does recall his earlier response to *And I thought that he was lovely!* Now I'm very glad of that response and the fact I answered as I did.

"Truly? Well, I won't swear to it, of course, but in spirit – why not? – I feel fairly open-minded concerning reincarnation. About a year ago I read *The Bloxham Tapes* and found it wholly fascinating. Unanswerable. I don't know why I never followed it up."

"Will you write that down for me, as well?"

I laugh. "Miss Pincher lives again!"

"No, she isn't dead – not so far as I know."

He says it quite matter-of-factly and I can't make out whether he's joking or not. I'm inclined to think he isn't but…well, one should never underestimate people. I'm suddenly full of fine ideals, although I think what I actually mean is that one should never underestimate Vince Peters. There's a complexity there despite what I've said about essential simplicity – is it possible to square the two? – and certainly a huge willingness to learn.

"Just because," he adds, still just as straight-faced, "you've recently read a book on reincarnation. A *wholly fascinating* book on reincarnation."

There you are, you see! Oh, there you are. You see?

"Are you laughing at me, young man?"

Now he does laugh. "Oh, I wouldn't do that. How could you possibly believe I would?"

"Mm." I'm not used to being teased any longer – not now that Ben has gone. "Well, I *did* find it wholly fascinating," I laugh.

"I know. You told me."

"And I suppose if I'd said Miss Pincher *rides* again you'd have said, 'That's right – she always goes everywhere on her bicycle.'"

"But she does! She really does! How did you know?"

"I'm psychic. I have mysterious powers."

"Prescient powers?"

"Yes." It's just as well I made that resolution…although, as prophesied, I really don't find it an easy one to stick to.

And at times, too, he's simply so transparent. The production of such an adjective was clearly something he felt inordinately proud of. Again, though, not at all off-puttingly. Totally the reverse.

"Like a fortune teller?" he pursues.

"Yes."

But then he shakes his head. "No. You're not a fortune teller! You and Miss Pincher – I'm beginning to believe you must be sisters."

He goes on without giving me the chance to think up a reply.

"Yes…your sister Miss Pincher… Mm. They always tell you it's a small world. And I suppose you know what she'll tell *you* when you next run into her? About not following up on that book which you found fascinating? No, not just fascinating – *wholly* fascinating! Pure laziness, she's going to call it."

I nod. "Yes, no doubt about it: pure and utter laziness! Vince Peters, I do believe you're telling me off."

"*I'm* not. Before long *she* may be."

"Oh, you coward. A big strong man like you hiding behind the skirts of such a little weak woman as her. But you're both completely right, of course."

I determine then and there that I'm definitely going to carry out research around *The Bloxham Tapes*.

"Little? Weak? I no longer believe you can be sisters."

He rubs his chest again. This time neither of us comments. "Anyhow," he murmurs.

And with that 'anyhow' I know the comedy is over.

"My parents?" he says. "You asked about my parents."

"Yes." Not entirely accurate but never mind.

He rows a bit further on in silence. I don't say anything, either.

"I never knew my dad."

"I'm sorry."

"But my mum always wanted to make a home for us together – just her and me, I mean."

I wait.

"The thing is, though, she used to drink a bit."

He's telling me his story very slowly. I remember thinking, after the advent of the squirrel, how he liked to take his time about imparting information. Yet this is clearly something completely different.

"But she vowed and vowed that she was going to give it up. And she did, too. At last she was really managing to get on top of it."

"What happened?" I almost hold my breath in dire anticipation.

"She had a temporary – I know it would only have been a *very* temporary – what's the word for it?"

"Lapse?"

"Yes. Lapse. And she ran away and tried to cross a busy road. And she was killed."

"Oh, Vince! Oh, *Vince!*"

I warn myself I mustn't cry, I mustn't cry, that wouldn't be helpful. Would be flagrantly sentimental.

But I sense there's something he's not telling me. My earlier inclination towards tact has altogether vanished.

"What was she running away from?"

"You mean, *who* was she running away from? She was running away from me."

"You were there? You saw it?"

"The last thing I said to her: 'Oh, Mum, please – you just can't let it get to you again!'"

His eyes are wet. If we hadn't been in a boat I would have stood up and gone to him and put my arms around him. Instead, I open my bag and fumble for my hanky. My own tears are about to spill over.

"How old were you?"

"Nine years ago."

Himself, he has succeeded in not crying. I try to pull away from that terrible scene beside the busy road.

"So they found you foster parents? Didn't your foster parents want to adopt you?"

"I was sixteen. There wasn't any poin*t.*"

I was sixteen. There wasn't any point.

"But I imagine you still see them?"

"Oh, yes, I still see them – I mean, I still see *her*. But Gran – I used to call her Gran because she seemed quite old when I first went to them; and anyhow I didn't want to call her Mum – Gran is in a home now. You see, she's…senile …and because of this she

235

doesn't always recognise me, although sometimes she does. And Granddad – well, he died last year, although for half a second I often forget, like I did just now, and then I start to tell him something, a bit of news or a joke I've heard which I think he might enjoy. I hope that carries on, even if, when you remember, you get another little pang, a new pang to add to all the others."

I describe what I myself have experienced, exactly the same as him. Everything that he confides to me seems to draw him that much closer.

'I hope that carries on.' Distractingly, this makes me wonder if Paul will be talking to me a little more after I'm dead than he does while I'm alive.

"Anyhow, I was lucky. Very lucky. They were nice people. Good people. Kind."

Which doesn't come as a surprise after what he's just been saying but I still feel as glad to hear this as I've ever felt glad to hear anything about anybody. I don't think I could have borne it (what utter nonsense, naturally – I'd have had to!) if he'd told me that he'd been treated without much sympathy or understanding.

"Poor Gran. It's sad to see the way that life can sometimes turn out."

"Yes, it is – very!"

I realise I'm talking about more than merely people with dementia.

"But by no means for everyone, Vince. Although you've had a pretty raw deal of it up to now – "

But he cuts short this intended banality. I get the feeling he's now on automatic pilot and scarcely even knows that he's still rowing.

"No. Like I said. I've been lucky. I was never one of them that was shoved around the whole time. Gran and Granddad would have kept me till I was ninety or a hundred-and-fifteen…"

"And what about your mother's parents? Aren't they still around?"

"No. Never were. I mean, I never knew them."

Oh, the backgrounds that some people come from! So far as I'm aware, I've never known anyone who was presumably illegitimate – and whose mother was presumably illegitimate as well.

Yet how can you be so cheerful when you tell me about it?

But this is a question I don't ask – because unexpectedly he's given me one of his broad smiles and I belatedly realise I've interrupted his train of thought about being lucky.

"And do you know what I say to Gran every time she doesn't recognise me – it always makes her laugh. I say to her, 'Gran, it's no wonder you don't recognise me! I was a skinny little runt when first you took me in. Just look at what your home cooking has gone and done for me!'"

I smile back at him. "I think it must have taken a little more than just her home cooking. Does she realise that?"

"I don't know. But it really doesn't matter. It makes her laugh."

Figuratively, it makes me laugh, too: the thought that he'd found something to give him a real purpose in life, just when he must most have needed it – and that he'd had the strength of character to see it through. (Of course, at sixteen he must already have been tall. I now picture him as gangly.)

"So was I wrong to call you a big strong man when Miss Pincher was sitting at her desk and being all severe? I think I was imagining you almost as you are now – face a little younger, maybe." I pause. "Just as in forty or fifty years' time I'll still be imagining you exactly as you are now. Face not one bit older, chest just as smooth as even Mr Bielenberg would require. Because it's dopy, isn't it? People never age in your imagination."

"Do you mean that in forty or fifty years you could still be remembering me?"

"Yes, most definitely!" Now there's not a second's hesitation. (Was there before? I don't recall.) "Poor fellow. You just can't get out of it! You're fated now to be one of the highlights of my drab existence."

"One of the highlights? Really?"

"Yes, one of the highlights. Really."

"And I can't get out of it?"

"'Fraid not."

I now have my compact out and am trying, none too obviously, to repair the damage. As I do so, another lyric occurs to me: one by Alan Jay Lerner for a song entitled *Too Late Now*. 'How could I ever close the door and be the same as I was before…?' Jane Powell again. *Royal Wedding*. 1951. For some reason, over here, we had to call it *Wedding Bells* – or, at any rate, we chose to do so. Might the Queen have objected? The wedding referred to was her own and Prince Philip's.

And by talking in this way about highlights, I suddenly wonder, does it mean that I'm flirting? It doesn't feel like it. It feels more as if I'm simply making plain statements of fact.

"Drab existence, Stella?"

I don't answer at once. He surely hasn't forgotten our very recent and light-hearted use of that phrase – no, clearly he can't have! – then, equally so, I don't need to tell him he may be stepping just slightly out of line.

"Now then, now then! I can feel myself getting all severe again!"

On the other hand, though, maybe drab means nothing other than plain dull. Doesn't *have* to mean bleak, empty, hopeless, does it? So maybe it's my own interpretation that's at fault? In which case he isn't stepping out of line at all.

But anyway, as intended, he immediately returns to the subject of Miss Pincher.

"Something that's always stayed with me… For two whole lessons she spoke about 'powers of prescience' – I really remember that word. Perhaps *she* saw that one day I was going to be a little more than just a lamppost. Perhaps *she* saw that one fine day…"

"What?"

"I was going to be a Glory Boy."

"Perhaps she did." I think at any rate she must have seen him as a rather handsome lamppost. I think she must have been very thankful – for however long or however short a time – to have him in her class. And not simply because of his handsomeness.

(I recall that at the start of the morning I had thought only that he had a pleasant face. How people change as you gradually get to know them! – although perhaps in this instance it wasn't so *incredibly* gradual? *Beauty and the Beast*, of course. Possibly the most appealing of all the fairytales.)

"Stella?"

"Yes?"

"I don't suppose you'd come and see it, would you? I could get you a ticket. I mean one you wouldn't have to pay for, they call them complimentaries. And there's nothing offensive about it – the show, I mean – honestly there isn't. You don't see any… you don't see anything you shouldn't. Mr Bielenberg who…who directs and choreographs more than half of it…that is, arranges the dancing and what they call our routines…he says it's all so clean it squeaks."

On this occasion – as contrasted to the one prior to our coming on the water – there isn't even one instant of hesitation.

"Thank you, Vince. I'd love to."

Seven

We disembark at the jetty. Vince springs out, then offers me his hand. Even holding onto this I rise a good deal less athletically and try to counteract the rocking of the boat – seemingly more pronounced now that I'm on my own. I step onto dry land and Vince puts on his T-shirt. Surprisingly, there's no one hounding us for extra payment, although I've taken out my purse and the old fellow who'd drawn us in must certainly have noticed. But he seems relaxed and amiable and is perhaps making the most of what may be a comparatively quiet moment. He says to me, "May I congratulate you, madam, on your courteous and nice-looking son?"

He's said it loud enough for Vince to hear – had probably quite intended him to hear – and I answer quickly, "Yes, you may indeed. Thank you." By then Vince has got so far as, "No, I'm not – ", but I rapidly cut in and with a presence of mind I only rarely achieve when I'm not in the singing business, overridingly complete the sentence: "...either courteous or especially nice-looking! Oh, stop being so aggravatingly modest, my love, and just try to accept it graciously, such a very kind compliment.

You're always getting them; you ought to be used to it by now!"

"Thank you, sir," Vince says to the boatman, "you're extremely kind," and we manage to restrain our laughter until we've each taken at least a couple of dozen steps. Already shaking, though – and when anyway it would be far too late to correct matters – I feel impelled to look back. But my trepidation is unnecessary: the boatman's now explaining something to an elderly Japanese gentleman who has two small Japanese children – grandchildren? – waiting patiently beside him.

"You didn't mind?" Vince asks.

"No, on the contrary. I feel highly honoured to possess such a courteous and nice-looking grandson."

I say this with an intended Japanese accent and put my hands together and bow in appreciation.

But I suddenly hear the echoes of that last word. Vince hadn't missed it either. It naturally renews our laughter.

"No, you look younger than Gran," he says.

"Is that because she has dementia?"

"You even look younger than – oh, you know – Elizabeth Taylor, who's also a grandmother."

"Thank you. I think *she* became a grandmother some ten or fifteen years ago."

"Well, what I mean is, you look younger than she did when she became one." He grabs my arm and gives it – for extra emphasis – a fairly exuberant shake. "*Some ten or fifteen years ago!*"

"That's very, very sweet of you." I keep up the Japanese accent. "I think you're most courteous English gentleman."

Oh, the foolish things which make you laugh – inexplicable to any outsider! Up until today, even when witnessing some acclaimed and witty farce or comedy, I've never in my adult life laughed so many times during so very circumscribed a period – laughed with so much of myself caught up in it, I mean. Not even with Maddie. Of course, she and I don't often discuss the courtesy and attractiveness of any of our grownup grandsons, nor the presence of werewolves on Regent's Park lake, nor the potential proliferation of male body hair. Clearly, we've been missing out.

"Though on the other hand…," I say.

"Yes? What? Out with it!" ('Out with it!', however, with a grin.)

"Mistaken for your foster Gran? Vince, I don't feel I can let you get away with that! Earlier, you told me I looked forty… maybe less than forty."

"I know I did. But why did you never tell me *I* looked about sixteen?"

"Oh, that's a very smooth reply. Smooth, neat, yet thoroughly dishonest."

"Okay. Forget sixteen. But couldn't I get away with twenty-one?"

"I doubt it. Still…at a push…maybe. If you had to."

"Shall we go back and ask him?"

"*No!*" I had no doubt that, if I'd said yes, he'd have been quite capable of doing it, gone before I could – oh, so ineffectually! – have reached out to restrain him. "Don't you *dare!*" I add.

So we settle, agreeably, for thirty-nine and twenty-one. We seem to be re-arranging our lives; me, most definitely for the better, I'm not so sure about him – would a man of twenty-five wish to be taken for twenty-one? But except for the fact we're so soon about to say goodbye (although now, of course, I'm going to have the theatre to look forward to), I'd claim we appeared to have got rid of two very major stumbling blocks: firstly, the huge discrepancy in our ages – simply by *confronting* it out of existence – and secondly, less explicitly, the tragedy of being sixteen and witnessing your true mother's violent death – by his spontaneous choice of that age in a very jokey bid to be of assistance. A dangerously simplistic assessment, I know, but one which my optimistic nature wants to fasten onto. I wonder if he's received counselling; or is just so healthy nine years later, and well-balanced and preoccupied, that he doesn't even require it. I'm glad his show is full of songs and that he too, apparently, finds it easy to laugh at extremely foolish things. I hope that all his succeeding shows will be equally as cheerful and as tune-packed. (I don't mean *Hamlet*, necessarily.)

At long last, however, we recover from our current bout of giggles; start to behave a little more like adults; and are able to straighten up and walk again in a respectable fashion.

Not only that. To add a fresh layer of seriousness to the situation – but certainly not one too heavy, as before – I ask him another question that rather loosely has to do with the entertainment industry…which undeniably he's very much a part of.

"Did you ever see a film called *Brief Encounter*? I mean, on TV? They made it in 1945, I think, or '46."

He shakes his head.

"One of its scenes was shot right here – exactly where we're standing now." We've paused together at the head of the lake, the site of the former boathouse.

"Who was in it?"

"Celia Johnson and Trevor Howard. The script was written by Noel Coward."

"Another couplet?"

"Sounds like it, doesn't it?"

"But it also sounds – or, at least, you make it sound – as though I should've heard of them." He has me take his arm again. I notice more than one couple giving us a curious look.

"Well, yes, you should. If you really mean to make a life in the theatre. As I know you do," I add hurriedly.

"Was it in black-and-white?"

I briefly pull my hand away and give him a punch on the upper arm. "You sound just like my children. Come to that, you sound just like my husband – except that, for him, black-and-white often has the saving grace of being French or Italian or Japanese."

"What about Russian?" But by now I know exactly when he's joking. Even though, in this case, he happens to have hit it precisely on the nail.

I tell him that naturally I never see such things as *The Terminator* or *The Sound of Music* with Duncan. (Or even *Manhattan* or *Annie Hall*.) If it isn't on my own or with the children (*The Sound of Music*, say) then it's usually with Maddie and her husband Bill. With Duncan I go to see *Rashomon* or *Pather Panchali* or *The World of Apu*, whenever they're revived.

Vince hasn't heard of either Kurosawa or Satyajit Ray. There's so much I'd like to teach him.

So much I'd like to introduce him to.

For the moment (but I'll be seeing him again this evening, I shall be seeing him again this evening! I shall be seeing him again this evening!!) I content myself with introducing him to a small bookshop I've occasionally been into, one that's just off Baker Street.

Where our quest proves eminently successful. The bearded assistant, whom unfortunately I haven't seen before, slips two slim books into a paper bag.

One is a book of poetry. The other a paperback concerning the Bloxham tapes – the same I have at home.

I'd guessed that this would be the place to come. If my confidence hadn't been justified we'd have had to keep on looking: Dillon's in Oxford Street perhaps; but not until after we'd had lunch, a rather late lunch: the time is nearly three. (One bit of me is even slightly sorry that this shop *did* have the books. Highly illogical and ungrateful. Oh dear, where has all my *niceness* gone, my appreciation, calm acceptance?) I look up from opening my shoulder bag to see that Vince is holding out his debit card. I push his arm away – or *try* to push his arm away – and say to the assistant, "You're taking mine, please. I'm the one who's paying for these."

But Vince doesn't falter.

"No. Please don't listen to her. I promise you I'll never come back unless you take mine."

The assistant gives a shrug and casts me a helpless glance.

"Madam, he's found our weak spot, got us where it really hurts. What can I say? Besides – he *is* a lot bigger than you."

"That's true," I agree. "I may *look* less terrifying. But what you don't know…my fingers are itching to press the trigger of this Colt revolver now pointed at your belly!" When I was a girl I used to read Peter Cheney and Mickey Spillane. "And if you cross me I shall have to spill your guts."

The young man accordingly turns away from Vince and accepts the card I'm left-handedly thrusting towards him. The other hand remains inside my shoulder bag. "Madam, I never could resist such blandishments!" Oh, yes, we've undoubtedly come to the right shop. Blow Dillon's in Oxford Street.

Vince says supportively, "I take it you know they call her the Shoulder-Bag Killer? There's a Wanted notice which you should put up in your window." Could anyone have given in more gracefully?

"Tarnation! In this silly dress there isn't any pocket." I state this ferociously but with the feeling I'm obliged to point out my defence. "So what would you have? It's shoulder bag or nothing!"

"Oh, life is hard, madam. It's a charming dress but, without pockets, Calamity Jane would never have worn it. However, there's an excellent tailor I could recommend."

"Huh! And I presume you get commission on every pistol-packing mama that you send along?"

"Just fifty bucks per alteration. It isn't very much. I suppose you wouldn't put in a kind word for me?"

All right, no pockets. But what I do have – and think I may have had it since well before noon – is a relative ease of self-expression. Being with somebody you like – particularly somebody attractive and, at least in your own eyes, charismatic (and, perhaps most importantly, somebody who clearly likes you back) – makes you a lot more articulate, gives you a turn of phrase and a fluency you'd almost forgotten you could sporadically lay claim to.

I unexpectedly wonder if Vince is also proving more articulate than usual. If Mr Bielenberg could hear him now, would he still flash that secret smile suggestive of a need for toleration? I just can't imagine he would.

Indeed, this whole episode reminds me of that scene in *Breakfast at Tiffany's* where Audrey Hepburn and George Peppard are setting out to do something neither has ever done previously: in this case, stealing from a five-and-ten cent store. What they're obviously doing is putting their new-found feeling for one another to the test – has it transformed them to the extent they can let themselves be laughed at in public? In grotesque masks taken from the merchandise – a cat for her, a dog for him – they creep around the various exhibits looking purposefully suspicious. They ignore the presence of the store detective.

And then they make a bolt for it, still wearing their absurd animal masks (unpaid for).

And once they're through the door – they run! Mission accomplished.

Of course, what *they* had was mood-setting music on the soundtrack. Indisputably a help. Potential bank-heist accompaniment.

Yet no. This was a first time for me as well: I'd never in my life threatened to spill the guts of any bookshop salesman. And had my accomplice ever conspired to spread the legend of some ruthless gun-toting outlaw? Vince makes a laid-back and quietly convincing confederate, who only last night might have waved goodbye to the Magnificent Seven.

Or even to the Glory Boys – they too are certainly up west.

So, Mr Henry Mancini! Who needs *your* assistance?

Eight

"But I've just got to pay for lunch," he says. Not especially eloquent yet heartfelt.

"No, you haven't. You'll be supplying me with two free theatre tickets."

He'd suggested it might be more fun to go with Maddie; had said there was a fifty-fifty chance the house seats would still be available.

"Or if they're not I'll phone you by six. But at the very worst would it be possible for you to come tomorrow night?"

"Yes, perfectly – please don't worry – or even one evening next week." (I'd work out what to say to Duncan.)

"And so," I say now, with the same determination I'd shown in the bookshop, "*I'm* paying for lunch. No arguments. You understand?"

He sighs. "No arguments. I understand. You still have your... Colt, was it?... and countless rounds of ammunition."

"And getting more trigger-happy all the time! You can now call me Calam. I shan't wear this dress again...unless I've sworn off plugging all the varmints for a while."

By now we're sitting in our mutually chosen restaurant and are waiting to be served.

"But I only wish this wasn't lunch," he says. "I wish that it was breakfast."

"What?"

He smiles at my confusion. I smile at it myself, albeit a little absently. I know there are many who might read an innuendo into a remark like that but I don't suppose for one moment there's any innuendo intended here. (Though naturally, being such a woman of the world, I've heard there *are* men who find older women sexually attractive. Deviants, would you call them?) Innuendo is cheap. Vince is anything but cheap.

'Deviant' is creepy. Vince is anything but creepy. Indeed, those must be the two very last things in the world which Vince is – cheap and creepy. In fact I suddenly realise I could write out a list of the *hundred* very last things in the world which Vince is. Unkind, uncaring, petty-minded, mean – oh, yes, and discourteous and plain – well, these would certainly make a pretty good start.

"Breakfast? What ever makes you say that? Is it because you're fancying bacon and eggs and fried bread?"

"No – you could hardly be further from it." He still smiles at my obvious puzzlement. "It's because you said hope makes a good breakfast but isn't much cop as a supper. So I suppose that even by the time we get to lunch it's losing a bit of its…of its…"

"Edge?"

"Particularly if it's a late lunch."

Very foolishly I want to cry again. That he should have noted, and remembered… (And applied; but I'm not at all insulted he's applied. I'm only aware of the empathy and the gentleness and the clear potential for understanding. Who ever said this man was thick? I know that in point of fact it was himself but if it had been anybody else my anger and my indignation – my anger? my *fury*! – might have been a little difficult to contain.)

"Vince, bless you. That's a very lovely thing to say."

"Is it? It was only meant as a..." Once more he flounders for the right phrase; plainly doesn't think he's found it. "...as *a very sincere thing to say*. In this life you don't have to be trigger-happy," he adds. "Just happy."

Again he looks as if he's about to say something else (more than once he's appeared on the point of asking some question or of making some observation which he's clearly then thought better of) but now as always his restraint – or sense of tact – is evidently a lot more reliable than mine.

Though later, when we're at the coffee stage, he indirectly refers back to it. "Stella, who said that thing about hope?"

"I don't know. I've forgotten. Perhaps we ought to have looked for a book of quotations."

I can tell that he doesn't really want to abandon this resurrected subject. But in case his tact isn't *completely* reliable I decide to help it out by the repetition of a recent question.

"Vince, are you sure you've had enough? Wouldn't you like a piece of fruit to finish with – or maybe some cheese? A little Stilton or some Gorgonzola?"

He shakes his head again, more emphatically than he'd done before.

"Goodness, no. That was a lovely lunch – filling, too. As it was, I shouldn't have ordered the pie. I should have followed your example, been just as strong as you were."

"What nonsense! You've been out in the open air all morning and had a great deal of exercise."

"This afternoon I'll need to have an extra hard workout."

My stomach gives a little flip – no longer such a pleasant one. It's the first verbal intimation that our time together is nearly at an end. And it's now just after four – how much of the afternoon can still be left? It's true, there's going to be this evening, but this evening isn't going to be the same. It'll then be the *public* Vince I shall be watching and no matter how intrigued I'll be, to see this new aspect of the man I've just been eating lunch with (and excited too; am I allowed to say excited?) we obviously shan't be alone and that will be so big a loss as to make it seem better, almost better, not to be there at all. But I've told him I'll be there and there's just no way I can renege on that.

And even if we go for a drink or a light meal following the show, Maddie will be with us and naturally that's going to change things too. Our time together is nearly at an end.

"Do you often go to the gym?"

The banality of it – and at a moment when the last of the sand is pouring almost visibly through the hourglass!

"Part of our contract. Every day we have to put in at least half an hour with the weights."

"And if I'm getting to know you I'd say you never skip a session – never make excuses or tell lies – but that on the contrary you normally put in a full hour or more."

"You are getting to know me."

"Is that the cue for another song? Again from *The King and I*."

"But I'm not nearly as – as noble? – no, not noble…"

"As virtuous?"

"Not nearly as virtuous as you make out. And I think I'm getting to know you, too." I'd been hoping he was going to say that. He smiles. "There's even a song from *Annie Get Your Gun*."

"What – 'There's No Business Like Show Business'?"

"Have you already seen us, then? Didn't like us much but couldn't bring yourself to say so?"

He pauses. Although I'd been hoping he was going to say what he did, he probably still guesses I'd prefer him to speak about the gym.

"But not a full hour with just the weights. I don't want to get muscle-bound."

"You always work out in the afternoon?"

That isn't what I want to be saying. I want to be saying: Tell me about your girlfriends, tell me about your love life. (Or do I, in fact? At least talking about the gym should be relatively safe.)

"No. The forecast said sun this morning, possibly rain later on. I usually try to work my day around that. Except Saturdays, when there's a matinee. What will you be doing after we've left here?"

I'm surprised there's only one matinee but I now want to ask him – a shade belatedly, I should have thought about this earlier – if he's ever been to the theatre museum or the transport museum, the National Gallery or the National Portrait Gallery? Churchill's War Rooms? The Planetarium? Madame Tussaud's; the Chamber of Horrors?

But dash it all, before I can even start on this litany, I realise that I need to do a wee. I want to ensure my maximum concentration and best possible powers of salesmanship.

"What shall I be doing? Well, when I met you I was thinking that later on I might wander down to Selfridges."

"You mean, when you met me in this life or the last?"

"Vince, when I met you in the last life Selfridges was still waiting for deliveries. I said I didn't want to be unreasonable – I'd give them time."

"If you're still going there, can I give you a lift in my taxi?"

"You may indeed. But right now, if you'll excuse me, Vince, I'm having to go somewhere else."

And I nod in the general direction of the Ladies'.

He stands as well; but isn't quite quick enough to pull out my chair, which I can see disappoints him. I resolve that when I return I must be careful to move less hurriedly.

But when I do return he has our waiter with him – and has just finished paying for our lunch.

"Vincent Peters! What *do* you think you're doing? I fully understood we had an agreement!"

"If you remember, though, you'd already told me I was crafty. Surely it's only right to show a lady she doesn't make mistakes?"

He takes a five-pound note from his pocket and gives it to the waiter as a tip. The waiter, an old man who looks as if he might be wearing a wig, and also looks as if he might be gay, is both delighted and appreciative. He looks as though he already loves this clearly generous – and considerate – and unassuming – and courteous – and *very* nice-looking… (Well, I could go on all afternoon.) I feel I should congratulate the waiter on his perspicacity and taste.

When he backs away, however, and I'm once again seated (but without having had my chair pulled out for me) I continue with my reprimand.

"That was low and underhand. I can't be getting to know you, after all. I didn't realise you were sneaky."

"Which is plainly just another bit of the whole picture. It's good you've been able to discover that. You ought to write one of those books."

"What books?"

"The ones where you look up a word and then they give you lots of other words which mean the same thing. Crafty – low – underhand – sneaky…and so on and so on. Cunning. Sly. I'm sure you could go on for much longer."

"Yes…well, before I do…" I am taking out my chequebook. "I haven't yet called you cunning or sly, have I, however much you may deserve it?"

"No, not yet, but I thought I'd try to be helpful and give you a bit of a hand."

"And to distract me a little at the same time? Vince, I'm going to make you out a cheque…"

But I know, of course, that he will only tear it up. I'll just have to pretend to myself – pretend to the two of us – that that's an idea which simply hasn't occurred to me. I start to look for the fountain pen which wasn't needed any earlier for the Herrick or the Shakespeare.

He doesn't tell me that he'll tear up the cheque. He puts it a bit differently.

"Listen, Stella. I was brought up to believe that gentlemen always pay for ladies – I mean, if the gentlemen can afford it. It would entirely spoil my pleasure if I let you pay."

"Oh, darling. That may have been true once. But times change, they really do."

That 'darling'…I'm appalled by the way it just slipped out. Yet what can I do, other than cling to a hope that in the theatre it no longer carries its rightful strength? An ironic hope – considering my not infrequent bursts of irritation at what's happening to the English language.

"Entirely spoil my pleasure," he repeats. Repeats it slowly and with stress. I feel relief: he mayn't have spotted that much difference between, say, Mr Bielenberg's form of endearment and my own. If he had, a word such as that could very easily ruin everything. I think fleetingly of Frank Sinatra: 'And then I go and spoil it all by saying something stupid like I love you.' At least I hadn't gone quite so far as that.

And I tenaciously hold on to that last phrase of his – Vince's, not Frank's (even if I also hold on to Frank's last phrase, but only in my heart) – and try to keep my voice as casual and oblivious as any voice can possibly be that's just said something stupid.

"How to demolish a person's whole case," I say, "in just a few well-chosen words! You must realise your pleasure is far more important to me than any silly squabble over which of us should pay." I put away my chequebook and my fountain pen. "I've enjoyed this lunch immensely. Thank you. Which is more or less the same as what you said to me yourself, in your duplicitous little way, a mere ten minutes ago. You ought to be thoroughly ashamed of yourself but I won't labour the point. I'll simply say again – thank you."

"And I'll simply say again: You are very welcome."

"You didn't say that before."

"No, I know I didn't. It was just a bit of – what do they call it? To make it sound a little better?"

"Poetic licence?"

"Thesaurus!" he says. "That book you're going to write which I couldn't remember the name of. It just came back to me."

In fact he's pronounced it wrong but I'm not going to tell him that – anyhow, not at this moment, not today.

"You know, Miss Pincher would be exceedingly proud of you, Vince. One of these days you're going to turn into an orator, become a real speechmaker. I can see it happening."

"I'll try," he says. "That's something you *can* say about me: I do try." And it seems he can even pass a comment of this kind without his sounding in the least bit smug.

"You don't need to tell me that. I've known it almost from the beginning. You try…and mainly you succeed. And will go on and on succeeding. I haven't the slightest doubt of it."

But something he isn't too good at as yet – despite what happened on the landing stage – is the art of accepting compliments. I take pity on his tendency to blush.

"Anyhow, thank you," I say again. "*Merci mille fois.* Those French are certainly inclined to exaggerate but on this one occasion I think they may have got it right."

"Why? What does it mean?"

"Thank you a thousand times."

"Mm. Yes. I think that could be about right."

"But even so, young man…"

"You don't? You really think it *might* be overdoing it? I see."

"That isn't what I was going to say."

"What, then?"

"Well, I'm still not sure that I don't feel a little like a maiden aunt letting her favourite nephew…"

"What?"

"Take *her* out on treats, rather than the other way about."

He's now become aware that, in a sense, I'm speaking seriously.

"No, you don't feel like that? Not really? Do you?"

And again I take pity on his fleeting yet transparent discomfiture. (I've obviously implied that the natural balance of things is slightly out of kilter.) "No. Not that I've ever been a maiden aunt. Nor indeed an aunt of any variety whatsoever."

He recovers quickly. In fact it seems to me he's learning to recover more swiftly every time. But I wouldn't swear to this; it may be only wishful thinking.

"Not that I've ever been a favourite nephew. Nor indeed a nephew of any variety whatsoever."

"What deprived lives we both have led!"

Oh God! Is that something to make a joke about? Remembering the life which Vince actually *has* led.

But the smile is still on his face; plainly he isn't thinking of himself. "Have *you* led a deprived life?"

"I was joking."

Again, I feel I have to be so careful here, although I'm sure that Vince wouldn't even want me to be. So I don't say it aloud – but hasn't everyone led a deprived life to some degree? Or, at any rate, hasn't the majority? In any case, I merely tell him I was speaking without thought…which, of course, I was. (And coincidentally – or maybe not so coincidentally – I think the deprived-life comment was a line I might have lifted from *Brief Encounter*.)

However, he doesn't let me get away with this. Or not entirely.

"You'd have liked to be an actress."

"Sure. I'd have liked to be a philanthropist as well. A great musician. A superb dancer and skier and diver and swimmer." *A fulfilled and loving and deeply appreciated spouse or partner. More than anything, a fulfilled and loving and deeply appreciated spouse or partner. That would be…now, that would be…well, heaven on earth, basically. Could any sane woman ever have asked for anything more – outside of happiness for her children, of course, and for all those she cared about? And could any sane man, either?* "In my wilder moments I'd even have liked to try hang-gliding."

"There's nothing whatever to stop you hang-gliding."

"But don't you see, Vince? That was just a sort of shorthand for all the things I feel I may have missed out on."

Oh, dear God. *Have* I led a deprived life! It's a possibility which has now just struck me more forcibly than ever.

"My little list of what-might-have-beens," I continue. "Like everybody has."

Yes, everybody. I'm no longer prepared to make exceptions. I think that if I did I might find it altogether more than I could bear. Far too depressing.

But again, of course, one *has* to bear. There's only one alternative, it seems. To kill oneself.

"We could make a deal," he says.

Although my heart leaps up at the implication contained here – that we *are* going to remain in touch beyond this evening or even beyond next week – I strive to sound cautious. Strive to suggest a sense of seventeenth-century coyness I'm very far from feeling. After all, I'm supposed to be an older person, aren't I, wise, mature, experienced? Someone you should always be able to rely on for that correct and totally disinterested decision? A sort of fairy godmother – if one wishes to be grittily pragmatic about it?

No 'supposed' at all necessary – I *am* an older person. (I'm not so sure about the rest of it.)

"Well, that depends…my sneaky, underhand and duplicitous young friend. What *is* the deal?"

"One black-and-white movie for every minute you're up in the air. Nothing sneaky about that."

"You mean, hang-gliding? Just one per minute? That's sneaky in itself. I should demand at least twenty."

"Twenty per minute?"

"Yes. Entirely non-negotiable."

"All right. Done!"

"You're an idiot, Vince Peters. We should go. You must get to your gym."

"I'll start with *Brief Encounter*. If it's as famous as you say it is, it's bound to be on video."

"You may find it very dated."

"Not if it's good I won't. Good things don't date. They just show you what life was like at the time they're set. 1945, I think you said."

"No, it was made in 1945. But set before the war. Must have been: not one army uniform on the street. Nor Navy nor Air Force." I've just remembered that he'd been thinking of applying to the Navy before he went into the library and saw that copy of *The Stage*. "No sign of shortages or ration books."

"Life in 1939, then – I'll remember. Or 1938 perhaps? The *year* doesn't matter so much; it's more the *feel* you're made to get that is important."

"You're very ready to meet people halfway, aren't you, Vince? Very relaxed about things."

And who says not very bright I want to add. But at the same time I don't want to suggest, not in any way at all, that this is something which could still occur to me.

"Very relaxed. Undemanding yet always on your toes. Mentally, much older than your years."

"Thank you," he says. "May I report back?"

"Nothing would give me greater pleasure."

I wonder if he guesses how much real truth resides in that short and pithy remark. Probably not – and much better, indeed, that he shouldn't…even if my awareness of this leaves me feeling suddenly chilled and suddenly rather lonely. I write down my address and phone number on a napkin. He looks it over, then folds it carefully, before easing it into a back pocket. "A souvenir," he says. "I shall put it into my address book." I imagine he's not referring to it as a variety of pressed leaf but I definitely believe he won't dispose of it too hurriedly. And this belief provides me with at least a glimmer of returning warmth.

I don't ask for his own address; I am now being determinedly relaxed myself, not merely playing at it. But, anyhow, when he sends in his report on *Brief Encounter*, as I know he will, simply because he's said so (I wish it didn't, yet it makes me think of Duncan when I first knew him), then of course I'll receive his address. (Dearest God. Please forgive me – I'm already wondering: how long will it be before I can expect a letter?) I know he lives in Stoke Newington; lives with an elderly couple he looks after to some extent, in exchange for a reduction in his rent. My instinct tells me he'd have been looking after them anyway; forget about reductions in the rent.

"So can I walk you to Selfridges? It's a good place for me to catch a bus."

The gym is just off Euston Road; I reckon that as soon as he's left me he'll probably make the rest of his journey on foot. The Euston Road isn't far.

"Of course you may. But oh dear – this lunch must have been expensive." In fact I know almost exactly how much it cost. "Taxi before the bill; bus ride afterwards."

"I didn't want to say goodbye until I had to. And I thought a taxi would sound better than just telling you we'd walk. Would Sir Lancelot have mentioned that you might need to walk?"

I don't ask him if – up West – they also have a tune or two from *Camelot*. I've stopped being surprised and I've also stopped (I hope) being patronising. I should like to say I've stopped being so boringly middle-class. But I know that *that* will probably be a degree harder.

"*You* don't have to take any tips off Sir Lancelot. Sir Lancelot would do well to take some tips off you."

But in fact what he's decided – and rightly decided – is that it wouldn't be worth our while to wait for a taxi. By the time a taxi had arrived at the restaurant, or by the time we'd ventured out to find one for ourselves, we could more than likely have been nearly there. The two of us are in full agreement.

We shouldn't have been, however.

As things turned out, it would have been better (might have been better) if I hadn't agreed with him at all.

But that's being wise in hindsight; and anyway would it really have made a difference? In the back of a cab it could have happened just as easily. Or when he got out to open my door and then to stand with me upon the pavement. For there's no guarantee he'd have taken the taxi on to Euston and the question which caused all the trouble hadn't occurred to him only since our finishing lunch. Apparently it had been worrying him for hours. Or no – he wasn't that specific – maybe not for hours but certainly for some time.

My own question came first, though – in truth not much more than just a piece of small talk of the 'Do you often go to the gym?' variety – harmless and yet, as it turned out, as it *then* turned out, extremely comforting.

"Why only one matinee a week? Today is Wednesday. Most theatres hold a matinee on Wednesdays."

"No, I explained it badly. Only one matinee a week for *me* is what I meant– well, for me and the rest of the cast that you'll be seeing tonight. You weren't wrong, though. There's another matinee that's actually going on at right this minute. But it's being done by all our understudies – the lads who are still in training for the provinces." He holds up my wrist and looks at the watch I wear. "And by now, don't you know, they've probably got as far as 'Shall we dance? – dum, dum, dum.'"

"Nor perchance?"

"That's right. Nor perchance."

'It's kismet,' I say to myself. I try to put it into words. "I'm *very* grateful, then, that you're now a seasoned professional and not still in training for the provinces."

"Me, too."

"Just think…!"

"I know."

We're silent for a moment. We're coming down to the junction with Wigmore Street. We're almost at the Food Hall.

"And the tickets," he says, "they'll be waiting for you at the box office from about six. Well, that's if I haven't had to phone you first – but I think the seats will still be free. Do you spell McCabe just like it sounds: MACCABE?"

"Perfect. Though we spell the Mac-bit without an A. Don't ask me why."

We've now arrived – no matter how I tried to slow my steps. (And Vince has always kept perfectly in time with me.) We shake hands.

"You won't mind the audience getting a little…wild?"

"Not a bit of it."

"It's all part of the fun, you see."

"Maddie and I will get just as wild as any of them. That's a promise."

Pause.

"Well, sir…"

"Well, madam…" He finally releases my hand.

"Vince, I've said it before and I'll say it again. My goodness but you're tall! Do you notice how everyone stares at you? No, I don't mean 'stares' but you certainly attract attention – I mean, attract it in a very flattering way…"

"Something I *have* noticed," he replies, rather slowly, "is that you're always trying to add to my feeling of confidence."

And what can one sensibly answer to that? I mean, if one only has a second or two in which to consider.

In fact I don't reply to it at all. "I've already thanked you for my lunch," I say – talk about evasion! "But thank you for the boat ride and the serenade. Thank you for the tickets. And thank you for leaving me just a little bit of my hand just now." I exaggeratedly rub the side of it, but he knows I'm merely teasing.

"Goodbye, Stella, and thank you as well. For the poems and the books. For the dum, dum, dums. (I'm going to speak to Mr Bielenberg – I think he's bound to offer you a contract.) For it all. Everything."

Yet he looks back after he's taken a few steps and when he sees I haven't moved returns to take hold of both my hands and bend to kiss my cheek. "Stella, there's something I've been wanting to ask."

"I'm listening."

And then it comes out – that question.

Preceded by a statement. (Or, at least, by part of a statement.)

"Little things you've said... Little things you haven't..."

Now I don't say anything. I wonder what little things I've said. I wonder what little things I haven't.

"Are you happy?"

I simply stare at him. And he repeats it.

Two minutes back he'd made a comment and I hadn't been able to produce an answer; but now, to a query like this, there should be any number of easy answers – possibly each one couched as a question itself and thereby giving away practically nothing.

Do you mean happy at this precise instant or do you mean happy as a general rule?... Or happy at odd moments, like when you see or hear something beautiful and moving; maybe unexpected?... Is anybody happy all the time?... But how are you defining it?... Perhaps you're thinking of contentment?

Yes, there should have been any number of different answers, none of them actually dishonest.

But I can't bring forth even one. No, not so much as even one. A single, solitary, isolated one. What's stopping me then? God only knows.

So in that case? How *do* I respond?

I respond by bursting into tears.

Why? In the name of all that's wonderful? Why?

Was it because he'd asked me at a particularly *unhappy* moment? Was it because, by filling such a large part of my day, he'd revealed to me how empty a large part of my life had now become?

Was it because until today I've experienced love at first sight only in novels and films; yet when it does come to me in my own life it's clearly something I can't pursue? Something impossible, something totally out of the question. Not on account of my being married. (I'm sorry, Duncan, that isn't it at all.) But on account of my being forty-nine.

Plainly, none of these things is an excuse. However, all of them are reasons.

So I burst into tears and he puts his arms about me. There must be scores of witnesses. Son comforting his mother – how very sweet! I push him away and run into the Food Hall.

He starts to follow (I can hear him), very soon decides that for a variety of reasons it might be better not to do so.

But he calls out.

"Stella, see you, then, after the show! And I'll be thinking of you – thinking of you all the time! See you, then, after the show!"

Although I keep my back turned, I do at least raise one hand in sorrowful acknowledgment.

Nine

Things are better again. Much. I've managed to pull myself together.

It's nearly six-thirty; he hasn't phoned to say the house seats are unavailable. He hasn't phoned to say I'm a highly neurotic woman and it might be better if I simply stayed at home.

I've taken a lot of care over my appearance – even more than I normally do. I think I look good. Which doesn't massively reassure me. No doubt because of what happened earlier, I'm having a small attack of nerves. I tell myself I'd cry off if I could. But I know that I can't – and, moreover, would never forgive myself if I did.

So I liberally anoint myself in Mitsouko – behind my ears and on my wrists. Duncan had given me a larger bottle than usual for my birthday – and naturally I don't mean just the toilet water.

I also put on a smile…a highly resolute and rather fixed sort of a smile…but wisely let it fade into something a lot softer before I get up from my dressing table.

"'I feel pretty, I feel pretty, I feel pretty and charming and gay…'"

That's far more in keeping with my smile – or grimace? – and I perform a lively little dance that takes me across the room and out to the top of the stairs.

"Watch out, you Glory Boys! The Glory Grandmothers are about to descend! Great news, lads: I think you've finally met your match!"

Oh, it's all so artificial.

Down in the sitting room, however, I help myself to a good dose of Dutch courage.

I stand at the mantelpiece for a moment, go to switch on the TV. See the closing credits of *Wogan*, switch it off again, return to the mantelpiece for my drink.

Which is a decent-sized gin-and-It. Good thing I've ordered a taxi! (I scarcely ever take the car when I'm heading into town. Especially if it's going to be dark before I get home.)

Then I look at my watch – yet again; do I really expect it to have changed that much since the last time? (Do I even remember what it said the last time?) Another ten minutes until the taxi arrives. It's true, I do feel somewhat nervous – in a way that owes *nothing at all* to what happened earlier. But am I now having regrets in regard to Maddie? Even before I'd returned to West Hampstead I'd decided I wasn't going to tell her about any of this. It's all too private and personal and precious.

It isn't so much that I mind her knowing I made such an utter fool of myself, actually crying on the pavement outside Selfridges, and then, in front of all those curious shoppers, having to hurry off to wash the still running tears off my face! It's more that I'm scared that – all unwittingly – she may cheapen things a little; if not by her questions and comments, then by the many unshared thoughts I'll be suspicious of. I hope I'll be able to find someone to whom I can give her ticket.

Though won't this be a shade unethical? Shan't I be betraying Vince's generosity – *and* the management's?

But, at any rate, I'm sure it's going to give pleasure.

Besides, Maddie's absence is obviously going to mean that after the show, if we go out for a snack and a drink as I feel confident we shall, I'll have the opportunity – which I so very badly need – to apologise for my behaviour. No way to explain it but to let him hear of my regret at having embarrassed him. Not that I believe he could truly have been that much embarrassed: he put his arms around me, didn't he, and if I hadn't pulled away he might have stood there a good deal longer? He called after me, too, without regard for what anybody was going to think – and the Food Hall was just as crowded as it generally is. He didn't set out to make any swift (and fully understandable) departure.

But anyway – whether he was embarrassed or not – I need to apologise for having subjected him to the risk of it. I need to apologise for having created so conspicuous a scene.

In any case, no longer will it be a question of the three of us. It will be a question of just Vince and me. Just Vince and me! That's what I've really wanted all along.

There's a ring at the doorbell.

Oh, God.

I pick up my tiny handbag, take a last look at myself in the hall mirror, wonder why I didn't go to have another (yet another) wee – so laughably unnecessary – then open the door with a smiling reprimand about to issue from my lips: "You're a little early, aren't you?"

But both the smile and the reprimand quickly disappear. There isn't any cabdriver standing on the doorstep. Instead of whom –

"Duncan? My God – *Duncan*! No, it can't be!"

My husband responds with a look of faint amusement.

"I've only been away for three days, yet you'd forgotten me already. How deeply saddening!"

Yet not so deeply saddening that after brushing his lips fleetingly against one corner of my mouth he doesn't walk across to check his correspondence. As usual when he's been away, there's a small pile of it on the table underneath the mirror. In a daze I close the front door.

"But you weren't due back till Friday!"

"How lucky, then, I'm early! If I hadn't come back till Friday – *and* claiming that I'd forgotten my door-key – mightn't you by then have been screaming for the police? 'Help! Help! Come quickly!'"

I try to laugh. "Oh, don't be so absurd."

"'Husband? – do I have one of those? No, no. Imposter!'"

He's now put down his suitcase and is already riffling through the mail that awaits him; doesn't seem to have noticed I'm wearing all my finery and could well be on my way out.

"Perplexing, though. I can't quite say I understand."

Ludicrously, I think at first he's referring to the envelope he has in hand.

But, no, it appears that he's referring to me. With a casual gesture he indicates the finery I thought he hadn't noticed.

"Incommunicado all day – and then, practically at set of sun, all dolled up and off to paint the town…?"

"Incommunicado?"

But then I realise. Before I went out I hadn't switched on the answering machine. I am always forgetting to switch on the answering machine. Indeed, if Duncan's not around I frequently don't bother.

"Oh, I'm sorry. Yes – stupid of me. Careless."

"Especially with your having been in absentia, it appears. Almost from dawn to dusk."

"Well, hardly that. But, as I say, I didn't suppose *you'd* be wanting to get in touch with me before Friday…"

Duncan never phones me from abroad but usually rings soon after his plane has landed, to ask about correspondence and to say what time he's likely to be requiring dinner.

Thankfully, the answer I've just given seems to be satisfactory.

"No, but things got a move on, thank God… The amount of superfluous mail one can receive in just three days – extraordinary!

My word, though, I'm famished. At any other time I might suggest our having a meal out but I'm sure that even at short notice you'll be able to rustle up something quite delectable… Now what the devil is *this* – postmark Canterbury? Oh, be a pet and pour me a large Scotch."

"Duncan, I… "

"And is there any pate' or smoked salmon? I wouldn't mind some nibbles while we wait."

I go back into the sitting room, pour him his Scotch. He comes in as I'm doing it, throws himself into a chair. "God, but it's good to be home!"

It's a mite unusual to hear this from Duncan: such a depth of feeling, such a depth of appreciation. "Was it as bad as all that, then?"

"Dull, dull, dull."

That reminds me of dum, dum, dum.

"But Amsterdam? You've never been to Amsterdam. Didn't you get a chance to – ?"

"No, of course not. When does one ever? These sudden calls for a series of totally useless meetings! This lot, I can tell you, turned out to be an almost criminal waste of time!"

"In what way?"

"Oh… Any answer to that would become so complicated you wouldn't stand a chance of understanding it. And I feel much too tired to go into it. Not to mention hungry."

There's another ring at the doorbell.

"Now who the bloody hell is that?"

"Taxi driver." I'd been looking forward to this as my chance to start explaining. "Shan't be a minute."

I head quickly for the front door but now don't take my purse as I'd originally intended. I ask the driver, instead of paying him off, whether he can wait a further few minutes. "Ten at the outside."

"What time do you have to be there, madam?" He scratches at the side of his bald head, a stocky and amenable fifty-year-old.

(Though I'm not always the most brilliant judge of age – just on the very rare occasion!)

"The play starts at seven-thirty."

Would you believe it, I'd even given the taxi company the name of the wrong theatre; but one just round the corner from the right one. Done this on purpose. I'm not yet quite as liberated as I'd like to be.

"Oh, no trouble, madam. We can do that comfortably."

I return inside. I suppose it won't even matter if I'm a little late; I'm sure it's not the kind of management that prohibits the entry of latecomers. (But, on the other hand, I should hate it if, despite the glare of the footlights, Vince were able to see well enough into the front stalls to distinguish a pair of empty seats.)

"Who was that? Somebody wanting to sell us something?"

On the front gate we have a little sign: *No Solicitors*. Myself, I'm almost embarrassed by it – or was at least, while it was still new. Duncan has said we ought to have another, despite its suggestion of conflict: *The woman who lives here is a complete pushover.* I told him I should much prefer it.

"No, no one like that. Taxi driver. You see, I was just on my way out…as you correctly guessed. But I've asked him to wait so that I can do you a cheese omelette if you'd like one. And, yes," *with my freshly washed and made-up face and my again-quite-steady voice after my reassuring talk to the lady in the cloakroom,* "yes, it's fortunate, in fact I bought some more smoked salmon just this very after– "

"Out? On your way out?"

"Well, you saw I was. You said – "

"Yes, I know I said you looked as if you might be off to hit the town. But I wasn't being serious. Where – out?"

"Maddie and Bill. Dinner."

"Well, that's all right, then. Only Maddie and Bill. I'm afraid you'll have to phone them. Cancel."

"I can't."

"Why not? It's only dear Madeleine. You see her every – "

"I mean – I can't phone. They're taking me to a restaurant; they'll already have left home."

I have to admit I'm feeling rather pleased with myself – or know at least that I shall be, when I have the time to relax a little and congratulate myself on having been inspired.

"Then phone the restaurant. Restaurants do have telephones, you know. Or so they tell me."

"I don't know which one." Perhaps that isn't quite so good.

"Stella, let me get this clear. You can't phone them? You're meeting them at a restaurant but you say you don't know which one?"

"Yes, of course I do. It's just that I've forgotten what it's called. It's a small place – French – opened less than a week ago…"

"Where, then? What street?"

I look at him sitting there with his well-nigh disbelieving expression – a smile, a smirk? – and think how can he not believe me. How can my husband of nearly thirty years not yet have learned to trust me? I feel indignant and insulted. This, after all, is the very first time. What's more, he plainly thinks I'm an idiot, someone who forgets or can't be bothered to turn on answering machines and who doesn't remember the name of restaurants or the streets they're in…when *she* isn't the one who either left her keys at home or in a Dutch hotel room or in an aeroplane lavatory or something… I'm about to remind him of this when he suddenly reaches over for the telephone.

"What are you doing?"

"Phoning Bill. It's possible they haven't left yet. He may have been late getting home from the office."

Oh, dear Lord. We both listen to the number ringing. (How on earth shall I put it, so that they'll instantly twig and play along?) It seems to ring for a very long time.

Nobody picks up.

Thank you, God.

Finally, Duncan replaces the receiver. "I suppose that in the end they may even get around to ringing *you*. In the meantime, they'll just have to sit there and twiddle their thumbs. Right?"

"No! No, I'm sorry, Duncan, I've been looking forward to it. You'll somehow have to manage without me, that's all."

And dammit – but it's your own fault – now there won't even be time to cook you an omelette.

"It isn't that simple, my dear." His voice has grown steely.

"Is it not?" My own voice matches his. There's no way I'm going to allow him to win this.

"No – when I couldn't get hold of you from the airport it occurred to me to ring Chrissie."

Christine is one of our daughters-in-law. Even Paul doesn't call her Chrissie – only his father does.

"You see, I thought you might be over there, spending time with your small grandson. But what do you think she told me? She'd been trying to phone you all day, wanting to ask if you could possibly take the baby overnight, because there's some very impromptu party she and Paul have been invited to, which they're desperate not to miss – apparently he, too, has been trying to get hold of you all afternoon. (Not very convenient, he'd said, on account of his having several meetings to attend.) I obviously told her yes…of course we'd take care of Thomas."

He looks at his watch.

"And they'll be here very shortly. But where were you, then, in Chrissie's hour of need? Or hours and hours of need, to be a little more exact?"

"What?"

"Where *were* you all the time she was trying to contact you? So that, apart from her anxiety over the party and Thomas, she was also having to worry about what might have happened to *you*. Naturally."

Piffle!

I want to throw something; I really want to throw something. I have never in the whole of my adult life thrown anything out of sheer anger. In fact I have invariably felt irritated when the rich heroines of mainly screwball comedies express their feelings thus – it's often perfume which they hurl and I'm aghast not only at the damage but at the sheer extravagance. Of course, they're never the ones who have to clean it up. But now – and literally for the first time ever – I feel I can understand. (Although I still wouldn't pick on my *Mitsouko*.)

Or if I can't throw anything, I feel that at least I want to shout out the truth. *Where was I? If you must know, I was in Queen Mary's Gardens, and then on the lake and then in a bookshop, and afterwards eating tender lamb chops and drinking wine – and even standing on the pavement of Orchard Street, outside the Food Hall at Selfridges, making a fool of myself; and, all of that time, I was either falling in love or had actually fallen in love. Yes, that's where I was and just what I was doing. I'm so sorry that no one could get hold of me.*

Well, this would give him a little something to think about. This would give them all a little something to think about.

Oh, if only.

And another thing. (And another thing, Duncan – and Paul – and *Chrissie*!) I am so tired, so terribly tired, of always being taken for granted. 'Not very convenient, on account of his having several meetings to attend.' How right you are: not very convenient at all! 'And she was also having to worry about what might have happened to *you*. Naturally.' About what might have happened to me naturally; without any intention whatsoever, or even wish. (Certainly no wish at the beginning…and even after the consciousness of wish, no intention.) In any case, Christine, you were never in the least bit worried about me. All that worried you, of course, was the thought of missing your wretched party.

However, I think of Vince…and then I manage neither to throw nor to shout. I instinctively know that if he'd been in a similar situation he would neither have thrown nor shouted. Just thinking about Vince calms me. Even the nerves I was experiencing prior to Duncan's homecoming wouldn't have survived, I realise now, if I'd only stopped and thought properly about Vince, not just about myself and my venturing on my own into unknown territory: amongst a *wild* crowd which I wasn't quite prepared for and felt in some way I might need protection from.

(No, my protection would be up there in front of me, not so many yards distant. I could imagine him striding down into the auditorium, in his fig-leaf or whatever, tanned and muscular and looking magnificent. And how lithe as he jumps down off the stage!… Perhaps it's just as well I'm not being given sufficient leisure at the moment to wallow in my fantasies. Even in my bath I didn't have much time.)

Therefore, calmed, I now repeat quite equably, "I'm sorry."

Equably and admirably – if indeed a fraction woodenly.

"The truth is, I must simply have been out, every time that someone called. Or else the line was out of order."

"Not according to the engineers. I checked."

Of course you did. "In any case, what does it matter? The thing is, this evening you'll have to look after Tommy yourself. Do a bit of bonding, tell him all about Amsterdam, make up a few of the details if you have to; he's not likely to run off and check in the encyclopaedia. He'll come in his carrycot and Christine – "

"Normally, of course, I would. Look after him myself. But Chrissie says he's teething – rather fractious – she knew you wouldn't mind. And unfortunately I've about six thousand reports to get through by the morning. It's a shame but there's nothing else for it. You'll merely have to explain to dearest Madeleine when at last she *does* telephone. I'm sure she'll understand. As you frequently make a point of telling me – she's always so *very* understanding."

Do I make a point of that? I hadn't been aware – evidently must now watch it.

Anyhow, I haven't the least idea of what to say next – can't think up any new arguments, no matter how implausible. "I…I'll go and fetch that paté."

In the kitchen I slam the cupboard door, slam the tin of paté onto the table, slam down the tin of dry biscuits.

Slam the drawer that holds the cutlery.

Back in the sitting room Duncan is still working through his correspondence. He doesn't look up when I re-enter but certainly looks at the plate I set before him. "My goodness, I hope you're going to complain about the state of these! Not that it matters. Bring me one of those little tables, will you, there's a good girl."

I do as he asks, behaving for all the world not only like a good girl but a most exemplary one – Vince would have been proud of me. "Where've you put the Times?" I fetch it in silence (the good girl is silent, and residually seething, but she is free to think of Vince and is gradually calming down again), then reach towards the telephone.

"I thought you didn't know the number."

"I'm phoning Christine. If Tommy isn't well they'll have to miss the party."

Now he does look up; he does look at me, as though I'm actually there in the same room.

"Stella! What's got into you tonight? It's not like you to be so...so, well I don't know...disobliging."

"I wouldn't call it that. I babysit for them a lot. For once, it won't hurt them to know it isn't so convenient. Won't hurt them – I mean, if they're really determined to leave their sick baby! – to look for somebody else." How often, I wonder, does Sonia babysit. Sonia is Christine's mother.

"At this late hour? Stella... You can see Madeleine any time." His tone has softened – has become tolerant, even kindly; he's being positively reasonable. "Paul and Chrissie don't receive party invitations every night of the week."

"Don't they? Sometimes it seems like it. They at least go out a lot more than we do."

"They're somewhat younger than we are. You'd expect it."

"Why?"

273

"Oh, Stella…!"

"Well, when Paul and Ben were babies how often did we get out? What's more, we would never have thought of going out if one of them was feverish. And tell me what's going to happen when they have a second child. Let alone a third or fourth. I don't like Christine very much."

That was both sudden and unintentional. I'm a little shocked by it myself: my own out-loud admission, never before voiced to anyone apart from Maddie.

I take my hand off the receiver…no doubt the result of shock. "Perhaps I don't mean that exactly…"

Coward! You mean it very exactly. (If very exact can be more exact than just exact, I mean it enormously exactly.)

"No, of course you don't. She's always been a very sweet daughter-in-law to both of us."

"Patronising. Especially to me."

"Patronising!"

"You're half-infatuated with her; you wouldn't see it. And these days Paul does it as well. They both patronise me."

Yet at least it's being helpful in a way: serving as a warning – and teaching me not to become patronising with others. I almost smile.

But only almost; at the moment I feel there's nothing that could make me actually do so.

"I wish to heaven it was they who were living in Australia – and not Ben."

Duncan remains seated but reaches out a hand that's supposed to be placatory. Dear Lord, he's continuing to be indulgent and reasonable. Can I bear it?

"Stella, is it still the change of life? I hoped that by now we'd got rid of all of that. Or is it just because – like me – you're hungry? Tired? Been missing me? I'll help you with the supper."

"No, I can do it; I'll find it easier on my own." Not all that tactful maybe; but who's trying to be tactful? Other than my husband?

"That's my girl. Then if you're certain, I think I'll go and take a shower. But see if you can't get a smile back on your face by the time Paul and Chrissie arrive. You know something? I always pride myself upon your smile. On that and your unselfishness!"

Well, bully for you. But perhaps it's just as well I don't say it; somehow we have to get through the rest of this hugely disappointing evening, even if I now feel I'd have given almost anything to be well clear of this house by the time he rang the bell. (And he'd have got in easily enough: some friends across the road have a spare set of our keys, just as we have one of theirs.)

This idly passing thought makes me remember the taxi driver. I snatch up my purse and rush to the front door a second time – thoroughly to put paid to all my hopes of happiness. Of temporary happiness.

Of temporary *partial* happiness.

Put paid to everything. That's practically the way it feels.

And for a moment – yet only for a moment – I almost wish I'd never met him. Vince.

However, I literally give myself a shake, then make a phone call. Now that Duncan's disappeared (and I stand on the stairs for an instant and listen to the sound of running water), now that Duncan's disappeared I really do make a phone call.

"Yes," she says, the woman in the box office. "That's right, Mrs Mc – Mrs McCabe – I've got them right here. With a note that you'll be picking them up just before the show. They're nice seats, too. Mr Peters wanted you to have the very best and we were lucky and had a cancellation…"

I wonder dully: isn't she supposed, then, to mention house seats? Would everyone be clamouring?

I tell her how sorry and disappointed I am but that I simply can't get there tonight.

"Oh, you don't say? That's such a pity, it really is. He *will* be disappointed… Yes, of course. I'll write it down."

Yet I'm not sure if she will; I imagine her winking at a colleague and taking on an expression of heavily comic irony – *oh, who do they think they're trying to fool, haven't we heard it all before?*

"You're sorry (I'm going to say), something very unexpected has turned up, you'll get in touch with Mr Peters as soon as… No, you don't want me to say that? Not any of it? Just that you're most terribly sorry. Right. And how enormously much you enjoyed meeting him."

Yes, now she's raising an eyebrow at that same enraptured colleague.

"Right. I'll see he gets it… Oh, you're ever so welcome. Perhaps you'll be able to come and see the show some other time? I'm sure you'd enjoy it. Thank you, Mrs…"

She's probably having to look again at what's written on the envelope at the second I ring off (I do so a little more abruptly than I'd intended, because I *would* have liked her to tell him how pleasant I sounded). But in my current mood I can only too easily imagine the dialogue that ensues.

"Well, what's that naughty young Vince been doing with himself, I wonder. Married ladies, eh? – and this one sounded rather posh. Bet that 'something very unexpected' was a husband. Well, I didn't think he was that sort of fellow, not our Vince. Still, just shows you, doesn't it? It's nearly always the quiet ones who – "

No, I don't want to imagine the rest of it – I arrange for her to have another customer. "Well yes, madam, as a matter of fact you're lucky. We do happen to have these two last seats, really excellent ones, less than a minute ago returned…"

Yes, lucky lady. And lucky friend of lucky lady. Just a slightly earlier getaway and those lucky people would have been Maddie and myself.

No, only me. I'd forgotten. Even Maddie would have been excluded.

And practically any moment now the curtain will be going up…

But just stop thinking of it, please.

In fact, I soon have to. I change into my housecoat, see to Duncan's supper (cook nothing for myself), and then, only a very short time later, am cuddling a most unhappy baby. And when you're cuddling a most unhappy baby – well, to be honest, unless you're thoroughly worn out by nights and nights of sleepless misery or else your name is Cruella de Vil... As you must know by now, I don't possess a very noble character but...well, with such an abject little bundle of humanity gazing up at me for reassurance, I find I can even put up with his mother and that's saying something.

At least I *think* I can even put up with his mother. Right now she is loftily addressing the rest of us – or perhaps not really addressing her husband so much, who in this situation at any rate is obviously a player having little to contribute.

I have to admit, though, she is quite unusually pretty. (I am regaining my nobility of character.)

"Oh, you poor things!" (That's to Duncan and me.) "I hope he's not going to go on like this all night. You're being perfectly foul, Thomas Archibald McCabe." (Where on earth did they get the 'Archibald'? Oh, yes. Her equally unpleasant father.) "It's vile of you to act this way; you've made your point; we know you're suffering." (But now it's back to me: I'm the favoured one.) "He's been a perfect brute all day. How unfair that men can escape to the office and even stay late, claim overtime! Though that's probably what he'll be doing himself in another twenty-five years or so – isn't it disgusting? Next time I shall come back as a man; just see if I don't!"

I manage to keep it to myself. *Yes, dear, that's all right – so long as you come back as something wholly different and somewhere as far as possible from us!*

"Parents-in-law, I think this party may have saved a murder from taking place. Stella, what should we ever do without you?"

"Christine," I suggest, "you don't think you ought to be with him while he's feeling so unhappy?" And believe it or not – I'm no longer thinking of the theatre.

"Good heavens, no. I'm the last person he wants; as I say, I'd only throttle the beast. Anyhow, you're always so much better with him than I am. He knows instinctively you've had the practice."

Paul puts in a word here. "Darling, it's not the practice, it's the disposition. Softness of nature, sweetness of character. Pity you're such a stranger to all the charms of true femininity."

Privately, Paul may not be my favourite son – and I realise, of course, that he *is* only joking – yet at the moment I could hug him to me almost as tightly as I'm hugging Tommy.

But I quite definitely couldn't hug Duncan.

"Paul, I don't know how you can say that, even in jest – rather tiresome jest. Your wife looks stunning; succulent; good enough to eat." ("To coin a phrase," I'd like to add.) "No one would ever know that Chrissie had been through such a very testing sort of day."

Now he slightly shifts his focus and talks to our own stunning little blonde Superwoman herself, size eight, green-eyed, pert-nosed, oh, utterly succulent and good enough to eat.

"I swear, there's not a soul who wouldn't think you'd just stepped out of a bandbox. You wouldn't like to ditch this boorish oaf and take up with someone who really appreciates you?"

"You know, Lord Duncan...I could certainly feel tempted. Enormously tempted."

Lord Duncan.

"Well," says Paul, "that's something you can both discuss another time. For the present, though – I'm afraid we'll really have to dash."

Now Christine actually nods at her own lord and master, drawing her attention – maybe reluctantly – well away from mine. But she's suddenly more businesslike. Stubs out her cigarette.

"Stella, just bung some of that jelly stuff on his gums every now and then – and put your faith in diluted orange juice and paracetamol. About three dozen, I'd advise. Goodnight, you little monster... No, Mummy didn't mean it. Give her a great smacky kiss to show her she's forgiven."

Paul is growing increasingly impatient. "*Do* come on, Chris!"

"Oh, these men, these men!"

She now delays only long enough to give Lord Duncan a peck on his cheek. "Not you, poppet, only the rest of them."

I, as nanny-factotum in residence, also get a peck. "Stella, you're an angel. Always have been, always will be. One of these days I'm going to get them to play a record for you on Radio 2. 'For the best mother-in-law in all the world – truly – without exception.' The whole nation shall be informed of it."

Duncan sees them both out. Still holding Tommy I cross over to the mantelpiece and snatch up one of the containers left on it.

"Paracetamol! At six months! I ask you!"

I actually say it aloud; and then – oh, Hollywood, at long last! – hurl the container down upon the carpet. It isn't of glass, so nothing breaks.

"Now, that's what we think about that, isn't it, my darling?"

I can't truthfully say that Tommy nods but he does appear compliant and seems to look around for something else that can be hurled. I know I haven't set a good example.

"Naughty old Granny! You see, she was cross. But even when you're cross it isn't right to throw things."

This is a statement, however, which causes me to reflect. 'Granny' – yes. 'Old' – no, most certainly not, life begins at fifty and Elizabeth Taylor was ten years younger than that when *she*... Whereas 'naughty' – well, wouldn't you have to define your terms; take into account contributing factors, pent-up emotions, unleashed motivations?

Or is that rationalisation?

Yes, most likely it is.

Shame.

Ten

Surprisingly, Tommy seems to sleep through most of the night. I need to go to him only four times – although, for me, it's clear that sleep just isn't going to come. I honestly believe – well, practically honestly believe – that I'll never have a good night's rest again. (The answer now is *not* to think of Vince but that's plainly impossible. He's in my mind every minute, almost every second.)

However, the morning dawns brightly and gives promise of another lovely day. Duncan is fed and out of the house by 8.25. Tommy is fed and out of the house, snugly bundled in his grandmother's arms, by 9.40. We get to my son's front door by ten. Paul, of course, will have left at least an hour earlier but I wonder a little maliciously whether Christine may have taken herself back to bed – that is, if she ever got out of it in the first place – in the hopes of luxuriously recovering from what may have been a pretty late night…and certainly she's still in her nightdress and dressing gown when eventually she comes to the door. (I don't get a kiss. For the time being, I've served my purpose.)

By 10.35, therefore, according to the clock on the Abbey National tower (and at roughly the same time as yesterday), I'm walking through the Baker Street entrance to Regent's Park – aware, I suppose, of the profusion of brilliant flowers on either side of me but definitely not experiencing any of my usual appreciation.

Then I cross the bridge that's nearly straight ahead and turn to the left on the other side – initially trying to forget it's the same path we walked along yesterday, Vince and I, though coming of course from the opposite direction. But not making a very good job of forgetting. Was it *here* he suggested that we go on a boat? Was it *here* he pointed out the slightly fuzzy hedgehog? And where's that painter with his easel and the picture we decided not to look at? Where's the youth who was sprawled up against his bike, sunbathing?

But these aren't the questions that matter.

There's only one question that matters: will Vince have returned this morning and gone to the same bench? That seems to be my notion of forgetting. (Confused and scarcely the same wench – there, sweetheart! – *couplet*! Every bit as good as Howard and Coward, yes? I wonder, I wonder. Will you be watching that today?)

I don't for one moment believe you'll be there – I *daren't* believe it – and yet if there should be even the remotest chance…

In short, are you thinking about me? Are you wondering what I may be doing; where I may be doing it? Could you be putting to the test any of those potential powers Miss Pincher must have spoken of, when making a well-remembered word the focus of two lessons?

If so, it wouldn't be too hard for you, would it, to sense that I've come back to the park?

I reach the path where our bench is.

I begin to walk a lot more slowly.

'Love… Love is all you need…'

I visualise that young couple again and listen again to their transistor. I try to smile at the complete cheesiness of such a lyric – I mean, if applied to the present context.

And at length I reach the final bend; I can't postpone arrival – not for so much as another minute. I strain for the scrabble of pigeons, for their cooing, for the throwing of nuts to squirrels… although what sort of sound, I ask myself, would *that* ever be likely to produce?

There seems to be nothing of the kind. Now…just a further few paces and I'll be there.

I take the final step – while doing everything I can to prepare myself for disappointment.

I remember how at this time yesterday I was almost praying for this bench to be empty.

But he'll believe I let him down last night. He'll believe I may have been playing with him. All froth and no substance.

Though surely he's a better judge of character than that? As I myself am. And my judgment of *him* says he'd never formulate such a judgment of *me*. I know that sounds conceited but it's true.

Of course, if that woman in the box office *did* leave him my message – and in a place where he could easily find it, since presumably she'd left the theatre before the show ended – then neither disillusion nor any test of prescience need have entered into it.

But either way – my absence – would it have caused him, after the performance, to speculate and worry? (For, please God, he'd have had no knowledge of it *during* the performance!) Did he keep on rootling around for possible reasons? The last time he'd seen me I was crying; might he have feared some inseparable connection? Did *he* manage to sleep?

Yes, I'm tired. So tired. I can't let myself get any more affected than I already am. *He is twenty-four years younger than me! He is twenty-four years younger than me!* I must go on repeating that. Endlessly. Ad infinitum.

I see him sitting there. I see myself sitting there. I was so very happy whilst I was sitting there.

Even, I mean, despite the fact I didn't immediately become aware of this. For I clearly hadn't been gathering my rosebuds with all the consciousness and perceptiveness required. I'd thought him kind and pleasant-looking but, except for that, had taken him basically at his own evaluation. Not very bright, he'd said.

I know now that I shall never do it again: I shall never again remind myself to gather rosebuds.

Something done for the last time. Is this then how it is with growing old: a gradual falling-off of things, things you know you'll never do again?

I shall never see *Brief Encounter* again. I shall never go rowing again. I shall never recite poetry again.

I shall never have a night of wholly peaceful sleep again.

I shall never see *him* again. Would it perhaps be better if I never did?

Such a confused and contradictory mess! That's me. Stella McCabe. I just don't know what I'm going to do with my life.

To go back to West Hampstead – what is there now but to go back to West Hampstead? – I turn in the direction of St John's Wood and Swiss Cottage. I can't bear to walk beside the lake. Shall I ever, any more, be able to bear it, that walk beside the lake?

Well, yes. I'm tired. I'm in a state of near-exhaustion. There'll come a day when I can look back on all of this and give a little shrug and – perhaps as well – a little laugh.

No, I don't want there to come a day when I can do that. Not ever. Not even when I'm old. Not even when it shouldn't matter any more.

Please God. I don't want it ever not to matter any more. (But if only it won't hurt me quite so much!)

I walk back to Parsifal Road, don't take a bus or taxi – walk *back*, not *home*, you notice. Somehow, now, I can't even think of it as home. Merely the place where I shall be on call to look after my grandchildren for the next fifteen years or so.

In fifteen years' time *you* will be forty, the moment at which life begins. (It's definitely not fifty any more – at fifty, life is finished.) Will you have met someone closer to your own age by then? Will you have married her? Will you have children?

Parsifal Road… Of course, you have a note of my address – I'd all but forgotten that. While I've been looking for *you* in Queen Mary's Garden, is there any chance you might have been looking for *me* in Parsifal Road? (This reminds me of *A Town Like Alice*, in which the heroine flies off to Alice Springs to look for the hero, at exactly the same point he's flying off to London to look for her.) In any case, that makes sense. You'd have rung the bell. Mrs Conway would have opened the door; led you through to the kitchen; given you a cup of tea. I try not to build up my hopes again; can't help building up my hopes again. You could be waiting for me at the house.

I arrive *back* – no, it's almost home again, *you* could have turned it into home once more, simply by sitting in the kitchen and chatting to Mrs Conway and drinking a mug of tea with her. (Yet I'm deliberately closing my eyes to any such incredible… no, to any such *miraculous*…possibility, even if I do believe in miracles, believe in them more staunchly, far less open-mindedly indeed, than I do in reincarnation, despite our having known each other in a previous life!) I arrive back home, then – though now walking a little more slowly again – a few minutes before twelve. Yesterday, we hadn't even left my favourite bench a few minutes before twelve. Perhaps never again my favourite bench; it all depends, doesn't it? It all depends. Like the lake and the landing stage, like the whole of Queen Mary's Garden – possibly like the whole of Regent's Park itself – I may now have little option but to stay away.

Yet I still have your bread wrapper at the bottom of my shoulder bag. How pathetic is that, how truly pathetic is that! What do I intend to do with it? (You see, my darling, despite what I said just a minute ago, I'm now quite closing my eyes to miracles. I refuse to encourage all those very foolish hopes for the second time in one short morning. Long morning – today, time has decided it wants to take its time. To make up, of course, for yesterday.)

So I wander down the road looking at front gardens – trying to concentrate on nothing except front gardens; some, of course, I admire a great deal more than others. George certainly keeps our own looking fairly colourful – as *I* request – and unfailingly neat, as Duncan does.

Mrs Conway is just about to leave.

No, she says, evidently a little surprised that I should ask (so far as I remember, I've never asked before) nobody at all has been; was I expecting someone? Yes, she thinks the phone may have rung a few times. She reminds me that this morning was her day for Hoovering – she doesn't always hear so well. After she's gone, of course, I check; but there isn't anything from Vince. *Why* isn't there? There was nothing on earth to prevent him from phoning me. In my depressed state I hadn't even thought about the ease with which he could pick up a receiver.

But perhaps it's been the same for him: sometimes when your mind's in turmoil the most obvious things simply don't occur to you. Logic doesn't get a look-in. Perhaps it's been the same for him?

Otherwise why – why, why, oh *why* – hasn't he telephoned?

When I saw her out, Mrs Conway had shown concern. (In this house she and I are the only ones who ever show concern. But I can't claim it's a gender thing. It wasn't like that while Ben was still around.)

"You're looking tired, madam. I hope you've not been overdoing it?"

Oh, yes, I've been spending several hours sitting on a bench in Queen Mary's Rose Garden, then reclining in the stern of a rowing boat – trailing my hand in the water, reciting poetry. Pointing a gun at the belly of a bookshop assistant. I think you *could* say that perhaps I've been overdoing it.

"So this afternoon, madam, why not plan to put your feet up? There may be a good film you could watch."

"Yes, thank you, Mrs Conway. Sounds restful."

Restful?

And of course I'll then have to make plans for this evening's dinner. Dear Lord. Another fifty years of making plans for this evening's dinner. (Do I have the will any more – or the energy – to continue thinking about renting a flat? Or about finding myself a job?)

The fact that he hasn't telephoned... I'm sure there's a good reason for it. I trust you, Vince. I trust you *implicitly*.

You're not like one of those frequently unreliable boyfriends I used to have before marriage.

Oh Lord. Please help me.

But why should you – when you have your hands so full of people who may be the objects of genocide or torture or earthquake or flood – pestilence, starvation? Not just like me, I mean, rich spoilt snivellers who have no understanding whatever of suffering almost *literally* unbearable. (Yes, now that word can be justified.) Imagine, there are still places which use beheading, stoning, crushing – yes, even crucifixion – as a means of execution. There are still people in those places knowing that they are shortly – next month, next week, tomorrow? – to be faced with one of them.

What was it Humphrey Bogart once said about three people's problems, in such a crazy mixed-up world, not amounting to a hill of beans?

(Has it always been such a crazy mixed-up world? I suppose, of course, it has.)

And at least *he* was talking about *three* people's problems.

I spend the next half-hour sitting at the kitchen table, with a pad of Basildon Bond in front of me and Miss Pincher's fountain pen. It will always be Miss Pincher's fountain pen – how odd that somebody I've never known and who's presumably still living in Manchester and riding about on her old beat-up bike (you never told me that but it's the way I've come to picture it, blue like that young fellow's in the park – blue, my darling, like the colour of your own eyes), how odd that this severe and influential woman, who might actually have been quite pretty if she hadn't been so very disappointed in love, that she should already have appropriated my fountain pen and become almost a part of my existence.

Is that the way people will one day talk about me? *She might actually have been quite pretty if she hadn't been so very disappointed in love.*

Never mind. I complete my letter, read over what I've written – read it over a second time, a third time, yet a fourth – then sigh and tear it up into small pieces. These pieces form a little heap on the corner of the table, waiting for me finally to make the effort to stand up and transfer them to the pedal bin.

I'm tired; I look tired; I think it's all too much of an effort. I cover my face in my hands and sob.

Since roughly four o'clock yesterday – what, in just a little over twenty hours? – I've probably done as much crying as in the whole of the past ten years. (It was back in '74 my mother died.) Of course, I'd started even a little before that, before the boat ride, when you told me about the death of your own mother… *Was* it before the boat ride? Yes, I think it was.

But I mustn't get confused. I mean *more* confused, though in a different way. I mustn't start to remember any of it wrongly.

And I don't want to forget what you look like. Not ever. Please God I'll always remember what you look like. (What you looked like on September 3rd, 1986.) Please.

Like I said, though, you'll still be twenty-five when I'm getting on for eighty. Ninety. A hundred.

Darling, I don't even know when your birthday is.

Anyway! This is absurd, it's all too absurd. How long can I continue to behave like this?

I sit up – push back my hair – blow my nose.

Stand up – cross to the pedal bin – leave the kitchen and go straight to the telephone.

"Hi, Mads… I was wondering – could we meet for lunch?"

Eleven

The Bunch of Grapes lies fairly near the Heath. It's a pub which serves good food and has a pleasant atmosphere, to go with pleasant surroundings. We sit on an outside bench in front of it, with our backs comfortably against the wall, the sun shining on us, half-pints in our hands.

I've decided to tell her everything. Or almost everything. I won't worry any more that she'll laugh – her laughter could only be affectionate. We were at school together; were often mistaken for sisters. She's reasonably tall (like me) and still reasonably slim (like me) but wears her dark hair in a chignon – when I've frequently implored her to do something a little more fashionable with it – and is inclined to slop around in old clothes which I admit quite suit her but which she chiefly picks up at Oxfam or Help the Aged. She doesn't use enough makeup – sometimes, none at all – but has a nice face and a ready smile and most people I know (with the notable exception of my husband!) consider her attractive.

"So in case it should ever come up…," I say.

"Unlikely though that is. As you know, Duncan and I are always careful to give one another a wide berth."

"But what if he ran into Bill someday in the City? Remember, it happened before."

"No doubt to their highly mutual embarrassment."

"Oh? *Was* Bill embarrassed? Duncan wasn't. He actually likes Bill."

"Sorry – me being facetious! So... When you didn't turn up last night, why didn't we phone?"

"You merely assumed I'd changed my mind; the arrangement hadn't been that firm. And unfortunately the restaurant – small, new, French – simply didn't make it. Was obliged to close down shortly afterwards."

"Because it never received our custom? Don't you feel rotten about that?"

I try to laugh but my amusement doesn't sound convincing.

"All right then. Now to the nitty-gritty... A man? Yes, it's got to be a man!"

"Oh, it's all so silly. I hardly dare tell you. We met yesterday in the park. He was feeding the birds. We went on the lake, had lunch together. Altogether I was with him for less than six hours."

"It doesn't sound in the least silly. It sounds lovely – charming – romantic. What was going to happen last night?"

"Just a show."

"Supper afterwards?"

"Maybe."

"And after supper?"

"No, it wasn't like that. It really wasn't."

"Oh, come off it, Stell. Of course it was like that. How could it not have been?"

I don't reply.

"Tell me about him." She takes a swig of cider, then gazes at me, waiting for my answer. "It doesn't seem to have made you very happy."

"No. It hasn't."

"Oh, love. And I was almost feeling envious. I've never had an affair; not since I've been married. And I wouldn't go out of my way to find one – Bill's sweet, I really love him, I'd never do anything to hurt him. But all the same. At times I can't help feeling... You know, just something light and frothy. And new. Before I get too old. And lose the chance forever."

"That's what Duncan said to me last night. My being difficult. He ascribed it to the menopause."

I'm not sure whether that's either accurate or fair. I decide it may not be accurate but on the whole it's fair.

"Well, Duncan would, wouldn't he?"

"You know, Maddy..."

"Mm?"

"I don't love Duncan."

"Well, darling, I'm sure you realise you have a sympathetic audience. Frankly, I can't stand him."

"No, he's always at his worst when you're around. I think he may be jealous – jealous of our friendship. He hasn't been a bad husband. Always a good provider. We haven't slept together in years."

"Oh God. I couldn't cope with that."

She adds: "Actually I've surmised it – oh, from little odds and ends you've occasionally let fall."

Little things you've said... Little things you haven't... Oh, it hurts.

"He never calls me 'darling' any more. No endearments. And now I've stopped using them as well. Just Duncan; just Stella; all rather businesslike. I don't know what I've done. I don't know what made him turn away from sex...although I do know, of course, he's always preferred women who were much younger – for him, a move to Stepford in the middle-Sixties would have been everything he'd dreamed of! But I think I usually tried to please him... A touch, just a brief affectionate touch; a spontaneous reaching-out; any kind of real physical contact...now all things of the past, totally things of the past..."

"Have you talked to him about it?"

"No. We've grown too far apart. We don't know one another any more. Maybe we never did."

"Well, then. Perhaps this has happened at the right time. Your handsome stranger." (*Oh, I believe it! 'My times are in thy hand.'*)

Again, I don't make any response. I just stare into my nearly empty glass. But her sympathy is helping; has prevented me from feeling so very weak and self-indulgent – incomparably weak, incomparably self-indulgent! I can even begin to believe that, entirely due to tiredness, I've been taking far too bleak a view of things. After all, there's nothing to stop me leaving him a letter at the stage door, a letter more carefully worded than the one I scribbled in the kitchen. And if I do it this afternoon – who knows? – I might even catch him as he comes in after his session at the gym. Comes in for tonight's performance.

"All right," she says, following my lengthy silence. "All right, he isn't handsome. Let's just hope he isn't married."

"No, he isn't married. And he is handsome."

"What about gay?"

"No, he isn't gay. At least…I didn't at all get the feeling that he was."

"And indeed – why should he bother if he were?"

"Why should he bother anyway?"

"Because you're a damned attractive woman, that's why! You can't let Duncan rob you of your self-esteem."

It takes half a minute or so but her indignation finally fades.

"Is he well-heeled?"

"Yes, he gets good money."

"Doing what?"

"I'm not sure exactly."

"Well, that doesn't matter. So long as he's not a crook?"

"I could as easily suspect the Queen of running a gang of pickpockets in Oxford Street."

"Hm. Well, I don't suppose she does, so that sounds *reasonably* definite. I think you're half in love with him already."

I let the 'half' go by.

"But how come he happened to be sitting in the park on a weekday? Is he a tourist? Soon returning to the States or Dubai or some place?"

"No. He lives in London. Comes from Manchester but lives in London."

"This is getting better all the time!"

"Oh, Maddie, it isn't. I don't know why we're even talking about him. It's all so completely pointless."

"Why, Stell? What's the snag?"

"He's younger than I am."

"So?"

"A lot younger."

"Who cares? He could be a whole ten years younger. Grab him."

"You can take that figure, double it and add four."

The sum itself probably doesn't take more than a second. The incredulous re-check perhaps accounts for a further two.

"Oh, my love! He's twenty-five?"

"It wasn't me who was talking about a new husband. It was you."

Actually it wasn't; it wasn't either of us. But I can scarcely blame her for being alive to some emanation of it in the ether – one I myself might well have put there.

"Twenty-five – only twenty-five – but, darling, he's a boy!"

"No – that, he isn't."

For the moment, I don't go into either physical appearances or mental attitudes. It isn't necessary.

"What," I say, "when at eighteen you can get called up, go off to fight for your country, be expected to lay down your life? No, at twenty-five you're not a boy. You're in your prime."

"Yes, of course. Forgive me. I wasn't thinking."

She stands up. For a second – I'm so sensitive right now, despite the way she's just answered – I half-believe she's going to walk off in disgust. *Maddie*? Walk off indisgust?

"I feel this calls, cries out, *shrieks*, for another drink for us both! Something infinitely more potent!"

We are now at a picnic table in the back garden of the pub – still with our glasses of cider (I had protested against her getting, for *me* at least, anything stronger) but now with pub-sized portions of bangers and mash in front of us. Despite my having eaten nothing last night, and not very much this morning, I haven't been able to cope with most of mine.

"It still seems to me that the timing is right."

"Oh, please don't go on. I shouldn't have told you about it. I wasn't going to."

"And I'd never have forgiven you if you hadn't! But listen, Stell, I'm being serious. An affair at this moment could be the very distraction you need. And what might be a certain disadvantage in a husband needn't be any drawback whatever in a lover. Hell, just the opposite. Twenty-five and tall and built like a Greek god. And handsome with it. Wow!"

"No. *You* listen, Maddie. You're turning this into something which it isn't. Sex wasn't on offer – or, at any rate, I can't be sure it was. Friendship was on offer. Affection was. Concern; education. Laughter. Understanding…"

"Education?"

"Yes. A two-way thing. He hadn't heard of Noel Coward or *Brief Encounter*."

"Two-way? What hadn't you heard of?"

"Hang-gliding."

"Stell, my love, you're off your trolley!"

She then holds her hands up, fast.

"But stay like that – for heaven's sake stay like that. Isn't it the most lovely way to be? Indeed, you could make this into a brief encounter to knock *Brief Encounter* into a cocked hat. Much as I liked Trevor Howard he wasn't built like a Greek god. And he was married, too. Come to that I don't see why it has to be so very brief."

"No. Thirty or forty years would be good. Fifty-one, if I live to be a hundred."

She doesn't appear to accept my sarcasm. "Okay, we'll do away with the 'brief'. But, darling, could you honestly look me in the eye and say you'd be happy to keep it platonic? And don't go all prissy on me. You never have before."

"But don't you see what you're doing? Just setting me up for a catastrophic letdown. Of course I'd like...he's wonderfully attractive...and he stirs me more than any...more than any favourite nephew ever ought to be allowed to stir a maiden aunt." I see a raised eyebrow but I don't stop to explain. "Yet I'd far rather it was platonic and we remained good friends than..."

"But don't you think you might get bored with him as nothing but a friend? The young can be so ignorant of all the small events that have helped to shape our lives...the people, attitudes – books, films, plays – even songs... How much does one actually have in common with someone who's a quarter of a century younger?"

"Okay, so he may not know 'A Nightingale Sang in Berkeley Square' or 'We'll Gather Lilacs in the Spring Again'. In any case, the answer's no."

"The answer to what is no? I must be growing senile."

"Like his poor old foster mum." Almost everything I hear relates straight back to Vince. "The answer is no, I wouldn't get bored with him. Not for an instant. He's... Oh, he's not well-educated – and he knows it. But he learns quickly – because he's curious and notices things. For instance, at the start of our meal yesterday he was holding his cutlery... awkwardly. He didn't say a word, neither did I, but just a minute later he was holding it correctly." I'm glad it's only Maddie who is hearing me say that.

"So up to now he simply hasn't known the right people?"

"Only if you define the right people as those who hold their cutlery according to some absolutely arbitrary rule of etiquette! Otherwise, he's known plenty of the right people."

I feel angry. His mum, his foster parents, Miss Pincher – and that's only the beginning. These are only the ones I know about.

"Don't be cross with me. All I meant was...well, what's the feminine form of Pygmalion? At least, I think that's what I meant."

"Plus – as well as curiosity – he has innate sensitivity. He has innate empathy. He has innate..."

She waits obediently.

I've already mentioned understanding; don't wish to repeat myself. Can't actually think of anything else right now but that's my deficiency, not his.

"Innate everything!"

I give a little laugh. It's only a laugh of rueful apology but thank God I can give one of any kind.

"My God, you have got it bad! A faithful wife for twenty-seven years –devoted mother – model citizen – everything you should be; and then in less than six hours – "

"No, no, no. I *want* to become everything I should be. Wholly integral aim."

I don't laugh again but at least I do smile.

"There. Now see what you're doing. You're making me ridiculous. Egging me on is not the thing I need... As a matter of fact, it again reminded me of *Brief Encounter* when I picked up the phone to you this morning. Doesn't Celia Johnson do exactly the same thing: ring up a friend to get her to supply an alibi?"

"Yes but let's do something Celia Johnson never did – at least not in the movie."

"Which is?"

"Let's go and see a show built around some male striptease. Let's go and goggle at some hunks. Let's go and do it tonight."

"No."

"Why not?"

"Well, to begin with – Duncan. I couldn't possibly go out and leave Duncan two nights in a row."

"But if you remember, you didn't exactly leave him last night."

"Not for any lack of trying. So don't you think that he might start…?"

Maddie ponders this – and finishes off her last mouthful of mash as she does so.

"But what if I got Bill to ring him? This afternoon, at the office? Bill was talking about a concert tonight at the Barbican. Given by the Chamber Orchestra of…Budapest, I think it was. I'm sure we could get tickets and Bill may not be some things but he's certainly a good sport. 'Duncan, I've been given these two splendid seats, Maddie doesn't much care for Schoenberg or Shostakovich but I suddenly remembered that you did, and so I thought…' Ten minutes later we'll have Duncan giving you the night off."

"It isn't only that."

"What is it, then?"

"I don't know."

"Oh, Stell, I understand exactly what it is. You're afraid that he'll be different. In place of all that gentleness and sensitivity you've spoken of… And I sympathise, I really do. But you accused me of building you up for an awful letdown. Yet if you can't take both sides of him – because, after all, this is something that Vince clearly feels quite happy with – then let's face it: this whole business is a non-starter. It doesn't stand a chance."

"Do you think I don't know that? But even so – "

"Besides. It will be fun. Tell you what? After we leave here, let's go to a film or something, then come back with me – to avoid getting the collywobbles, like you did last night – and the whole thing will be a riot from start to finish. You can ring Duncan from my place. What's more, you can buy a new dress. Damn it, we both can."

*

I still write him my letter of explanation. I do this in Maddie's kitchen, not my own (is it because of her Aga that we often tend to sit there when it's just the two of us?), and this time compose a letter which she, wearing her glasses and the look of a school examiner, eventually passes as being 'unreservedly beautiful!'... and which then, following another car drive, I leave at the stage door just around from the Aldwych. But I don't see him. It isn't any longer so important: I'm given firm assurance he'll be handed the envelope as soon as he arrives and, besides that, with any luck at all, I shall be seeing him later on tonight. Equally, it doesn't seem so inhibiting that Maddie will be with us.

From the stage door I walk into the theatre itself and immediately approach the box office.

"Good afternoon – my name is Stella McCabe. I think I spoke to you last night?"

It is indeed the same woman. She's roughly my own age: plump, red-cheeked, a little thin on top. She smiles and says, "Ah, yes." She isn't the type I now picture as being scoffing and superior – I'm sure she left Vince the note exactly as she said she would. I apologise wordlessly.

And also not so wordlessly.

"I'm sorry I've given you so much trouble. But now my problems of yesterday have resolved themselves and I'm wondering if by any chance you might have another two seats? For tonight? I know I don't deserve them."

They don't really have any seats left for tonight, she says; but my disappointment's held at bay both by that 'really' and the fact I can see she's looking at me rather speculatively – I think I know what's going through her mind. It's something I myself had even been prepared to mention (very tactfully) if I'd had to.

"But I wonder," she says. "Mr Peters...yesterday...two very special seats... it's *possible* they're still available tonight..."

"I wouldn't mind how much they cost me."

In the end, however, I get them for nothing; so I go to buy a large and expensive box of chocolates and because there isn't room to slip it underneath the glass partition, Katherine opens the door alongside and shakes my hand and perhaps takes in all the details of my appearance so as to be able, later, to pass them on; but I don't mind, I now feel sure this won't be done salaciously. I return to Maddie, who's waiting in her car (earlier, she had followed as I drove mine back from The Bunch of Grapes to Parsifal Road) and tell her the good news.

"Stella, I knew it was going to be okay. Methinks you have a guardian angel."

"You mean he just waved down and blew a kiss and gave you a jaunty thumbs-up? That was kind."

She shakes her head. Her voice is disapproving. "You're sounding far too cynical. It must be Vince who has the guardian angel."

In any case, I should prefer that. Much.

We have decided we won't go to the cinema or even buy new dresses; not enough time. But the phone call to Duncan passes well. He's pleased to have heard from Bill and is still being entirely reasonable. He even suggests I should stay at Maddie's for the first part of the evening: he doesn't suppose he'll get back from the Barbican much before half-past-ten.

Maddie also has a suggestion. But for me, not for Duncan.

"How about our dropping into a séance? I'm sure they hold them in the afternoons. Then we could ask Noel Coward to write a sort of sequel to *Brief Encounter*. He could call it *This Time A Bloody Lifelong Encounter* and naturally – he'd scarcely need to be told! – furnish it with the loveliest happy ending."

"Thanks but *This Time A Blessed Lifelong Encounter* would be a lot preferable. If you don't mind."

It's blessing enough that from now on I'm determined actually to *count* my blessings, no matter how this situation will finally resolve itself.

Easy enough to do, of course, if everything turns out as I'd like it to; a little more difficult if the reverse proves to be true.

But at least I'm feeling confident again. This evening I shall be wearing the same getup that I wore last night...which is a shoulder-padded, baby-blue silk blouse, with matching slacks, self-coloured belt, kitten-heel sandals. As I've already said, Duncan always insists that for the theatre I wear something long but I don't think the Glory Boys are going to demand it.

It's a getup, of course, quite suitable for going wild in.

Well, we shall have to see.

Twelve

It's about twenty-past-seven as we get out of our taxi. (Maddie doesn't like driving in the dark any more than I do.) I give the driver a large tip, because I already know it's going to be that kind of an evening – although I'm none too sure what I mean by that – an evening when one shouldn't count the cost, presumably? 'The Glory Boys Up West,' say all the posters. 'A Musical With Muscle!' There are photographs too – plenty of large, blown-up photographs – but I guide Maddie past them. I don't want to point out Vince in just a picture.

The crowd standing in the foyer is predominantly female, although there are one or two ebullient escorts who are possibly indulgent husbands, possibly homosexual pals. The sense of expectation is high; everyone seems fully set on having a good night out. There are pinup calendars on sale – five pounds – and several women are already carrying them. But I shake my head at Maddie. (Tell myself I can always come back at some later date if necessary.) We make our way through to the stalls. Fifth row and a little bit off-centre. Just couldn't be better.

The show starts promptly. The rising of the curtain precipitates gales of welcome even if the dozen or so young men lining the back of the stage, and ranged along both sides of it, are all fully clothed. They're wearing tan slacks and linen jackets, long-sleeved pink shirts – whose cuffs, of course, are visible – brown leather moccasins. They even wear ties.

Vince is at the back and slightly to the left, though actually sharing centre with a man of the same height; he's one of the four directly facing us. (Yes, there are exactly twelve.) On catching sight of him I gasp – Maddie turns to me in sharp reaction. I'd been prepared for disappointment, because I knew that in my mind I'd probably built him up, physically, to even more than he actually was. Yet there isn't one iota of disappointment. He looks beautiful; tall, tanned and with that sort of nonchalant grace which is remarkably sexy. All the Glory Boys are reasonably tall; all of them, naturally, are tanned and well-built and nice-looking – but I think Vince would be my favourite even if I didn't know him. With a feeling of indomitable pride I point him out to Maddie.

"Oh, Stell. May I have him, please, when you're quite done?"

This isn't offensive; nothing tonight could be offensive. Even the most tasteless, tactless, jokes in the world…I shan't take exception to a single one of them. I feel I'm no longer the slightly anal Stella McCabe. I'm the potentially liberated woman striving to be everything she ought to be. It's a pretty wonderful feeling.

I'm aware he won't see me, not just because of the footlights but also because he won't be looking, doesn't even know I'm in the theatre. But all the same it's as if he's gazing straight towards me; and I soon find myself believing that he is. Whether or not he ever got Katherine's note I'm immensely relieved to think that by now he'll certainly have read my letter.

He was right: the music being played is plainly a medley of Rodgers and Hammerstein or Rodgers and Hart; and, shorn of all lyrics, is soft and pleasant and ideally suited. Up until now the men have all stood stationary but suddenly they wave at us – there is an answering explosion of approval from every part of the

302

theatre, and in all likelihood hundreds of reciprocated waves.

So now they're a little less stationary…yet not significantly so, each of them still keeping to his individual spot. I soon appreciate, however, that every movement – every turn, dip, raise of the knee, tap of the shoe – is not only flawlessly in unison but very carefully timed to the beat of the music.

Of course, it isn't long before things start coming off – their buttonholes to begin with, twelve red carnations. A glamorous young woman wearing a green bathing suit and looking like a conjurer's or magician's assistant enters from the wings and – also keeping time to the music – parades around the line of men, letting each of them cast his buttonhole into her gardening basket. She goes around a second time, not simply collecting all the ties but with a smile and a small curtsey on each occasion, undoing the top button of every shirt.

Then she goes, only to return ten seconds later with a similarly clad partner, the two of them receiving six jackets apiece, neatly folded by its wearer and placed cheerily across extended arms. (I think of the hours of patient ironing before the next appearance of such – originally! – smooth white linen.)

All this takes time but there's no feeling that it might be taking too long. Even the regular handclap that's now emanating from the audience doesn't indicate impatience, only a gathering momentum that is very much a part of the music; cornily – but effectively! – Rodgers has now been replaced by Ravel.

Maddie and I, both smiling a little sheepishly, have also been drawn into the handclap – well, didn't I virtually promise Vince? But, anyway, how could we sit there and not participate? Not *want* to participate?

The ties and now the cufflinks – who ever dreamt that the removal of a cufflink could become so tantalising? Even these small things have been choreographed: it's in perfect unison that they're thrust into trouser pockets, the pockets provided with a terminating pat.

After which, the slow rolling up of sleeves…all synchronised and all revealing tanned forearms, none of them visibly hairy.

Next, the undoing of all shirt buttons, equally deliberate. A simple act you'd think but my goodness how easy for an audience – or for Mr Bielenberg! – to observe if anyone lags behind or at any point muffs the unfastening. I feel sure all my sleep would be shot through with the fear of ignominious dismissal.

(A final goodbye to *The Glory Grandmothers Up West*, therefore. All this is too professional.)

8.25. Sweet heavens, it's only at this moment that the shirts themselves are going to be removed…how long has it taken? One could believe that none of us had ever set eyes on a man's naked torso before. Well, multiply this by twelve that are so very well developed and maybe we hadn't. Not all at one easy and comfortable viewing, that is. (More or less easy and comfortable viewing. One hopes they're supplied with theatre glasses up in the gods.)

The shirts are swung around this way and that, with much syncopation, much melody, much movement of the arms and hips; at long last to land up on the floor behind their wearer's back – so as, we infer, not to clutter up the centre of the stage.

Need I go on? Shoes, socks, belts, trousers, briefs – all dispensed with in that order and with the maximum of elegant gyrations; also with dance steps apparently reined in for now but conveying the impression that all twelve men are simply desperate for the moment when they can burst out unrestrained.

And once these discarded items – pink shirts included – have been borne away by our two smiling girls in bathing costume, once the clutter's been removed, then all those small-scale and frustrated dance steps do indeed develop into large-scale and liberated movements, with everyone expending lots of energy, whirling round, doing the splits (Vince doesn't do the splits), then eventually advancing into the middle, advancing, retreating, interweaving – forming a square, two lines of three intercutting two lines of three – you'd think it wasn't enough but the results are intricate and pleasing.

But as Vince had told me yesterday, this doesn't mean the men are now bare. They still wear posing trunks…or pouches… or jockstraps, I'm not sure what the term should be. (Maddie, likewise.) And by the time the interval arrives, the audience is in tumult. To shed everything but those pouches – or are they G-strings? – has taken nearly ninety minutes; one wonders what the rest of the show can do to cap it. At the descent of the curtain, Maddie voices her surprise at the amount of sheer *talent* that's just been on display. How many incipient Gene Kellys up there, she asks – if only they'd all been lucky enough to be in the right spot at the right moment! I agree – though I think at least one of them is a good deal more attractive than Kelly. Plus, it comes to me as no surprise that he has exceedingly nice legs and feet, to go along with the rest of him.

The only real surprise, maybe, is that the episode with the yellow balloons lasted for maybe less than thirty seconds and seemed so natural and so easily performed that I'd forgotten Vince had ever worried about it. Now I find it hard to believe that anything, *anything*, even so long as a year ago, could seriously have rocked his confidence.

(Oh, possibly the fact that he can't do the splits!)

As Maddie and I leave our seats the orchestra happens to be playing 'Stella by Starlight'. Which is something else I'd forgotten…whether its presence might be due to synchronicity, or to just plain everyday coincidence.

We spend the twenty-minute interval at one of the very busy, very noisy bars. And we eavesdrop quite shamelessly.

"The trouble is," says one woman, "it could make you feel so thoroughly dissatisfied with what you have at home."

"Which one would you pick," asks her companion, "if you could spend a fortnight on a desert island?"

"I'd want to take all twelve; draw up a duty roster."

"No, no, that's cheating! I'd take the one who let off the balloons. I like his face – his smile – his personality. I rather like the rest of him too, but obviously we're ladies and respectable and we're here to rise above the animals. Even when he's dressed I'm sure he has a very nice personality."

Again, I feel so proud. *Ridiculously*, I feel so proud. You'd think that instead of having known him for merely a matter of hours I was the person who'd brought him up and turned him into what he is today. Even if I had been, I couldn't have felt prouder.

"Here," continues the second woman, "hand me the programme... I don't care for his name so much. But he could change that, couldn't he, after we'd passed a charming little hour together and I'd coaxed him and bewitched him and driven him *madly, wildly – agonisingly* – out of his senses?"

The first one gives a laugh. "Vince? What's wrong with Vince?"

Maddie says to me: "Sure. What's wrong with Vince?"

The second half of the show elicits clapping possibly more abandoned than the first...that is, if I were competent to measure. This half has more to do with athletics – hand stands, somersaults, back flips – and routines with different coloured wooden clubs and china plates; several times it turns into a twenty-four-handed and wonderfully rhythmic piece of juggling. But since every movement has undoubtedly been choreographed to show off twelve young bodies at their peak of fitness, and since by this time all the men are glistening with a sheen which surely owes more to sweat than to baby oil, there is no feeling that the form of ballet now taking place – complex, harmonious, nakedly aesthetic – is in any way devoid of masculinity. Again it seems to me that the fear of one dropped club, one dropped plate, one misdirected movement, could so easily become the stuff of nightmare – and I wonder we don't have a dozen stressed neurotics in front of us rather than the relaxed and smiling people they appear to be. But I tell myself, and Maddie later on confirms it, that there must be a procedure to deal with any mishap: some form of comedic response – pretend beating of the culprit, mock hysteria, exaggerated mayhem? – which will undoubtedly draw laughter and applause from a hugely sympathetic audience. Obviously it's something we shall have to ask.

The exercises aren't done with. A vaulting horse is brought on; there's a game of leapfrog; a full minute of one-armed press-ups – these men are immensely strong. There's also a lot more music, more precision dancing, more clever interweaving – once more (I'm obsessed!), if the timing at any point went wrong there'd be complete chaos. 'Shall We Dance?' is performed with a dozen floppy dolls – rather funny.

Squeaky clean, however? Throughout, there's an indisputable desire on the part of the audience that those posing pouches – or G-strings or whatever – are going to work themselves loose. There's plenty of encouragement for the performers to make themselves comfortable and experience the joy of total freedom.

Indeed, the climax would seem to pander to this. A frenzy of horseplay develops, during which two gangs are formed – and now the music is from *West Side Story* – each gang apparently intent on removing every last trace of modesty from off its opponents. Both factions grow increasingly warlike: they growl, they crook their fingers into claws, give convincing portraits of rivalry and hate and of the will to win – yes, even Vince could be thought to look sadistic. For the first time, his ambition to be an actor doesn't seem so terribly far-fetched.

But all the coverings remain intact; illusorily, they must be very well secured. At curtain call the glares turn into smiles, the snarls into laughter, arms around shoulders, hands no longer poised to snatch and humiliate and delight. Even the two women in the front row who've been keen to rush on stage and help out with the removals – but who at last have been held back by uniformed attendants (unquestionably a put-up job) – burst into laughter and wave at the audience. The whole cast is waving; I only wish that Vince could've known I was there! Gracious, they must all be feeling so very tired (no wonder there's only one matinee per week) but the smiles and waves are so good-natured you might think it was a party that we'd been attending: a family party made up of exceedingly game relatives – cheering relatives – grandmothers most certainly included. The Glory Boys don't want to let their family go. Their family – oh, my goodness! – doesn't wish to *be* let go. It must take literally all of five minutes, maybe twice as long, before the curtain finally stays down, the lights come on, the show is absolutely over.

But there's still soft music to accompany us up the aisles and out of the auditorium.

One suspects it's been a really good evening for everybody. People will undoubtedly treasure their programmes and their memories.

Maddie and I decide that on our way out we're each going to buy a programme. Yes, and a calendar, why not? I wonder whether I might even show one of them to Mrs Conway.

Outside the theatre there's nearly as much confusion as inside. We start to walk along the Strand in the hope of picking up a taxi.

Otherwise, we can maybe catch a tube at Charing Cross.

It's ten-thirty, already night-time dark. But even so, before we've walked very far:

"You know, it isn't too late, Stell. You could always change your mind."

"I know I could. But I'm not going to."

"Spoilsport. Are you scared that once he sees me…?"

"With all the disfigurements you'd soon acquire? You wouldn't stay pretty very long."

She laughs. "Admit it, then: we did right to go. You're a lot happier now than you were this afternoon. *Would* you have gone to his dressing room if I hadn't been here? I could easily perform a disappearing act."

"No, don't do that. And, anyway, he'd hardly have his own dressing room, would he? Imagine me barging in…and finding all twelve of them either in the shower or just getting out of it!"

"Okay. I *am* imagining it. I'll make that my assignment for tonight."

"Besides. When I wrote to him this afternoon I wasn't sure we'd be able to get tickets. If I'd known, I might have suggested we all meet."

Something occurs to me.

"Actually, it wouldn't have been any different last night, would it? He'd called out, 'See you, then, after the show!' but hadn't said where – and you know how one's always reading about people going backstage to congratulate the star on her performance, and finding the dressing room already brimming over with well-wishers…?"

"Or, in this case, naked men?"

"Obviously, we're not the most organised of couples."

That final word… There's no justification for my using it – none at all – but, still, it pleases me.

"Well, last night," says Maddie, "wouldn't we have waited at the stage door? Isn't that what he'd have meant? And you could always do the same tonight."

"No, no – he mightn't be leaving on his own. And he might find it embarrassing."

Yet I don't suppose he would, remembering what, to the best of my belief, he hadn't found embarrassing at Selfridges.

"So how did you leave things in the letter? I've forgotten."

"Simply by asking him to get in touch. He has my address, he has my number. Besides, Mads, on thinking about it, we could hardly have met him tonight; I really ought to be getting back before Duncan does."

Even Maddie accedes to this.

"But we're all right so far, aren't we?" I'm suddenly anxious. Until this moment I haven't given much thought to the time.

"Oh, yes, I'm sure we are. But there may be a limit to how long Bill can keep him in the pub."

We cross the Strand.

"In any case, Stell, I bet we had a lot more fun than they did at the Barbican. And were a much more appreciative audience, even if one that may have seemed...just a *soupcon*...less cultured."

Thirteen

When we leave the underground at West Hampstead we're lucky and soon pick up a cab. Since Maddie lives much further on than I do, halfway along the Hendon Way, we stop first at Parsifal Road. She's already giving the driver her own address when I suddenly notice something which neither of us had expected. I tap on the window and she lowers it.

"Maddie, isn't that Bill's car?"

She leans towards me and confirms that it is.

"Then you'd better come in and have that cup of coffee."

I start to pay off the driver. Maddie gets out and even as she does so the door of the house opens and Duncan appears, framed in light.

"Ah, I was sure I heard a taxi!"

He calls back inside; Bill's most likely in the sitting room. "Yes, I was right: it *is* Stella! Oh, and Maddie, too. What a surprise. Full house."

Maddie says, "Hello, Duncan, how are you? I see that Bill's here."

"Indeed he is. We've been back half an hour. Pondering a mystery."

The taxi drives away, the driver raising his hand in farewell.

"Hello, Duncan," I say. "Have you had a good time?" I raise my voice as I step into the hall. "Hello, Bill!... What mystery?" But this is more to Duncan.

"One which you alone appear to hold the key to."

I close the front door, leave my programme and calendar in the cupboard where we hang our coats and umbrellas and follow Maddie into the sitting room – where Bill, of course, is still standing. He's about the same height as Duncan, a shade overweight, with thinning sandy hair, a smattering of freckles and a perennially kind expression. He's dressed in a brown sports jacket over a green pullover – rather than, like Duncan, in a dark suit with sober tie. I cross the room and kiss him on the cheek. "I'm so glad you're here. I don't feel I've seen you for ages."

"Yes, yesterday – last night – everything went so awry," murmurs Duncan, sympathetically. "And all because of me! Or, rather, all because of Thomas and his inconsiderate tendency to teethe."

I turn away from Bill.

"Or, rather, all because of Paul and Christine and their inconsiderate tendency to go to parties when they *know* he's teething."

Perhaps I shouldn't have said that, yet I'm glad I did – despite no one having an answer and the ensuing silence feeling a bit uncomfortable.

(Maddie in fact does murmur, "Oh, children!" But whether she's referring to Paul or to Tommy isn't clear. She herself doesn't have any children – which may rather limit the field.)

In any case the silence doesn't last.

"What mystery, Duncan? What are you talking about?"

It now strikes me that this slightly uncomfortable air may already have been present.

"Oh, sit down first, everybody – make yourselves at home. All will be revealed. You're looking very smart, Madeleine. You've obviously been on the town, the pair of you. I thought you were going to spend a quiet evening sitting cosily by the fire. What can we get you to drink?"

Maddie ignores this last question. ("With our tatting or embroidery?" she'd apparently come very close to asking. *Me*, I'd been about to inquire, "With our *knitting* or embroidery?" This shows how pretty much alike we are.) She's reluctantly taken a seat – and I notice, gratefully, that she's hidden *her* programme and calendar beneath her handbag – but she looks to Bill for elucidation. "Sweetheart, what's all this sudden cloak-and-dagger stuff? What have the two of you been up to?"

"Oh, no," says Duncan. "Oh, no. It's not what *we've* been up to."

Then he again becomes the host.

"Gin? Sherry? Scotch?"

This time she accepts, although her acceptance seems a little absent-minded. "Gin, please. Tonic."

"And you, Stella?"

"No, nothing." But then I amend this a little. "Thank you." It's as well to be polite. Moreover, it's as well to be politic – especially when you're worried something odd may be afoot.

"Oh, yes," he says to me, "go on! You must have something."

This, again, contributes to the oddness: the *really* good host, the *really* attentive husband? Is he doing it for the benefit of our guests? By now I'm growing seriously alarmed. (But how can it have anything to do with Vince? Vince can't have been here whilst Duncan was around. Obviously, Vince would have been on stage.)

"Besides… I consider that you might need it."

"Duncan, what *are* you talking about?"

A smile. Nothing but a wholly inscrutable smile.

"Bill. Please tell me what he's talking about."

"A rather common little voice. Wouldn't you agree, Bill?"

For a moment I actually think he's talking about mine – the reverse of when he'd been holding a letter in the hall and I'd thought he was talking about *that*.

313

Which naturally comes to me as something of a shock. It's not the sort of thing you say to a friend regarding your own wife.

But the shock is short-lived and doesn't prevent me – all at once – from realising what's occurred.

"Maddie, darling," says Bill, "I think perhaps we ought to go."

He's already started to rise – beer unfinished on the small table beside him – but I instantly reach out an arm and Maddie shakes her head. Bill sits down again.

"No. Please. Don't go," I say. "Who has a common little voice?"

I don't at all agree with the assessment but I know perfectly well the person being referred to. There has to be a message on the tape.

"Yes, who indeed? Now that's what we're hoping *you'll* tell *us*. As I say, you're the one who holds the key. I'll do the drinks – Bill, you switch on the machine."

But neither of these tasks is seen to by the men. Judging from Bill's hesitation and the fact he doesn't again attempt to rise, Duncan would have had to see to them both. (Even then, I feel the slightest twinge of sympathy: he'd clearly relied on having a confederate.) I myself walk over and activate the tape.

On this occasion, the usual faint whirring sound seems to last three times longer than it possibly could have done.

After that, there's something vaguely surreal about hearing Duncan tell the caller that no one's home at present.

"But if you'd like to leave a message, whoever it concerns will speedily respond. Thank you."

There's still a wait. Then finally –

"Stella, this is Vince."

Even under these circumstances the sound of his voice releases an instant surge of welcome.

"What happened last night?"

I think: By now, thank God, he's very well aware of what had happened last night (and of a great deal more besides: mainly, of why I'd reacted as I did after he'd asked about my happiness).

"Anyhow, that doesn't matter. I know there must have been a good reason. Can I come round tonight after the show? No, *may* I come round tonight after the show? I mean, for just a short while – maybe half an hour? If not, leave a message at the theatre or even a bit of paper pinned to your front door. But I've got to see you – I've just got to see you! Please. I think that it's important."

After that there's a silence. It's as if he doesn't quite know how to say goodbye. I often have the same problem. 'Goodbye' itself seems formal. 'Love, Stella,' makes it sound as though I've been writing a letter.

"Anyhow, see you later – I hope. By the way, I'm going out now to try and get that video. It's only about one, so who knows? – may even have a chance to watch it this afternoon!"

I receive the impression – for which I'm grateful – that he doesn't want to put the phone down.

"I don't like talking into these things; guess I'm just not used to them! Sorry if I don't sound natural. Stupid of me, I was even a bit thrown to hear your husband's voice. Don't laugh: I had to ring off and prepare myself and ring up again. Anyhow, I hope you're happy. That's another word I use too much, isn't it?" (I think he's going to say *happy* but he says *anyhow*.) "Yet anyhow" – he chuckles, briefly – "I hope you're happy. Goodbye, Stella. See you later on…perhaps?"

There follow three or four seconds while I wonder if he's going to say anything more. But – no – at last he brings himself to break the connection; and I too at last, as though awakening from a trance, bring myself to move away.

One particular set of words is running through my head, of course: "I've got to see you – I've just got to see you! Please." He likes me, I tell myself. He really does like me. He makes me think he wouldn't know what to do if I were suddenly to say…if I were suddenly to say, for instance, that we *couldn't* see one another again. It almost sounds as if he may like me nearly as much as I like him.

But how I do wish he had telephoned me earlier – I mean, before I'd left the house with Tommy. For a moment I feel again some of the desolation I'd experienced in the park…now so incredibly, so amazingly, unjustified!

Yet maybe Vince had been upset as well? Maybe he hadn't slept much better than I had? Maybe – mindful of the freshness he feels morally obliged to bring to each performance – he'd decided that he must try to sleep some more? I recall how Paul and Ben, after merely some party on a Saturday night or just a lengthy session at the pub, would often, in spite of their father's irritation, decide to stay in bed for the whole of Sunday morning and even half of Sunday afternoon.

Slowly, I turn back to face the world.

I even give a little laugh.

"Sorry to disappoint you. I'm afraid there's no great mystery to any of *that*! It's only someone I met yesterday while walking in the park. A nice young man about Ben's age. He was feeding bread to the pigeons."

"About Ben's age?"

"He's twenty-five."

"Thank you – I think I know how old my son is."

"I meant Vince, of course, not Ben."

"Feeding bread to the pigeons? Oh well, that's that, then. A sort of rustic idyll. Sun-kissed. Homespun."

He pauses; puts a hand to his chin, as though deep in meditation.

"Except… 'What happened last night?' asks this young man of about Ben's age and suddenly it may not sound *quite* so innocent or idyllic. 'Anyhow, that doesn't matter.' But I'm afraid he's mistaken about that, isn't he? It does matter. Our two friends here must have grown increasingly perturbed whilst waiting for their dinner in that little French restaurant whose name you had forgotten."

Oh, Duncan, this isn't the way to regain a confederate. Do you *want* to be out there entirely on your own?

"No – it wasn't Maddie and Bill's fault. They had nothing to do with it. Hadn't the least idea of it until today."

"Well, maybe not. I can accept that."

Then possibly he *doesn't* wish to be out there entirely on his own.

"So last night did you have a little tryst with this twenty-five-year-old champion of the pigeon world?"

"He wanted me to see the play he was appearing in. He was leaving me a ticket at the box office."

"Ah. Another small point clarified – and proving me wrong. 'After the show,' he said…but, you see, I didn't think he'd be an actor, not with that rather common little voice. I wondered if perhaps he'd be a stagehand; move little bits of scenery about – tear up tickets at the door. That sort of thing."

"Duncan, I just don't understand what makes you call a regional accent common. Myself, I rather like it. I assure you, there is nothing common nor little about him at all. Not in any way."

"My God. What *did* he get up to in the park, besides feeding those pigeons?"

"Now, if you want to talk about common, or maybe in this case I ought to say cheap, I didn't mean that and you know full well I didn't." I realise that calling Duncan cheap is really going to hurt and I feel glad of it. "You know full well I didn't."

"No. I know nothing. Why did he want you to see him in his play?"

"Why not? To me it seemed utterly natural. I'd told him you were away – wouldn't be back for another couple of days – "

"I rather thought you might have."

" – and he may have imagined I was lonely. Thought he might be doing me a good turn. And I thought so too. There was nothing…shabby or underhand about any of it."

"Nothing underhand?"

"No."

"Oh, did I miss it, then, when you said to me on my return: 'Darling, I met this young man in the park today and he wants me so much to go to the theatre tonight'? Was I merely hallucinating when I thought you said: 'Actually Bill and Maddie have invited me to this new little restaurant and I feel I can't let them down.'?"

"Yes, well."

"Well, what?"

"*That* was a little underhand. But not in any sleazy sort of way – which I think you're sleazily implying. If I *had* told you about Vince, can't you just imagine how you'd have reacted – not so differently, indeed, to the way you're acting now? Because everything you say is either snide or cheap or sarcastic. And into the bargain you'd have stopped me going. So what would've been the point?"

"Yes, of course. And also tell them how I'd have twisted your arm; locked you in a cupboard. Don't leave out the details. Have you been to see him in this play of his tonight?"

"Yes."

"And did you go backstage afterwards?"

"No."

"So he mayn't even have known you were there?"

"I don't suppose he did."

"In which case, perhaps we can still expect a visit? Well, that should be illuminating. 'I've got to see you – I've just got to see you! Please. I think that it's important.' What might he consider so important?"

"I don't know. Haven't the least idea. But we shan't find out tonight. I'll write him a note and tack it to the door."

"Oh, no. That wouldn't be fair to the rest of us. We're all agape to hear the answer."

However, I'm about to leave the room. Bill now rises again. This time he makes it to his feet.

"I think you'll wish in the morning that you'd kept all this to yourselves."

"Bill…," says Maddie, plainly doubtful. But she's looking more at me than at Bill.

"Sweetheart, all this is just between him and Stella."

"Between *Duncan* and Stella," says Duncan.

Bill ignores this pitiful interruption. "I feel the two of us are pretty much intruders."

"Between Duncan and Stella and Vince," continues Duncan, inexorably. "Oh, we mustn't forget Vince."

There's a further short silence.

"Though it's funny about names, isn't it? Vincent Price, Vincent van Gogh, Vincente Minnelli. It's only when it gets shortened, I suppose, that it becomes somehow…less dignified."

He's too canny to reintroduce the word 'cheap'. And I simply can't be bothered to take issue – partly, I imagine, because if he'd been talking about anyone other than Vince, *my* Vince, I might previously have agreed. I remember that woman's comment during the interval. But names change, I think, just as much as faces do. (And I wonder if Duncan ever came across that salutary little reminder in regard to everything we say: is it true? is it kind? is it *necessary*? Perhaps I'll write it on a card and lay it carefully beside his pillow, for him to wake up to and intermittently ponder during the course of a busy day.)

"Bill," he asks, "did you know where Madeleine and Stella meant to go tonight?"

"Yes."

"Then the sad thing is, one of the sad things is, we were having such a remarkably pleasant evening, you and I – one of the nicest I've had in many a long month… Well, never mind. Times change, times change. Twenty-seven years ago she never used to call me snide or sarcastic. Then it was a case of 'gentle', 'sweet', 'reliable'. But now you'd never think, would you, that we once made jokes and danced together and did everything we could to find new ways of pleasing one another?"

"True enough," I say. "But it isn't times that change. It's people. Time only reveals how wrong we may have been in not foreseeing such a big potential for change: that stripping away of all the onion skins."

319

Is it merely the concomitant of a new love that with Vince I don't feel there can be anything awful to conceal? No latent sarcasm or malice.

No, it isn't merely that. In fact, I feel the same concerning those other two people in the room.

Now Maddie also gets up – reluctantly – programme and calendar still artfully hidden behind handbag.

"If I were you, Stell, I'd hurry up and pin that piece of paper to the front door. Bill and I could handle it. I'm not too sure whether Vince could."

"Hm – interesting," says Duncan. "If he were a bit thrown by my voice on just a tape I wonder how he'll react to hearing it all live and unrecorded…"

He looks at the rest of us, pensively, as if actually awaiting somebody to give their opinion on the subject.

But then he shakes his head.

"No, not on your life! No little bits of paper!"

"Oh, God, you're such a bastard." Maddie's tone is almost conversational. "Come on, Bill. We're going. I was wrong a moment ago. I don't know about you or Stella but I'm no longer sure if *I* could handle it."

"Ah ha? Clever, Madeleine – oh, clever! (Stella's lucky to have a friend like you – I readily admit it.) You post yourselves outside the gate and intercept our visitor. You think I'd fall for that?"

"Well, there's not a damned thing you can do about it." Bill walks purposefully towards the door; Maddie gives a quick squeeze to my hand, somehow endorsing the notion that of course they're going to wait on the pavement. Intercept Vince.

Already practically out of the room Bill suddenly turns back.

"But, Duncan, you're right about one thing. We certainly did have a pleasant evening. Perhaps we can do it again sometime… after all this dust has settled and when the two of you…?"

Bill, it seems to me, would most surely hit it off with Vince.

"Yes? When the two of us…have what?"

"Oh, I don't know. Just try to keep things in perspective, that's all. *Act in haste; repent at leisure. You'll feel better in the morning.* And several other assorted *bons mots*."

Then he shrugs – with both a smile and a suggestion of apology.

"Yes, I know. All a little glib. But at the same time very true and worthy of remembrance."

A sentiment at once corroborated, it seems.

By the doorbell.

Fourteen

What follows is an undignified race between Duncan and myself to get to the front door first, a mad scramble in which Maddie and Bill, who'd both had the bad luck to be standing in our way, must have found themselves not merely whirled about but practically knocked down.

Kind people that they are, however, they've simply returned into the sitting room.

But in the hall I make a grab for Duncan's sleeve.

"At least let *me* be the one he's going to see first."

Surprisingly he utters no protest.

"There's only one reason why I've kept so close," he says. "To make quite sure you won't send him off."

I give him my word that I won't do that.

So…almost an Armistice. The door is opened less hurriedly than would previously have appeared likely.

Nevertheless a reception committee of two, even if Duncan is now standing a few paces to the rear, and even if our hallway is by no means an especially narrow one – this must be making the entry space seem quite unusually restricted.

"Well – oh, my goodness!"

"Paul!"

This exclamation emerges in such perfect harmony that Mr Bielenberg might have been in the cupboard with my calendar. Conducting us.

"My mum and dad together! How often does that occur? Talk about history in the making!"

But our having done so well in regard to timing has obviously taken its toll. For a couple of seconds both Duncan and I dry up.

Yet Paul doesn't appear fazed. "Yes, talk about a warm welcome!"

"In fact we were expecting someone else."

"Gee, Dad. Thanks."

"Darling, it's a bad moment. Why've you come?" And at *this* hour, too? – but I don't add that, although by now it must be eleven-thirty at the very least.

"Oh, it's Chris! She's lost her cigarette case. Been carrying on about it all evening. Suddenly wondered if she might have left it here."

"Yet couldn't it have waited until morning?"

Had the caller actually been Christine herself, that question would certainly not have been asked.

"Well, if you must know, Dad, it gave me an excuse to get out of the house – and I know you two have never been early bed-goers. So I told her I'd bloody well come and search for it myself."

"Then, darling, of course you'd better come in." I say this because Duncan is still barring his entrance. But at least my words oblige his father finally to move aside. "It's very nice to see you. How's Tommy?"

"Seems better. Thank God."

"Poor little love. And your party last night – how was that?"

It's at this instant, though, that Bill comes into the hall. He's followed by Maddie. Now there really is a feeling of congestion.

"Darling, I was just about to tell you that Maddie and Bill are here."

"But that Maddie and Bill are just on the point of leaving. How are you, Paul?"

"Fine, thanks, Bill… Maddie, you're looking very smart."

"Thank you. My Thursday best."

"Nice. But I'm sorry it has to be a case of only hello and goodbye."

"Yes, so are we."

However, the rest of what she's about to say suddenly tails off, because Duncan hasn't yet closed the door and we can now all see there's a taxi slowing down on the other side of Bill's car.

"Is this your visitor? What a *very* sociable night you're having!"

"Yes, aren't we? You all go in, please. He doesn't want the whole of London lying in wait."

There still seems a bit of a hiatus.

"I'll bring him through in a moment, Duncan. I've promised you."

It's clearly these last words which cause our son to look unexpectedly surprised and to make him glance at me inquiringly.

Maddie says, "No, darling, I think we'll just slip away quietly. If that's okay."

"I'd much rather you didn't. I think he's going to need you both. I know that I am."

Her decision is instant.

"We stay. Duncan, please for the sake of all of us – for your own sake – be kind."

"Here. Who *is* this visitor?" asks Paul.

But I suddenly feel grateful for his presence. Because of it – and I'm sure only because of it – Duncan allows himself to be swept back into the sitting room; swept back between the three of them…although it can't properly be said that anybody leads or that anybody follows.

Notwithstanding, before I move onto the path I hear him give a response to Paul's question.

"Who is he? He's your mother's toy boy."

"What!"

I'm forced to stay put a moment.

"Well, that was certainly kind!" snaps Maddie.

"Oh, don't expect to hear any kindness around here tonight, Madeleine. But I'm sorry, Paul. She's right. I shouldn't have sprung it on you like that."

"And *not* her toy boy, either." Bless her, that's Maddie again. "A friend, Paul – simply a friend. Can't think where your father gets all his rather weird ideas."

But that's the last thing I hear before someone – probably Bill or Maddie – shuts the door of the sitting room. And by then, anyway – obviously having seen the hall light shining onto the garden path, as if purposely trained there in order to greet him – Vince has settled up with his driver and the taxi is about to pull away.

I run to the gate and open it.

"It isn't too late, is it?" Without greeting, he repeats anxiously what he'd said on the tape. "I promise you I won't stay long."

Naturally I'm now wishing, and have been wishing for the past hour, that I'd written about Duncan's premature return, not just about Tommy's illness and his parents' urgent desire to be elsewhere. But alongside this regret, I'm fully aware of my pleasure at having him so close again. I'm fully aware of *his* pleasure, too, and of his overriding relief at not being turned away by a dark house and an explanatory note. "Hello, Stella," he now says, as if belatedly aware of his – to me, perhaps, more than to himself – highly understandable lapse in manners. "Stella by starlight."

"Not quite. Stella by sodium-vapour streetlamp, more like."

Tonight he's wearing a sweater in place of a T-shirt – a sweater which is pale blue, V-necked and, again, pretty form-hugging. Though at one time I might have considered this a little in bad taste, 'at one time' certainly isn't tonight. Tonight, in fact, I feel glad. He's looking great – just as great as he did yesterday and (albeit in a marginally different fashion) earlier on this evening.

He must sense, however, that there's something which isn't quite right.

"I *haven't* come at a bad time, have I?" He's almost echoing the words I'd used earlier to Paul. "You haven't got company or something?"

"Darling, either you've come at an incredibly bad time or you've come at an incredibly good time. We shall have to see."

It's only the instant after I've spoken that I realise how I've just addressed him. But, again, I feel glad. It doesn't seem in any way unnatural.

(On the other hand, natural-seeming or not, I realise I shouldn't feel glad. I realise I have a real need to try to discipline myself.)

"You're right: we do have company. My husband has come back from abroad – he wasn't expected until tomorrow."

"Had I better go, then?"

"No. I promised I'd take you in. And one of our sons is there as well – our elder son Paul. Also, my best friend Maddie, along with her husband Bill, both of whom I think you'll like a lot. Maddie and I came to see the show tonight – were given the house seats which (thanks to you) we'd have had yesterday. We thought the show terrific; really and truly terrific. And we thought *you* just about the best thing in it."

"Thank you. But what has he said about me? Your husband? What did you tell him?"

"He was the one who first listened to your message. Naturally he was curious. So I told him how we met and how old you are and how you'd invited both Maddie and me to see your show."

"Did you tell him I was a Glory Boy?"

"No, I said you were an actor."

He answers quickly.

"You're not ashamed of it, are you? Of me being one of the Glory Boys?"

"Oh no, Vince, anything *but*! Indeed, he must have sensed it was completely the other way about: how proud I was and how very much I liked you. I think it may have made him jealous."

"Stella, I need to talk to you about things! But not out here; not like this."

"I know. Not out here; not like this. Maybe tomorrow we can meet in the park again – same bench – about twelve?" The arrangement is made more hurriedly than would otherwise be normal.

"Yes, I'll be there – and on the lookout for you, supposing the bench is full."

"Darling, your coming into the house and meeting my husband, meeting my son, I know that this isn't going to be easy but – "

"You called me darling. That's twice in three minutes you've called me darling."

"Listen. Don't be nervous. I think you're very fine. You've got great dignity."

"I think you're very fine as well."

I want to say: "I love you, Vince." I know I mustn't. I believe he might reply in kind, which would be wonderful – everything, indeed, that I could wish for. Miraculous. But it wouldn't be fair. It would *not* be fair. He's only twenty-five; he's only twenty-five. He still has a whole lifetime ahead of him.

No, I'll settle for "I think you're very fine as well." Those are incredibly sweet words, which I shall cherish and keep snug and undoubtedly remember far more often than I should.

And, later on, I must somehow find a way of telling him: No, I *shan't* be meeting you tomorrow.

I've thought about this. Even in the theatre; even on the journey home. Last night; this morning. Percolating through all the pessimism and all the hope; percolating through all the dreams, percolating through all the fears.

What am I to do? When I'm sixty he'll be thirty-five. (All right, thirty-six…big deal!) What am I to do? I'm still so incredibly mixed up… But, basically, my clear bounden duty – the one mature and truly altruistic thing I ought to be able to do…

I want to be strong. I want to be everything I ought to be.

(Oh, but I have such a very long way to go. What on God's earth could ever have possessed me to call him darling – and, as he noticed, not just once but twice? Dear Lord, please help me do the right thing. The needful thing. Please help me give him up.)

"Vince," I say now, still at the gate. "I feel you ought to know something. I've decided to leave my husband. In no way is that your responsibility. It would have happened very shortly anyhow."

"But had it *nothing*, then, to do with me?"

His evident disappointment, his evident eagerness, are both so difficult to resist.

"No. Nothing. He may say some very hurtful things to you within the next ten minutes. You mustn't let them hurt you. You really don't have to stay here more than five or ten minutes."

He pauses before answering.

"I guessed that you weren't happy. I *knew* that you weren't happy. I really couldn't stand it."

My expression. He mustn't get to use it himself, *must* become aware of its essential banality.

"Vince…"

"If you're leaving him anyhow, may I take you away with me tonight? My landlord and my landlady have a nice spare bedroom."

Oh, stop it, darling. Stop it.

"No," I say. "You don't even know me, Vince. The two of us are strangers. You – owe – me – nothing."

"Yesterday morning you said we'd known each other ever since our meeting in a previous life."

"Yes, well. That was yesterday morning." How can a mere half-dozen words be so devastatingly difficult to get out? "Yesterday morning was yesterday morning."

In fact, we're both wrong. It was yesterday afternoon.

"Two minutes ago you called me darling. Which do I believe?"

It would be so easy to tell him what he wants to hear; to tell him what I'm so desperately keen to tell him. And I know it would give him confidence, help as nothing else could to get him through the ordeal which I'm sure lies ahead. Would help (as nothing else could) to get us both through the ordeal which I'm sure lies ahead. *But he is only twenty-five. He is only twenty-five!* In fifteen years' time, when he's still only forty and still at that very place where they say that life begins…

"Vince, we must go in now."

"When did you change your mind then? Was it after I left you at Selfridges? Was it when you couldn't sleep? When did you change your mind, Stella? Change it so completely?"

"They'll think we're not coming. We really have to go in right now."

"You mean, because you promised them you'd bring me in?"

"Yes."

"All right. I'm ready. I'm sorry about all of this."

Is *he* actually apologising?

"It isn't your fault, Vince. I promise you. Absolutely none of this is *your* fault."

"But if I hadn't left that message…"

Darling, I love you. There is no other man on this earth I could possibly love half as much.

But I say it only inside my own head, while praying dispiritedly that some emanation of it may reach out to provide him with the courage which he needs.

The courage which we both need.

We go into the house.

Fifteen

"Everyone, I'd like to introduce you to Vince – Vince Peters."
But the very moment I say it, what strikes me first is how frightfully middle-class I sound.

Yet even if while Vince and I were coming up the path and walking through the hall and I was planning the nature of my opening remark – even if I'd known how frightfully middle-class I'd sound, could I really have done very much about it? In civilised society, is there any alternative?

The second thing that strikes me, though, is considerably more gratifying. It's the unmistakable astonishment on everyone's face, other than on Maddie's.

So is it possible I've already grown accustomed to this man's height, to the fact he often has to bow his head when walking through a doorway, to the breadth of his shoulders and the narrowness of his hips? I both hope and believe that I haven't, for I myself should like to go on being surprised. (Though how can I hope for this to happen, if I'm never going to set eyes on him again?) I remember the pride I'd taken in strolling at his side the previous day, the number of admiring glances he'd attracted

– even if it's true that in my current state of stress I may nearly have forgotten it, despite the impact of his pale blue sweater only a short while previously.

But I think I heard a gasp as he followed me into the sitting room. Yet if so I'm not at all sure from whom it came. I only know (because old habits die notoriously hard) that I can't endure the fact I shall shortly have to say goodbye – that, in a way, I already *have* said goodbye. There could hardly be a more despairingly divided woman than me.

(How am I ever going to get through the next days and weeks and years? How am I ever going to get through the rest of my life – no matter if it starts today or tomorrow…which in any case, I now see from the clock on the mantelpiece, begins in about eight minutes? Not a huge amount of choice there, I'd quibble with the experts. *Feel the Fear and Do It Anyway.* I don't want to feel the fear even if I know I'm going to do it anyway. Perhaps I mean to get bolshie.)

For the moment, though, I am a credit to my upbringing.

"Vince, this is my husband – Duncan. My son – Paul. My dear friend Maddie who was at school with me, and Maddie's husband Bill. Bill Gordon."

Bill and Maddie, who've now been sitting on a sofa by the fireplace, are the only ones to rise. Maddie, being a woman, needn't have done so, but I guess she's deliberately making a point. For although Vince had certainly moved towards Duncan and Paul as each was introduced, it had soon become clear that neither intended to shake hands with him, let alone to get up. Indeed, I'd been vaguely surprised to see them both seated, rather than pacing about like caged animals expectant of nourishment…but perhaps their decision had been taken in the realisation they could then make the gesture of *not* standing up when the nourishment was brought in.

But this isn't without its irony. How extra tall he must appear from the very depth of their low seating!

Maddie is concerned to fill the silence.

"Stella and I – we saw your show tonight. We loved it. Haven't seen anything so wonderfully enjoyable since… Well, to be honest, since I can't remember when."

"Thank you, Mrs Gordon."

"Maddie. Since *My Fair Lady*. That was the last thing I think I enjoyed possibly as much."

"Yes, *My Fair Lady* was good," agrees Bill. "Of course, it wasn't the original production. No Julie Andrews. No Rex Harrison."

"I must be the only person in the world who's never seen it," I put in. "Original production or otherwise. I saw the film of *Pygmalion* though. That was good."

"I'm sorry – what's the connection?" asks Vince.

"It's a play by Bernard Shaw. *My Fair Lady* was based on it."

"What's a Pygmalion?"

"It's not a thing. It's the name of a character in Greek mythology who carved a woman out of ivory – *was* it ivory? – and then hoped to breathe life into her. But the play's a comedy, just doesn't have the music."

"'I Could Have Danced All Night'" says Vince.

"Yes, that's right."

"We have it in the show."

"Oh, do you? I'm afraid I didn't notice."

"Nor me," says Maddie. "There was so much going on."

"And the film…is it in black-and-white? Perhaps I ought to get the video?"

Oh, darling…don't!

I attempt a laugh. "Well, I brought you in, Vince – introduced you. I think you're now at perfect liberty to leave. Whenever you feel like it."

Bill makes a suggestion. "Though if that's not within the next ten seconds," he smiles, "and, heaven knows, I have no wish to rush you – well, then I might ask you to sit down. Or even *beg* you to sit down. It's unfair the advantage some men have, when they've done nothing whatever to deserve it. What gives you the right just to stand there – and *tower* – and make the rest of us have to crick our necks and feel inadequate? How tall *are* you?"

"Six-six? Six-six and a half? Something like that. May I share the sofa with you both?"

"Of course you may," says Maddie.

We all sit. I'm in an armchair closer to the centre of the room. I think he is behaving so very beautifully. My goodness, how he's showing up my husband and my son.

Duncan, at least, now feels impelled to contribute something. "Are all actors, I wonder, advised to be so nonchalant when asked for personal details? It seems to be quite common but I'd wager most of them know down to the very last hair's breadth: their own height and chest measurement and waist measurement, et cetera. What's the name of this show which you're appearing in?"

Perhaps that's not exactly small talk (and not *exactly* inoffensive either) but my son may think it is and may have decided he wants to hear something a little more to the point than all our comments on Pygmalion.

Because before Vince has even started to reply – simply hasn't been given the chance – "Will somebody please tell me what's going on here? Tell me *precisely* what's going on here?"

"Yes, I shall, Paul." This *is* my province, I believe. "What precisely is going on here – and I'm sorry, darling, but you've got to know it – your dad and I haven't been getting on too well for many years now, and it looks like you've walked in at the moment when we're finally about to split up."

"Because of him?" He looks toward the sofa.

"Because of Vince? No, not at all because of Vince. I met Vince only yesterday."

"Then what's he doing here?"

"He's here because your father seems to have gone cuckoo – no other word for it. But, anyway, all that matters is that we've now decided to separate – "

Duncan briefly cuts in. "You may have decided that. I haven't."

" – and in truth we should only be talking about this through lawyers, not turning it into a general discussion with even one of our own children present."

I glance at the sofa again.

"Maddie, may I stay with you and Bill tonight?"

"Yes, of course you may. And for just however long you want to."

I nod my thanks. "Then, Duncan, I think it'll be best if I come back tomorrow, to pick up my things while you're at work. A few of my things. That way we can spare ourselves – and everybody else – the embarrassment of any long drawn-out slanging match. Drawn-out and utterly pointless."

"Good," he says. "Well, thank you, Madeleine. Thank you, Bill. And since that seems to be settled so very satisfactorily, would you both mind waiting in the car? There won't be any bullying or violence – I can give you my word on that. But as you realised earlier…this is all, in truth, rather private; not dirty washing to be done in public."

His dismissal of Vince is far less diplomatic.

"You too. None of what I want to say has anything to do with any interfering stranger! You can see my wife tomorrow – that is, if she has even the slightest desire to see *you*. I honestly can't imagine why she should have."

Vince doesn't respond. He merely turns towards myself. "Do you think you'll be okay?"

"Yes. What he says is right – basically – although I hate his way of saying it; and I apologise for such plebeian uncouthness. It *is* best that you should all go. Vince, will you write down your address and phone number and leave it with Maddie. I'll ring you in the morning."

I say this extra clearly, so there's no way Duncan can possibly miss it.

Vince also expresses his defiance…although not in a fashion that can really be labelled as such.

"You don't need to ring, Stella. Don't forget we're meeting at twelve. Or wouldn't it be better – we don't know what the weather will be like – to make it one and instead of the park, at the restaurant where we had lunch yesterday?"

"All right. That would be good. I'll see you to the door."

"No, don't bother," says Maddie. "We'll see ourselves out. Come on, Vince. We'll give you a lift home and then come back to pick up Stella."

I understand her reasoning. It would have been awkward saying goodnight to Vince, even with only Bill and Maddie as an audience; equally awkward to have asked them – or hoped for them – to go and sit in their car whilst I said it.

And Vince appears to understand it, too.

"Goodnight then, Stella."

He also says goodnight to Duncan and Paul but of course – my heart goes out to him; again I feel so proud – without his receiving any acknowledgment whatever.

The three of them leave. Maddie doesn't wish anyone goodnight and Bill only murmurs indistinctly. I hear the front door open and close and feel that a part of *me* has also departed. The room seems suddenly much barer. Colder. Wholly foreign and unhomely.

"Paul, you as well. I'll look for the cigarette case in the morning. This is between your father and myself."

"No thanks. Damn that cigarette case! I think I also am entitled to some say in this!"

"Well, as you like. To be honest, I just couldn't care less."

I feel tired, inexpressibly tired, and I'm not surprised my manner should suddenly reflect this.

Duncan stands up – and not before time, either!

"Now that they're gone I don't know what to say."

He shrugs.

"Well, how about another drink? Paul, you haven't had one. Oh, neither have you, Stella. Now that they're gone I don't know what to say."

This – the repetition of it – strikes me as pathetic; in the sense of being pitiable. So I don't point out what I'd been about to point out: that even while they were here he'd said absolutely nothing of importance. His whole performance had struck me as woefully lacklustre.

Is this how it had also struck Paul, I wonder. Pathetic? Pitiable?

An issue which he totally evades. "I do, Dad! I know *exactly* what to say!"

"Oh, yes?"

"But not to you. To *her*."

He fixes me with the kind of glare which – whatever the situation – I'd never have received from Ben. I feel quite sure of it.

"You're leaving Dad because of *that*?"

He obviously either hasn't registered, or else believed, any of my earlier protestations. "He looks even younger than I am."

"A year younger," supplies Duncan. His tone is both complacent and obliging.

"My God! I'm so ashamed."

"Vince is merely the catalyst," I explain – despising myself even while I'm saying it. (And yet I do need to sound authoritative.) "Neither he nor his age has anything to do with it. You could say that he may have hurried things on a bit. But that's the very most I shall allow you to say."

Paul appears unexpectedly reassured.

"Then he isn't your boyfriend?"

"No."

"And you don't see him as becoming one?"

"No."

Strange woman that I am, however, at least I'm gratified by his acceptance – strongly unwilling acceptance – that such a possibility hadn't, not by any means, been unimaginable.

"No, I don't see him as becoming one. For his own sake rather than mine." I reclaim a little of my self-respect.

"What does that imply?"

"Well, as you've just gone to such pains to point out, he's a year younger than Ben. That's what that implies."

"But he's someone who you like?"

"He's someone whom I like enormously. He's a truly unselfish and straightforward human being."

"How can you tell that, if you only met him yesterday?"

"One can often tell these things in merely a matter of minutes. It's just something that one *knows*."

"And what about attractive? Do you find him attractive? Sexually attractive?"

"I think the majority of women would." *And a goodish number of men as well.* But I stick to what's relevant.

"The majority of women of *your* age?"

"Good heavens, why are you so obsessed tonight with age? Age is just a number – or so I've heard so many people say." (I'd like to believe it.) "But yes. At any age. One doesn't lose one's libido just because one's growing older. People can start affairs at eighty."

"Oh – just wait until Ben hears of this! Wait until Granny hears of this!" Paul is referring to Duncan's mother, with whom I now get on surprisingly well, although it's seldom quite the same as having your own mother still on hand. "No, you can't have thought it through. Granny's eighty-four and age isn't just a number, not in her case. The shock of it could kill her."

By saying, 'not in her case', is he admitting that in my own it's clearly rather different? I realise that, in the context, this is hardly a very noble thought. Poor old Norah, the last thing I'd want is to give her any shock that could seriously pull her down. But at least I can try to soften things a bit, prepare her for the fact of my wishing to divorce her son – and why should there be the slightest need for Vince or his sex appeal ever to be mentioned?

Besides, we all have our own lives to lead. That's unarguable, obviously. Therefore...so long as we're not talking about young children, or someone who's physically dependent on us, why should we need to feel responsible for the attitude of one single other person – mother-in-law, husband, son – or even mother if the case applies?

"And what about your friends: Tim and Elaine, John and Mona, the Wilkersons? You're going to be a laughing stock in their eyes. We all are."

Actually it's Duncan who responds to this. He doesn't say, *We all have our own lives to lead – would Tim and Elaine, John and Mona or the Wilkersons ever consider otherwise?* What he says, a little more succinctly, is, "Paul… This isn't helping."

But Paul is clearly as confused about it as I am – and have been – and most likely always shall be.

"Dad, she's got to be made to see how disgusting this is. Good God, I don't know how I'm going to break the news even to Chris. And can't you just imagine what Sonia and Barnaby are going to say?"

This really is scraping the bottom of the barrel; Duncan has never had much time for Christine's parents…regardless of whatever the feelings he may entertain for their daughter.

"I think there may be slightly bigger problems than what Sonia and Barnaby are going to say."

"And does he have a job? He looks to me like a layabout."

"Then you clearly need glasses!" I want almost to hit him. "A *layabout*? Because he isn't dressed in a suit and tie and nice stiff collar?"

"He's an actor," says Duncan.

"An actor! Then an out-of-work one, I'll bet. And doubtless on the lookout for an easy meal ticket from a gullible and well-heeled woman."

"Who shortly," I say, "isn't going to be in the least well-heeled. I'm sure he understands that – simply by listening, which is something you yourself don't appear to go in for, judging from your ignorant remarks."

But it's time to put an end to all of this.

"And in fact he isn't yet an actor. He's a performer. He's a male stripper."

"What!"

"Paul, that's a joke. Your mother's just having her little joke. Getting her own back."

I'd forgotten that this shocking revelation is as much a piece of enlightenment to Duncan as it is to Paul. And it doesn't even sound as if Duncan is believing it. My goodness, what *would* it do to Norah?

(Though – as I say – why does Norah even need to know?)

Yet it's strange how quickly I myself have come to think of male strippers as being – well, perhaps not exactly a normal part of life but certainly a healthy and a pleasure-giving part of it. If the Wilkersons for instance, who have a daughter of marriageable age, were suddenly to tell me that Lydia was dating a Chippendale, I now think my reaction might surprise them. Well, naturally enough, of course – but I'm still delighted at the speed with which it's happened. (One's always being told old dogs can't learn new tricks, a leopard doesn't change its spots. And so on. How depressing if that were true. I've actually thought for a long time that even in heaven we shall go on developing. How boring if we're never to learn anything new or never to be faced with any fresh challenge. How boring if we shan't frequently be called on to re-jig our own attitudes.)

And now I have proof I'm readily adaptable. Glorious proof. *I'm in love with a male stripper – not a doctor nor a solicitor or an accountant.*

(But I wouldn't say any of this to the Wilkersons. I'd have no wish to be stealing poor Lydia's thunder, if she ever meets that Chippendale.)

Yes, muddled, wavering, irresolute. In fact, at the moment I feel the age thing is all that's standing in my way. I may feel just twenty-five on the inside but I can't constantly be telling the world to look more closely. *Hey, that's me in there, still only in my middle twenties – you mustn't be fooled by the crow's feet or the lines or the wrinkles!* (Which I honestly don't believe there are too many of as yet. Thanks to *Oil of Ulay* and *Visible Difference* and all the others.)

On the other hand, there's no getting away from the fact that I *may* be tying him down and compromising the freedom that's a young man's due. (And I don't apologise for all of this being repetitive. That's what happens when your brain keeps on going around in circles.)

But on the other hand *again*...if I receive support, encouragement and help – and naturally I mean *his* – I'm as willing to learn as anybody could be, even as Vince himself could be, and with any luck might then become a far better and more interesting person – hopefully more self-effacing too – and in every other way much fitter to encourage *him*.

He could be Pygmalion; I'd be Galatea. Or turn and turn about. But only now and then. It wouldn't be wearily unremitting.

I'd even take up hang-gliding. If that was going to help him.

Truly, I feel I've never been encouraged before. Not, at any rate, since I've been grown up – or supposedly grown up. Not since my mother died.

"No, Paul, it isn't a case of my just wanting to get my own back. It's not a joke."

"Well, if it is, it's a remarkably sick one. And if it isn't, then you've clearly taken leave of your senses. Of all the cheap and vulgar and degrading – "

"Vince has a fine body. Why shouldn't he show it off, if it gives the public pleasure? And it does give the public pleasure. I can vouch for that."

"No, you can't. You're only one particular and degenerate member of it. That public which you're trying to vouch for."

Should a son ever describe his mother as degenerate – in any circumstances short of her brandishing an axe perhaps, whose sharpened blade might still be dripping with gore?

But people get angry and jealous and hurt, of course. Nor can it help that Vince is so very close to Paul's own age. (And I suddenly remember the cards he used to draw for me at school – he was far more conscientious than Ben and spent a lot more time on these – and I remember the string of pearls he gave me when he was seventeen, not real ones naturally, and how much trouble he'd taken to make sure that it was the best he could possibly get. In some ways it's still the one item in my jewellery box I really appreciate and value.)

"No, darling. Maddie and I went to see his show this evening." I'm no longer taking it on trust that either he or his father has absorbed everything spoken of earlier. "And we enjoyed it, very much enjoyed it. It was fun – lively – great."

"Oh, yes, I'm sure – *great*!"

"And anyway it pays him more than most people expect to see at twenty-five. So he hardly needs that rich and gullible old woman you so clearly had in mind."

"But you do know what people are going to say, don't you? They'll say you're a slut. They'll say you're sex-starved and deluded."

Like myself, he's plainly going around in circles; but, again, I feel he's bolstering me, rather than what he intends to be doing. "The happy slut," I think wistfully. Yet I'm suddenly not sure whether I need to be feeling wistful…even need to be feeling melancholy. I'm meeting him for lunch tomorrow – is there truly any call to cancel?

Duncan has now returned with our drinks.

"Paul, that's enough – that really *is* enough! I won't have you calling your mother these things."

"I'm only saying it's what other people will be calling her."

"And supposing they do? Will you let them?"

"Well obviously, Dad, it won't be to our faces! A male stripper, for God's sake! And probably queer into the bargain."

I smile. "What an added incentive for any woman who's a sex-starved slut!"

And while he's been talking I've discovered something else that ought to make me smile: I don't *care* what people are going to say about me. I just don't care any more. Not so long as I'll think it unjustified. How liberating to discover the only opinions worth listening to are my own and those of the few people I truly love. Vince, Maddie, Bill... Ben, Jane... It's an incredibly small number.

And although at the beginning of only this week I'd have said, "Yes, I care very much what people say about me," I'm now beginning to believe I don't know myself any longer. I always used to think I knew myself through and through. ("Know then thyself, presume not God to scan; the proper study of mankind is man." Hadn't I quoted that in the boat only yesterday – well, the day before yesterday?) Now I suspect I'd better assume I'd got quite a lot of it wrong – that vaunted self-knowledge. In one way this thought is rather scary. But in another it's...yes, it's challenging. And very welcome. I have a new woman to get to know, and make better than the old.

"*What an added incentive!* You don't even take it seriously. A male stripper. Queer. And younger than your own children."

How seriously *ought* I to take it? That's the comment which first occurs to me. How seriously ought anyone to take anything that basically affects only themselves? One's own life is more or less absurd. Other people's...well, when they lose loved ones, when they suffer from crippling disabilities, when they come face to face with pure evil or with sheer misguided humanity...that's obviously something else altogether.

But it isn't the comment which I choose to make.

"Not queer. Nor even gay. And no younger than Ben. I think indeed that Ben would rather like him; the two of them might get on rather well."

"Sure. Bosom pals – I can see it! I used to think that you had class. Intelligence. Culture. I used to believe you were refined."

"Oh Lord, oh Lord! How horrible!"

I'm sorry if it seems I'm making fun of him. But in all honesty he's not giving me much option. How long does this have to go on?

That same question must have occurred to Duncan.

"Paul, shut up. You don't know what you're saying. I think you should apologise. For twenty-six years your mother's been a first-class mother to you; for twenty-seven she's been a first-class wife to me. She hasn't thought of anybody but us. Until tonight you've always been aware of that; you've always loved her. Isn't that right?... I'm asking you a question. Isn't that right?"

"Oh, I suppose so. Until tonight."

"And now just because of some silly and unimportant little incident ...? Everybody's human, Paul. Everybody makes mistakes."

"Not with male strippers only half their age!"

It strikes me – though not for the first time – that Duncan has been quite civilised over this stripper business; can that be a part of *his* development? – and that over the past ten minutes, also, he's been dealing fairly admirably with Paul. (Not that I like 'silly and unimportant little incident'. Not that I like 'mistakes'.)

However, he continues to be quite civilised – and to deal fairly admirably.

"It's late, Paul. I think you ought to be off home and getting back to Chrissie."

I've been disposing of my Scotch quite quickly. "Duncan, I think I'd like another, please." While he's in the mood, I feel grateful to be waited on.

"All right, Dad. I'll leave – in fact will willingly and very gladly leave."

Yet when Paul turns back to me he's somewhat less accommodating.

"But I warn you, Mother. If you go through with this I don't think I shall ever want to see you again." I know he isn't referring only to my separation from his father. "That goes for Christine, too. And of course that means you won't see your grandson any more – of whom you profess to be so fond."

Paul has always been a person inclined to make threats and offhand I can't think of any which hasn't eventually proved groundless. (The one concerning Christine can be kept to, if he likes.) I'm not unduly worried; yet I still remonstrate to some degree, feeling I ought to show him I believe in what he's saying.

"Paul. Paul darling…"

"No, Mother, I mean it. Goodnight, Dad. I really do feel very sorry for you. After all these years you've been served a pretty damned rotten trick. And you never deserved it, what's more. Neither did I."

And then something utterly awful happens.

Awful – unexpected – heart-breaking.

Paul is actually out in the hall when, on a repetition of his final three words, his voice catches… and a hugely audible sob bursts out of him. We hear the front door slam.

Sixteen

At first it's simply as if we hadn't heard that parting sob, although my own eyes are wet – just as I'm sure Paul's were – and I suspect Duncan's may not be entirely dry. But he's busying himself with pouring out my second Scotch, even if I'm not certain that I still want it...it won't help matters if either of us grows tipsy. But, anyhow, by the time he hands it to me I feel a little more composed; and possibly he does as well. He's also brought himself a Scotch – one practically as generous as my own. Earlier, like Bill, he'd been drinking only beer.

I say: "They'll be back any minute, Maddie and Bill. We don't want to delay them."

I'm doing my best to keep everything as impersonal as I possibly can...which is why I haven't referred to Paul's departure.

"I ought to throw some things into a bag."

But it's as though he hasn't heard me.

"Stella, you mustn't mind all that. Whatever he says...once he's calmed down a bit – tonight when he doesn't sleep – he'll start remembering all the million things you've done for him, all the sacrifices you've made, all the endless bits and pieces which have turned this into such a very happy sort of home. He'll remember all the treats and games and outings, all the special celebration meals you've cooked. Those fantastic birthday cakes. The fact that you were always there when he needed you."

One phrase stands out. *Such a very happy sort of home.* Is that what it was? Intermittently, maybe, but surely that's the only word to use: *intermittently.* Had I really done enough; consistently done enough; put myself last, put my family first?

No, I hadn't.

Oh, periodically I might have tried. There'd been times during which I could honestly swear I'd done my utmost, but there'd also been times when I felt I'd simply given up, had wanted to run away, had concentrated fully as much on my own concerns as upon anybody else's. A phrase like that could make me feel extremely guilty.

But give him his due – Duncan isn't trying to have that happen. No, indeed. Quite the opposite, I'd call it.

"All right," I at last concede, "I think that by and large I've been a reasonably good mother. I'm not too happy with the way Paul's turned out – but, yes, I've always loved him and in his heart, despite those unjustified little jealousies he's often felt towards Ben, he must certainly be aware of it."

Unjustified? No, perhaps that isn't altogether true.

"So all right, I've been a good mother. But equally I'm fully conscious I haven't been a good wife – not for the past ten or twelve years, anyhow." (How stupid: talk about plumbing the depths of stupidity: I'm deliberately saying 'anyhow' and not 'any*way*'!) "Any more than you've been a good husband."

"Granted!" he replies. "Well, obviously the one results from the other. But I can change, Stella; and heaven help me, I mean to. You see, I still love you. I know I haven't always shown it."

"The pity is, though, *I* don't love *you.* You've killed it. Perhaps we both have."

"But you loved me once. If we could just get back to where we used to be…?" He spreads his hands – from him, an exceedingly rare act of supplication. "I wouldn't mind; I'd work at it. You'd find I could be patient."

Yet I'm damned if I'll let him get away with it quite so easily as he hopes.

"Patient? *You*, maybe – but I'm not sure that I myself could manage it. The best years of my life are gone. I want to use what's left; I want to use it now and to the full. I don't have any time for patience."

"No, but they needn't be gone, Stella, those best years of your life."

He makes it sound like an exercise in logic; gentle reasoning from a lecturer to his first-year students.

"In fact, they could be just about beginning. An entirely new start; a fresh slate; second honeymoon. After all, just look at where we stand today! No responsibilities; no encumbrances. If we chose, we could almost *literally* throw our money all around us. Left, right, and centre! Best restaurants, best theatre seats, best everything. Travel; round-the-world cruises; back and forth to Sydney as often as you like! We could throw wild parties, have other people do the work, put Mrs Conway in queenly charge, even on Wednesdays."

"And Sundays, don't forget."

"And Sundays too. Give hundreds to all those charities of yours. Live like there was no tomorrow."

"That's what you say tonight." Duncan was always so articulate. I already regret my jokiness concerning Mrs Conway's days off. I remember the sign he'd suggested putting on our garden gate. *The woman who lives here is a complete pushover.*

"Yes – and it's what I'll say tomorrow night as well. And for a million other nights to come."

"Moreover, I don't doubt you'd do your best. But human nature says it wouldn't last. Can a leopard change its spots? An old dog learn new tricks?"

Oh, Stella – just listen to yourself! Isn't hypocrisy one of those very first things you'd want to be shot of?

Duncan shrugs.

"I don't know about spots. Tricks. They can certainly change their attitudes. They can loosen up – learn to get interested in country walks – museums, cathedrals, stately homes. Get interested in Coward, Priestley, Rattigan. They can even grow to be quite romantic…remember how *this* particular leopard once used to be? Darling, don't you understand? I need you. I don't care what I have to do to win you back."

"'Darling'. Suddenly it's darling – almost as though you meant it."

"I do mean it."

In any case, I stand up.

"Well, I'll think about it. At all events I can promise you that much. I'll think about it. But for now I'm tired. Bill and Maddie will be here at any minute. I really have to collect together a few things."

"But you don't still mean to go? Surely?"

"Of course I do. At the very least we need to be away from one another for a bit."

"But we have to talk. There's so much we have to talk about. We haven't really talked for…"

"Roughly a decade?"

I had taken advantage of what I knew would've been only the very briefest of pauses. Duncan doesn't like to be interrupted. What am I doing in this instance? Boldly – recklessly? – testing the water?

"There you are, then." Not one sign of resenting my interruption. "A whole decade that now has to be atoned for…"

I feel his eyes skewering into my back as I head towards the door.

"Stella. You can even see him, if that makes a difference. I mean, see him as often as you like. Here at the house – anywhere – I shan't be asking any questions. I'll treat him as… He'll be a friend of the family. I won't make fun of what he does."

"That's certainly generous."

And I don't mean this ironically.

"I think it's impracticable," I add, "but I appreciate the intention behind it. Actually, though, I feel that in many ways…"

This isn't easy.

"…I feel that in many ways…"

"What?"

"It might possibly be better if…if I *don't* see him again. Cold turkey, perhaps? I don't know."

"Well, that would clearly be something for you – and for you alone – to make up your mind on. Nothing too hurried. I feel you need to think things over."

"Yes."

"Stella, I need you."

"I have to go and pack."

But he follows me as I leave the sitting room and walk towards the stairs. "And I think you need me, too."

"Oh, yes? In what way do you think I need you too?"

"Well, if at present in no other way…at least for all the good things that you enjoy in life."

"You mean for your money?"

"Isn't it possible that after all these years you may have come to take our bank account a little bit too much for granted? But if suddenly you hadn't got it…? And, Stella, he isn't going to marry you. Though even if he did…"

Duncan is staying at the foot of the stairs; I'm nearly at the top.

"In another ten years…," he says.

"In another ten years you think he'd leave me?"

"I wasn't going to say that. I was only going to say he might be unemployed. In that line of work hasn't there got to be an age limit? But as for me…although by then I'll be coming up for retirement, we'll still be well provided for. I won't be having to sign on."

"Well – as I said. I'll take all that into earnest consideration. I'll sleep on it."

"Yes, but Maddie…"

"No, I won't let Maddie try to influence me. I'll make a point of asking her not to. I'm certain she'll respect that."

He calls after me as I go into my bedroom.

"And remember. You were the one who spoke about his leaving you. And when he's the age that you are now – well, you'll be getting on for eighty."

"No, Duncan."

I'd like to be able to say I drew myself up to my full height. People should always draw themselves up to their full height at moments such as this.

"I shall be seventy-three."

"Eighty? Seventy-three? Same difference. He'll still be in his prime."

"Thank you." I remember Paul on the doorstep saying, "Gee, Dad. Thanks." There are so many facets to every individual. Duncan… invariably articulate. By no means so invariably the essence of tact.

But on the other hand. Is tactlessness a cardinal sin?

He even apologises – semi-apologises. "That may have sounded brutal. Yet a person has to be realistic."

"Does she? But, anyhow, what I meant was" – an out-and-out lie, of course, but too tempting to be jettisoned – "thank you for suggesting that right now I'm in my prime."

"Darling, I was talking about men. It's different for men."

"I see. So *you're* still in your prime…but *me*, I'm well over the hill by now? A depressing old has-been? Whatever happened to Women's Lib?"

He's now standing in the doorway to my bedroom. "No, no, no. You're trying to pick a quarrel!" (Didn't he see that I was being facetious? I think Vince would have seen it.)

By this time I have my overnight bag open on the bed. I'm folding a nightdress to transfer into it.

"I wish you weren't doing this. As Bill remarked earlier – however banal it might have sounded at the time – all we need is a sense of proportion. We don't have to separate for lack of that."

He comes up behind me while I'm tucking my slippers beneath the nightgown; puts his arms around my waist.

"I haven't felt you close like this for such a time," he says. "You just don't know how good it feels; you don't know how very much I've missed you. Turn around a moment, darling. Let me hold you properly. Let me see your face."

"No, Duncan. Please. You're rushing things."

I break away but he follows me into my bathroom, where I'm collecting spongebag and flannels and toothbrush.

"I beg you not to keep me at a distance."

"Well, how can you expect me to do otherwise, after so many years of abstinence?" I keep my back turned.

"I didn't want that abstinence."

"But it was you who moved into the other room."

"Yes, because of my insomnia! That whole big shake-up at the company – and so many men much younger than myself suddenly being made redundant! It woke you up whenever I grew restless. What's more, I couldn't even put on the lamp – though naturally without light I wasn't able to read. And if I got out of bed…well, that disturbed you, too."

Reasonable, reasonable. Insidiously reasonable. Indeed, it had been partly my own idea for him to move, so that he *could* turn on a lamp without his needing to worry. I didn't remind him of this.

"But let me ask you – after all of that was over, did you ever make the slightest attempt to come back?"

"You never seemed to want me. And a man has his pride."

"Pride? Mere pride? Often, I also sensed hostility."

"But not directed at you. At the world maybe. But not at you. Or at least… only on occasion."

Despite myself, I'm impressed by his honesty. Yet I'm still determined not to make it plain sailing.

"It wasn't easy to distinguish."

"I've really missed you, darling. Do you know that? I've really missed you."

He must have seen me waver. I'd been looking at him only in the mirror of the medicine cabinet. But he must have seen me waver.

"Just now you packed your nightie. Why not put it on instead? Isn't there still that bottle of Moet in the cellar? Let me pop it in the freezer for a minute. Champagne is definitely what's called for at a moment such as this."

"Duncan…"

"Oh, and with any luck Bill and Maddie will arrive while I'm down there and I can let them know you've changed your mind. I'll shake them by the hand and assure them there are no hard feelings. I'll invite them round for dinner – say, tomorrow night? I'll tell them how much I admired the way that Maddie stood up for you! I was a pig. I've always been a pig. We'll drink to the end of all such piggery. She and I may really get to like one another."

He goes lightly from the room. At first I hold out a hand as if to restrain him but then I let it fall. He calls to me from some point on the stairs – or maybe he's already at the bottom. "Till death us do part, remember? We'll drink to that as well."

Unexpectedly he laughs.

"I think you also promised to obey."

"Then, if I did, what a total fool I was." But this most certainly isn't intended as facetious; no link to humour whatsoever. "I think just now *you* promised to be patient."

Again, a statement of unwavering seriousness.

"Then – if I did – oh, what a total fool I was!"

He pauses…maybe in the hope that I'm going to betray a modicum of amusement. Reluctant or otherwise.

"But anyway it wasn't quite a promise," he points out. "Nor did you seem to welcome it. You said you hadn't time."

I can still hear his laughter as he moves into the kitchen – I think it's the kitchen – presumably now making his way down into the cellar. I give a sigh. I feel exhausted. I no longer feel like twenty-five. No, right at this moment *ninety*-five might be closer.

And right at this moment, too, the idea of looking for a flat… the idea of looking for a job…

I'm sorry, Vince. But this is truly how it has to end.

Perhaps it's as well, I think, that Duncan should be laughing. Perhaps it's just as well he sounds so resolute, so optimistic, about the making of a fresh start. I suppose there must be thousands of middle-aged women – thousands? millions! – who'd declare I neither recognised nor appreciated my own practically unheard-of (and, yes, wholly unmerited) good fortune. At heart he must really be a good man – an unusually good man; that's what these women would declare.

And – who knows? – I may even be starting to agree with them.

Seventeen

Shamefully, of all the many points he's raised, it's those about travel and the general throwing around of money which have impressed me most. How superficial! How untimely! Just when Stella McCabe might have been on the brink of becoming a new woman! Now it seems improbable she's ever going to change – well, certainly not in any truly meaningful or positive a fashion. She's more likely just to be accepting of the prevailing status quo, rather than to put up much resistance to it. Perhaps doing what she can to make the most of things and simulate enjoyment?

And possibly that's as it should be. After all, under the circumstances there wasn't any real alternative, was there?

And possibly, too, before very long I shall even have learned to count my blessings – *again*!

Principal blessing? That at present, for example, there should still have been room for this very rapid build-up of reasonable argument – this brick-by-brick expansion of sheer common sense – and that I hadn't altogether destroyed its obvious potential. I don't love him any more but it seems he still *is* a pretty decent man at heart and I suppose that – in the face of such goodwill – love can gradually return. Quite plainly, I should start showing some goodwill of my own. During the past ten minutes or so, all of it's been coming from him; been coming *only* from him.

'Till death us do part…' Is that where reality lies? So maybe *this* is the beginning of my ultimate development: that I should now be ready to face that reality and – if not for the moment exactly to embrace it – at least to take one step closer to the true acceptance of it. The *mature* and responsible acceptance of it.

Courageous, positive, clear-thinking.

Yes!

If life is all about acceptance…which categorically it ought to be. Not resignation, clearly. It doesn't have to feel like that. Tomorrow morning when I'm fresher, that's the very first thing that I'll attend to. (I solemnly promise myself.) *One's character is built upon the ashes of one's despair.* I can't remember who actually said that – Rousseau? I'm almost sure it was – but this vaguely comforting edict has been with me ever since I was a teenager. It spoke of development arising out of misery…and it was universal, all part of the human comedy.

All part of the human comedy. Possibly my original mantra, or at any rate the first I can remember. I think I used to change my mantras roughly every week.

I start to unpack my suitcase. There isn't much in it. I return some makeup to the top of my dressing table. And as I do so, a tear runs down my cheek. I brush it away, impatiently. The telephone rings.

Oh my God, I think. It's Vince.

But that's crazy. Why should it be Vince ringing at nearly one o'clock in the morning? It wouldn't be like him at all. He'd have far too much consideration.

Yet he knows I'll still be up, or anyhow suspects it, and there could be some desperately important reason – perhaps simply because he's sure it'll bring reassurance and will help me sleep? Dear Lord. Sweet Lord. Vince is my first and only thought. It has to be Vince.

There's an extension on my bedside table. I suddenly realise I must get to it before my husband picks up. This could be vital; the one deciding factor. (Deciding *what*?) Duncan could still be in the cellar.

But he isn't in the cellar. He's just beaten me to it…by the fraction of a fraction of a second! And it isn't Vince, how could I ever have thought it would be? Of all the people in this world whom (God alone knows) we really don't need to be in touch with right now –

Christine!

"Oh, Duncan, I've only just heard. I can't tell you how terribly shocked I am. I still can't bring myself quite to believe it."

"Ah, Chrissie… Chrissie, my dear. That's very sweet. But not to worry. I've –"

"I know I shouldn't be saying this – but, Duncan, she's such a bitch! Poppet, you're worth twenty dozen of the likes of her. I've always thought so. I can't think how you've stood it for so long. I really can't."

"No, no, my dear. You're very kind and sweet and sympathetic but you don't yet know what's happened. The situation is – "

"And as if all that wasn't enough, oh my God, you're just so good! There's no one else I know who'd still be such a gentleman after all you've just been through. You really are the most amazing man. And so attractive too; I think she must be gaga. Sometimes I've even thought that if you hadn't been Paul's father… And she goes for a boy – an ignorant peasant from Liverpool or somewhere who's still wet behind the ears and who actually makes his living (no, please tell me that this can't be true!) in the sleazy world of Soho striptease and gay pornography – goes for *him* in preference to a…! Well, let me only tell you this. It's the very best thing that could have happened to you, Duncan – especially while you're still so young and vigorous and bursting with energy. Darling, when this gets out, the scores of women you'll be having to fend off! The scores who'll be lining up outside your door and cutting off their arms and legs in order to hurl themselves at your feet!"

She warms to this theme; now she even has them bending over backwards.

"I can see I'm going to have my work cut out, just looking after your interests. Any one of them will appreciate you more than Stella ever did, but this time we're going to see you end up with the absolute best. That's what you deserve, you saintly Duncan. And that, my love, is what you're going to get."

I have been standing there, quite woodenly, listening to all of this, but now I lay the receiver down on top of the duvet and walk quietly down the stairs. Still quite woodenly, I think – even robotically. I stand in the open doorway to the sitting room and watch my unsuspecting husband as he sinks luxuriously into his usual armchair.

"Chrissie, my sweet, you certainly know how to boost an old man's ego – no, no, please let me finish – and I've always been aware of the warmth and tenderness beneath your sometimes joshing ways. Paul's a very lucky man and it would be seriously unnatural if I didn't at moments feel a little envious. But you *must* allow me to explain. The situation's changed. Stella isn't going; I've won her round, we're going to make a fresh start. Good common sense has reasserted itself and from now on it's going to be nothing but blue skies. We're just about to drink to it – I mustn't keep her waiting. But there's one thing I must say before I let you go. I shan't ever forget the way you rallied round like this, when you thought I was in trouble; I always hold it's when the chips are down that you find out who your true friends really are – true, and honest, and eternally dependable."

I go silently upstairs again, retrieve the underwear and tights I'd put back in a drawer, my makeup from the dressing table, my washing things and other bits and pieces from the places where they normally reside – where they normally *used to* reside. I close the bag and return with it to the doorway of the sitting-room. Duncan is still talking.

"Oh, no, I feel quite sure we've seen the last of him. Really, it wasn't any contest. Just a gift-wrapped set of muscles, every bit as gormless as you'd expect. But of course we'll have to give her a brief period in which to wipe all that egg off her face. How about this: one day you and I could go to see him do his act, pelt him with rotten tomatoes – well, at least have a jolly good belly laugh? Our own little secret; our own little assignation! Darling, I really must go. Bless you for phoning and for being so nice... Yes, yes, I will, I promise... Goodnight, then, and sleep well... Goodnight... Yes, yes and you... Goodnight."

He puts down the receiver, continues a moment to sit there on the edge of the table to which patently he had removed himself whilst I was still upstairs. He sits there, swinging his foot and smiling.

Then he gets up; turns round and sees me.

But he doesn't see my packed bag, which I've set down in the hallway, beyond his line of vision.

"Stella! What're you doing down here? I'm sorry that I've been so long. That was Chrissie on the phone – just couldn't get rid of her! But her relief at hearing that our little contretemps is now over! I wish you could have heard it. I think you'd have been really quite moved."

"Mm."

"And, dearest, I thought that you were changing. You've been just as slow as I have!"

"No, Duncan. There you're actually in a class of your own. But a person has to be realistic, you know. Though you're not even gift-wrapped or beribboned. Oh dear. Did no one consider it worth the trouble?"

Eighteen

I think there must be a patron saint for bridge-burners; for even as I pick up my bag and walk to the front door there comes the long-awaited knock.

Long-awaited…but oh such very beautiful timing! Despite the fact, scarcely noticed, that it has now started to rain. Fairly heavily.

At the kerb is Bill's car.

But it isn't Bill who's standing on the doorstep.

Nor is it Maddie

Vince leans forward to take my bag from me.

"Am I dreaming? I thought you'd be back in Stoke Newington by now, safely tucked up in your bed! Actually, I thought you'd have been there at least an hour ago."

"No. Maddie didn't take me to Stoke Newington. Nor did Bill. You can't trust them. They're not people of their word."

"But I don't understand. Why are you *here*? Where've you been all this time?"

"At headquarters," he says. "Being grilled."

"Scotland Yard, you mean? MI6? Wormwood Scrubs?"

"Worse."

"Hendon Way?"

He nods.

"Grilled about what?"

By now we're at the car and he's holding open the door of the passenger seat. None of this seems real.

"About whether I'm worthy of you or not."

"Darling, this is mad."

But I can't help asking. "And are you?"

"What? Mad?"

"No. Worthy of me."

"Apparently I am. And to prove it I shall be given the Good Housekeeping Seal of Approval. But naturally I had to lie before I could get it. Lie my socks off."

His socks must have been returned to him. I get a glimpse of them while he's settling himself into the driving seat. His manoeuvres remind me of Rock Hudson in *Pillow Talk* – who was also much too tall to fit in easily behind the wheel.

"You wouldn't know how to lie," I say. "You wouldn't have the first idea."

"Well…perhaps not in comparison to you."

I glare at him. I glare like my son Paul or even like Miss Pincher herself. "And what exactly do you mean by that, Vince Peters?"

"This is exactly what I mean by that, Stella McCabe. After she'd gone on and on about *me* – Maddie – the conversation then turned more interesting and we started talking about *you*. And she assured me – *assured* me – that you'd been lying when I first arrived, lying to me and making me feel miserable…and all because you thought you were doing it for my own good. Was she right about that?"

By now, I'm altogether past the lying stage. It's nearly two o'clock in the morning. I no longer have the energy.

"Only about one hundred percent."

"Is that all? But, anyhow, I'm the one who knows what's best for me; you don't – please remember that! And added to this, Maddie claims to be the one who knows what's best for *you*! I'm afraid that for the moment there's nowhere that you, Mrs McCabe, can even hope to get a look-in."

I'm so fed up with arguing – I mean, arguing with myself more than with anyone else – I don't mind there being nowhere I can even hope to get a look-in. Not on those terms.

But I decide to keep it practical. "By the way, Vince. I've decided to revert to my maiden name. Stella Dodd."

He's started the car. I take his arm and lean against his shoulder. Hampering him already, I think – *crowding* him, almost pushing him into a corner. He doesn't object. On the contrary, he touches my forehead with the fingertips of his left hand, lightly running them across.

"Where are we going?" I ask.

"Stoke Newington, of course. I told you that my landlords have a spare room."

"So you did."

"Although I'm rather hoping…"

"What?"

"That we shan't be needing it."

I snuggle up a little closer.

"Shall we drive?" he says. And indeed, having put the question, he immediately starts to do so.

"Dum, dum, dum," I reliably, and most professionally, put in.

And there's not the least requirement for me to give any additional response.

But, instead, I inquire about something a little different. "On a wet road of music, shall we drive? Dum, dum, dum. Shall we drive?" I know I'm exceeding my remit.

"Or perchance – when that last little star has left the sky – dum, dum, dum. Shall we then say goodnight and mean goodbye?"

He's exceeding his, as well – probably because he thinks I'm tired – but even so…no, we can't have that. I wait for him to do a repeat. Vince the consummate performer, even after a three-hour show.

And I'm not disappointed. I *know* him. "When that last little star has left the sky…," he reprises.

My moment. I hastily step in. "Shall we still be together, with our arms around each other, and shall you be my new romance? On the clear understanding that this kind of thing can happen…"

"*All* of that? *All* of that?" he breaks in. "My goodness, aren't you hogging it a bit?"

"No. Simply getting my own back." (Can you hear me, Paul?) "Simply getting my own back, pure and simple. Wreaking my revenge."

I can see him thinking about that word, 'wreaking'. But all he says is: "Revenge for what?"

"Oh, a slightly more sensitive person wouldn't even have to ask. But – naturally – my revenge for your having commandeered all my dum, dum, dums. And hoping that I wouldn't even notice."

"It's true, I didn't think you'd notice."

"Or that I wouldn't guess your motivation."

"My motivation? What was my motivation?" he inquires, obligingly.

"Nothing but jealousy! Pure jealousy!"

After a moment he admits to it. "All right. But I can't always be the backing singer. I want to be the star."

"Tough! What's more, you may have *said* you were going to get me a contract from Mr Bielenberg. But did you actually do it? Ha!"

"Tomorrow, lady! I'll do it tomorrow!"

"And you expect me to believe that? Still…you can reckon yourself lucky. I have a *beautifully* forgiving nature. So…shall we drive?"

"Shall we drive? On a wet road of music shall we drive?" And without even a single dum-dum-dum's encroachment.

"Shall we then say goodnight and mean goodbye? Or perchance…" I leave the rest of it hanging. There's no need to endlessly repeat ourselves.

We drive. We're now heading towards Chalk Farm and Camden Town and Euston. I wonder if Maddie and Bill advised him on the best route back to Stoke Newington. (Indeed, they've even given him a little map. On top of this has been written, 'Temporary Good Housekeeping Seal of Approval – please expect something more permanent to shortly take its place.' Like me, when it sounds necessary, Bill doesn't at all object to splitting an infinitive.)

I still have my head comfortably against his shoulder. "At any rate I hope you noticed something just now? That it was I who had the last word. Shape of things to come?"

"Darling, by any chance…are you flirting with me?"

Not strictly. Merely being provocative and sounding maybe sickeningly smug. But who cares? That 'darling'…it was slipped in so very casually. The first time he's done it. My present reaction is pretty much the same as when he'd first called me Stella. How can I possibly be so happy? How can *anyone* possibly be so happy? It's only an hour or two since I believed my world to be irretrievably lost. How can everything have changed so quickly? And all because the sun came out on Wednesday, therefore I decided to take a walk in Queen Mary's Garden, happened to be a little later than I might otherwise have been? Can life really depend on such apparently thin and unimportant threads?

He adds: "I am sorry. I'll have to struggle with that jealousy. You know – in truth – I feel I could get to like the star. Really like her. Given enough time."

"Darling, by any chance…are you flirting with me?" This is such a long way from any conversation I ever held with Duncan. Or, come to that, with absolutely anybody.

"Stella and the Prince of Stoke Newington," I observe. "One up on the King of Siam."

"Why only one? Did *he* ever watch 'Brief Encounter'? I watched it this afternoon. *And you never even asked!*"

"I'm sorry. I may have had a couple of small things on my mind. Did you enjoy it?"

"Yes. It was touching and I liked the detail: the station, the restaurant, the cinema – all of that. The bit of grit in the eye. The drying of socks on the radiator in the boathouse."

He hardly leaves a moment's pause.

"Oh – and by the way, I'd like them to play that Rachmaninoff concerto thing at our wedding." Now he does pause – a whole five seconds' worth. "I mean, instead of Stella Dodd…why not Stella Peters?"

"Are you sure?" And I'm not referring simply to the music.

"You see, I've recently been given some pretty good advice. About marriage. It would be silly not to take it."

"What sort of advice? And who gave it to you? Maddie?"

"No. *You* did."

By this time, not surprisingly, I am sitting bolt upright. "Vince, I never! I would never do such a thing! What can you possibly think I said?"

"I admit, only indirectly, but still… It made good sense. I didn't feel I could ignore it."

"What?"

"'Then be not coy, but use your time;
And while ye may, go marry:
For having lost but once your prime,
You may for ever tarry.'"

"Oh. You idiot." I relax a little but still remain mindful of his original question – the one concerning surnames.

"Please, Stella. I don't want to lose my prime. And when I know I've met the right woman and could never meet another who came anywhere near her in absolute rightness…"

"A woman whom you've known for just two days – "

"In *this* life."

"You're very stubborn, aren't you? You won't let go. You don't forget."

"No, I won't let go – unless I have to. And, in this case, do I have to? And I certainly don't forget."

" – and furthermore, who's old enough to be your mother…"

"Not yet. Not by a long chalk. For the past ten years – *nearly* ten years – I've looked on Gran as my mother. But, still, you *will* get older. We mustn't give up hope."

I put my head back on his shoulder, absently watch the windscreen wipers. Do I suppose I'll be able to think more logically that way, be *hypnotised* into providing the right answer?

"In any case," he adds, "it's going to be a very long while before you lose your prime."

I want to say something about his real mother but I can't think what – and feel that, anyway, this may hardly be the best moment.

"Will you, Stella?"

"Thank you, my darling, for asking me. Thank you. Well, we'll just have to see, won't we?"

He seems to take this for a yes; and I don't do anything to discourage him.

"And if he could only have been a couple of years older – is there no way you can hurry him up? – we'd have had your little grandson as our pageboy. Tommy, isn't it?"

Quickly I acquaint him with Paul's threat. Vince has an almost instant remedy.

"I'll go and do a strip right on their doorstep. For all the neighbours. Free of charge. (And for the police as well if I have to. I think it would only mean a day or two banged up.) Don't you think that this might help them reconsider?"

I have a distinct feeling that it might. "Then that's the only thing – now – which is left to wish for: my being able to see Tommy."

"Nonsense. Have you got dementia?"

"Yes, I knew it! You already see me as your Gran! And all because I referred to you as my grandson when we left the boat? However – have I got dementia? – yes, that's very sweet of you to ask. But why?"

"Because there are a hundred other things still left to wish for – are you saying you've forgotten them? Yes, you and Gran will get on wonderfully."

"What things?"

"Well, for a start, we need to get you enrolled at drama school. Then you can play Laura Jesson when they do a remake."

"They already have – starring Richard Burton and Sophia Loren – disastrous! But I'll certainly apply to drama school if you will." I hesitate. "Should that be before or after we go to visit Ben and Jane?"

Indeed, by the time we're passing through Islington we seem to have a great number of the details sorted. Which is just as well. There'll only be another ten minutes or so before we reach Stoke Newington.

Later on that night – again I'm not getting a lot of sleep but now it no longer seems to matter, not for one single intoxicating moment – later on I'll wonder if there might also be a patron saint for those middle-aged women who go off to live in Stoke Newington with young male strippers whom (despite everything that this particular young male stripper says about Rachmaninoff's Second Piano Concerto) she thinks she'll never tie down in marriage but whom she'll most sanguinely hope to spend the rest of her life with. They'll be endlessly good for one another and extremely good, in fact, for a great many others – even for their landlord and landlady, before the landlord dies and they take his wife to live with them in Yorkshire. Perhaps there'll be no more talk of bungee-jumping or hang-gliding (not *serious* talk, that is) but there'll be lots of poetry and black-and-white movies and rewarding study – yes for both of them, at drama college – lots of travel and general broadening of horizons…again, for both of them, very much for both of them…and occasional visits to Queen Mary's Rose Garden, where Queen Mary in her toque and long fur-collared overcoat had so carefully positioned their bench…with one last, God-Almighty heave?…far softer-natured than people often gave her credit for.

And although that striptease may never take place on anybody's doorstep Tommy will often come to visit us when he's old enough to be independent; and we have a loving family in Australia, a family which always make us feel extremely welcome. Moreover, there's not a single day that passes without the Pride of the Glory Boys telling me how much he loves me, and without my telling the Pride of the Glory Boys how much I love him back.

Plus, even by late-afternoon on Friday 5th September 1986, I've made quite sure (but oh so tactfully, of course!) that it's no longer only white sliced Mother's Pride that ends up in the bread bin in the kitchen of our happy new household; and I've been to see Mrs Conway and asked her, amongst other things, whether she and her daughter might like to see a certain show playing at the Aldwych Theatre, near the Strand.

One never knows where anything is going to finish – of course it never does. If I were going to give this little book a title, I might well borrow half a dozen words from Shakespeare.

The owl was a baker's daughter.

Okay. Beat that!